ALSO BY LEE MOLER

Baltimore Blues

BONE MUSIC

LEE MOLER

SIMON & SCHUSTER

SIMON & SCHUSTER
Rockefeller Center
1230 Avenue of the Americas
New York, NY 10020

Designed by Elina D. Nudelman
Manufactured in the United States of America

1   3   5   7   9   10   8   6   4   2

Library of Congress Cataloging-in-Publication Data
Moler, Lee.
Bone music / Lee Moler.
p.   cm.
I. Title.
PS3563.0396B66   1999
813'.54—dc21   98-46826   CIP
ISBN 0-684-84355-2

ACKNOWLEDGMENTS

Special thanks to Albert Zuckerman: agent, adviser, mentor, friend. I would also like to thank Gordon and Connie Moler for their unflagging support, and my daughters, Stephanie and Caitlin, for their courage, character, and humor.

1

MORNING in northern Montana: A wave of early sun taking flight off the floor of the plains, warming the sky from night-indigo to diamond-blue, crystals of overnight ice hanging in the air like angels, but a hellish stink in the air.

John David Jefferson stood on a little hill overlooking the forty acres where 150 of his pedigreed Angus lay dead. Their carcasses were scattered outward like shrapnel from a bomb, wild looks in their eyes, mud in their noses, and grass between their lips. Small trees were trampled, yards of ground pawed down to the dirt, as if the animals had gone berserk before they died.

"Well," said Jefferson's foreman, Pete Haskins. "I guess you could look at it like they was born to die anyway."

Jefferson was a big man, six-four and 220, but he spoke in a low Southern drawl.

"Yeah, Pete," he muttered. "And you might say love is eternal because half of all divorces end in remarriage."

"Ain't so much the cattle that's bothering you, is it?"

"It was a prize herd."

"But it's her that's really gettin' under your skin, ain't it."

"That's enough."

"Sure, boss. But you got to relax. She'll be back."

Everybody was full of advice after your wife left you. Where was Pete with his advice before she left? Why hadn't he told the boss man that he was about to lose the thing that made his life his own and not someone else's?

This was not the way his life was supposed to work out. The way he had it planned, forty-nine was the age when all he'd have to do was stay rich, love his wife, ride a good horse, read some poetry, drink some whiskey, and generally ignore the heart-felt horseshit stories of love, hate, and overweight trauma that flapped on a media string between New York and Los Angeles like ugly laundry in a gimpy wind.

Now he had to ask himself all the questions he'd avoided along with one other big one: Why had 150 head of prime beef cattle died in a single night?

Jefferson hunkered down on the heels of his custom-made Luc-ceses and reached up for a drag of Pete's smoke, knowing without looking that he had one and that he'd give it to him.

Jefferson had always harbored a quiet admiration for Pete be-cause he was born in Montana, where people knew the difference between opinions and truth. As Pete put it: "Opinions is from peo-ple, the truth is from the weather."

There weren't many people in Montana, and fewer still who needed to lay their lame-duck opinions on you while they got a later set from the new experts who would soon be old news.

Pete didn't mind laying a little nugget of philosophy on you, though, usually in times like this, when you least expected or wanted it. That would have been an annoying habit if what he said weren't often dumb enough to be harmless but smart enough to be interesting.

"My woman came back and so will your'n," Pete said quietly. "Women is a lot like horses—sometimes they just get spooked."

The cellular phone on Jefferson's belt chirped, and he flipped it open.

"Judd?"

A jolt of electricity went through his belly when he heard her voice.

"I can't talk now, Celine. I'm busy with a field of dead cattle."

"Have you talked to the children lately?" she asked.

Why was she asking him questions she knew the answer to? Of course he'd talked to the children. Was he going to send them off to school in Switzerland and then quit talking to them just because their mother had lost her mind? She was after something here—maybe just a reason to talk to him.

"I talked to Keith night before last. He wanted to come home when he found out. I told him to stay there, that it was between you and me. Delia didn't say much of anything. You know her."

"She thinks I'm deserting you."

Delia. Daddy's girl. Chestnut hair only a little darker than her mother's auburn cascade, dark eyes like his own, but soft as summer. Delia held herself in like her grandfather, Colonel Jack Jefferson. She'd broken her first horse at the age of fifteen, sneaking out of bed in the middle of the night so she could do it by herself. Jefferson had sensed something in the corral and had gone down, intending to scold her for doing it alone, but she was so proud all he could do was smile. Delia shared the smile with him, and he went back to bed.

"Now, why would she think you're deserting me?"

"This isn't easy for me, Judd."

"What do you want me to do, Celine? Tell her it's all right?"

"Just don't turn her against me."

"Where did this idea come from that I'm a threat to you?"

"Now, don't get angry."

"I'm not angry, I'm frustrated. I've done the best I could since I moved you out here from Virginia. I thought we'd done pretty well."

"Think back."

"What?"

"Think back to those first weeks we spent together, Judd. I could see something coming for you. I've seen it coming all these years, and now that it's here, I can't stand it."

"Maybe it's just age."

"I may be forty-four," she said with frosty dignity, "but I'm not the one getting in bar fights and strangling strangers. And I didn't call to get into this."

"What, then?"

"I just wanted to ask about the pre-Colombian piece in the front hall."

"Take it."

"You're sure?"

"See you soon."

Jefferson clicked off the phone, walked up a slight hill to a cotton-wood tree, and slammed his hat against the trunk.

He heard footsteps behind him and felt a hand clap him lightly on the shoulder.

"She'll come back, boss."

Jefferson looked straight into Pete's baked-apple face.

"What if I'm the one who's spooked?"

Pete stuck the cigarette into his mouth and talked around it.

"Well, boss, a spooked stallion, sometimes you just got to let him run it out."

Jefferson straightened the brim of his hat and returned his attention to the dead cattle.

"What do you think about this?" he asked, waving an arm at the pasture.

Pete kicked at a clod of dirt and rubbed the back of his neck. "Never seen anything like it," he said. "A whole herd don't go down at once. It's like they was poisoned. Deliberate."

"Or accidentally."

"Accidentally, boss?"

Jefferson was about to answer Pete, but the state vet was walking up the hill, a slim Swede wearing a dark blue state jumpsuit and long rubber gloves. He pulled the gloves off as he walked and dropped them near his van.

"Mr. Jefferson," he began.

Jefferson straightened up out of his slouch to take the news.

"Yeah?"

"I took some samples of saliva, and later today we'll be sending out a truck for one of the carcasses. We'll do an autopsy, and you should hear something in three or four days."

"What's your best guess?"

The vet rubbed sweat from his eyes and stared at the cattle, shaking his head.

"Strange," he said. "The random pattern of the bodies, the trampled condition of the area, the contorted postures. All of that would indicate some type of brain lesions, meningitis, mad cow disease, even rabies."

"But they were all inoculated."

"I know; I'm just using rabies as an example. I don't really have any idea at this point."

"What about poison? PCP or mercury leeching into the streams?"

The vet rubbed his jaw as he looked around the area.

"Maybe, but where would it come from?"

Jefferson pointed west at a faint wisp of white smoke rising from the horizon.

"What about that plant over there? It opened three months ago and now this happens."

"But they make computer chips, don't they?"

"So they say."

"Well, I don't know much about that business, but from what I've heard, it's one of the cleaner industries, and they'd have to file an impact statement with the EPA."

"But we could be dealing with a pollutant?"

"I just don't know."

Jefferson seized the man by the upper arm and held him, squeezing tight with one bearlike hand.

"I want an educated guess," he said. "I've got fifteen thousand more acres out there. I need to be thinking about what to do."

The state man looked down at his arm, then up at Jefferson.

"Don't shoot the messenger, Mr. Jefferson."

"Just make me a guess."

"A brain lesion . . . probably a pathogen, but maybe a pollutant. That's the best I can do for you right now."

The vet pulled his arm free, walked quickly to his van, and stopped by the door.

"I'm sorry to tell you this, Mr. Jefferson, but we're going to have to quarantine the whole ranch until we get the answer."

He jumped quickly into the truck and drove away.

Jefferson sailed his hat into the tall grass to his right.

"Goddamn!" he said. "Did you hear that, Pete? Quarantined."

Jefferson was mad enough to sweat steam. If all the cattle died he'd still make it, but Pete and Pete's friends would be out of a job. He would have failed them, and not only would he be a failure, he'd be a lonely one. Celine had bailed, and now this. Maybe she was right and something was coming for him.

"Lucky thing you got other herds," Pete said. "Maybe we ought to ride out and check on 'em, boss. Maybe take us a bottle, smoke some cee-gars, and cuss the bears. How's that sound?"

"You see that, Pete?" Jefferson asked, pointing west.

"That plant's been there for months, boss. If it's poisoning the water table, how come we ain't dead too?"

"Maybe it just takes longer for us."

Pete turned pale under his leathery tan.

"C'mon, boss. You're scaring me."

Jefferson turned on Haskins with a thick-browed scowl.

13

"I don't feel too easy about it myself, Pete. The damn thing opens up, then forty acres of cattle die. What's next? By God, I'm going over there."

"Boss . . ."

"I'm going over there, Pete."

AS HE DROVE up Highway 89 toward the plant, Jefferson thought of his son Keith; six-two, athletic, hard-jawed kid with a head to match, stubborn as his father, willful as his mother, with Celine's red hair and gray eyes and the old man's temper—a dangerous combination. But a sweet kid, really, always ready to agree that the measure of a man was forbearance, but only after he'd told a teacher where to get off or gone chasing wolves in Canada for a week without telling anyone. Maybe the Europeans would put a little shine on him.

It was good that Keith was away, because Jefferson was about to do something he'd blast the kid for doing. But Keith didn't have several hundred people depending on him, and he'd never known his grandfather, Colonel Jack Jefferson. If Colonel Jack had sent young John David to Switzerland, it would have been to invade the place. A bitter smile crossed Jefferson's face as he remembered his father standing tall in a yellow spring sun as it turned his marine greens to gold, finger pointing down, burr-head bent forward, voice loud as a drill sergeant's:

You WILL go over to Frankie Bradley's house, and you WILL get your football back by whatever means necessary. Do I make myself clear?

Frankie Bradley was two years older. But that cut no ice with Colonel Jack, who had been a platoon lieutenant in the First Marines when they fought their way through a quarter million Chinese troops to get back from the Chosin Reservoir in 1952.

Jefferson and his friends had been playing three-on-three with the football Colonel Jack had given him for Christmas. Frankie Bradley had seen the younger boys choosing up sides and invited himself in. He'd knocked the smaller boys around until dark. Then he'd simply picked up the ball and walked away.

Frankie's mother was at one of her three jobs, so Frankie answered the door. Jefferson could see his football lying on the couch.

He asked for it back, but Frankie told him with a smile it was now his football. Jefferson was caught between Frankie and the old man and at that moment he hated them both, and the football, and Christmas. He felt surrounded and miserable, with no way out but to attack.

Jefferson hit Frankie in the jaw with all the power in his ten-year-old body. Frankie slammed against the door frame, and Jefferson hit him again in the small of the back. Frankie let out a moaning whine and sank to his knees, the front of his pants turning dark and wet.

"I got a kidney condition," he wailed. "Now I'm gonna die."

Jefferson was so horrified that he couldn't feel his feet on the floor as he walked over to get the football.

He ran home on a cushion of cold panic, sure that Frankie was dying on the floor of his house and that his ghost would come out of the closet at night to drag him into eternal blackness.

The old man nodded his head with satisfaction when he saw the football.

"I hit Frankie and he's gonna die," Jefferson blurted.

"Is that what he said?"

"He's got a kidney condition."

"Bullies always come up with a condition when you hit 'em. Don't go soft on him now, John D."

Jefferson had gone up to his room and crumpled in a corner, feeling used and ashamed. He hated the old man that night for showing him pain and humiliation. And he hated him for not coming upstairs. He'd actually approve of this, God bless his shiny brass heart.

THE PLANT WAS cobalt-blue steel and loomed squarely off the flat plains like a giant headstone. A man at the gate waved for him to stop, but Jefferson just waved back and rolled on by. At the top of the road he pulled into a half-full parking lot, got out, and headed for a set of double doors cut into the front of the building.

A sign on the door announced the place as Unitel Incorporated. Harlow Rourke had built the place to produce fuel from the methane in cow manure, but then the bottom dropped out of the shit business. Harlow had been looking for a sucker to buy the place ever since.

Jefferson had never heard of Unitel Incorporated and couldn't imagine why they would choose to locate in the middle of Montana ranchland.

Inside the double doors was a glass partition set into the side of a long hallway, which led toward the rear of the plant. Behind the partition was a plump young woman with crow's-wing hair and a flat copper face, a girl from the Blackfoot reservation.

"Good morning," she said with rehearsed cordiality. "May I help you?"

"I'm looking for the plant manager," Jefferson told her.

"Mr. Chang?"

"Yes."

"Do you have an appointment?"

"No."

The girl stared at him blankly.

"Just call him, will you. My name is Jefferson. I own the property adjacent to here. Tell him I have a matter of possible liability to discuss with him."

Chang was interested in possible liability. He came down the hallway and escorted Jefferson up a flight of stairs to a second-floor office with a window facing Jefferson's property.

"Now then," he said in heavily accented English. "What is this matter of liability?"

Chang didn't look much like a businessman. He was short but athletic-looking, had his hair cut in a hip 'do that hung to his shoulders, and he sported a thin mustache. He also had a thin scar running from hairline to cheekbone that looked more like barroom fight than boardroom stress.

"Forty acres of beef cattle," said Jefferson. "Dead in one night and downhill from here. What's in your waste water?"

"Nothing harmful, I promise you," Chang said with a placating gesture. "We meet every EPA standard. I have the certification right here."

Chang reached into his desk and pulled out a sheaf of papers with the EPA logo on top. He tossed the papers casually onto the barren desktop. Jefferson picked them up and saw they were authentic. He owned gas wells, silver mines, and reams of EPA boilerplate just like the ones he was holding in his hand.

"You make computer chips?" he asked.

Chang stiffened a little in his chair. Obviously he was a man not used to answering a lot of questions.

"Yes."

"And the smoke?"

"From the heating system, mostly. It's cold at night. And we incinerate our trash. Read the certification."

"I don't have to read it. I can see they certified you. I also know that the people who do the certifications are a bunch of hog-nosed geeks who can't find their ass without sitting down. Half of them can be bought off with a subscription to *Penthouse*."

Chang's eyes narrowed to slits and his scar turned from white to red.

"I'm not going to argue about it," he said.

"I don't think you have enough authority to argue about it."

"You're a very rude man," Chang said.

"Give me a name, someone who can actually help me."

"Mr. Jefferson, I have showed you the EPA certification. That was more than I had to do. Now I'm asking you to leave."

One part of Jefferson's brain told him to leave, but it was a part that was way in the back. The blood all seemed to be rushing to the front. He moved forward and stood over Chang's desk. His hands began to tingle and his vision zoom-focused onto Chang's face.

"No," he said. "I want a name, the CEO, someone on the board. I want to talk to someone who actually owns this building. Give me a name. One way or another, you're going to give me a name."

Chang looked a little surprised but not at all afraid.

"Mr. Jefferson, are you threatening me?"

This was going to be the fortune cookie thing all over again, only worse. Jefferson knew he should be backing off, acting his age, but it felt so good coasting toward the line. He looked toward the multi-button phone on Chang's desk.

"You going to call security?"

"Maybe I'll call the sheriff."

"Good. His name is Bob Wagman. He's a sixty-year-old fat guy I shoot quail with three times a year. He owes me five hundred bucks from a poker game, and I know he's been on the take for years. Do you want me to dial the number?"

A little smile played across Chang's face.

"Maybe security, then. They're not sixty or fat and the only person they owe is me."

Over the years Jefferson had lost a lot of faith in conversation. It always seemed to go around in circles. He was done talking.

"I want a name."

"You're trespassing. We don't have to be gentle."

The blood receded from Jefferson's eyes and went to his hands. He felt loose and relaxed. He was glad for Chang's implied threat. It made his decision easier.

Chang's hand darted toward the telephone, but before it could get there, Jefferson reached forward, grasped Chang's necktie, and yanked the man forward. He pulled the necktie over the front edge of the desk, pinioning Chang's head.

"Odd behavior for men of our station, isn't it," he growled into Chang's face. "But I like it. I'm forty-nine and my wife has left me and a lot of my cattle are dead. If you don't tell me who I can talk to, I'm going to throw you out your office window."

Jefferson pulled Chang across the desk, and with his right hand still on the necktie, he grabbed Chang's belt with his left hand, flipped him around, and headed toward the window.

"All right," gurgled Chang. "All right. Put me down."

Jefferson dropped the man against the wall but held on to the necktie.

Chang took a few deep breaths and tried to recover his composure.

Jefferson tightened his grip on the necktie.

"The name."

"We don't even own the plant. We lease it from Harlow Rourke."

Jefferson breathed a sigh of relief. Harlow was a hard piece of work, but they'd known each other since Jefferson hit Montana in 1970. They'd even been friends once. He'd see the old goat just as soon as he could figure out a way to let go of Chang.

"Thank you, Mr. Chang, that's very helpful. But we've got kind of a problem here, don't we?"

"I'd say you're the one with the problem."

He was right. Jefferson had what he wanted, but now he had to get out of the plant without encountering security.

He looked around the office and saw a red fire alarm on the front wall. In the event of fire, security would have to man the extinguishers and make sure people got out. Jefferson would be glad to oblige. He let go of Chang, ripped the phone cord out of the wall, then pulled the handle. The plant erupted into a cacophony of bells and sirens. A recorded voice began booming out the message that this wasn't a drill.

Jefferson left the office and began running toward a fire exit sign. He passed several other people running in various directions, all wearing white lab coats. He heard Chang behind him yelling down the hall for security just as he hit the fire door and blasted through it onto a set of steps. He took them four at a time and stumbled out a bottom door on the side of the building.

Workers wearing blue coveralls were jumping off the loading dock and heading for the parking lot. Jefferson joined them, looking over his shoulder for Chang. He thought he saw a light-suited figure waving some security men toward the lot, but by that time he was already jumping into the Rover.

He roared down the gravel road in a rooster tail of dust.

"Well, Colonel Jack," he said. "How'd you like that one?"

2

HARLOW Rourke's ranch was twenty miles down Highway 89. It took fifteen of those miles for Jefferson to settle out of the adrenaline rush that had started when he grabbed Chang by the necktie.

The rush was over now and he'd switched from enjoying the memory to worrying about the consequences. Sheriff Bob Wagman wouldn't do much on the say-so of a bunch of outsiders, but they could sue him, he supposed.

Then he thought of how it was going to be to face down Harlow Rourke, a man who, like Colonel Jack, thought buckshot was the only thing that stayed crispy in milk. Harlow didn't think much of his own two sons and had once offered Jefferson a chance to be his partner.

Hell, boy. I could teach you how to be a king out here—make politicians, break 'em if need be. You don't know what you're turning down.

After Jefferson refused to go partners with him he'd quit calling him Son, but hadn't tried to run him out of business or used the cops to plant crack in his coat pocket. Maybe that was because he still had some fantasies about having a surrogate son.

What the hell? If Harlow wanted to think they were alike, let him. There was even a little truth to it, but then porpoises were a little like sharks. Only the people who got eaten could fully appreciate the difference.

AS JEFFERSON DROVE through the entrance to Rourke property, he caught a glimpse of the dogs—descendants of the dingoes Harlow had smuggled in from Australia in 1945. They had bred with wolves and coyotes to become mutant gargoyles, all yellow eyes and long teeth.

They roamed around and killed a few head of cattle, but no one ever called Natural Resources, because they knew it wouldn't do any good. Harlow owned the Montana senator who chaired the Resources budget committee. And nobody wanted Harlow mad at them, because he was dog-wild himself.

A streak of gray fur melted through the trees. The damn dogs seemed to be everywhere.

"HOW'S THE bourbon?" Harlow inquired.

He was a tall man who still had powerful shoulders even at seventy. He also had a full mane of white hair and a hawk face that looked like it should be on a stamp. He was sitting behind a boat-sized desk running his big roper's hands through the white hair.

"The bourbon's fine. What's the deal on that plant?"

Harlow looked down at the desktop and shook his head sadly.

"I've noticed over the years that you got a tendency to be rude under stress, Judd."

Like everyone but his employees, Harlow called him Judd, long for J.D.

The office was an appendage to the main house and was paneled in the same oak as the desk. It smelled of oiled wood and cigar smoke. There were pictures around the walls of Harlow with various politicians, giving or receiving awards. Behind the desk was a gun rack flanked by bookcases filled with whiskey bottles, cigar humidors, and a collection of brass cowboys on horses.

"A tendency toward rudeness," Harlow said again. "Man of accomplishment like you doesn't need that."

Harlow the seducer: warm bourbon and flattering advice.

"The manager of your plant called me rude right before I threatened to throw him out his office window."

"It's not my plant. I just . . . you threatened to throw him out his own window?"

"Yeah, that's the only way he'd tell me you still owned the place."

Harlow looked into Jefferson's face and chuckled. "I'll be damned, Judd, if you ain't a pistol. Sometimes you remind me of me."

"I don't think so."

"You don't like to admit it, but only someone like me would have screwed me like you did on that land deal."

Jefferson groaned.

"You loaned me the money, Harlow. You practically begged me to take it. And I paid you back."

"With that gas under it, it was worth ten times what you paid for it, but it's not the money, it's the principle."

"Harlow, one thing I've learned about you—when you say it's the principle, it's the money."

Harlow took a pull of his own drink and looked deep into the bottom of the glass.

"Not exactly true, Judd my boy. I got some principles with men I admire. Damn few of those around, though. You're the only one comes to mind."

It was touching the way liars seemed so eager when they were telling the truth. Honest people told the truth often enough that they didn't expect to be loved for it.

Jefferson leaned forward and looked through the whiskey warmth in Harlow's amber eyes to the outlaw underneath.

"You want to know why I didn't go partners with you when you asked me?"

"I thought it was because you didn't trust me."

"You'd have started to think we were family."

"I already thought of us as family!"

"And I knew we couldn't be."

Harlow smacked his palm against the desktop. "Why not, goddamnit?"

"Because I knew there'd come a day when you'd try to be my daddy instead of telling me the truth."

Harlow sighed, but his amber eyes took on a hard glitter. "One day you may find a daddy's better than the truth."

"My real father taught me different."

Harlow looked away quickly and glanced out the window as he spoke. "Well, daddy or not, Judd. I feel for you in your situation with Celine. I think your emotions are a little out of control."

Jefferson set his whiskey glass down hard onto Harlow's desk, the sound cracking off the walls. "This conversation has nothing to do with Celine, and you know it. Now, what's going on at your plant?"

Harlow's eyes returned from the window with a surprised lurch. "I don't know. I only leased it to this Unitel outfit because I'd rather make something on it than pay to have it torn down. You said the man showed you the EPA certs."

"He showed me a smile too, but I didn't believe that, either."

"What do you want me to say?"

"I want you to say you'll pull some strings in Washington. Have them send out some people to really go over that place."

"I don't run things quite as directly as you seem to think I do, Judd. It's true I'm owed some favors, but that only goes so far."

"You're getting more than meets the eye out of this, aren't you, Harlow? Either that or you're afraid of something. Which is it?"

Harlow pushed himself out of the chair and went to a window. As he looked at the tops of the Rockies shading the high blue sky into deep opal shadow, he took a handkerchief from the pocket of his white shirt and mopped his forehead.

"Getting warm early this year," he said. "The heat's bringing the dogs up close to the house."

"Why don't you get rid of them?" Jefferson asked. "Have Natural Resources kill them, or do it yourself."

"Hell, they're out there breeding with coyotes and wolves right now. They'll always be here. I don't kill those dogs because they're just like me. We go where we want to, when we want to."

"What about my cattle, Harlow. Why won't you help me?"

"Things live and die in their own time and in the long run it don't make no difference."

"It could be your people. It could be you."

"I'm the lead dog, Judd. I'm going to die last."

"Then you won't help me?"

"I'm trying to help you right now by telling you this."

Harlow raised his eyebrows and spread his hands helplessly. Jefferson felt the anger rising red from his feet. "Well, let me tell you something; when the shooting starts, the lead dog is liable to be the first one hit."

Harlow rocked back on his heels as if he'd been punched in the gut. "Goddamn!" he said. "The man I like most in this world. The man who took what I gave him and turned it into a fortune. Not only does he turn on me, he threatens me!"

Harlow pulled a gold pocket watch from the pocket of his striped pants.

"Time for you to leave, Judd. I've got someplace to go."

With no plan, there was nothing for Jefferson to do but dig in his heels.

"I'm not going anywhere until we get this plant thing ironed out."

Harlow's amber eyes turned wild-dog yellow and his upper lip curled into a snarl, voice going from rumble to roar.

"By God, you're talking to the man who run the Indians off of any land he wanted. And I didn't have no cavalry to help me either, just the dogs and any lowlifes I could whip into some kind of shape. You think 'cause that was back in 1945 now you can talk to me any way you want? I'm Harlow fuckin' Rourke, and woe be to any son of a bitch that forgets it."

Harlow had risen to his feet and now he was standing, big-knuckled hands turning white as they gripped the edge of his desk, body leaning forward in a vein-pumping, spitting rage.

"I'll kill you . . . I'll kill you if you don't stop pushing on me. I don't want to, but I done lots of things I didn't want to."

The hair on Jefferson's neck stood straight up. He felt like he had on his first night in Southeast Asia: in the dark and on someone else's turf. He'd been prepared for resistance, but not this. Time to regroup.

"Well, since you put it that way, Harlow. I think I'll be going."

Harlow relaxed his stance.

"Some things just are the way they are," he said almost apologetically. "Some people too. You got to know when to back off, that's all."

HALFWAY TO THE highway, at the top of a hill, Jefferson pulled the Rover to the side and looked back. From this vantage point he could see the helicopter lift off its small pad in back of Harlow's house and swing around to the front. He could even see Harlow walk rapidly out his front door and get into the chopper, which pointed its nose to the north and headed off in a rising arc.

A cold breeze blew down Jefferson's neck, and for a second he wished Colonel Jack were here. But a mortar shell had put him in the ground outside Da Nang in 1966. Before that, he'd boot-kicked young John D. through academics, football, and his own made-up backyard sport—pugil-sticking.

He had brought home two of the thick oak sticks with fat padded ends that the marines used to teach bayonet fighting. He would drag Jefferson into the backyard and pummel him until he started pummeling back.

The Colonel gave out a lot of "Well done"s in those years but never a hug or even much of a smile. Jefferson never got to have that talk with the Colonel in which he'd tell him what an asshole he was. After 1966 he was a dead asshole, which meant it was too late to do anything but love him. Colonel Jack had taught him how to live without a daddy, and maybe he'd done it because he knew one day it would be necessary.

From behind him Jefferson heard a low growl and sensed something moving through the scrub pines. He shuddered and spurred the Rover toward home.

3

ON the top floor of the Unitel plant there was a room that was off-limits to all employees. Inside the room was a glass-walled cubicle with its own air supply. There was no furniture in the cubicle. There was nothing but a young woman who was dying slowly, too slowly.

C. K. Lone looked at her through the glass wall and shook his head. The girl had been beautiful once—five feet ten inches of cream-colored curves and wild blond hair. For three days she'd been throwing herself against the walls of the cubicle and biting chunks out of her own flesh as the rabies virus burned up her brain.

"This is no good," Lone said to Chang. "Do you know how many people she could infect in three days?"

"It's not likely anyone would come close to her after the first day," Chang answered lamely.

"Stop talking to me like I'm a fool. All they have to do is breathe the same air. It is airborne now, isn't it?"

"Yes, yes. The test with the cattle proved that, and they were all dead within a few hours."

Lone winced; the goddamn unauthorized test. But how was Chang to know he'd be dealing with Jefferson when he decided to kill a small herd of cattle?

"Then why is it taking so long for her to die?"

"A problem getting human cells to capture the virus. I'm sure Vanek will explain it when he talks to you."

Lone lit his fifteenth cigarette of the young morning. "Vanek hasn't seen this?" he asked.

"No. I put her in and sprayed the aerosol myself."

"Then how does he know there's a problem?"

"He and his people can read the virus like a book."

"Why did you test it on the girl? Don't you trust Vanek?"

"Not entirely. I think he's been having an attack of conscience."

"You think he wants to quit?"

"I think it's possible."

"Let's go. I want to take a look at the laboratory. Then I'll talk to Vanek."

26

Lone and Chang left the room as the girl slammed herself onto the floor of the cubicle. Blood flowed from the corners of her eyes.

ABOVE THE LAB was a circular catwalk. Lone peered down into the fluorescent-lit room, appreciating the cleanliness and the electric hum. White-smocked attendants manned keyboards, while figures in white spacesuits bent over the controls to a set of robotic arms that swung back and forth inside eight enclosed cubicles.

Lone looked down on the bowed heads bent to electron microscopes as they spliced genes, attached them to other genes, and created new life forms. Silent history being made, for him, C. K. Lone, fifty years old, slim, tanned, powerful, one of the most powerful men in the world if the project was successful—a big if now that Jefferson was in the picture.

He took a handkerchief from the inside pocket of his custom-made silk suit. He straightened the suit with a spasm of his shoulders and wiped his forehead. He needed another cigarette.

Motioning for Chang to follow, he exited the workroom into an outer hallway. There, he blew smoke in Chang's direction as he spoke.

"Yesterday's problem with Jefferson shouldn't have happened."

"Your instructions were to establish this place as a computer chip factory. I thought it was best to follow customary business practices. I was wrong."

Chang was wrong, but only because he expected to meet a normal person, not Jefferson.

"We have to speed up our operation," he said. "I want a fast-killing virus ready for sale in ninety days."

Chang's eyes widened in surprise.

"All this because of Jefferson?"

"Believe me, he won't stop."

"You know this man?"

"Since Vietnam," Lone said bitterly. "The market in children was an important part of our business. Jefferson was an army policeman. He blamed me personally for the fact that the children were born poor in a country that sold its poor. He hounded me day and night, raided my brothels, even followed my people into the hills where we bought the children. Eventually, he shot me, but missed the kill shot. But I hated him even before then. He turned someone I trusted against me and then almost killed me. The triad saw that as weakness, not bad luck. I should have spent the last twenty-five years in Hong Kong, next in line for the leadership. But I'm still doing the same job I did in Vietnam, dealing in bodies and drugs. But that is soon going to change."

"Because of the project?"

"Now that the Communists are taking over Hong Kong, they'll force out the triads just like they did on the mainland. It's time for us to come to America, and if we work together, we can be more powerful than the mafia ever imagined. But it will take a leader with vision."

Chang smiled thinly.

It didn't bother Lone at all that they were conspiring to break two of the thirty-six triad oaths: number eight—*I must never cause harm or bring trouble to my sworn brothers. If I do I will be killed by myriads of knives*—and number sixteen—*If I knowingly convert my sworn brothers' cash or property to my own use, I will be killed by myriads of knives*. Death by myriads of knives: slashed across all the main muscle groups—calves, thighs, biceps, forearms—then chopped up by the triads' trademark weapon, a meat cleaver.

What bothered Lone was the reappearance of Jefferson. The man was a curse. How else could he have known Sylvie was ready to turn traitor? The whore bitch! Twenty-five years, and it still scalded inside.

Lone lit another cigarette and walked down the hall toward the stairs to Chang's office. At the bottom of the stairs he stopped and stared through the drifting smoke at the blank wall in front of him, thinking of different smoke on another morning, the worst of his life.

"Why not just kill this Jefferson?" asked Chang.

Lone whirled and stared, still in a partial trance. Why not, indeed? It should be easy, but nothing about Jefferson had ever been easy. If they failed, there would be open warfare, and the sound of it would get back to Hong Kong. One thing the project couldn't stand was attention from Hong Kong.

"No," he said to Chang. "First we finish the project. From now on, you operate around the clock."

"Vanek will object."

Lone looked up the stairs and remembered why he was there.

"No one touches Jefferson until I order it," he said. "He's my problem. He always has been. Now, give me a few minutes and send Vanek up to your office."

Inside Chang's office, he looked out toward Jefferson's property, thinking he should have expected this. He and Jefferson were each other's disease. One of them would have to die before the other could live. How could he have thought they wouldn't meet again?

Lone jumped as the phone buzzed and a female voice told him Dr. Vanek was waiting to see him. Vanek was a Russian with a body like a sack of bones, hair like raked weeds, and the teeth of a dead man. Like the rest of the Russian scientists, Vanek was an overnight whore, selling what he knew, but what he knew was priceless. Vanek could not be allowed to quit.

The Russian was soaked with sweat, his skin as white as bad pastry. He wanted to quit and was afraid to say it. The logical solution, thought Lone, would be to kill him as an example to the other workers, but he was head of the project. There was nothing to do but bluff.

Vanek said nothing but blinked rapidly, like a rabbit.

"Something wrong with your eyes, Doctor?" Lone asked in English.

"Uh, no," Vanek said, attempting a wide-eyed stare.

"So, what's the problem with the virus's kill-speed?"

Vanek was on home ground now and his eyes narrowed into shrewd slits.

"Vell, a virus lives only by transferring from one host to another. If host A dies before the virus can be transmitted to host B, it is an unsuccessful virus. By asking it to kill within minutes we are, in effect, asking it to perform a suicide attack."

"Chang says you have a problem."

Vanek crossed his legs nervously, revealing a stretch of hairless white leg above a short black sock.

"Vell, the rabies virus is not good at traveling through the air, so what we haff done is remove sections of DNA from a large harmless virus called the vaccina virus and implanted the mutant strain of rabies virus that exists in the atmosphere over this part of, uh, what is dis place called again?"

"Montana."

"Yes, Montana. As I was saying, the standard rabies virus gets into the nerve cells at the neuromuscular junction when a carrier bites the victim. Then it works its way to the brain. Normally, this process takes from three to ten days. But the mutant strain found here is able to invade blood cells passing through the circulatory system of the lungs. Blood from the lungs is the quickest route to the brain, so, the virus travels via the blood to the cells of the meninges, the membrane which surrounds the brain. There, it destroys the meninges and crosses directly into the cells of the brain."

Lone picked up a piece of paper from the desk, wadded it into a ball, and bounced it off Vanek's head.

"I'm getting bored with the lecture. Why won't it kill humans as fast as cattle?"

Vanek's face blotched red and he swallowed hard.

"You are familiar with the term *endomitosis?*"

"No."

"Vell, in the body, healthy cells sometimes . . . sweep outside molecules into themselves. They do so because these molecules contain things they need. They recognize what they need by various protein indicators on the surface of the molecules. Often a virus is able to, ah, imitate these indicators so closely that the host cell cannot differentiate them from the molecules it seeks and sweeps them in. Do you follow?"

In spite of himself Lone was fascinated. What Vanek was describing sounded almost like criminal cunning.

"You mean viruses can . . . think?" he asked.

Vanek smiled condescendingly.

"Vell, no. The process is mediated by mutations in the viral DNA, chance if you vill, or more accurately quantum mechanics."

"Stick to the subject, Doctor. What is the problem, and how long will it take to fix it?"

Vanek squirmed and wiped sweat from his forehead.

"That is one thing I vanted to talk to you about. I . . ."

Vanek, rumpled and sweaty, was looking around the room, blinking wildly at the walls. Lone knew from experience that a well-groomed man was always at an advantage. He made it a point to rehearse for the day in front of a mirror, assess himself, and appreciate what he saw: five-feet-ten and 165 pounds; tan skin; knife-blade cheekbones; milk-jade eyes, slanted. He got up and walked to the front of the desk, stood above Vanek.

"I hate hedging, Doctor. Hedging is lying, and lying is something I don't tolerate in my employees."

Vanek looked down and examined the backs of his hands as he spoke. "The virus must look like what the cell seeks, and so far, we have been more successful in making it look like what cattle cells seek than what human cells, uh . . . seek."

"But you can do it?"

"Of course. Yes. It is just that, at all levels, the human is much more complex than other life forms."

"How long will it take?"

Vanek shook his head sadly. "I cannot say. Maybe you should get someone else to run the project. Yvgenitch would be a good choice. He is younger. He . . ."

Lone looked directly into his face. "Vanek, are you trying to desert me after taking all the money I've already paid you?"

"Vell, Mr. Lone. I'm having . . . second thoughts about working on this project."

"Let me guess. You're worried that these viruses will be used to kill innocent people."

"Vell, in a manner of speaking."

"The question is, are they innocent enough for you to sacrifice your life for them?"

Now Vanek didn't look so puzzled. "You vould . . . kill me?"

"Yes. But who knows? You might save some people. How innocent would they be then?"

"But . . ."

"Doctor, if there is such a thing as innocence, you have long since left it behind. The sooner you finish, the sooner you can walk away."

Vanek's eyes quit blinking. He slumped in his chair, satisfied that he had no choice, comforted by thoughts of his money.

Lone heard the thrum of a helicopter warming on the pad outside. "Now, Doctor. I have a business appointment and you have work to do."

Vanek walked out the door like a crab.

Lone checked his watch. He still had time to be in Calgary a half hour before Harlow arrived, take a shower, and get a fresh shirt. Harlow was a whole other animal. He was going to want something. He always wanted something.

4

DOWNTOWN Calgary, top floor of the Canadian Trust building. A third of that space was the office. A forty-foot-long room carpeted in muted green with an opulent teak desk on a raised dais, but none of the luxury made a dent in the fact that Lone hated Calgary. He was marooned in a flat city full of flat white faces stunned into idiot cheerfulness by the cold.

Just the same, he supposed he should be grateful to Hahn, the fat dung-eater. If he hadn't sent him here on what was intended to be a fool's errand, he wouldn't be on the verge of the biggest coup in triad history. Iraq would pay $20 million for a fast-kill rabies aerosol. When Iraq had it, Iran would have to have it, then Libya, then Israel, then the U.S. The total take would be more than half a billion dollars.

Thank the gods Hahn had wanted to send him somewhere he would be no threat. If it hadn't been for that, and an opium-addicted college professor with a demented theory about viruses, someone else would be sitting on this opportunity.

He'd develop the virus in Montana, set up full-scale production in Argentina, and start selling. When the money started to flow, the triad would beg him to be leader. He would accept under one condition: the death of Hahn, in any way he named.

Lone poured himself a drink. Harlow's helicopter was landing on the roof.

GODDAMN HELICOPTERS ALWAYS messed up your hair. Harlow knew that appearance was important to old C.K. He watched everything like a snake, moved his head instead of his eyeballs, just like a damn rattler. That was okay. You always knew where you stood with a rattler. Harlow smoothed his hair and went into Lone's office.

"Have a seat, Harlow," Lone said, standing behind the raised desk. "Can I offer you a drink?"

"Bourbon'll be fine."

Lone shoved the glass to the front of his desk, and Harlow leaned up to take it.

"Things going all right for you at the plant?"

"Yes. Why do you ask?"

"That herd of cattle that went down the other night."

"That was just a little field test."

"You picked the wrong man's cattle."

LONE HAD HATED Harlow Rourke ever since their first meeting in the lawyer's office where they'd signed the lease for the plant. He'd thought the old man looked like a vulture that should have its neck wrung. But since Harlow's plant was at the exact center of the boundaries laid out by Hahn's drugged-out professor, he'd had to do business instead of kicking the old bastard in the balls.

"I'll handle any trouble from Mr. Jefferson," Lone said easily.

"Cut the crap, C.K."

"Crap?"

"Yeah. I'd say there's somethin' about Judd Jefferson that you ain't got any idea if you can handle."

The old fool should be worried about what he could handle. He wasn't even safe from himself. No man was, who had an addiction like his. Lone had discerned it that first day. He'd proposed a series of thirty-day leases. Harlow had agreed. They had several drinks to seal the deal, and Harlow had gotten talkative about his sexual tastes, which ran toward sadistic pornography. That's when Lone invited him to the sex circus he ran in a warehouse at the stockyards. The circus brought in money, but Harlow didn't want to pay. Instead he offered a report by a professor named Vandivier.

Judd's name had made Lone nervous. And when people got nervous, they did things they wouldn't do otherwise. That could be good if you knew how to work the situation.

"You're a smooth one, C.K., but you're scared of Jefferson, and you ought to be scared."

Lone was beginning to hate Harlow almost as much as Jefferson. If it weren't for the thirty-day leases . . . but he thought he'd be saving money. Who in their right mind would have given any worth to the idea of viral mutations caused by a hole in the ozone layer? He'd thought it was something Hahn's professor imagined in an opium dream. Then Vandivier's report had said the same thing. It had to be fate.

Lone jumped out of his chair and leaned across his desk.

"Listen, old man. I know more about Jefferson than you ever could. He hounded me for two years in Vietnam. If he knows I'm here, people will start to die. There will be noise, police. The plant will have to close, and neither you nor I will get what we want."

GODDAMN! LONE AND Jefferson had a personal grudge. A bystander might make out real well on this fight. Letting a reptile like Lone get one up on Judd didn't sit right. But, damnit, there was some kind of death bug right over Rourke property. A man had to think of his family's future. Problem was how to unload fifty thousand acres of land for enough to keep the Rourke name big as it always had been. The thing to do was squeeze a deal out of Lone.

"So, C.K., I tell Judd that you're in town and we're both out of what we want."

"Exactly."

"But I ain't never told you what I want."

Lone reached for his cigarette pack. "And what is that?"

"To sell my land for a whole lot of money before word gets out about these bugs in the air."

"Yes?"

"Vandivier's report is bound to leak out, and when it does, my land will be worth about as much as hot air in August."

"That's possible."

"What I need is a buyer, someone who could come in right now and buy me out with no muss, no fuss. Hell, I guess you can see what I'm driving at, can't you, C.K.?"

"I hope for your sake I don't see, Harlow."

"Come on, C.K. You got twenty-one days left on your current lease, and if I tell Judd your name, you won't have that long. I know a man over a barrel when I see one."

Lone had to think fast or lose. He was going back to the triads as Shan Chu or he wasn't going back at all.

"Do you know who you're fucking with, Harlow? Tsendai Holding Co. is a property of the Wo Shing Wo triad. We've been in operation since 1644. We taxed the opium trade between China and Britain in the 1850s. The Japanese paid us not to bother them during World

War Two. We controlled the black market in Vietnam. We taxed every business in Hong Kong and Malaysia, and by the year 2000 we'll control the West Coast ethnic gangs and the East Coast mafia. We'll have five legitimate companies on the New York Stock Exchange."

Harlow gave him a yellow-toothed smile and spread his arms in a friendly shrug. "Hell, an outfit big as yours won't even miss the price of my land."

"How much?"

Harlow leaned back and rubbed his chin. "Well, let's see. Fifty thousand acres at a thousand an acre comes to fifty million, give or take a few acres' worth."

Lone almost gagged. The only way Hahn would authorize that kind of payment was if he knew the project was working—and then he would take control.

Harlow couldn't be killed, so he'd have to be seduced out of his land deal.

"There's no use trying to lie to you, Harlow. I am over a barrel. I'll buy your land, but I can't just write you a check. That much money will have to be approved by the Tsendai board of directors. They'll do it, but they'll want a legal deal; a survey of the land, a notarized contract . . ."

"I'll give you twenty-one days, C.K. We can sign the agreement the same day we sign the next lease."

"And the plant property will be included in the purchase agreement."

"You think I don't know them thirty-day leases are the only thing keepin' me alive? No sir! The plant stays in my possession, and I keep leasin' it to you."

"You're making me lose face, Harlow."

"Don't take it personal, C.K. It's just business."

Lone made a disgusted noise and shrugged.

"All right, Harlow. We have a deal. We sign in twenty-one days."

Harlow grinned wolfishly as he shook Lone's hand. Lone sat on the edge of his desk and lit a cigarette.

"You know how to take advantage of a situation, Harlow. I must respect that. In some other time and place . . ."

Harlow licked bourbon off his lip and laughed. "You trying to say we could be friends, C.K.?"

"Not yet. We're still dealing. Do you remember your . . . special night at the circus?"

HARLOW REMEMBERED, all right. It wasn't no circus at all. It was more like being inside one of them dreams you got on a hot night: men, women, boys, girls, animals, different combinations, all shiny with sweat in the lights. The specialty act, though—that was the one. They had brought out the girl and tied one of her wrists to the bedpost, then came a man waving silk scarves in the air, asking for bids to use 'em on her any way you liked, highest bidder . . . whatever you wanted.

Hardly even knew what he was doing when he jumped up and bid fifty thousand, and then on the bed, all of it a blur now, tying her tight, turning her every which way, sweating with the fever, her tied down like a split trout and one more scarf on the bedpost . . . slipping it around her neck, pulling it just a little, then harder, her face going red, then dark, him watching the colors, pulling tighter all the time . . . until he let go inside himself . . . then let go of her, and knew she'd never move again. He'd been the last thing she would ever feel, and he was still here and kickin'. It made you feel like you'd beat the odds . . . beat your age. No feeling like it. . . . The only thing left you couldn't buy just anywhere.

Harlow looked up warily. "Yeah, I remember. So what?"

"You'd like to do it again, wouldn't you?"

One day you get to a point where there's no more thrills, there ain't nothing ahead but the end. There had to be some reward for all that sweat and strain.

"I bet it'd cost me something, wouldn't it?"

"Well, you just drove a hard bargain. You've got to let me save a little face."

"Do I?"

LONE PRESSED A button on his phone and spoke a few words of Cantonese. In a few minutes his old friend Ling came through the door with a girl. He walked her to the center of the room and pulled off the kimono she was wearing. She was fifteen years old. There was a golden glow to her skin. She had small breasts, but they were round as teacups and had black-cherry nipples. Her black hair fell to the tops of her slim buttocks and matched the small Asian bush between her legs. She was perfect. Harlow had to be squirming inside.

"What is it you want?" Harlow croaked.

"Just a little face, that's all. You get your $50 million deal and you keep on leasing me the plant property, but you do it for one dollar a month. We'll probably only be there another four months. Giving up the present rate of sixty thousand a month will cost you $240,000, but each one of those months I'll give you a girl just like this one. With the land deal, you'll never miss the money."

Harlow sucked in his breath as he looked at the golden young flesh.

"Just a little something to let me save face," Lone said pleasantly.

You sweat, strain, lie, deal, get and more get. Then both boys turn out to be slugs and Judd spits in your eye. Nothing like you planned it, and too late to start over. Only one way to get that feeling. Harlow swallowed some whiskey to clear his throat.

"Okay," he said. "You got a deal."

"Good. Mr. Ling will drive you and the girl to the warehouse."

Harlow's hands shook as he pushed himself to his feet. He looked away from the girl. "See you in twenty-one days," he said, placing his glass on the desk.

Harlow walked out of the room, afraid to look at the girl. Lone motioned Ling forward.

"When you get to the warehouse, turn the tape system on," he said quietly. "I want a video of everything that happens."

Ling smiled and nodded, then hurried the girl out of the room.

Lone sighed deeply and poured a half glass of straight scotch. He drank and felt himself settle comfortably into his body, crossing a line with his mind, everything calm, even as a sea horizon, a level, endless pale between sky and water, no color, nothing. Nothing was good.

5

JEFFERSON'S office was a big rectangular room papered in pool-table green and trimmed in pecan. An L-shaped mahogany computer station dominated the center, and two leather sofas faced each other in the east end by a fireplace.

Jefferson felt a mighty temptation to back off and let things take their normal course, but he'd already seen the beginnings of the normal course in the red-rimmed sulfur of Harlow's eyes.

Something dark was spreading toward Montana, and it had already reached Harlow. Who would stand in its way if not John David Jefferson?

Montana had given him wealth and respect. If he turned away now, he might be able to keep the money but he'd lose the respect, which he liked.

Maybe he was Colonel Jack's boy after all, needing a zone of silence around himself, needing to keep a river inside from running dry. In any case, he knew he was going to fight just like the Colonel would have. And if it came down to killing?

Jefferson blinked his eyes rapidly and shook his head. He hadn't thought seriously of killing anyone in twenty-five years. Now here he was in his expensive house staring at his expensive computer and pondering murder.

Maybe he was crazy; the cattle had just caught a cold, and Celine would be here soon with a couple of guys in white coats. Actually, a couple months on Thorazine and a vegetable diet was beginning to sound pretty good.

Jefferson exited the spreadsheet and decided to do a little surfing on the Internet. He logged on and did a search for "Montana cattle." At the bottom of the list he ran across something called "Montana Millennium." He was about to investigate when he heard footsteps at the front of the house. There was no mistaking that familiar quick clatter. It was Celine.

"Judd?"

"Back here."

A combined surge of lust and tenderness rocketed through him when he saw her: sky-high legs in black slacks and pumps; white silk blouse under green blazer; small breasts pushing outward when she breathed; long-jawed, wide-mouthed, high-boned face surrounding calm gray eyes and haloed large by all that long auburn hair.

God almighty, he didn't know what to do. What he wanted to do most was jump up and get naked, but the telephone tone in her voice told him she hadn't come for any of that.

"Judd, I came to pick up a couple things."

"Yeah, I guess you tend to leave a lot of things behind after twenty-five years."

She ignored him and walked a few steps toward the desk, staring at the computer screen.

"What're you doing there?"

"I was trying to figure out what it would cost if the whole Angus herd went down."

"The Angus herd?"

"I told you on the phone. A hundred and fifty of them went down in one night."

"The state come out?"

"Yeah. It's something respiratory. They don't know what."

"The new pressure regulators come in for the Red Dog field?"

"Yeah."

"Thirty PSI difference?"

"Yeah."

"Just like we figured."

"They'll still save . . ."

"A million-five a year."

"Just like we figured."

"Alllll right!"

She smiled and wound up for a high-five, smacking his palm hard, and then catching the heat in his eyes as their skin touched.

"Congratulations," he said. "Those regulators were your idea."

Celine shrugged her tailored shoulders. "I just happened to see an article about them."

"Just like the one you read about the gene-spliced Angus and the high-pressure pipe and Rand Trucking."

"Just stuff I read."

"You've got a discerning mind. I depend on it."

She backed away from the desk and smoothed her jacket. "Well, you could have fooled me, Judd."

"I've always listened to you."

"Except about the really important things." Celine looked down at the floor, red hair falling over her eyes.

Jefferson rose from his chair and walked around the desk, moving forward as slowly as he would with a wild horse.

"Something big is happening, something bad, and it has to do with the cattle and Harlow and that little plant he built out in the western range."

She looked up and her eyes widened a little.

"I'm getting feelings I haven't had since I was in Vietnam."

"Then see someone about it, please."

"Listen, damnit! It's not flashbacks. It's more like Vietnam is coming here, and I have to be ready."

Tears welled in the corners of her gray eyes. She dropped her guard for a moment, and he stepped in close to her, sliding an arm around her waist, supporting her back with the other one.

"Come home, Cee."

Her arms hung limp at her sides, then moved up to the back of his neck, ran lightly along the tops of his shoulders, pressing, remembering. He bent to kiss her, but she pulled her arms in and pushed him away.

"No! I can't."

"Why?"

"I can't depend on you."

"How can you say that?"

"Damnit, Judd. I thought that no matter how tired or down I might get I could always rest in you."

Jefferson felt like the air had been sucked out of the room. He opened his mouth, but the words wouldn't come out. Then he backed away and tried again.

"You're talking about that fortune cookie thing, aren't you?"

She threw back her head, letting her hair fall down her back in a way that broke his heart.

"That was only a symptom."

"You know I didn't mean to hit you!"

"Judd, people who don't know what they're doing need help."

"Maybe you're the only kind of help I need."

She came forward a step, started to reach out to him, then clenched her fists and put them to the sides of her face.

"No! I can't. Everything in me wants to hold you until this thing in you passes, but I tried that for months and it didn't work. You've got to help yourself."

Jefferson sighed and went back to the desk. He sat heavily in the chair and reached into the top drawer for a cigarette.

Celine walked to the front of the desk, thighs pressed against the wood, marvelous thighs, forty-four years old and not a ripple of fat, not a varicose vein, strong and smooth, pinch against your sides like a velvet vise. He took a deep drag of the cigarette.

"I bet you're smoking a pack a day," she said.

"Come back, and I'll quit smoking."

Her smile was crooked and wan.

"No you wouldn't. There's something wrong inside you. You always had a temper, but you . . . you had such a light inside. Lately you're . . . I don't know. You tell me what it is."

"I've been trying to tell you."

"Dead cattle, something with Harlow?"

"He threatened to have me killed, Celine."

She was stunned for a second, but then she rubbed the back of her neck and laughed nervously.

"He was probably drunk. And I'm sure you said something to bait him."

"That's not the way it was at all. He was sober and completely serious. You know about him and the Indians in 1945."

"Yes, but . . ."

"He's got some kind of financial interest in this plant, and he'll do whatever it takes to protect it."

Celine put her fingertips on the desk and leaned forward. "Tell the law about what he said and then leave it alone. That's what anyone else would do."

Jefferson's fist slammed onto the desktop. "I'm not anyone else, damnit! I never wanted to be and I still don't."

"All right," she said, spreading her hands. "I think I'd better go."

Celine was right. This wasn't the way, throwing words at each other like rocks. In twenty-five years hadn't they made a home for themselves inside each other? You didn't throw rocks inside a home. You might break something.

He swiveled his chair away from her and clicked on the address for "Montana Millennium." What he got was the home page of a man named Vandivier. It contained a message:

> Behold! I will bring a sword upon you.
> And I will destroy your high places.
> Anyone who has heard of unexplained
> animal or human deaths, fevers,
> dementias, or localized epidemics, please
> contact me immediately with details of same. I have
> information to offer in exchange. . . . James Vandivier.

The message was followed by an E-mail address that was suddenly louder than Celine's voice.

"I'm going now, Judd," she said from behind him.

He swiveled his chair toward her and shrugged. "I love you, Celine."

She drew her fingertips across the desktop the way she'd often drawn them across his face. "I have to go now," she said.

She turned on her heel and walked out of the room. Jefferson turned back to the computer and sent an E-mail to Vandivier:

```
A herd of my cattle died in exactly the
kind of unexplained epidemic you asked
about. Contact me here.
```

Then he leaned back in his chair, wondering how he was going to wait until Vandivier contacted him. He lit a cigarette and considered getting a bottle and heading out on the plains for a few days—push it all out of his mind and then come back to see if there was really any Vandivier. He blew some cigarette smoke at the computer screen and saw he didn't have to wait a few days, or even a few hours. He got a message back that said:

```
Jefferson, received your message. If you
want to know what's going on meet me
tonight at the Lewis and Clark monument.
I have to see you in person. Ten o'clock.
Yes or no?
```

Jefferson stubbed out the cigarette and typed:

```
Yes.
```

TWENTY-FIVE HUNDRED miles away, in a suburb of Philadelphia, Joe Donnelly was in his basement computer station talking to Eddie Marcuse, his bookmaker. Eddie was thin, dark, and nervous. He paced back and forth as he talked, drinking the scotch Donnelly had given him.

"You know it ain't me," he was saying. "You know I ain't the kind of guy who'd threaten you. Hell, I'd just cut off your action and eat the twenty-seven thou. But I laid it off to my guy downtown, and he's connected. If he don't get his money, somebody's gonna get hurt, and, Joe, it ain't going to be me."

"I'll come up with it, Eddie. You know I always do."

"Where you gonna get it?"

"Credit cards, same as always."

"You got that much credit left? The way you been losing?"

"I told you, I make my own credit."

It had always been no problem. Donnelly was thirty-five and had built his first computer when he was fourteen. He'd dropped out of high school to go to an electronics trade school when he was sixteen, worked full-time as a programmer when he was eighteen, and had been running computer operations for First National Fidelity since he was thirty.

That was day work. His night work was hacking. He'd hacked into all the banks in town, Social Security records, Blue Cross, the credit bureau, the Department of Defense, and, most important, his own

MasterCard and Visa records at banks from Philadelphia to Fargo, North Dakota. He owned five credit cards with credit lines up to ten thousand each. Over the past five years, with Eddie's help, he'd maxed them all out three or four times, but it was no problem. He'd simply get into his files, write in large payments on all the cards, and start all over again, like now. He was maxed out and had just suffered a weekend when Roger Clemens, Greg Maddux, and Jack McDowell all lost. Three Cy Young winners losing in one weekend. What were the odds against that? Whatever they were, they had come in. He was maxed out and $27,000 down. And there was a problem.

"So," suggested Eddie, "maybe you better get started."

Donnelly pulled a Camel from his pocket, lit it, inhaled, and waited for the heart attack. A heart attack would be a fitting end to his weekend—maybe it would even help him. How could they expect him to come up with the money if he was in the hospital with a heart attack? He took another deep drag and then a big hit of scotch.

"No problem," he said, except there was one.

The banks that issued his credit cards all had their own security programs—cheeseboxes, which must have been put together by local high school teachers. That's why he'd chosen those particular banks to be his lending institutions. But now they had double-crossed him. MasterCard and Visa had apparently hired their own consultants to install an overall security program, and it was a murderous maze of switchbacks, false trails, and cul de sacs. Worst of all, Donnelly had the feeling that they had installed tracking features which would lead them back to him.

"Good, good," said Eddie. "So how about we take the cards and go get some money?"

"Well, you know. I can't get it all at once."

"Ten, then. That'll cool my guy out for a few days."

"Right. I'm maxed right now, but all I have to do is get in and show some payments. You know how it works."

"So, do your thing, Doctor."

Donnelly glanced at his wristwatch. It was already two in the afternoon. If he could stall Eddie until the banks were closed, it would give him time. Maybe if he worked all night he could crack this thing.

"I've got to wait until the banks close in Fargo, Eddie. If I start messing around while they're open, they'll notice."

Eddie took a couple nervous drags of his cigarette. "So what're you telling me? You can fix it tonight and get it tomorrow?"

"Sure, exactly. I just have to wait for some downtime out there."

"When tomorrow?"

Eddie was nervous, which meant his layoff guy must be very connected. Donnelly felt a queasy loosening in his bowels.

"Noon."

Eddie glanced at his watch and stubbed out his cigarette. "Understand something, man." he said. "As a friend, I'm telling you that's high noon. After that, I'm out of it. I got my livelihood to protect, people depending on me. Ten thou by noon and everything's cool."

"No problem," said Donnelly as Eddie let himself out the basement door.

Donnelly lit another Camel and went to work. At five he heard Elaine come in, followed by the clatter of the two girls. They knew not to come downstairs when Dad was working. At six-thirty Elaine opened the door and asked if he wanted dinner. He didn't. By nine he was bathed in sweat and had a headache. At eleven he drank more scotch to get rid of the headache, and by midnight he knew there was no way he was going to crack the security program by the next morning, or any other morning. He was thirty-five, ancient for the hacking game. Young blood had beaten him.

He thought of Elaine: lovely little woman with wavy hips and a wonderful smile, which he rarely saw anymore. She knew he was going down, saw it in his tortured squirming as he watched the games on TV. Fights all the time, even more than before. Had he gotten into the gambling because of the fights, or was it the other way around? He still loved her, which meant nothing when you were twenty-seven down and they were going to come after it.

He could get a second mortgage on the house, but that would take Elaine's signature. Would she do it? Could he ask her? What would they do to him? Beat him up? Surely they wouldn't kill him. He should have asked Eddie, but that would have tipped him off. It was over. How could he be Daddy anymore to his two girls when they knew he'd lost the chance for them to go to college?

One thing he knew from talking to Eddie—they wouldn't go after the family. That was the rule. The debts were the bettor's. They wouldn't go after the family. Eddie had said so, and Eddie had never lied to him. Eddie had even told him to chill on the betting, but why should he when it was a game played with the bank's money?

The game was now over. The marriage was over. Maybe it had been over for a while. They were going to come after him, and he needed someplace to go, somebody to be. He would give anything not to be Joe Donnelly. But he had nothing to give. It was all gone.

With a despondent flick of his hand, he let himself out of the credit security program and logged on to the Internet. Surfing around, he saw something called "Montana Millennium." He pulled it up and read:

> Behold. I will bring a sword upon you. And I
> will destroy your high places. . . . The stink of
> corruption will cover Montana like a fog.

Donnelly was Catholic in what was left of his soul. He still kept a Bible among his computer manuals, and now he dug it out and flipped through the prophets until he got to Ezekiel. He read until he got to the sixth chapter and found it: *I will destroy your high places. And your altars shall be dissolute, and your images shall be broken.*

The nuns had said things like that all the time, only in more modern language. He'd always thought it was meant for someone else, but now here it was, on his computer screen. And here he was, altars destroyed, images broken.

Donnelly slumped in his chair, overcome by a sense of deliverance. Ever since his boyhood, the computer had been his closest friend. Why shouldn't it be true that now, in the most dangerous moment of his life, it would save him? What was God if not the whole of cyberspace? Where else could you talk into the void and get an answer but on your computer? Who else could be speaking to him now if not God? *The stink of death . . . Montana.*

Apparently, he wasn't the only one filled with corruption. Montana was full of it too. And where there was sin, there was the opportunity for redemption.

The computer had spoken. And best of all, it was twenty-five hundred miles from Philadelphia. They would never look for him that far away. They would call it a loss and leave Elaine alone. But he couldn't tell her where he was going. She would yell, scream about his selfishness, tell him what a fool he was—the same things she said when they fought over the laundry.

He had to leave. He had to leave tonight. He'd never find redemption in a hospital bed, which is where he would end up if he stayed in Philadelphia.

Take the one credit card with a few hundred left on it. Take most of what was in the checking account. *Sorry, Elaine, but it's for everyone's good.*

Donnelly went quietly out the basement door and got into the station wagon, parked next to Elaine's Toyota. He released the brake and let the wagon drift down the driveway. He took a last look before starting the engine: two-story Colonial, lights ablaze against the soft spring night, angelic without the corruption of Joe Donnelly. It was a good thing he was doing. He felt better already.

6

THE Lewis and Clark monument was a six-foot granite obelisk on top of a hill overlooking miles of grassland. It marked the spot where the explorers' expedition had turned back after their party was attacked by Indians. The monument was a couple hundred yards off Highway 9, in the middle of the Blackfoot lands. At ten o'clock, there was no light but the moon and no sound but a shush of wind along the ground.

Jefferson pulled off the road and up the narrow lane to a small gravel parking area. Vandivier's car was already there, a beat-up gray Volvo circa '86. Jefferson got out of the Rover and looked in the Volvo's window, but there was no one inside. He turned away and walked up the hill to where the monument glowed blue in the shuttered light of a half moon. Vandivier was standing downhill with his back to the monument, staring north into the black sea of moving grass. Jefferson walked a few steps past the top of the hill.

"I'm Jefferson."

Vandivier spoke without turning around. "I wonder if it was the Indians that made them turn back or the immensity of it all."

Vandivier turned and came up the hill: thin body, concave chest, bald except for a ring of hair that fell to his collar, white shirt with cowboy snaps circled by a bolo tie. His wire-rim glasses glinted in the pale light like two quarters.

When he got to the top of the hill, he stuck out a hand and shook with a firm grip. There were lines around his eyes and little pouches under his thin jaw. He looked like he was in his early sixties, but there was a hippie quality about him, as if he were a college professor who'd stayed young by smoking weed with his students.

"You said you lost some cattle, Mr. Jefferson?"

"A hundred and fifty in one night. Perfectly healthy during the day, dead the next morning. The state man didn't know what to make of it."

"I guess you're quarantined at the moment."

"That's right."

"Well, I wouldn't worry about that too much. I don't think they'll find anything that will keep you that way for long."

"Why not?"

Vandivier walked to the monument and sat on its base, hands hanging between his knees.

"I'm a biologist," he said. "Came out here from Penn State to do doctoral work in 1956 and never left. I got a job teaching biology at the U of M. Got married and divorced, then did the same thing again. Two years ago I retired."

"Uh, yeah, but . . ."

"Yes, the point. What I'm trying to say is that I did whatever it took to stay in Montana. It's close to paradise, geographically as well as metaphorically."

"Geographically?"

Vandivier stared quietly at Jefferson, his eyes hidden by the moon reflected in his glasses.

"Yes," he said. "I believe these are the end times and the apocalypse is starting here."

"You with a survivalist group? Came here to fish, stayed to die?"

Vandivier laughed, deeper than Jefferson would have imagined. "I told you, I've been here since 1956. I was a member of the United Brethren Christian Church over in Flathead, but we only had thirty-five members. Some moved, some died. There weren't enough left to maintain a church. But Jesus said, Wheresoever two of you are gathered in my name, there also will I be."

"You think he really talked that poetically?"

Vandivier laughed again. "It's what he said that counts, not how he said it."

"Amen."

"Are you a believer?"

"Why don't you tell me something, and we'll see if I believe it."

Vandivier sighed, as if he was used to dealing with infidels.

"All right then, how do I begin? Do you know anything about viruses?"

"They're like germs, except they can't be treated with antibiotics."

Vandivier rose to his feet and looked into Jefferson's face. The moonlight shifted and his eyes showed for the first time, wide and bright with a far-off light of their own. He was a believer, all right.

"Actually," he said, "they're nothing like germs at all. Bacteria are what we commonly think of as germs, and bacteria are single-celled living organisms. They have their own cell membrane, their own genetic material, and their own cytoplasm. That's a semiliquid material that makes up the bulk of any cell."

Vandivier stopped talking and looked up. The sky was a fall of sapphire stars down a dome of blue night. He sighed and shrugged. "But viruses," he continued, "aren't cells. They have no nucleus, no cytoplasm, no membrane. They're just bits of genetic material, DNA or RNA surrounded by coats of protein. Every single one of a certain type is exactly the same size and shape as every other one of that type. In the traditional sense of the term, viruses aren't really alive."

Vandivier's voice took on more emotion as he talked, as if he were reciting a favorite poem.

"Not alive?"

"No."

"Then how do they do anything?"

"They hang around the atmosphere cocooned in their protein coats, waiting for dust particles or the drops of a sneeze. They're like travelers on a rocket ship in suspended animation."

"Waiting to get into my cattle? Is that where we're going with this?"

"You said they were alive at night and dead in the morning?"

"Yeah."

"Any bite marks, signs of a fight?"

"No, nothing."

"Were they lying in a group or scattered?"

Jefferson began to feel uneasy. The man knew something. "Scattered. Some of the grass was trampled, like they'd been running in circles."

"Something is very wrong, Mr. Jefferson."

"That's why we're here, Dr. Vandivier. Tell me."

Vandivier stuck his hands in his pocket and plowed ahead.

"Listen carefully. I'll try to make this as simple as possible. To reproduce, the virus has to get inside the cells of a host. Once inside, the viral genes get into the DNA chain of the host and direct it to start manufacturing more viral genes, then assemble them into viral proteins, which ultimately become a string of new viruses, which are released into the host's bloodstream."

Jefferson's mind was searching for some way to square what he was hearing with his experience of the world. "So, what are we talking about here—little brains? They plan this?"

Vandivier stared at Jefferson and cocked his head. "You're asking me if they think? The answer is no, they respond chemically. For example, a part of the body's immune system is a cell known as the killer T cell. Every killer T is programmed by the thymus gland to bind with one particular virus type. Because of this programming, people are born with T cells able to fight at least a million different invaders. Every killer T carries on its surface a protein that locks on to only one particular virus. When this happens, the infected cell is destroyed."

"Sounds like a certain kind of love," Jefferson said without thinking. "You know, opposites attract but end up destroying each other."

A shocked look crossed Vandivier's face. "I never thought of that, Mr. Jefferson. If I had, it might have prevented two bad marriages."

"Maybe you couldn't help it any more than the viruses and uh . . ."

"T cells."

"Right."

Vandivier scuffed the ground with the toe of his hiking shoe. He leaned against the monument. "There is a well-regarded theory that says viruses are bits of our own DNA which, eons ago, either worked themselves outside the body or were cast out."

"You mean they're us?"

"You seem familiar with the Bible, Mr. Jefferson. Do you recall that Satan was the angel Lucifer before he was cast out of heaven?"

"So . . . the Devil killed my cattle?"

Vandivier stepped up onto the monument's base and stared down at Jefferson, mercury-colored moonlight flashing from his glasses again.

"Well, death is the Devil's business isn't it?"

"You're not the most level-headed scientist I ever met, Doctor."

"Religion and science always cross at their outer boundaries, Mr. Jefferson. I need fifty thousand dollars."

"For what?"

"The Devil is coming to Montana, and I want to leave."

"No, I mean what would I be paying for? It is me who's supposed to give you the fifty K?"

"Fifty thousand is reasonable for my information."

"So far I haven't heard anything I couldn't find in the encyclopedia or the nearest church."

Vandivier jumped down from the monument and walked toward Jefferson, lowering his voice to a hoarse whisper, which blended with the wind.

"The rabies virus is poetically vicious. It's transmitted in the saliva when a carrier bites a victim. Then it gets into the nerves at the neuromuscular junction and travels to the brain. It invades and destroys the part of the brain that controls the impulse to bite. This takes time—sometimes two weeks, time enough for a vaccine to work. But right now, high up over the place where we're standing, common rabies viruses are mutating into ones that can settle into the lining of the lungs, then pass into the bloodstream, then to the lining of the brain and into the brain itself, all within a matter of hours."

Suddenly, Jefferson realized how hard it was to judge a learned man's sanity. Vandivier might be a lone genius or a lonely nut. "My animals all had rabies shots."

"A vaccine simply introduces the immune system to the invader so that when it attacks for real, it will be recognized. The mutant virus wouldn't be the same one used in the vaccine. It would be unrecognizable."

"I think there's a good chance you're insane."

Vandivier threw up his hands in frustration and kicked at a clod of dirt. "Listen," he said. "For several years the National Weather Service has known about a sizable ozone hole over this area of Montana. But you can see how they might not want to publicize such a thing."

"So?"

"The earth's ozone layer filters the ultraviolet radiation that streams in from space. The rabies mutations are probably due to the increased ultraviolet."

Vandivier was close now, and he looked as sure of himself as a snake eyeing a mouse.

Jefferson took a couple steps backward, trying to think. "Why aren't we all dead, then, like my cattle?"

Vandivier closed the distance between them, glancing over his shoulder as if someone might be listening. "The virus can't survive long outside a host. By the time it falls to earth, it has dried up and become inactive."

Vandivier fell silent but kept staring into Jefferson's face, waiting with a grim half smile. "You do see, don't you?"

Jefferson was afraid he did.

"If they would normally be dead by the time they reached the earth, but they were live enough to kill your cattle, it means somebody took them before they reached the earth and then . . . altered them."

Jefferson turned away, squatted, and looked into the darkness.

Vandivier gave him a few seconds to think then began talking again. "I arrived at my theory about the mutations two years ago but I couldn't reproduce the virus in the lab. The university's government funding was drying up and they weren't about to commit money to a man who was on the verge of retirement, especially when, just like you, they didn't consider me very level-headed."

"So, you waited two years and then decided to tell me?"

"Not at all. I wrote a report and tried to decide who to give it to. Then I thought of Senator Hairston. I went to a fund-raiser for Hairston in Bozeman and managed to give him the report I'd written summarizing my findings. He seemed interested, but two weeks later I got a visit from two FBI men, who told me not to say anything more. They said it was a matter of national security and that if I created a problem, they could put me away for as long as they wanted."

Jefferson turned and looked at Vandivier. "Without a charge or a trial? You bought that?"

"They reminded me that people disappear all the time. After they hit me in the ribs a few times, I started to believe them."

Jefferson was no great believer in government good faith, but he doubted the FBI would roust a citizen over a report that could be made to look like it came from a religious crackpot. If Vandivier was telling the truth, the men he had talked to were more likely sent by Harlow Rourke. Hairston had spent his whole career in Harlow's pocket and would have asked him what to do with Vandivier's report.

But if Harlow had gone to all that trouble, it meant he believed the report, which meant he'd checked it out and there was something to it. Jefferson felt a cold knot form in his stomach as a drop of sweat trickled down his back. He stood up, and when he spoke, his voice was louder than he meant it to be.

"Listen. If it turns out that my cattle died of rabies, then maybe we can talk, but if you think I'm going to hand you fifty thousand because I trust you, then you're even crazier than you seem."

Vandivier was holding up his hands and backing away as if he expected to be hit. "Fair enough, Mr. Jefferson. Wait until you get the diagnosis. But if it turns out to be rabies and you want my report, footnoted and cross-indexed, contact me via E-mail. But be prepared to spend fifty thousand dollars. That's enough for me to leave the state and settle in Alaska."

Jefferson walked to the monument and stared into the grassland beyond, wondering if Vandivier was just a religious nut with a bad case of paranoia, knowing he was wrong, feeling a foreign rustle in the wind . . . moving curtains in front of a closed window. More sweat ran down his back. He turned to face him. "Okay, it's a deal."

"You may not believe this," said Vandivier, "but I hope I'm wrong. I'm not, though. The beast is coming."

Vandivier turned toward the parking lot and disappeared into the darkness.

Jefferson looked out into the long flat night and realized it was where he needed to go—away from science and money and spoken religion. He'd take a bottle and some cigars, cuss the bears because they had the good life. All they did was eat, sleep, roam, and mate. Maybe if he stayed out on the plains for a few days he could figure out how the bears had gotten so lucky.

7

JOSEPH Far Lightning was thinking about General George Custer, or rather a famous picture of Custer: big hat, long hair, the floppy mustache all the old bully-boys wore to hide their weak mouths. It was the eyes, though, that told on his soul—lightless as a poisoned pond. All the old Indian killers had dead-man eyes. Too much killing of women and babies would do that to you.

The three cowboys at the bar had the same kind of faces as Custer and his syphilitic Seventh Cavalry. Ten to one there was going to be a fight unless Far Lightning left now, which he had no intention of doing.

He was sitting in a back booth of the Buffalo Wallow Bar and Grill, a high-toned place, or at least as high-toned as places got in Wild Gap, Montana. It was large and clean and the furniture was as blond as the big-bosomed Swede waitresses. They gave you a glass with your beer, and everyone was careful to spit his snuff into a paper cup.

It was two in the afternoon. There was no one in the place except Far Lightning, the three cowboys off the Rourke ranch, some women real estate agents, and that crazy Donnelly bastard who'd shown up a month ago in a 1984 Chevy Celebrity station wagon, which he'd been living in ever since. In the evenings he'd bump the thing out through the scrub toward Glacier Park. In the morning he'd wash naked in a stream while grabbing at trout, then head back to the Buffalo Wallow.

The white people said he was crazy, but they said that about everyone who made them nervous. Their next step was to lock you up or kill you. Usually, they hired the truly crazy to do it for them, people like Custer. Far Lightning began to hum an Oglala hunting song.

"What the hell's that noise I hear?" said one of the cowboys at the bar.

"Maybe it's me," answered Donnelly. "Did I say something?"

Far Lightning was beginning to think Donnelly was a Heyoka, a sacred clown. Heyokas had to do everything backward. If the day was hot, they wore heavy robes and complained of the cold. In the dead of winter, they jumped naked into freezing streams. They walked backward, rode facing the rear of their horses, and lived apart from the rest of the tribe. But they saw visions of the future.

Of course, the Bureau of Indian Affairs had been murdering Indian culture for a couple hundred years, so most Indians didn't believe in Heyokas anymore. But Far Lightning knew there were visions. He'd had a few himself. Even some white men had visions, men like Jack Kerouac and Neal Cassady. Beatniks, the other white people called them, but they were really white Indians, nomads, changing cars like horses. It was good to remember that not all whites were nervous weasels.

"I'm telling you," said the ugliest of the three cowboys. "There's some kind of animal sound in here, like something that ought to be throwed out."

"Did I say something again?" asked Donnelly. "Sometimes things come to me lately, but jeez, I didn't kill anyone. It wasn't like I killed anyone."

Donnelly looked into his glass of whiskey like he was searching for his eyeball, then drained it off, gasping for another before he'd even finished swallowing. The cowboys paid no attention to him; they'd heard his spiels before.

Donnelly's hair was a reddish color, but it was hard to tell because it was covered with a powder of red clay-dust, just like the rest of him. He had a lot of hair, though, and it stuck out in all directions. He was mid-sized and he wore Eastern street shoes instead of boots. The heels were worn to the ground, which made him move in a jumping trot like coyote. Far Lightning wondered if Donnelly could stay free long enough to act out his vision.

Far Lightning took a drink of beer and kept on with the hunting song. He wondered how long it would be before the three cowboys worked up enough guts to fight. He wondered why he had come into Wild Gap at all. Some tourist was always wanting to take a picture of you holding a rubber tomahawk. Or a Custer-faced moron would want to fight.

Far Lightning was fifty-two years old, but his six-one frame carried 190, and very little of it was gut. He'd won most of his fights because he had to. If you were an Indian and ended up on the floor, someone would come to lock you up. Then your three ex-wives would show up wanting back child support. Why should wives stay with their husbands when they could get child support? Child support was one more corruption brought by the whites, like whiskey and smallpox.

Far Lightning evaded his ex-wives by living alone on the high plains east of Glacier National Park, listening to the voice of the earth, looking for visions. Sometimes he went to the reservation for some social life. Sometimes he went to Las Vegas to gamble and buy a woman. Buying a woman was not as satisfying as marrying one, but it was a lot cheaper. They didn't tell you that in college. They didn't tell you much of anything in college. He'd been three years to Stanford on a do-gooder 1960s scholarship but quit when he found himself subscribing to *The Wall Street Journal*. Finance made you nervous, and the more you knew, the more nervous you got. Pretty soon you couldn't look at the rain without thinking how it would affect the commodities market. Foresight was no substitute for vision, so now he spent most of his time on the plains. The only white man he saw much of was John David Jefferson.

It would be night and Far Lightning would be studying the light around the moon to find the weather, then a black shadow would pass along the horizon. The next day Jefferson would ride into camp with a bottle of tequila, which they would drink together, making bets on the shifting of the wind.

Whether or not Jefferson was his friend was something both of them were still trying to decide. It was a tough question. Jefferson was white, and Far Lightning was half in love with his wife.

Two years ago, he'd used some of his Stanford reputation to get a job at the U of Montana extension campus in Great Falls. He was short on cash and thought maybe he could do some good teaching a course in Native American studies.

Celine Jefferson took the course, and he hadn't been able to forget her. She was a redhead out of the East with a half-moon profile like an Egyptian queen. She was tall and long-limbed, spring-butted, a racehorse woman. The first time she came up to his desk, her eyes made him deaf. They were pearl-gray, wide-set, and kind. She had a light.

He was the teacher, she was the student. That was all. At the end of the semester they exchanged a handshake and went home. But he remembered, especially when he was drinking with Jefferson. He wanted to ask about her but didn't, and Jefferson knew there was something unspoken being said.

Far Lightning took another drink and kept humming.

"Goddamnit, now, I hear it again," said the ugly cowboy, a beefy dirtbag whose idea of politeness would be to let the manure dry on his boots before entering your home.

"Yeah," chimed in a younger, rangy guy on his left. "Some kind of animal. Animals ain't allowed in here, are they?"

The third guy, the smallest of the three, just laughed and lit a cigarette.

"And, by God," said the first one. "I believe I know where it's coming from." Then all three of them turned toward Far Lightning.

Yeah, here came the bully-boys. They were always so sure they were going to win. But the gold rush was over and the great father in Washington was far away. Custer had forgotten that, too.

Far Lightning lit a cigarette and puffed it up to a hot ash. That was for the first one's eye. Then he lightly tapped his jacket to locate the handle of his blackjack. It was for the rangy one's kneecap. His long-necked bottle of Coors was for the little one, but the little one didn't look all that anxious.

"Hey there, Chief," the first one said. "You got some kind of pig under the table. Even Injuns ain't allowed to bring pigs in a bar."

Why the hell did they always want to call you Chief before trying to beat the crap out of you?

8

CELINE Jefferson was sitting in a corner banquette only half listening to Marylin Torborg review development plans for the Jensen ranch. Ordinarily, she would have dived into the discussion, but her mind was on Judd. She hadn't been able to put aside what he'd said about Harlow threatening to kill him.

Celine had the vague feeling Marylin was saying something to her and she was trying to concoct a response when male voices mentioned a pig and the room's tension level rose. Three scuzzy cowboys were gathered around a booth, jawing at someone seated there. She couldn't get a look at the seated man through the cowboys, but she'd bet it was an Indian. These cow-chip commandos always started on Indians if one was stupid enough to show up anywhere he could be had for cheap. Also, she could see a hint of graying braids through the shit-shufflers' backs. God! They'd gotten hold of one who was middle-aged. She glanced around the bar to see if the Indian could expect any help, but there was no one except the bartender and that crazy Donnelly bastard.

"I can say what I want," Donnelly was yelling at the oblivious cowboys. "I didn't kill anyone, damnit."

"Someone should do something," Marylin said, taking a sip of her gin and tonic.

"Yes," Celine agreed. "Anyone got a gun? We could shoot the whole boys' club and get on with the meeting."

"As if you were listening anyway," Marylin answered, sucking in more Tanqueray and Schweppes.

Someone should do something. What would Judd do if he were here? *What the hell do you think he'd do? He'd probably be the one person in the room who actually did have a gun.*

The cowboys were crowding closer to the table, building up enough energy to make the first move. The Indian was still seated. She didn't think he was saying anything. Maybe he was too drunk to move. More man crap! Why the hell couldn't men get it through their heads that nobody cared about all their fightin', fuckin', fartin' bullshit? Did they think God cared who could beat up who? Was he going to move them into the big time if they won enough fights? Or was it money? Maybe if they all had money it would help. But Judd had money and he was impossible. Someone should do something.

Celine stepped over Dorothy Werner and jumped out into the middle of the floor, taking her purse with her. When she hit the middle of the room, she opened the purse and took out a wad of fifties she had withdrawn to go shopping in Great Falls. Crumpling them like spitballs, she started throwing them at the backs of the cowboys while screaming at them:

"Here, you dirt-surfing, dog-breath bozos. Take some money, have some money, put it in your pants. It'll be the most valuable thing you've ever had in there, that's for sure."

She was yelling as loud as she could, but none of the men paid any attention because the fight had just started for real. In a movement that shocked her into silence, the Indian's arm shot straight out and jabbed a lighted cigarette into the eye of the biggest cowboy, who bellowed like a castrated bull and shot backward from the booth, crashing into an empty table, scattering chairs like shrapnel. Celine was still trying to take this in when she heard a shriek from the taller cowboy and saw him go down clutching his knee and uttering a continuous high-pitched scream. But the Indian had been forced to bend over to do whatever he did to the tall cowboy, giving the little one a chance to kick him in the ribs, rolling him out of the booth and onto the floor, where he was making a maximum effort to get up when the first cowboy got over the initial pain of his burn and came for him.

Apparently, the Indian had missed the slug-bucket's eyeball, because he seemed perfectly able to see as he swung a chair at the Indian, who had risen but was forced to fall back into the booth to avoid the chair. The tall cowboy was out of action, but the big and little ones now charged the Indian, who was trapped inside the booth. He managed to clip the little one underneath the chin with a swing of his boot, but the big one pinned him and was reaching into his back pocket for a folding buck knife when, out of the space behind her, Celine saw a red missile launch itself into the air with a scream.

It was that crazy Donnelly bastard! He literally flew headfirst past Celine and into the back of the big cowboy, knocking the buck knife out of his hand and the wind out of his body. With a huff like a punctured bladder, the cowboy went down under Donnelly, while the Indian slid out of the booth and came up in back of them both. The

Indian took time to grab the little cowboy and smash his head against a corner of the booth. Donnelly was on top of the big cowboy, gouging at his eyes and screaming something about odds.

"Come on," she heard the Indian say to Donnelly as he pulled him off the big cowboy. "We've got to get out of here before the cops come. Understand?"

The Indian shook Donnelly as he talked, putting his hand over his mouth to make him listen.

"We've got to get out of here, Heyoka. They'll lock us both up."

Then Donnelly shut up and looked at the Indian like he understood. Turning on his run-down shoes, he headed toward the door at a dead run.

"Fuck all odds," she heard him yell as he reached the parking lot.

By this time the big cowboy was trying to get up, but the Indian hit him in the kidneys three times and he went down again, moaning when he was able. Then the Indian turned and ran toward her. She knew she should get out of the way, but her feet couldn't seem to pick a direction. He stopped just in front of her, staring with shocked eyes.

"Celine?" he said.

"What?"

"Celine Jefferson?"

"What?" she stammered again.

"I'm Joseph Far Lightning. U of M extension class? Two years ago?"

God yes, it was her soft-spoken instructor. What was a nice guy like him doing in a fight like this?

"Yes," she said. "Now I remember."

"So nice to see you," he said, as if they were at a faculty tea. Then he took her hand in both of his and shook it.

"Well, I have to go," he said. "The cops, you know."

Then he was out the door.

Celine wandered back to her table and drained off what was left of her scotch and water.

"Well," said Marylin. "Courtly fellow, isn't he, when he's not committing mayhem."

"I'd pick that money up before the police get here if I were you," advised Dorothy. "You know how they are."

9

CELINE was on her way home in her Chevy Suburban. Further discussion of the Jensen property had been tabled. Instead, they had four more rounds of drinks, during which her frustration had come out as anger and she'd participated in an impromptu seminar on the stupidity of men.

The consensus was that men lived in a fantasy world where they were durable as robots, when in reality they were brittle and breakable; always in the midst of a countdown for the unguided missiles between their legs, their computers checking for malfunctions, always online to the women at mission control but refusing to acknowledge they were even wearing headphones.

Celine had become bored with the whole rant before it was over. Hell yes, men were everything women said they were. Women were so much more mature than men, so much more knowledgeable. But all that knowledge got boring.

Men were a whole other country, but if you got past the border, they could be downright majestic in the scope and variety of their landscapes. They were wilderness areas, full of wild beauty and hidden violence, horse muscle at noon, wolf eyes at midnight, maniacal motion or absolute rest. And Judd was beautiful in either state.

She thought back to that spring day in 1970 when she first saw him. It wasn't so much that he had been incredibly handsome, though he was: six-four, broad shoulders, thick black hair, a jaw like the front of a ship. It was the way he had been standing—his head tilted back, he was staring into the upper reaches of a large magnolia tree.

He was wearing a loose white shirt with sleeves that flared like wings over his black jeans, making him look as fanciful as a prince in a poem. She instantly moved toward him, trying to connect with him somewhere in the magnolia leaves.

He didn't look down as she approached, but he did stop turning. "Promised myself I'd do this," he said.

His voice was a Southern M&M: hard baritone shell; sweet, soft center.

"Do what?" she croaked, still looking into the tree.

"Come back here, take in the smell of this tree."

She took a long draught of sweetened air. "This particular tree?"

"This very one. I've been away. This tree came into my mind a lot, so I promised myself."

"You graduated from here?"

"Got halfway through my senior year."

"I'm halfway through my senior year."

They stopped looking up into the tree and began looking at each other. His eyes were black onyx shining through a sea of magnolia perfume.

"Why this particular tree?"

"Because this is where I opened my draft notice."

"Oh."

"You're not gonna run off now, are you?"

If only she could have, but she felt as rooted as the tree. "Now, why would I do that?"

"Don't know. Everybody does, though."

Of course they did. It was 1970, and when a guy told you he'd been to Vietnam, you shifted into neutral and coasted for the nearest exit.

"Why don't you just not tell them?"

He looked at her with mild surprise, shrugged, and said, "I don't, usually."

Her throat tightened. She could barely manage to speak the question.

"Why tell me?"

"Even before I looked at you, it seemed like I'd thought of you, just like the tree."

It sounded like a pickup line. She started to laugh, but the sound never got past the lump in her throat.

They sat under the tree and shared a tuna sandwich she was carrying. He was only going to be in Richmond for a week, then he was returning to Montana. When he was discharged from the army in Seattle, he'd decided to rent a car and drive home. Then, when he got to Montana, he'd realized it was home. He was leaving in three days.

But he didn't. Instead, he stayed for three weeks, which seemed like three days. She quit going to class and spent the time with him in a series of hotel rooms along the banks of the James River. The scent of magnolia was everywhere, and the flower scent soaked into the sweat of his body to create a musk so lasting she could still smell it when she wanted to, only now she didn't want to. But it was there anyway, lodged in the front of her head, just above the tears running down her face.

She pulled the car to the side of the road and sat staring at a blurred wash of sunflowers that flowed toward the Rockies in a three-mile wave. She licked a tear from the corner of her mouth and its salt reminded her of how summer used to mean the sea.

When she was young, before Judd, her parents had always taken the family to spend part of the summer at Myrtle Beach, where five o'clock was her favorite time of day: the beach nearly deserted, the sun low and gentle, afternoon breezes mellowing into a constant caress that played with the hair at the back of her neck, making her stretch her long legs toward the setting sun and dream of something sweet to hold between them. Well, she'd found something sweet and held it, so tightly that it now seemed she was permanently weak in the knees.

He could have stopped her from leaving. All he had to do was let go of the darkness that was driving her away. All the drinking, the brooding, the damn "Space Invaders." He'd spend hours in the game room playing "Space Invaders" on a secondhand machine he'd bought from an arcade that was going out of business. And then there were the bar fights. A forty-nine-year-old man didn't get into bar fights unless something bad was happening to him.

Something was even wrong with the sex. Sometimes he'd whale away at her like a crazy man, slamming her head against the backboard, going on and on like he was trying to kill something. She always came, but there was no satisfaction in the coming. Still, she stayed—until the thing with the fortune cookie.

She and Marylin had been trying to sell a piece of grazing land to a representative of a big cattle company. He was a big guy named Baker and looked a little like Marlon Brando. Marylin was half attracted to him and thought it would be a good idea to take him out to dinner. Celine invited Judd to make it a foursome, and they'd gone to a Chinese restaurant in Great Falls. During dinner Judd had been congenial enough, engaging Baker in conversation about cattle and places they'd seen. Baker's company supplied meat to the fast-food industry, and he traveled all over the hemisphere in search of burger fodder.

After dinner came the complimentary tray of fortune cookies, and Marylin had insisted that everyone open one. Celine didn't remember what hers said. She remembered Baker's though: *The family's wealth is found in its children.*

Generically uplifting, maybe even true. Baker, probably trying to impress Marylin with his wit, chuckled and said, "Yeah, but too many of 'em and you got a problem."

"How's that?" Judd asked quickly.

Celine sensed what was coming and tried to head things off by suggesting another round of drinks, but there had been too many drinks already. Baker picked up the note of challenge in Judd's voice and was moved to respond. He said he bought a lot of cattle in Brazil and that down there, kids roamed all over the streets, little kids, seven, eight, ten years old, running in packs, begging and hustling.

"Really clog things up, huh?" Judd said, baiting him.

"That's the word for it, all right," answered Baker. "It's scary. Their families send them out to bring home the bacon and they're hanging all over you, plucking at your clothes like weasels, ripping and tearing at you. It's scary. They're out of control. You get so you wish a big vacuum cleaner would come along and just sweep them up."

Judd's hand shot across the table and locked around Baker's throat, pinning his head against the back of the booth.

"One does come," he said as leaned into Baker's throat. "Government death squads. They pick up the kids, take them away, and kill them. That good enough for you? Is that good enough?"

Judd was half standing, leaning with all his weight as Baker turned bloodred and pawed at him.

"Got to keep the tourists happy, don't they?" Judd hissed, oblivious to the fact that Baker's face was changing color.

"Judd," Celine shouted, and grabbed his arm with both hands, tugging with all her might. Then it happened. He released his grip on Baker's neck and swung his arm back as if he were batting away a mosquito. His forearm slammed into the side of her head, knocking her backward into the wall.

Instantly, he was all over her with apologies, caressing her face, pleading for her to say something, but all she could do was stare at him with blank terror, looking through friend, husband, and lover to something deadly. Judd turned and opened his mouth to apologize to Baker, who was too busy gulping air to pay any attention.

"I'm sorry," he said to the room in general, then got up and headed for the door.

Baker left as soon as he was able, and Celine spent the night with Marylin. The next day she phoned Judd and told him she was leaving. He thought it was because he had hit her and said it was an accident. She believed him, but it didn't matter.

She wasn't ready to follow him into the darkness, and that's where he was going. Hell, she had probably known it even in those hotel rooms along the James River. She'd wake up and see him standing in the smoky evening dusk, naked in front of an open window, drinking from a bottle. She'd look at his face, and, tracking the look in his eyes, she'd see that he was searching for the approach of night. His head would tilt gradually as though he could follow the leading edge of darkness as it came for him.

Back then, it didn't bother her. He was just back from a war. He had some private things to work out. There was never much doubt in either of their minds that she was going to Montana.

MONTANA WAS OLDER than history, bigger than life, and empty as death, six hundred miles of tableland running out of the east on a wave of grass. Then it ran into the Rocky Mountains. They rose from the flatland in a jagged curtain of shifting light reaching from the Canadian border to Colorado, a dreamscape that made the waking world seem false.

But if you stayed long enough, you enlarged to fit the land. She and Judd had made one hell of a team. She read and suggested. He acted and invested. Pretty soon there were gas wells all over their land, then more land, cattle, timber in Oregon, interstate trucking, mining in Alaska. The first million dollars surprised her; the later millions didn't.

. . .

CELINE LOOKED UP with a start and realized her head had been resting on the steering wheel. Long mountain shadows were beginning to cover the wash of sunflowers in front of her. She glanced at her watch. Five P.M.

Automatically, she twisted the key in the ignition, then remembered there was no one waiting for her. Home was now the cabin up near Lake McDonald where she and Judd used to take the kids in the summer. Damnit, she couldn't stop thinking about him. It was like she could feel him next to her, and something next to him, dangerous, alive, tangible as footsteps in a dark room.

"Guilt," she said. "Only natural. You did the only thing left for you to do."

Then she noticed a hole in her slacks, small, about the size of a dime but something about it held her attention. She kept staring at it and the patch of tanned leg beneath it. It was time to turn the car onto the road but the patch of leg was staring back at her. There was something in the hole. No, something the shape of the hole, something without skin, rising from the floor of the car, hovering in the darkness of the passenger seat, something that could see her. It was watching, waiting, getting bigger.

It was nothing, nothing but shadows and imagination and alcohol. She looked resolutely at the road and turned the wheel, but she could still see it out of the corner of her eye. When she tried to look at it directly it slid away as if it were imprinted on her eyelid. She snapped her head to the right, trying to catch it, but it slid away again, down toward the hole in her pants, making her nauseous and shaky. Something was watching, an eye-shaped darkness now everywhere in the car but nowhere.

"Stop it, goddamnit," she screamed.

She flipped open the glove box and pawed papers and tissues onto the floor until she found a pack of Camel Lights. She had a hard time fitting the shaking end into the car's lighter, but she finally managed to light one and drag deeply. The bite of the smoke in her lungs and the rush to her head cleared the thing away, forcing it somewhere to the extreme rear of the car. She chain-smoked all the way to the cabin, and by the time she got there, her vertigo or whatever it was had been replaced by a comforting nicotine headache.

She threw her pants into the bottom of the clothes hamper, had a hit of straight scotch, and went to bed. In the half light at the edge of sleep she saw the thing in the car fading away. She plopped back onto the pillow and drifted toward sleep, hoping for a dream. These days her dreams were more real than life, and more welcome.

10

PETE Haskins's cigarette croak sounded like a chicken over the phone.

"Well, boss, I guess if the world was flat we'd understand it better."

Jefferson tried to understand this Pete-ism but couldn't.

"How's that, Pete?"

"It was rabies. All them cattle had their shots, but it was rabies anyway."

"That's what the state man said?"

"No, I wrote down what he said."

Jefferson could hear Pete rustling a piece of paper.

"Okay. He said it was a mutated form of the rabies virus with an abnormal nucleotide chain, which directed the production of atypical protein indicators not found in the normally administered rabies vaccine, thus rendering the mutated virus impervious to the animals' immune systems."

"Good job on those words, Pete."

"I been practicing. Any of that make sense to you?"

"Yeah, Pete. I'm afraid it does. What did they say about the quarantine?"

"Nothin' shows up in two weeks, we're in the clear."

"Thanks, Pete."

"Right, boss."

Jefferson clicked off the cellular phone and felt something cold in the middle of his back.

"Jack, stop that."

Jack paid no attention. He only did what he was told when you had a spur in his ribs. Jack should have been gelded, but the big buckskin had a glimmer of intelligence in his eyes that might go out if his balls were cut off.

"Damnit, Jack. I said stop it."

The horse kept nudging him in the back with his muzzle, and it felt scratchy and cold because Jefferson was naked. It was June first, warm, about 75 degrees, blue sky, eagles circling through wispy cirrus, air sweetened by a warm chinook out of the west. All of a sudden it had seemed like a good idea to chuck his clothes and spend the morning outside listening to "Mr. Tambourine Man" on his portable tape player.

He and Celine had listened to that Dylan tape all the way down the James River and then sung the songs together on the drive to Montana. How could she turn her back on their history? He couldn't, even with the help of tequila and Layla Bright.

Layla was a big girl with a heart-shaped butt and rocket breasts. Her blond hair curled wild and loose around a full-lipped face. She loved to laugh. Her only problem was age. She was just twenty-eight—not even born when Jefferson and his high school friends had tiptoed through the Cuban Missile Crisis wondering if they'd live to be eighteen. She was two years old when he was pulling dead bodies out of the Mekong River, three when he and Celine were leaning out the window of his van bellowing Dylan songs. Layla got Jack Kennedy confused with Bobby, and wouldn't listen to Dylan because he sang through his nose.

But she said she loved Judd Jefferson, said the gray in his hair was like streaks of light, the veins in his hands like rivers on a map. She even laughed when he did his Jack-Nicholson-reads-the-Bible bit.

He loved all that, but he didn't talk to her when she wasn't there, and he couldn't feel her when he was alone or see her when he looked in the mirror. He couldn't feel years of himself inside her when they had sex—and they had plenty of sex. Maybe more than he'd had with Celine, because it didn't leave him satisfied like it did with Celine. It was good. It was fun. It was hot. But it wasn't love.

He reached for the bottle of tequila lying on the ground next to him, took a mouthful, and listened to the sound of the spring wind as it lofted the Rockies and rode the spangled morning, sweeping down on him clean and bright. Two circling eagles rose high enough to be almost out of sight. A half mile away, the stream would be running fast and cold with melted snow from the peaks where the eagles lived. Just below the peaks were the glaciers, always there, the last legs of the ice age.

Damn, he loved Montana. People here did what they had to do—like old Jack Nord, who got stranded in an upland cabin once and shot off his frostbitten toes when they began to look gangrenous.

People stuck it out here, and Celine was going to cut him loose because of some article she'd read about post-Vietnam stress syndrome?

That's what she was hinting at with all her talk about counseling. She'd read an article about stress syndrome and decided he had it, but he didn't. You had to repress your memories to get it, and he remembered everything: the Criminal Investigation Division; the black market; the heroin trade; the triads; and C. K. Lone, dealer in children, bought cheap and sold high. How could you forget twelve-year-old whores and snuff films? He remembered it all clear as to-day's sky—especially Lone. He'd been remembering Lone a lot lately. Most of all, he remembered a hot Saigon morning, heat waves, smoke, an oily fire, and the smell of Lamh and Sylvie watching their own bodies burn.

Lamh was a proud man. What a humiliation it must have been for him. Sylvie was probably as calm as one of those monks who burned themselves alive, comforted by the knowledge that Lone knew she'd taken his money while risking everything for Lamh.

Jefferson would never get over the fact that he'd had Lone in the sights of an M-16 that morning. Just a hair more patience and the bastard's head, not his side, would have had a hole in it.

The realization would hit him at odd times, like when he was standing next to the drinks table at a wedding reception or in church on Christmas Eve: Lone was still alive. When the full moon eased over the peaks, you could feel him sending death wishes into the graveyard light. He was out there somewhere.

Jefferson took another hit of tequila and started putting on his clothes. Time to get on Jack and ride.

IT WAS TWO in the afternoon. Jefferson was riding northeast, toward an intersection of property lines where his land came to-gether with the Blackfoot reservation and the outer reaches of Gla-cier National Park. He stopped to take in a spot where the land swept away toward the Rockies in a wave of grass that broke sharply onto distant groves of aspen and birch. He was marveling at the baby-hair smell in the air when he saw a rider emerge from the trees and head toward him.

He pulled out his binoculars and uttered a short laugh when he recognized Vincent Gionfredo, wearing a huge cowboy hat that made him look like a table for two. He was also sporting boots with red toes and one of those shoelace ties worn by people who thought it was a real shame Hoss Cartwright had died a virgin.

Gionfredo was a fast-talking New York guy who'd been around for about six months. He'd bought a big house off Route 83 near St. Mary but seemed to spend all his time hanging around the Four Chiefs diner, where Layla was the cashier. A couple times he'd asked Jefferson about the ranching business, but it was really Layla he had on his mind. He'd kid her about tough steak in a tender voice and hand her a tip. He always made sure he handed out his tips, never just left them on the table. Layla liked that. Jefferson didn't. He supposed one day he and Gionfredo would have to fight over Layla. As silly as it seemed, he guessed he'd do it when the time came.

Jefferson put the binoculars away and replaced them with the tequila bottle. He took a large mouthful and felt the wings on his head grow a little wider. He was getting fairly drunk and liking it.

"That outfit looks like square dance night at the dude ranch," Jefferson said to Gionfredo as he reined in the aging bay he was riding. "You buy it with your horse's Social Security check?"

Jefferson was cracking himself up, so he had another hit of tequila.

"You're drunk, Jefferson," said Gionfredo. "This is a hell of a time to find you drunk."

"A helluva time all right," Jefferson said, offering him the bottle. "Have one."

"Don't want one. Listen . . ."

"Have one, damnit. It's the code of the West. You don't take it we have to fight."

"I'm tryin' to tell you somethin'."

"Have one."

"Awright, awright."

Gionfredo grabbed the bottle, swallowed hard, winced, and gagged it down.

"Jesus, tastes like somethin' I'd put in my car. You wanta listen to what I got to tell you now?"

Sweat was pouring off Gionfredo like rain off a barn roof, and there was a hard place in back of his eyes.

"Yeah, sure. Tell me."

"There's a guy just over the rise who's running up balloons over your property."

Jefferson took another drink and wondered at the strange turn the day seemed to be taking.

"Balloons? What kind of balloons?"

"I dunno . . . balloons, on a cable. He's got a drum thing in a van. He winds 'em out and fastens them to the ground. You gonna just sit here an' ask me questions?"

What did Gionfredo expect him to do, ride down and shoot the guy?

"Whall, pardner," he said in his best John Wayne. "There'll be no balloon herders allowed in these parts. This is cattle country."

"It ain't gonna be so funny when you find out who it is," said Gionfredo.

"You know the guy?"

"Not the guy, damnit, the outfit he works for."

"You talked to him already?"

"Yeah, before I saw you."

"Let me ask you something, Gionfredo."

"Every time I see you I tell you to call me Vinnie, but you never do."

"I've got my reasons."

"More code of the West shit?"

"Maybe. Why are you so interested in what happens on my land?"

"I got my reasons. You gonna go and talk to this guy, or you gonna let the fish rot right under your nose?"

"What's that mean?"

"The code of the East."

"Okay, let's go."

IT WAS A van, all right, and it had a kind of winch outfit in the back, which was playing out wire cable to what looked like a weather balloon. Five of them were already anchored in place

74

with eye hooks driven into the ground. An Asian man wearing a Dodgers baseball cap was working the winch. As Jefferson rode up with Gionfredo, he stopped what he was doing and bowed slightly.

"Hello," he said. "My name is George Yohiro, and you are?"

"His name's Jefferson," blurted Gionfredo, "and he can bag your ass up and ship you back to Yoko Ono or wherever it is you came from."

Jefferson took one more drink and realized he was now seeing the two other men through a tequila window that made them look like cartoons. That's what this was—a cartoon, cat and mouse, Vinnie and George. Jefferson remembered his favorite cartoon as a kid was Yosemite Sam, cowboy hat, red beard, two six-shooters. Then he remembered the .44 magnum in his saddlebags and smiled.

"I say, what's the deal here?" he asked in a Yosemite Sam voice as he pulled out the gun. "Why don't you tell me what you're doing here."

"I'm just taking some air samples."

"You're on my property."

"Yes, yes, but it's for your own protection."

"How's that grab you, Jefferson?" Vinnie asked. "Your own protection."

"I'm head of the plant safety program," Yohiro added quickly. "The manager got a complaint about some dead cattle."

"That would be the computer chip factory a few miles southeast of here?"

"Yes, Unitel computer chips."

"I'm the one who made the complaint, and I didn't say anything about the air."

"We're just covering every possibility."

This was getting really strange: Japanese balloon guy, rocking horse Italian cowboy, air samples when no one had complained about the air, all of it on his land. This was definitely a case for Yosemite Sam.

"Yahoo," he said as he shot two of the balloons. The thin wire cables fell to earth, and Jefferson rode over to them. Attached to the remnants of the balloons were what looked like automobile oil filters, wire cages lined with layers of paper.

"It's just an air sampler," Yohiro blurted. "It captures pollutants, foreign particles. Checks the air quality, that's all."

Jefferson rode back to him, pistol dangling at his side, sloppy smile on his face.

"He's lying," Gionfredo snapped.

Jefferson turned and looked at him. "What is it with you and this guy?"

"You heard who he works for."

"Unitel."

"Tell-Shmell. It's owned by the Tsendai Corporation. Ask him."

Jefferson looked at Yohiro, who nodded his head nervously.

"Tsendai," Gionfredo said bitterly.

"So what?"asked Jefferson.

"They build theme parks. In 1996 they wanted to build one of them Chuck D. Doughnut parks up in Buffalo. Only some . . . organizations in New York control the construction unions. Tsendai doesn't want to pay the going rate, so they have some union trouble. After about two weeks the cops find the president of the ironworkers' local stuffed in a drain pipe with a bullet hole in his head. Point is, they ain't exactly the Disney company."

"I know nothing about that," Yohiro protested. "I'm head of plant safety for Unitel."

"Doesn't matter," Gionfredo said. "We need to send 'em a message, right now."

"What do you suggest?"

Gionfredo had the face of a Mediterranean priest, but his eyes were starting to glow red.

"Kill him and dump him. I didn't see nothing."

You try to have a nice outdoor drunk and all of a sudden you run into a Martin Scorsese movie. Gionfredo actually looked serious, and Jefferson was drunk enough to find out how serious. He twirled the gun until it was butt first and tossed it to Gionfredo.

"Here, you do it."

Yohiro turned as white as the overhead sun as Gionfredo aimed the pistol at his face.

Jefferson undid the rope hanging from his saddle and prepared to swing it at the gun.

"Please," begged Yohiro. "I've got a family."

Gionfredo dropped the barrel and let go two rounds into the ground. Yohiro jumped into the air and ran toward the front of his van.

"Go on, get out of here," shouted Gionfredo. "I can't shoot your worthless ass, not today anyway."

Jefferson hung the rope back on his saddle. "Why didn't you kill him?"

Gionfredo spat into the dust. "You were gonna do something to stop me, weren't you?"

"That why you didn't shoot?"

"Nah."

"Then why?"

"I came out here to get away from certain things."

"Certain things, huh. Like the mafia?"

"Hey, there's no such thing as the mafia. There's just family businesses. Sometimes these businesses form associations."

"Maybe. But I'm not holding my breath until you open that little Italian restaurant everyone's waiting for. Have a drink."

Gionfredo took a drink and gritted his teeth. "Let's say I got an uncle. I work for him. He likes me, but he's got a daughter and she's married to a guy who wants my job. My uncle wants his daughter to be happy. I can fight it, in which case people get hurt, maybe me. So I go to the uncle, I make a deal. I take what's mine plus a healthy bonus. The golden parachute, just like any other company."

"Uh-huh. So what about you and Unitel?"

"Tsendai, and they could just be making computer chips for all I know. Chuck Doughnut was a legit business. But check this: T is the twentieth letter of the alphabet, right? If you add that to the numbers of the other letters, the total is seventy-two, and seven plus two is nine, and seventy-two is divisible by nine. You ever hear of the Chinese triads?"

"I spent a year trying to put them out of business in Vietnam."

"Then maybe you know nine is a lucky number to them. Put that together with the way they handle their problems, and you can see what I'm sayin'."

The tequila window was transforming itself into a clear vision of Jefferson's immediate future. He was about to become a problem to Tsendai.

"We should talk about this," Gionfredo said.

"It's my business."

"You're gonna need help—professional help."

"I've got to go now."

"Yeah, well you're just freakin' welcome."

"Talk to you later."

Jefferson turned Jack's head toward the mountains.

"You better make it sooner," Gionfredo yelled after him. "Tsendai ain't no velvet glove."

Jefferson kicked Jack into a trot, feeling remarkably sober now, aware that he was almost glad about what was happening. Maybe he couldn't do anything about Celine, but he could do something about that damn plant, something that would lift the black cloud that had settled over him. The ice age ended when the first glacier retreated the first inch. Tsendai would have to move back.

11

FAR Lightning swung his old pickup truck onto a back road to Indian lands. He looked left and saw Donnelly's station wagon by the bank of a stream. On impulse, he jerked the wheel and coasted in its direction.

Donnelly was sitting on the stream bank staring into the water. Far Lightning got out of the truck and walked over to him.

"Just thought I'd stop and thank you."

Donnelly's head whipped around and he sprang into a runner's crouch.

"It's all right. I'm the guy you helped back in the bar . . . yesterday . . . remember?"

"Uh, oh yeah."

"I want to thank you. My name's Joseph Far Lightning. If you hadn't jumped in, I might be in the hospital right now—or in jail."

Far Lightning walked forward and extended his hand. Donnelly took it warily, but his grip was strong. For a few seconds he forgot to let go. "I've never been much of a fighter."

"Well, you did pretty good."

Donnelly's eyes blinked too much, and there was a tic in his left jaw.

"You on the run, Donnelly?"

Donnelly stopped glancing around and stared at Far Lightning, his eyes focusing for the first time. "I don't know. Maybe."

"It's okay. A lot of people are on the run out here, some for the right reasons."

"Reasons?"

"You know, the things that make people do what they do. You got any?"

Donnelly turned his back and walked toward the stream.

"I'm only asking because I owe you. Maybe I can help."

Donnelly was staring into the water again.

Far Lightning walked over and crouched next to him. "You're not an easy man to talk to."

Donnelly turned. He was staring hard, like he'd just realized an actual person was talking to him.

"Haven't had a conversation in a while, have you?"

"I've got reasons," Donnelly said.

"Yeah?"

"Why do you want to know?"

"There's a person in the Native American religion who's called a Heyoka. He does everything backwards, a real clown, except he's seen a vision. The vision is the only thing that's important to him. Everything else is backwards."

"You're an Indian?"

"Oglala Sioux. This is all Blackfoot land around here, but I like it."

"You're an Indian."

"Yeah, I'm an Indian. Native American is the official name now."

"I was born in Pennsylvania."

"What did you do to put you on the run?"

Donnelly's dusty eyebrows lowered into a puzzled frown. "I didn't kill anyone."

"Didn't think you did."

"I'm just . . . crazy I guess."

"Maybe you're a Heyoka."

"I'm from Pennsylvania."

"Ever heard of the beatniks? They were white, but they rode over the country looking for visions. I read about them in a white school and started to look for visions myself."

"Beatniks," Donnelly said experimentally. "I'm a Catholic."

"Ah, then you've sinned."

"Yes," said Donnelly fervently.

"You went to Catholic school?"

"Yes."

"Then you should remember how sinners become saints?"

Donnelly frowned, trying to remember something from long ago.

"Paul, on the road to Damascus, remember?"

"Yes," Donnelly murmured. "He went blind."

"But then he saw something."

"God."

"A vision."

"Yes."

"And then he acted it out, for the rest of his life."

"He was redeemed."

"Redeemed, yes. Have you seen anything, Donnelly?"

Donnelly turned. He looked looking straight into Far Lightning's face, but his blue eyes were blank and wide.

"I will send a sword against your high places. Your altars shall be broken, your images destroyed. Death will cover Montana like a fog . . . I saw that."

"In a vision?"

"In Philadelphia, on my computer screen."

"It just came on the screen?"

"It was on the Internet: Montana Millennium."

Donnelly's face was hammered flat by an idea. He'd definitely seen a ghost in the gray of his computer screen.

"Montana? It said Montana?"

"Death will cover Montana like a fog."

"Why did you come here, then?"

The clouds moved away from Donnelly's face and he almost smiled. "Redemption," he said. "Redemption before the end times."

The end times, Armageddon, the world laid waste and a new world formed. The reason whites were always looking over their shoulder, and the reason an Indian might believe what his own prophet said: The white man's world will one day be rolled up like a carpet, and the buffalo will return. That was a long time ago, but what's time to a prophet?

"So, Donnelly. How can I help you?"

Donnelly shrugged. "I don't know."

"You want to come with me? I've got food and shelter."

Donnelly stared into the water like he hadn't heard. "I guess not. I've got to keep going."

Far Lightning knew it was no use to ask where. "Well, I'll probably see you again sometime."

"Maybe," said Donnelly, taking a quarter out of his pocket and skipping it off the water.

Far Lightning walked back to his truck thinking about prophecy. What if the white man's world was rolled up like a carpet? What then? The old ways would then be new ways. You'd have to be ready. But was it a real desire or just beatnik poetry? This would take some looking into.

12

IT was 3 A.M. and there was a new moon, total darkness, the kind of night when Jefferson was glad he put up with Jack's personality. The big horse was not only strong; he was surefooted. The ground sloped upward, and Jack picked his way along as if he liked it.

Suddenly there was a smell of wood in the air and a distant crack, like a twig breaking. Jefferson pulled Jack up and listened. There it was again. He dismounted and slipped a pair of hobbles onto the horse's legs.

Magnum in hand, he began to work his way up the slope. There was the sound again, something familiar in it, a cushioned crack, then silence, then another crack.

Near the top of the hill the cracks stopped. Jefferson flattened against the ground and listened. Nothing. He removed his hat, put it on the ground, and moved his eyes level with the top of the hill. Then something green streaked through the air and smacked into the left side of his head. Before he had time to yell, something hard and metallic was pushing against his back.

"This is a Callaway Big Bertha," someone said in a soft baritone. "Keep your left arm close to your body on the backswing and you won't get hurt."

"Goddamnit," he said to Far Lightning. "You're lucky I didn't shoot you."

"You're lucky I didn't wrap this golf club around your head. What're you doing sneaking around in the dark?"

"I've had a weird couple of days."

"Come on up and hit some balls."

Up on the plateau, Far Lightning pointed to a bucket of golf balls painted phosphorescent green. He had been hitting green golf balls into the night. Some rancher in the valley would be reporting UFOs.

"Got a Callaway Big Bertha and couldn't wait to try it out," said Far Lightning. "It's so good I threw my old driver over the hill."

Jefferson took the driver from Far Lightning and teed up a ball. The loud plink of metal on golf ball sounded in the darkness, and a long green streak shot into the distance and turned sharply to the right.

"Is it true about your wife?" Far Lightning asked.

"Yeah. She left."

No wonder Jefferson couldn't hit it straight. White men were always thrown when their wives left them. Didn't they notice how many female animals chase off the male after they breed? Plus, Jefferson would be a tough man to live with . . . big temper.

"Jefferson, you remember that cattle broker in Denver?"

"Which one?"

"The one out at the stockyards. I pulled you off him before you killed him."

Jefferson teed up another ball and hit it. "It wasn't my temper that caused her to leave."

"Maybe it was your slice."

"You think that's funny?"

"I think it takes a tranquil spirit to hit a golf ball straight."

Jefferson teed a ball, relaxed, swung with all the smooth he felt from the seamless night, and watched the green streak curve 45 degrees to the right. "About that cattle broker," he said.

"Yeah?"

"He wanted to run the price up on a Mexican bull in exchange for getting me some young stuff from Minnesota. Fifteen years old, he said—hardly been touched."

"And that's when you went for him?"

"Yeah."

"And you're telling me now."

Jefferson teed a ball and looked over the edge of the bluff. A northwest wind curved in off the mountains with a sound like flapping silk. He took off his hat and let the air cut the sweat from his eyes. Then he took his stance, forgot everything but the flow of air over arms, and hit a rising rocket that cut a laser hole straight into the smoky black.

Far Lightning walked to the edge of the bluff and looked over.

"You want something," he said.

"Not long ago I lost a whole herd of beef cattle in one night . . . from rabies. They'd all had their shots. The state man said it was a new kind of virus. The vaccine didn't work against it. You know that old fertilizer plant of Harlow's? Now it's owned by something called the Tsendai Corporation and I think they might be a problem."

Far Lightning turned away and walked into the northwest wind, which had become steady enough to drive a sailing ship. It was as strong a reaction as you were likely to get from him, so Jefferson left him to it. It was a full minute before he turned and spoke.

"I will take a sword to your high places," Far Lightning said. "Your altars will be broken, your images shattered."

"Jesus! Where did you hear that?"

"From a white Heyoka named Donnelly."

"That crazy bastard who lives in his car?"

"He saw it on his computer screen in Philadelphia."

"I saw it too. Then I talked to the man who put it there. He predicted a new virus."

Far Lightning stared into the darkness over Jefferson's shoulder but said nothing. Jefferson wondered what he was thinking, but knew it would do no good to ask.

"You think the virus is coming from Harlow's old plant?"

"The water table falls downhill from there."

The northwest wind died suddenly and was replaced by a sweat-sucking humidity that seemed to come from the ground itself. Far Lightning squatted on his heels with the creak and groan of aged leather and aging knees.

"So," he said, "you're going to war against a big corporation and you're looking for recruits."

"You still raising rodeo horses?" Jefferson asked.

"Got to have some greenbacks to survive in the white man's world."

"Next time it could be your horses that go down."

"I don't care much about the horses."

"What do you care about?"

"Visions."

Jefferson walked to the opposite edge of the bluff. How were you supposed to communicate with a man who kept half his brain back in the fifteenth century? "That's going to be the way you decide what to do?" he asked, knowing the answer.

"I don't separate my religion from my life," answered Far Lightning.

84

Jefferson wanted to ask him how his religion fit into his trips to Vegas and the cheating on his three ex-wives and the neglect of his eight children and the horse scams he pulled at rodeos. He wanted to ask him but he didn't, because he knew there had to be a vision for each one of those things. The man lived his life on the goddamn cosmic Internet.

"Well, consider this. A brand-new virus might be someone else's vision."

Jefferson picked up one of the balls and tossed it to Far Lightning, who caught it and waved it back and forth, drawing a glowing green arc against the night sky.

"There are bad visions," he said.

"Then why don't you help me."

Because it might be the old prophecy coming true—that's why. The white man's world was being rolled up like a carpet. No more box-bound nuclear family society. No child support. No taking away a man's ability to be a man because he married wrong. The tribe is the family. It takes care of us and our ex-wives and our old people. No more dollar-mind. Then again, it could be a warning.

"What is it you want me to do?"

"I'm going to try and get some hungry reporter to come out and stir things up enough to get the EPA interested."

"You want some Indians carrying signs so the do-gooder liberals will write letters?"

"I was hoping more for phone calls."

Far Lightning walked over and sat in front of him. "Then tell me your vision. What do you see? What do you know?"

Far Lightning didn't kid much, and he never kidded about the vision stuff. Jefferson knew he'd better come up with something if he wanted help. "It's just a feeling, like something big is coming—something I can feel but not see."

Far Lightning stared hard into Jefferson's face. "Let me know when you see it."

"Then you won't help me?"

"Without a vision, you'll be walking in circles."

"Give me a straight answer."

"I'll think about it."

Jesus! One time Joseph had said he was going to think about buying a brood mare and then went off to Las Vegas for two weeks, lost the money to buy the mare, and said he was glad because she reminded him of his second wife. But this was as straight an answer as Jefferson was going to get.

"You'll let me know?"

"You'll let me know when you see your vision?"

"First thing." Jefferson smiled crookedly, but Far Lightning just looked at him and nodded an end to the conversation. A red-eye sun was rising over the edge of the plains, and he could see Jack biting at the hobbles on his forelegs.

"Well, thanks for the golf," he said. He began walking toward the edge of the hill.

"I'll be in touch," said Far Lightning, teeing up a golf ball.

Jefferson put on his hat and headed down the hill toward Jack. After Far Lightning, the horse would seem like the soul of reason.

13

BE HERE WEDNESDAY AT 3 P.M. BRING THE
MONEY WITH YOU. CASH ONLY. THIS POINT
IS NOT NEGOTIABLE . . . VANDIVIER.

Jefferson stared at his computer screen and took a few minutes to think about this latest E-mail. Fifty thousand dollars was a lot of money, but this was the same man who had predicted not only the dead cattle but the virus that had killed them. Of course it could be a con, or it could be a rip-off. The man seemed harmless but a little desperate. It wouldn't be a bad idea to take the pistol. He leaned forward and typed a reply and hit the key to send it back.

AGREED. I'LL BE THERE AT THREE. PROOF
BEFORE PAYMENT.

AT 2:45 ON Wednesday, Jefferson pulled the Rover to the side of Highway 424 thirty miles northwest of Kalispell. According to Vandivier's directions, he was supposed to turn due east and drive five miles. The problem was, there was no road, just a long stretch of rocky scrub leading upward into a stand of pine at the top of a ridge.

Feeling a little foolish, Jefferson levered the Rover into four-wheel drive and rattled off into the scrub. The ground rose at a steep angle until it reached the pines and then leveled off into the rutted semblance of a road, which led across a plateau covered with aspen and birch. It was a clear day but unusually hot for the high elevation. Jefferson began to feel very alone, and it occurred to him that no one knew where he was going and he didn't know what he would find when he got there. He had the magnum, but he couldn't very well walk into Vandivier's place waving it around—if it was really Vandivier's place.

The rut-road turned north along the high ground, then banked down into a hollow, which led to a stream. Above the stream was a log house with a stable in back, just where Vandivier said they would be. The road ended about fifty yards above the house.

Jefferson coasted to a stop and looked the place over. The stable looked okay—a low log building that matched the house. There were four stalls facing front, horses craning their necks out of three of them. Directly in front of the Rover were an old Volvo, a rusted Ford Bronco, and a Dodge Ram pickup with a rack of floodlights on the roll bar.

Jefferson opened the door and had one leg on the ground when he wondered what to do with the magnum. He had a holster, but it always made him feel like he was wearing a Halloween cowboy outfit. The place was calm as a church anyway. Still, people got laid to rest in churches all the time. He stuck the gun between his jeans and the small of his back. To cover it, he put on the cotton sport coat he'd brought. Then he picked up the briefcase with the fifty thousand and got out.

Jefferson crabbed his way down the hill and walked across the lawn to the front porch. He stepped up to the door and knocked. No answer, so he knocked again.

"Vandivier," he shouted in the direction of the stable. Again, no answer.

Jefferson pushed at the door and it swung open. He stepped inside and called Vandivier's name again. Then he remembered something he'd seen as he passed the Dodge pickup: a thin blue piece of paper on the dash, with dim carbon writing—a rental receipt.

Jefferson turned on his heel and started out the door, but his path was blocked by a man in a blue suit, a tall thin man wearing sunglasses and holding a thin blue automatic pistol. The pistol was pointed at Jefferson's belly.

"My name is Smith," said the man. "What's yours?"

Rip-off! But no. If it was, they'd know his name.

"James," he said. "Bob James. I had an appointment to discuss some insurance with Mr. Vandivier."

"Uh-huh," he replied. "I've used that line myself, and I look a lot more like an insurance man than you do."

"Maybe they look different where you come from."

"They look the same everywhere, and they don't look like you. Come on in the kitchen and let's try this again."

The man motioned Jefferson through an alcove and up three steps to a large sunny kitchen. A sink and countertop ran along a wall of windows at the back of the room. A wooden table had been pushed to the side of the room, leaving a lone chair in the middle of the floor. Several lengths of clothesline lay at the chair's feet. Jefferson walked to the center of the room and turned around. Smith's blue suit was cheap, and he had a homemade star tattoo on the back of his hand—a prison tattoo.

"Look," said Jefferson. "I came to discuss insurance with Mr. Vandivier."

"Cut the crap," said Smith. "I think you're here for the same reason I am."

That was it: Smith was here for the report, and he would have a partner—someone who was holding Vandivier in another room; someone who had tied him to the kitchen chair at one point. A familiar noise was coming from outside the window, but Jefferson didn't want to turn his head away from Smith to see what it was.

"You came for the report, didn't you, bud?" asked Smith.

"I told you . . ."

"And I told you to cut it. You're too big and your hands are too rough for an insurance salesman."

Jefferson said nothing, but Smith must have noticed a look of surprise. "Yeah," he said. "I notice things. I was going to be a private detective, only I couldn't get a license. Once you commit a crime, you have to make a career out of it 'cause they won't let you do anything else. What's in the briefcase?"

"Insurance papers."

Smith smiled. There was a gap where one of his canine teeth should have been.

"Now, let's see how good a detective I could have been. I come to get a certain report from Vandivier, along with the names of anyone he might have talked to about it. Then a great big guy with cowboy's hands shows up carrying a briefcase and says he's an insurance man. I'd say you're some rancher and that you're here to buy the report and that briefcase is full of money."

Suddenly Jefferson thought of something important he'd learned in the war: Bad things really do happen. Smith was going to kill Vandivier, and him. It was really going to happen unless he did something to stop it. The gun was still tucked into the back of his jeans, but he'd be dead by the time he got it out. What else? Jefferson felt his mind beginning to lock up with fear.

"Now, put the briefcase on the floor and kick it over here," ordered Smith.

Smith was going to kill him—right here in a sunny kitchen on a beautiful blue day in the middle of the prettiest country anywhere. Mortal fear . . . a near-death experience . . . white light and slow-motion clarity . . . his mind on the ceiling looking down at him and thinking, sending him one perfect thought: Use the fear.

The noise was coming from outside the window again. Jefferson glanced to his left and saw a familiar object in its rack on the counter.

"The briefcase, bud. Slide it over."

Jefferson dropped the briefcase at his feet but didn't slide it anywhere. Instead, he began to stammer.

"I'm an insurance man . . . believe me . . . please . . . don't shoot me . . . I've got a wife . . . I've . . . please don't shoot . . ."

He choked. He clutched his chest in pain and began to gurgle in his throat, breath coming hard, grunting with the effort, groaning with the pain, like the guy with the heart attack he'd seen once on the sidewalk in Great Falls. Then he began to slump to his knees, on top of the briefcase, grabbing at the front of his shirt, holding his breath, sliding left down the counter toward the familiar object: a white Braun mixing wand, the kind shaped like a long thin gun, with blades on the front.

"Jesus!" said Smith as he took three steps across the room. He peered down at Jefferson. "A damn heart attack. Good-bye, bud, and get off the briefcase."

Smith switched the automatic from his right hand to his left and began to shove Jefferson aside with his right hip and shoulder. As the man touched him, Jefferson reached out with his right hand and grabbed Smith's left wrist. With his left hand, he grabbed the mixing wand from its rack, pressed the trigger, and shoved the blades into the front of Smith's face.

Smith screamed through the circular spray of blood and let go of the pistol to grab at his face. Jefferson dropped the mixing wand, snatched Smith's pistol, and stood up. Smith didn't notice, because he was rolling around on the floor gibbering wildly through the bloody mucus where his nose and lips used to be.

Jefferson looked out the window and identified the noise he'd been hearing. It was muffled screaming. Down the hill by the creek, a man on horseback was dragging another man over a patch of flat rocky ground. The man on horseback was wearing a blue suit that shone cheaply in the sun.

Jefferson looked over his shoulder at Smith, who was now whimpering in the corner like a whipped dog, and stepped out onto the back porch. The man on horseback had to be Smith's partner. The man being dragged must be Vandivier. The two of them were about seventy-five yards away, a long shot for a pistol, but there was no way to get closer without wasting time, and it was clear that Vandivier didn't have much time. Even from this distance, he looked like a pile of bloody rags.

Jefferson used Smith's pistol and emptied ten of the fifteen rounds in the direction of the creek bed. The man on horseback reined in and looked up at the porch. Jefferson fired off the automatic's remaining five shots, pulled out the magnum, and waited. The man on the horse ducked, took out a knife, and cut the rope that attached him to Vandivier. Then he looked up.

Jefferson fired a round from the .44 and a rock exploded not more than ten feet from the horseman. He yanked the horse's head toward the woods west of the creek and took off.

Jefferson waited a few seconds, bounded down the steps, and ran toward Vandivier. When he got to him, he could see it was bad, very bad. They were always dragging someone behind a horse in western movies. Then they'd stop and the guy would get up with some dirt on his face and a few strands of grass in his hair.

It wasn't like that at all. Vandivier's clothes were torn off, and so was his skin. His chest was raked down to naked breastbone, and the side of his skull was showing through a wadded grunge of muddy blood. One eye was completely missing from its socket, and his right shin was perpendicular to the rest of his leg, its shattered bone shining blue-white with gristle.

Vandivier had been in his sixties, but now he was a lot older. He was dying. Jefferson thought of running inside and calling 911, but he'd seen men die before. It was a long time ago, but he hadn't forgotten the look. Vandivier had it—the clear, bright, knowing look in his one remaining eye. A man his age couldn't stand these kinds of injuries, and he knew it.

Jefferson stroked the side of Vandivier's face. "It's Jefferson," he said. "I'm sorry I didn't get here sooner."

Vandivier's eye swiveled onto Jefferson's face and regarded him kindly. "It's all right," he said. "I'm not afraid to die. I'm a Christian."

Jefferson stroked Vandivier's face again but could think of nothing to say.

"I was right about the virus, wasn't I?" asked Vandivier.

"Yes. You were right."

"I didn't tell them who was buying the report, but I told them where it was, and they took it. I'm sorry."

"You couldn't help it."

Vandivier groaned, his body deflating. Jefferson leaned closer.

"All life," Vandivier whispered. "All life is a form of virus ... DNA ... parts of ourselves ... whether we want them or not ... we think we're higher but . . . Your altars will be destroyed, your images broken."

The pain left Vandivier's face, along with his life. Jefferson could see the man underneath the injuries, peering out like a face beneath cracked lake-ice. He hoped when it was his time to go he'd do it with as much composure.

As Jefferson laid Vandivier's head on the ground, he was jolted to his feet by the sound of a truck starting in front of the house. He raced across the lawn and up the back stairs to the kitchen, cursing all the way because he knew what he would find—or, rather, what he wouldn't find.

"Goddamn!" he bellowed when he slammed into the kitchen and saw that not only was Smith gone, so was his fifty thousand.

He ran to the front door and listened. Over the crest of the hill he heard an engine's whine and saw a dust puff rise into the air. He knew he should go after the man and get back his fifty thousand. The problem with that plan was that it might succeed. What would he do if he caught the guy? The best he could hope for was a squad room full of bumpkin cops trying to question their way onto tabloid

TV. One of the nicest things about having money was that you could afford to lose some of it.

Jefferson went through the house and out to the back, where he retrieved Vandivier's body and carried it inside. After leaving the man as neatly as possible on his own bed, he went to the kitchen and checked the refrigerator. Two Budweisers in the back. Thank you, Jesus.

When he was done with the beers, he washed any fingerprints off the bottles and slogged his way back to the Rover. On Highway 424 he got a room at a motel and made an anonymous call to the local sheriff's office from the pay phone outside. Then he fell across the bed, thinking of all the ways you could make yourself sick—bad ideas, sleazy desires, perverse self-destruction, rejection of love. Put them all together and they might be the Devil, riding in on bits of excreted DNA, the defenders needing not altars or images but a clear vision of themselves. *Do you have a vision, Jefferson?* That's what Far Lightning had asked. *I'm looking,* he thought as he fell asleep. *I'm sure looking.*

14

JUNE 5. Calgary. It was 70 degrees and the sun was out. The sidewalks were crowded with whites, blacks, Indians, and even a few Asians, all of them stealing glances at the sky to catch the heat on their faces.

Lone felt good, confident, and quick. He'd just come from a kickboxing session at a downtown gym in which he'd flattened the instructor with a kick to the solar plexus. He was lethal, and he was ready for his meeting with Harlow.

Lone put on his sunglasses and looked up. A balloon floated overhead, bright red against the blue sky, string trailing in the breeze, its end twitching like a nerve. He started to move fast toward the Canadian Trust building and his meeting with Harlow. It was lease-signing day. Harlow would find out who was over a barrel now.

Lone entered the building and took an elevator to the second floor. Harlow had insisted the signing be held in a standard bank conference room and not the Tsendai offices. "You wouldn't be dumb enough to do something to me where people could hear it," he had said.

As if the old bastard couldn't be killed in five seconds with no more noise that it took to drink a glass of water. Lone's first weapon had been a knife and he had one in his pocket now, a gravity spike with a six-inch blade. One fast thrust into the throat was all it took, right above the collar button. The only noise would be a gurgle as the person tried to scream. They always got such a funny look on their faces when they realized they weren't making any noise.

The conference room was furnished with a long table and twelve matching chairs. Ling had placed the television and VCR at the far end of the table. He was pacing the room, holding the videotape in one hand and smoking with the other.

"Thirty minutes until the meeting," he said.

Good old Ling—big, bald, broad-shouldered. He was totally dependable and loyal down to his liver.

"Let's see it," said Lone.

Ling pushed the tape into the machine and flicked off the lights.

The camera was near the ceiling and had a big lens, so it could see anyone on the raised stage at the center of the room. The stage was for the performers and the equipment: bars, beds, leather and chrome, straps and buckles. The customers liked it when the sex seemed to be part of the equipment, but there was no equipment on the video. The only thing on the stage was a steel-framed bed, and in the bed were Harlow Rourke and the Thai girl Lone had given him to seal their deal.

There was no doubt it was Harlow. His face was clearly visible as he held the girl down with his knees and tied her arms to the bed frame. There were many angles after that, showing every side of Harlow's naked body and the nasty side of his personality. Lone considered himself an expert, and he was impressed with the varieties of misery Harlow inflicted on the girl before wrapping the silk scarf around her neck. The muscles along the old man's back were still impressive as he pulled the scarf tight and kept on pulling.

Lone turned his attention to the girl, drawn by her futile struggle to free an arm or leg for leverage. She looked like a sleek fish struggling for oxygen . . . a fish caught in the Yangtze River when Lone was seven, his sister beside him, six years old, laughing and clapping her hands, looking at him like he was a hero. Father standing over them both, voice firm and encouraging, Lone unable to remember his face, just the legs, leaning against them as he almost fell. Steadying himself, reeling in the fish against the strength of the legs.

Father's face forgotten, then remembered, the way it looked as it was taken away, smooth skin, high brow, full lips, broken glasses hanging from his ear as soldiers pulled him away, Mother and Sister shrieking.

Communists, Mother said. No more Father. Then Hong Kong. Dimwit Mother swindled out of all their money, living in the walled city of Kowloon; fifty thousand people sharing apartments only a few feet square, buildings twelve stories high with only a few inches between them, and that space filled with garbage to a height of thirty feet. Solid mass of buildings, alleys dark even at noon, running wet with sewage and animal guts thrown from one-room factories turning out fishcakes.

The main alley—Pak Fa'an Gai, White Powder Street . . . heroin, street. No-go for Europeans or the police; no-go for anyone without triad connections.

Lone and Sister gutting fish on a slimy floor, buying heroin and taking it to Mother, her eyes blank and thankless, then running heroin through the alleys, then money, then messages, then came Hahn, Fu Shan Fu of the second-largest triad in Hong Kong. Hahn noticed how hard he and Sister worked and how close they were. Hahn liked children. He knew other people who liked children. He had a proposition.

They ate well at Hahn's, and Mother got her heroin for free, as long as Lone and Sister played their games, like tag really, a lot of touching, naked in front of Hahn's friends, Sister making little gasping sounds, Lone learning to like them.

But he never liked it when Hahn made him leave Sister and go to a room with men from the audience. They thought they were having him, but he wasn't even there. He was up near the ceiling, circling slowly around the room and dreaming of how a knife would look in their throats, wondering if Hahn would give him permission to kill one of them, then asking. "What are you willing to do to repay me?"

"Whatever you ask."

Hahn smoothing his fat tiger's face with the back of his hand, then making another proposition. "I have a request from a client who has seen almost everything. There is only one thing he hasn't seen."

HARLOW WAS PULLING on the scarf with all his strength. The girl's eyes stared somewhere into the distance over Harlow's shoulder, looking for help from above. None was forthcoming. Then there was a moment of realization when she knew she would never have a boyfriend or husband or babies.

For a few seconds after that, the terror in her eyes changed to hatred and she stared at her killer with radioactive malice. A woman could cut off a piece of your life with that look, like Sister had taken a piece of his. It was Hahn who should have paid the price. It was Hahn who should be seeing Sister's hatred in every woman's face.

Sister: looking at him with bright full eyes, her hero even in Hong Kong, looking at him for guidance, holding on to him and making the little gasping sounds, trusting him when he said it was for Mother, believing him when he said there was no other way to escape the alleys of slime.

She believed everything he said, and she learned, just like he did, that there was no way back to the riverbank. She learned too well and became hard-faced at twelve, even suggesting things that would bring more favors from Hahn. Lone hated her suggestions, and hated seeing her stick the needle in Mother's arm, hated her for sticking it in her own arm.

He wasn't her hero anymore, and one day Hahn would have offered her a deal, too, and she would have thought, like he did, that everyone had to die sometime. He had a chance to rise, while the best she could hope for was to become a white-powder madam, shriveled and croaking.

Sister had kicked and cried as he pulled the scarf, just like the girl with Harlow. Then, just before the end, a grown woman's hate had jumped across the space between them.

Sometimes he thought Sister's last look had taken away the little bit of extra joss that made the difference between success and mediocrity. The idea had pulled at him ever since Jefferson got to Vietnam and began dogging him, never able to stop him, but eating at his confidence.

The virus project would give him the joss it would take to kill Hahn and take his place. And it was something that had to be done, because of a secret Hahn tried to keep. Lone had found out anyway: There had been no client who wanted to see him kill his sister. It was Hahn who had wanted it and he'd taken a piece of Lone's joss to get it.

Lone lit a cigarette and blew smoke toward the television screen. The Thai girl was dead. Harlow was looking around the room, not knowing what to do next. Ling entered the picture and escorted him off the stage. Then the screen went blank.

"Excellent, Ling," Lone said. "I owe you a large favor."

Ling shrugged slightly and rewound the tape.

"You could let me kill Rourke," he said. "If the time ever comes."

"Done."

The phone on the wall buzzed and Ling answered it.

97

"Bank security says Harlow Rourke is here."

"Well then, tell them to send him up, and rewind the tape while we wait."

Harlow entered the room without knocking. He took a look around, then made his way to a seat in the middle of the table, humming under his breath.

"Your man got a drink for me?" he asked, nodding at Ling.

"No. This occasion is strictly business."

Harlow tapped his fingers on the table. "Well, I don't see no papers."

"I read about Vandivier's death. That was stupid of you."

Harlow looked like he'd bitten into a lemon. "What makes you think it was me?"

"Vandivier had information you thought would leak. You didn't want it to leak. So you did what most bumpkin amateurs would do."

Harlow frowned and inspected the gold rings on his fingers. "Looks like you already got it all figured out."

"You changed a retired crackpot into someone people will be interested in."

"People like who?"

"Like the police, or Jefferson."

Harlow growled deep in his throat. "Sumbitch had been puttin' out the word on the Internet that he'd sell his report. Gave it to me, and now he wanted to sell it for fifty thousand. Guess who was ready to buy?"

A pain ran down the left side of Lone's head.

"Don't look so surprised," said Harlow. "Judd likes to surf the Net. Soon as I saw Vandivier's message, I knew Judd would see it too. Couldn't let him buy that report, could I?"

"How do you know he didn't?"

"If he'd gotten anything, he'd be bangin' on my door again, and he ain't. Nope. I can still give him as much or as little info as I want."

A satisfied smirk flitted across Harlow's beaked face.

"And you're counting on that."

"Well, C.K, it does kind of keep things balanced, land deal–wise."

Harlow was way too old to be so confident, too bent with debts. He had to pay. Everyone had to pay . . . finally. No more of these old bastards. "There will be no land deal."

Harlow's head snapped around, lips drawn back in a half snarl. "Come again?"

"No land deal. No fifty million dollars."

Harlow's snarl got bigger. "You're makin' me real happy I got Jefferson in my pocket."

"You won't tell Jefferson a thing."

"I think I will."

Lone gestured to Ling, who lowered the lights and turned on the VCR. The air went out of Harlow in a long sigh as the image of the bed appeared on the screen.

"You can turn it off now," he said when he saw himself.

But Lone didn't turn it off. He ran the whole tape. Harlow started to get up, but he couldn't resist watching the girl's death. When the tape was over and the lights came up, he sat looking at the back of his hands on the table.

"Not much trouble identifying the star, is there, Harlow?"

"Tapes are faked all the time."

"But the same labs that fake them can prove they're real."

"You send that tape out, and I'll have Jefferson all over you."

"I'm not going to send it out as long as you say nothing to Jefferson and give up any idea of an expensive land deal."

Harlow rubbed his right fist into his left palm. Lone fingered the knife in his pocket.

"Jefferson could ruin your project."

"That's murder on that tape, Harlow."

"You release the tape, and there'll be no leases, no project."

"Things will fall apart anyway if you tell Jefferson or keep distracting me with swindles."

Harlow's face turned purple along the outer edges. He stood up and pointed a long finger. "I'll tell you what," he croaked. "You're makin' a mistake pushin' Harlow Rourke to the wall. You hand that tape over to me, or you got two weeks to get off'n my property. Take it or leave it."

Lone leaped out of the chair, put a hand on the back of Harlow's head, and pulled it toward the blade, which was coming up from below, its point at Harlow's throat, heavy enough to draw blood but not to kill. He walked the old man back across the room while digging a little deeper. When the old man pulled his head away, he pinned it against the wall.

"You'll sign," Lone hissed. "You'll sign or I'll stick this knife through your throat and watch you stagger around the room trying to hold the blood in with your hands. You'll make a gurgling sound and jerk like a chicken. And I don't even care about hiding your body, because if there's no project, I don't care what happens. I'm tense. I'm very tense. So reach out with your right hand and take the pen Ling is handing you."

Harlow reached carefully, and Ling placed a pen in his hand.

"Now, Ling is going to hold up a clipboard with the lease on it. Sign where you see the *X*."

Harlow's eyes moved to the clipboard, but his head stayed perfectly still. He signed. Lone backed away, folded the knife, and sat down. He wished he'd known going into the meeting what he was going to do. Then he could have had a ninety-day lease ready.

Harlow was using the wall to hold himself up.

"You said take it or leave it, Harlow. I decided to leave it."

Harlow took a handkerchief from his back pocket and dabbed at the blood on the front of his neck.

"Sit down," said Lone, motioning Harlow forward.

Harlow stood where he was.

"I said sit down."

Harlow walked to the table looking every year of his age. He eased into a chair, and some of the color came back into his face.

"Never threaten a triad member," Lone said.

Harlow licked his dry lips but said nothing.

"Now that you've signed, I'm prepared to keep my part of the deal. There's another girl waiting for you at the warehouse right now."

Harlow looked like he might vomit. "No. Not today."

"You're sure?"

Harlow's eyes locked onto Lone's for a second, then slid away.

"I guess our business for this month is done then."

LONE STOOD IN HIS office holding a drink and staring at his computer. Harlow was now a bitter enemy. At some point he would side with Jefferson. Lone shook his head, thinking he had only twelve reliable men. Harlow and Jefferson together might be an insurmountable problem. One of them had to die now, and Harlow was still necessary. That left Jefferson. But how?

Lone keyed in the address for Vandivier's home page and left a message for Jefferson on the bulletin board. Sooner or later he would look there again.

```
JEFFERSON: I AM AN ASSOCIATE OF
VANDIVIER'S. HAVE INFORMATION YOU SEEK.
FOR OBVIOUS REASONS CANNOT REVEAL MORE
ON THIS VENUE. IF INTERESTED CONTACT ME
AT 12:30 P.M. MONDAY. IT IS NOW FRIDAY
AFTERNOON.
```

Lone gave his E-mail address and logged off. It could work. It would work. Jefferson would pay a hundred thousand dollars for his own death.

15

CELINE tried to move but couldn't, tried to scream but no sound would come, tried to breathe but no air would come. Something hard and hairy was on top of her, breathing fast and giving off male musk. She clawed and tried to kick without parting her legs, because that's where the thing wanted to go and she couldn't let it.

She arched to the side and tried to roll away from the temptation to give in, relax, and betray herself, and betrayal was what the thing really wanted. When that happened, she'd become a silent soulless husk and they'd call it madness but it would be death; floating in eternal darkness.

With a final spine-wrenching effort, Celine pulled in some air and screamed, arched, swam up and away, out of the bed, and onto the floor, panting hard and sweating, alone in the early morning light.

"Jesus," she said. "That was the worst one yet."

The worst what? That was the question. If she were to tell anyone, she'd have to call it a dream. But it was more real than that. It didn't go away like a dream. It was always there, lurking just beneath the surface. She shuddered when it occurred to her that maybe this was the beginning stage of insanity.

In a panic, she jumped up and started throwing on her clothes. She had to get out and go somewhere familiar and friendly. She had to see other people doing normal things and be normal with them. Max's. She'd go to Max's.

THIRTY MINUTES LATER Celine was in the car heading for Max's Western Wear at eighty miles an hour. Max's was located in the Cut Bank Mall in the town of Cut Bank, which consisted of the mall, a gas station, fourteen houses, and a nondenominational church. The town was surrounded by thousands of acres of ranchland. The collective population was a couple hundred, all of whom shopped at Max's. They roamed through the barnlike space catching up on each other's doings as they tried on the biggest variety of yoked, brocaded, and spangled clothes west of the Grand Ole Opry.

Actually, Celine hated all that Nashville cowgirl crap. She bought her clothes in Denver or from the Nieman-Marcus catalog. But she loved the social atmosphere of Max's and dropped by sometimes to talk and play a little machine poker in the casino bar that adjoined the place.

Cut Bank was forty-five miles east of Wild Gap, about a five-cigarette drive now that she was smoking again. She thought she'd kicked nicotine for good, but now it was a defense against the nameless presence that would neither leave nor announce itself. It just hovered around her like morning in the badlands on a tornado day.

She'd be sitting in the cabin trying to read and an area of low pressure would ooze under the window on the far side of the room and hang there waiting for her to look away, and she had to look away. Then, when she looked again, it would move nearer, forcing her to leave. She'd dropped ten pounds from an already thin frame because she couldn't be still long enough to eat. Maybe a lot of loud clothes and whoop-de-do conversation would get the stalking specter off her back.

No such luck. She felt it lurking under the floorboards all the way down from Wild Gap and out across the Blackfoot lands, where the road ran straight and high like a dike between seas of grass.

There were no white lines on the road. The only indication of her speed were the telephone poles snicking by the side window. Small white crosses had been erected next to most of the poles, marking the spot where high-speed drunks had killed themselves. Feathers or effigies were attached to the newer crosses, giving the whole stretch the aura of an Indian burial ground.

The telephone poles moved by with the hypnotic regularity of carousel creatures. Ground winds snaked through the grasslands, making the eagle feathers stand out from the crosses at impossible angles. Over it all arched the white quiet of souls surprised by death. The road was a vacuum that drew the thing from under the floor. It hid in the back under the luggage cover, the dead spot at its center imposing itself on the corner of her eye, forcing her to look away from the road.

Celine glanced toward the rear of the car to convince herself the thing wasn't there, and of course it had moved. She snapped her head to the front and saw a telephone pole moving toward her at seventy miles an hour.

Celine spun the wheel back toward the center of the road with all her strength, whipping the front in counterpoint to the Suburban's desire to go over the side. Finally, she fought it to a standstill and stopped, panting with exertion and mightily pissed off.

"Goddamn you!" she screamed. "I'm not going to cry. Do you hear me? I'm not going to cry!"

She pulled the car half into the narrow berm and got out, slamming the door with a force that boomed through the dry afternoon like a cannon shot.

"You just tipped your hand, you bastard," she yelled to the inside of the car. "I know you're real, because you just tried to kill me."

She circled the car looking in the windows, kicking the tires and banging on the sides with her fists. No response. She turned in a quick circle, trying to catch it hovering in back of her head like it did at home. Nothing. She clutched impulsively at the air by her ears, thinking maybe it was trying to enter there or get out.

Jesus, was that where it lived—inside her head? It couldn't happen back east, but she'd been in Montana for over twenty years: two decades of long white summers and winter winds slicing down from out of the ice age, of bears looking you in the eye, elk munching down your fence line, and eagles hanging in the air with the nonchalance of kites. And the Indian stuff—thousands of years of it: spirits and visions and talking to dead relatives in the guise of animals.

Joseph Far Lightning had said in class that some Indians believed the spirit world would give them eventual victory in their war with the white man. Oh, he'd been very academic about it, but she got the feeling he believed more than he said. Maybe it was that blissful little smile he got when he was thinking of what to say. Very sexy, that little smile.

She'd had an impure notion or two about him back then. But once the class was over, she hadn't given him much thought until the other day. The structure of his face was that of a cliff—flat planes and oblique angles, a stern overhang to his eyes.

She lay back on the grass and remembered what he'd said about the spirit world being the real world. A small hot wind licked at her ankles. The air overhead hung dead and dry. She wanted desperately to go, but she was afraid to drive. She wished for some traffic, but what would she do—bolt into the road and ask for a ride? Where? Why?

Come on, Far Lightning. What did you say? In class that day. You were talking about visions. You'd starved yourself in a hole or something until you got one. Why weren't you afraid? A light heart, that's what you said.

Celine jumped to her feet and walked to the car. She put her face against the window and smiled.

"Hey, big boy," she said. "I'm on my way to Cut Bank for a drink. Want to ride along? I bet you've never seen anything like Max's in the otherworld, or maybe you have. I always wondered where all that fringe came from."

She winked through the glass, then got into the car, looking cautiously around the interior.

"All right," she said. "I'll take that as a yes. Here we go."

She started the engine and headed back out onto the road. She turned on the radio, sang along with a few of the songs, talked to the absent thing when she wasn't singing.

But that couldn't be what Far Lightning meant by a light heart. It was too much like whistling by the graveyard. What had he meant? He owed her an explanation.

God! All this had started the day she'd seen him in the bar. She had to see Far Lightning. But the only person who might know where to find him was Judd, and how would she tell him about this? Of course she didn't have to tell him anything. They were separated, weren't they? Well, weren't they?

"Yes damnit. Yes," she yelled. "But that doesn't mean I want him to die."

She clapped a hand over her mouth as soon as the words were out. What had made her say that? Judd wasn't going to die. She was the one with the thing in her head.

"Jesus," she said gratefully as the mall came into view. "I need a drink."

Gunning the car into a space by the bar, she jumped out, locked the door, and headed for the entrance. As she was stepping onto the sidewalk, she caught a movement out of the corner of her eye and looked to her left. Fifty feet away, a small man emerged from behind a support pole and pointed a camera at her. She froze. Then the man lowered the camera and walked quickly away. He looked Japanese, probably a tourist from Glacier Park. What the hell would he be doing here, over sixty miles away?

The opening of the camera's long lens had looked a lot like the thing in the car. Celine rushed into the bar, a fugitive seeking sanctuary.

16

JEFFERSON was spooked by what had happened at Vandivier's place—not so much because it happened, but because he couldn't quite gauge his part in it. When he fired from Vandivier's porch, had he been trying to hit the man on the horse or just scare him? After twenty-five years, was he really ready to kill if he had to? He'd thought about it enough. He decided that if it happened again, it wouldn't be his aim that was the problem. The last three days had been spent target shooting with the magnum.

He'd gone nowhere, eaten only what Eliza the housekeeper made him eat, and done a lot of soul-searching in the office.

On Saturday night he'd been idling through a game of computer solitaire when he decided to check Vandivier's home page one last time. And there it was—a message from someone who said he knew Vandivier. Apparently, even weird scientists had friends.

AT 12:30 ON Monday, Jefferson keyed in the instructed address. After establishing contact using the bulletin board's conference feature, he asked a question that had been bothering him:

> Who are you? And how do I know you're a
> friend of Vandivier's?

> Call me Chuck. I know you wanted the
> report, and I know you were going to pay
> him for it.

> Okay, let's assume you are a friend of
> his. Why did you contact me?

> I know what he knew.

> You have a copy of the report?

> Yes.

> How much do you want?

> One hundred thousand.

That's absurd.

I have to get out of the country. They'll
kill me too.

Who? Do you know who they are?

Not who you think they are.

Jefferson blinked at the screen. Who did he think they were? He
didn't know, so how did this guy know?

Who do I think it is?

No answer. Jefferson typed the question again.

Vandivier was informed of your cattle.

An oblique answer, and one that brought up another question:

How?

He received computer printouts from the
state.

Do you work for the state?

I'm Canadian. The source of your problem
is here, not in Montana.

What is the source of my problem?

That is an answer for which you have to
pay.

Jefferson frowned and shook his head. The last time he had tried
to pay someone, it almost got him killed. He was in no hurry to go
traipsing off to some isolated spot carrying a suitcase full of cash.
Aside from that, the guy was giving him nothing but footwork.

First you have to prove you know
something.

I know it all.

Prove it.

I don't have to prove anything. I can
sell to someone else. I'm risking my life
just talking to you.

Is it Tsendai?

Pay or remain ignorant. I have to go now.
Working from laptop computer. I'm moving
around to keep them off me. I will
contact you soon.

Jefferson wondered if the information could really be worth a hundred thousand and if he was talking to a scientist or a con man. Then he realized he didn't care, because the whole thing had gotten very personal. What was it Vandivier had said about viruses? They were parts of ourselves that we had rejected eons ago. Something was coming home to roost, and he wanted to reject it again.

But there was something not quite right about the man at the other end his computer modem. He had an oblique way of talking. It made Jefferson uneasy, as if he were playing poker and had forgotten which card was wild. In a case like that, there was only one sure way to find out: Shove your hundred thousand across the table and make the other man show his cards.

17

JOE Donnelly took a huge hit of the unfiltered Camel and sucked the smoke into his lungs. His hands shook and his head got light. Another hit and then a familiar dull pain in his right bronchus. It had to be the beginning of cancer, but he didn't seem to care. He wanted to care, but he kept hitting the Camels because they had the same effect on him as Elaine—anxiety, nervous tremors, loin rushes, and probably death.

She'd ragged and nagged and generally gnawed his flesh like a weasel for ten years, telling him the exact opposite of what she had told him before they were married. Then, his sloppiness had been manly and his stupidity was eccentric genius.

He wasn't a genius and he wasn't stupid. A place in the middle— that's all he'd been looking for his whole married life. Every time he got near to it, Elaine would start a bogus fight.

The laundry. Elaine would moan and whine about what a chore it was. Then he'd offer to do it and she'd tell him no—he wouldn't do it right, and besides, he was only trying to shut her up.

They'd fight, and two days later he'd have to apologize or she'd never get over it. Then they'd make love, but the laundry problem wouldn't get solved and he'd be even further away from knowing whether Joe Donnelly was slob or lover, brute or wuss.

Now the sun was going down behind the mountains, and he was sitting in the jump seat of his Celebrity station wagon. It was going to be a chilly night. He should be planning a way to get some gas in case he had to run the heater. But first he had to figure it out. How did a middle-class systems analyst become a degenerate gambler? What day was it when he had said to himself, *Donnelly, today you're going to start living by chance and your wits. Today you're going to stop trying to figure out who you are and let fate decide.*

Donnelly started upward in the jump seat and banged his head on the roof of the car.

"Christ!" he said aloud. "That's it. I let something else decide. Was it God?"

He got out of the car and paced back and forth, wondering if what other people called bad luck was really the will of God. What was chance, anyway? You sacrificed yourself the way Abraham had been willing to sacrifice his son. Abraham rolled the dice and came up rich and righteous.

He might have been the last one to do it, too. Every time you found a guy who was supposed to be lucky, it turned out he was just lucky enough to get back his repossessed car.

What had the sisters taught him back in Catholic school? Something would get you if you didn't watch out. Where was the something that got you, unless it was your wife making you wonder all the time who you were and who you wanted to be?

For a while, he had thought Elaine was the manifestation of Catholic mystery. She was always making him ask the infinite questions while preventing any answers. What the hell did she really want to do about the laundry? If he couldn't answer that, how could he tell who he was? She controlled his very identity.

"Jesus, Elaine," he said, pacing the length of the car and back again. "I wasn't trying to screw things up. It's just that you goddamn well flatly refused to tell me what you wanted to do about the laundry except fight about it. Around and around about the laundry and my habits. In bed, things were okay; out of it was another story. You made me feel like two people. You had no answers. It was all circles: bed or laundry; stay or go. You never told me to kill Isaac, but you never told me to stop. Goddamnit, Elaine. You made me feel like there was no God."

Donnelly stopped pacing and dropped to his knees. He looked up into the pastel vastness of the sunset and prayed aloud:

"Oh, God. Are you the forbidden fruit? Tell me the answer so I can tell my wife and daughters. It's all I can give them now. Tell me, am I Donnelly or was I Donnelly? I'm sorry for asking. I'm sorry I ever asked. I'm sorry, Elaine. I should have just done the laundry."

Donnelly put his forehead to the ground and listened for a deep slow voice. He heard nothing but the drip-drop of his tears falling into the dust. He sat back against the side of his car and lit another cigarette.

He watched the smoke as it curled out of his mouth and rose into the crescent sun now dipping into the night. The dust lay calm as sand on a beach. Donnelly heard his breath and held it; complete quiet. Nothing moved except the smoke from his cigarette. It wavered faintly, then dispersed horizontally, becoming a foggy mesa.

The last light of day shot through the smoke, creating a columned hall of beams leading away toward the Canadian border. Donnelly wanted to rise through the air and walk down that hall, toward color, toward clean, toward a deep voice.

He dropped the cigarette and looked at the ground, which rolled away under the smoke. It was dry and fairly flat; not too many rocks. He'd drive real slow.

18

LONE closed the detective's report on Jefferson and smiled. The marital problem was good. Sentimental people were always off balance during times of marital stress, and Jefferson was bug-eyed with sentiment. Why else the obsession with his job in Vietnam, as if each peasant child were a personal acquaintance?

Jefferson was a true believer, recruiting his own little army, infiltrating, corrupting employees, even Sylvie: French eyes, mocking wit, moonlit complexion, long fingers, tasteful as they guided you in. Then Jefferson and his dog, Lamh. Burning Lamh alive the most satisfying moment of life; burning Sylvie, the most painful. No. The most painful was learning Jefferson had sent Lamh into Sylvie's bed.

She'd risen from brothel whore to assistant and lover, a queen brought down by lust for the ordinary. Nothing would ever be truly right until Jefferson was dead.

Lone picked up the remote, flipped on the news from Billings, and jerked spasmodically to his feet. There on the screen in front of him, gray in his hair, face fuller but still the same shooter's eyes, was John David Jefferson.

He was being interviewed by a square-jawed blond woman about the death of his cattle, and they were standing outside the Unitel plant, complaining that the manager had refused to speak to them. Jefferson was blaming the plant for his dead cattle, demanding an EPA investigation. Then a few platitudes from the woman reporter and the piece was over.

Lone hit the off switch on the remote and sat staring at the empty screen. Jefferson . . . what a stupid bastard. A wealthy man incensed about the loss of a few cows, as if they were Vietnamese children. Everything to him was life and death. *So be it, Jefferson. So be it.*

Lone went to the computer room and logged on. *Careful, don't overplay.*

JEFFERSON CLICKED OFF the television and felt his face with his hands. They said TV made you look heavier, and they were right. His cheeks had looked like he was storing nuts for the winter. Mary Braun was the reporter's name, and she couldn't be older than twenty-three. Even off camera she'd called him Mr. Jefferson.

It made him feel old, and feeling old had brought Celine to mind. Why didn't he just drive over to the cabin and ask her to come back? How hard could that be? Just burst in and say she was right. She'd throw her arms around him and tell him to take her home, but what then? Was he going to grow a paunch and tell the youngsters to accept what they couldn't change? She wouldn't like him that way, no matter what she thought.

Jefferson kicked himself out of his chair and poured a drink. Maybe he'd get a little drunk and play some "Space Invaders." First check the E-mail. Sit down, kick back, and then . . . an E-mail from Chuck.

```
Jefferson . . . important. Contact me on the
Montana Millennium bulletin board.
```

Jefferson quickly posted a message on the board to tell Chuck he was there.

Lone jumped when he saw Jefferson's reply on the screen. His face became flushed, his stomach queasy. He took deep breaths and rolled his neck to relax. This was a rare opportunity but delicate. Push too hard, and Jefferson would get suspicious; not hard enough, and there would be more reporters outside the plant. One more deep breath, then he leaned forward and typed.

```
Jefferson, saw your piece on television.
It's a dangerous thing you're doing,
especially for me. They know there is a
leak. Now they'll be looking for me twice
as hard.
```

The reply was instantaneous.

```
You're a part of Tsendai?
Yes. I know what they're doing and who is
doing it.
```

114

```
Is there something going on which is
larger than just the plant?
```

Lone waited, considering how to hook Jefferson with his own arrogant concern for the little people.

```
A lot of innocent people are going to die.
```

Innocent people—not just people, but innocent people. There was that familiar thing again, like someone knew which of his buttons to push.

```
Do I know you?
```

Time to back away. Jefferson was thinking of people who knew him, and who knew him better than C. K. Lone?

```
I know only that you're interested in
Tsendai and that you have a hundred
thousand dollars.
Only if you're for real.
```

Now was the time. Make him stop the news stories.

```
I'm for real, but I won't be for long
unless you stop troubling them. If TV
stories continue, they will begin to
search out anyone with information and
destroy them. And they know I have
information.
```

Chuck dropped the article *the* before the word *TV.* Intentional, or was he foreign?

```
All right. But only until I get what you
have.
```

Right. First some breathing room, then the kill.

```
Agreed. We have to meet soon in person.
You bring the money, in cash, and I will
have not only the Vandivier report but
Tsendai intentions, with names.

When and where?
```

The answer would take some thought. It would have to be a spot agreeable to Jefferson but one where he would have no chance of survival. Isolated yet familiar.

```
I will let you know the place when I am
ready. Keep watching your screen. I will
contact you soon.
```

All right, let Chuck pick the time and place. Take his word that he's at risk, but don't give him enough time to cave in.

```
Two weeks, or I start making noise again.
```

Wave the cape, watch Jefferson charge. How had someone so predictable lived this long?

```
Agreed. I'll be in touch.
```

The screen went blank, and Jefferson lit a cigar. What was he going to do for two weeks? Maybe get back to normal life. Do some business, and see Layla. It had been—what—a week, ten days? She'd left several messages on his machine, but he'd waited until he knew she was working before he answered.

He picked up the phone and got Layla's machine.

"High, Layla. Sorry I've missed you on the phone. I've missed you other ways, too. I'm heading down tonight. See you when you get off work."

He started toward the bathroom, stripping off his shirt as he went.

116

19

IT was a fifteen-mile shot down Route 83 to Wild Gap, where Layla lived in a bungalow overlooking the ninth fairway of the Jasper public golf course.

Jefferson kept the Rover at seventy-five and would have punched it to ninety if he hadn't been towing Jack in a horse trailer. Tomorrow he'd take an early morning ride with Layla, then in the afternoon, he'd play a quick nine holes. His golf clubs in the back, his horse in the trailer, beer in the cooler—the modern-day cowboy in action. Jefferson laughed out loud at his own satisfaction.

He had a key to Layla's house and planned to have a drink and watch some TV while he waited for her to get home from work at eleven-thirty. But even though it was only nine when he got there, her jeep was already in the drive.

Jefferson took the front steps in a single jump and had his key in the lock when the door swung open and there was Vincent Gionfredo standing in the middle of Layla's living room swinging a golf club and wearing a bathrobe—Jefferson's bathrobe.

"Hey," said Gionfredo, speaking without thinking. "I might take up golf."

"What the fuck are you doing here?" growled Jefferson. Then Layla came in from the bedroom wearing nothing but a towel and a guilty expression.

"Judd," she croaked. "What are you doing here?"

"I thought we'd go down to Great Falls for some entertainment. Looks like you've already had plenty of that, though."

Jefferson took two steps into the room and stood with his hands on his hips. He felt foolish, but he was unable to stop himself.

"His car was getting fixed. I gave him a ride," she said lamely.

"I can see that," bellowed Jefferson. "I can damn well see that."

"Hey, wait a minute," Gionfredo said. "There's no need for a big magilla here."

Jefferson noticed that the golf club in Gionfredo's hand was part of a set he'd given Layla for her birthday. It was time to get stupid.

"Don't tell me what there's a need for, motherfucker," he said to Gionfredo.

"Hey now," he said, putting down the club and puffing out his chest. "In the city, that kind of talk means you want to get it on."

"Means the same thing out here," Jefferson answered, acutely aware that what he really wanted right now was a cheeseburger. If only the man weren't wearing his bathrobe. He edged forward looking for an opening.

Gionfredo stood his ground but made no move to swing. "Whoa there, cowboy," he said. "I got a few years on ya."

"Let's see how much good that does you."

Layla came forward like a schoolteacher scolding a student.

"Judd Jefferson, you're twice his size."

Gionfredo turned and walked calmly to the sofa, Jefferson's tall-man bathrobe bunching around his feet as he went. He looked like one of the seven dwarfs. Jefferson would have laughed if he hadn't seen the snub-nosed .38 Gionfredo pulled from his coat on the sofa. He waved the gun casually as he spoke.

"Ain't as big as that cannon of yours," he said, "but you don't want to fool with it at this range."

Jefferson was dumbfounded. Shooting someone in the living room of her house was no way to impress a woman.

"I ain't about to give her to you just so you don't have to get your pillow wet over your old lady," the little man said.

"I give me if there's any giving to be done," screamed Layla.

"You're the real deal," Gionfredo said to her. "That's why I love you."

"Vinnie," Layla stammered. "This is so sudden."

Jesus, she'd really said that. This was turning into an old movie.

"She's had enough of you playin' with her," Gionfredo yelled.

"Goddamnit, Vinnie," Layla said. "Stop talking for me."

"Sorry baby," he answered. "But I been watching him play you for cheap since I hit town."

Jefferson started toward him, but he pointed the gun like he meant it.

"Back off, Jefferson. Don't get hurt over something you don't even want."

Jefferson looked at Layla and saw her slump to the floor in tears.

He felt as bad as if he'd knocked her down. Enough was enough. He turned and walked out the door.

He got into the Rover. He even put the key in the ignition. Then it struck him that there was no place he wanted to go. If he left now, he'd only wish he hadn't. If he stayed, he'd wish the same thing. This was a movie, all right, and a man had to do what a man had to do, even if he wasn't sure what it was. Life, love, man, woman—the whole thing sucked. You couldn't win. It was enough to make you bash your head into a wall, or your car.

"What the hell," Jefferson said with a hopeless grin.

Then he threw the Rover into gear and gunned it toward the picture window of Layla's living room.

The big Rover crashed through the wall in an explosion of glass and splintering wood. It came to rest against the far wall, cutting the living room in half and causing Gionfredo to scream in frustration as he tried to get to his gun on the other side of the truck. He was attempting a scramble over the roof when Jefferson swung open the driver's door and knocked him onto his back.

Layla, now in jeans and a T-shirt, was jumping with rage.

"My house! You goddamn crazy bastard! You wrecked my house."

Gionfredo jumped onto the roof, still going for the gun. Then Jefferson remembered that the .44 was back in the horse trailer with Jack. He jumped out of the cab and sprinted for the trailer, which was sticking out the side of Layla's house like the tail of a dog. The .44 was in the saddlebags under Jack's blanket, but Jack was throwing a royal fit. He was kicking hell out of the side of the trailer while staring out of dinner-plate eyes that saw nothing. There was no getting past him to the gun.

Jefferson bolted out the back of the horse trailer expecting to be shot, but then he saw Gionfredo pulling futilely on the drawer of an end table. The table was pinned against the wall by the truck, meaning that a quick left hook would allow them both to go back to acting like people and call their lawyers.

"Oh no," Gionfredo yelled as Jefferson approached. "You're not going to beat on me like no dog."

He scrambled across the hood of the Rover toward a golf club that was propped against the wall. The silk bathrobe came undone as he did so, revealing bare butt. He looked so stupid that Jefferson felt sorry for him, then realized he was about to get brained with a golf club.

He turned and yanked open the rear door of the Rover. His own clubs were on the backseat, but he couldn't seem to grab one until he picked a number. Three? Five? No . . . a seven iron. It was longer than Gionfredo's nine iron but short enough to handle. Just as he placed his hand on the club, the head of a nine iron shattered the truck's window.

Jesus! The little bastard had a smooth swing. He stopped long enough to tie the robe's sash, and Jefferson slammed the truck door into him and made for the outside, where the seven iron's reach would count.

Out on the lawn they began slashing away in earnest, grunting and panting, clanging shafts as they moved across Layla's front lawn to the ninth fairway. The son of a bitch was in good shape, and he kept coming.

"Never been beat up," he gasped. "Not going to start now."

Jefferson believed him and swung harder, aiming to bend the club and not Gionfredo's head. Enough already with the movie. A person could get hurt.

Layla was screaming for them to stop and, seeing they weren't listening, took off across the golf course for the Buffalo Wallow, following Jack, who was out of the trailer and heading full speed for anywhere.

It only took a few minutes for the men to bend the hell out of their clubs, but they kept hacking away with the bent shafts, Gionfredo staggering forward in his billowing red robe and Jefferson becoming as rumpled as a homeless drunk, hat off, hair wired at odd angles.

"Wyantcha go home, Jefferson?" Gionfredo gasped. "You're no John Wayne."

"You're no Italian Stallion."

"Fuck you."

To that, Jefferson took a vicious hack, which missed with such force that it tore the club from his hand. He winced as it sailed off toward the moon.

Gionfredo responded by throwing the nine iron far out onto the golf course. Then he got into a fighting crouch, breathing hard, barely able to hold up his arms.

Jefferson's own arms trembled and his chest heaved.

"Come on," Gionfredo said. "You may be bigger, but I got right on my side."

"You got right on your side?" Jefferson asked, dropping his arms. "Who do you think you are, King fucking Arthur? I bet you went to see *Camelot*, didn't you? Admit it."

Gionfredo collapsed onto the grass and looked up. "Yeah well, I was datin' a chick who liked musicals. But I'm right and you know it."

Jefferson flopped onto the grass beside him. "What makes you so sure?"

"I love her, man," Gionfredo said. "And you love your old lady, and there ain't nothin' either of us can do about it."

Jefferson rolled onto his back and looked up into the stars, which began at the horizon and stretched across the night.

"I love her, and I love this freakin' place," Gionfredo declared. "Real sky. Real stars. A real woman. Anybody pollutes this deserves to die."

"So?"

"So I seen you on TV."

"Yeah?"

"So if you need any help, I'm your man."

Jefferson rolled onto his side and looked at Gionfredo, who was sucking blood from a cut on the back of his hand. "After this?"

"Ahh, this wasn't nothing but a little Valentine to our old ladies."

Jefferson realized with a shock that Gionfredo's personality was a lot like Jack's—and his own.

"Well, shit. When you're right you're right, Gionfredo."

"Call me Vinnie."

"Just one thing, Vinnie."

"Yeah?"

"You don't get to keep the robe."

20

"THAT'S Jack," Celine said as the big horse smashed through the screen door of the Buffalo Wallow. Tables, customers, and steaks scattered in a spray of silverware and screams as Jack bolted from one end of the room to the other.

"Goddamnit," shouted Hal, the bartender. "I'm going to shoot the son of a bitch."

He was reaching beneath the bar for his shotgun when Celine jumped up and ran toward him.

"Don't shoot," pleaded Celine. "You don't have to shoot him. Just turn on the TV."

"What?" Hal shook his head like he was trying to clear his ears.

"The TV. It'll calm him right down. He's been like that since he was a foal."

"Well, Celine," Hal asked sarcastically. "Is there anything special you think he'd like to watch?"

"ESPN. He loves sports."

Hal turned and flipped on the television above the bar. He clicked the remote to ESPN.

Jack pricked up his ears and quit hammering the bar with his hind legs. He walked to the center of the room and tilted his head, twitching his tail as he watched water skiing.

"Them water ski gals is real purty, ain't they?" said a drunk cowboy at a corner table. "And where'd you get that fine-lookin' horse, Hal?"

At that moment Layla Bright burst through the same door as Jack. She looked wildly around the room, saw Celine, and rushed toward her.

"Oh my God," she gasped, seizing Celine's arm in a death grip. "You've got to come with me. Judd and Vinnie are at each other over at my place. You've got to talk to Judd before someone gets killed."

"Take your hands off me, Layla," Celine said through clenched teeth.

"Celine . . . they're hurting each other. Now, quit being a bitch and come on."

Layla ran out the door without waiting for an answer and Celine followed.

"Hey," shouted Hal. "I'm going to call the sheriff about this horse."

"OH CHRIST, DON'T let them be dead," Celine heard Layla say as they approached the golf course.

She could see two bodies sprawled on the grass in the dark. Celine recognized the one on the left as Judd.

"Check on Vinnie," she said, pushing Layla to the right. Vinnie seemed all right and they wandered back toward Layla's house.

Celine walked up to Judd and knelt a couple feet away. "Judd, are you hurt?"

"Celine," he said drowsily. "It's great to see you."

His sugared Southern baritone went well with the night.

"Are you hurt?"

"Nah, golf's not a contact sport."

Celine glanced up and saw Judd's trailer sticking out of Layla's house. "Judd, did you by any chance drive your truck through the wall of Layla's house?"

"I did do that, didn't I?" he said, as if he couldn't believe it himself.

"Are you drunk?"

"Haven't had a drop."

"I don't know whether that's a good sign or not."

"If I was drunk, I might have forgotten to fasten my seat belt."

"You're a genuine card, Judd. What is it you think you're doing here?"

He rolled up on his elbow and looked into her eyes. "Kiss me," he said, reaching out.

She brushed his hand away. "Judd, why did you drive your car through Layla's house?"

He sighed and rolled onto his back, running a hand through his thick hair. God, what hair. What a body for a man nearing fifty.

"Because I've had a very rough week, and I found Vinnie there wearing my bathrobe."

"Got yourself a little generation gap?" she asked with more relish than she intended.

"No," he said, rolling up to face her again.

"What, then?"

"What do you think?"

Starlight sparkled off his dark eyes like the moon off the James River. She sat on the grass.

"What do you think?" he asked again, leaning closer.

"About what?"

"Why'd Layla go behind my back with Vinnie?"

"He's a better driver?"

"Both of them know I'll love you until the day they put me in the ground. Everybody knows that except you."

His soft tidewater accent brushed her face. She wanted to dive into that voice and never come up. But what difference did it make if someone loved you till the grave if he was in too much of a hurry to get there?

"That's the reason," he said. "Wouldn't want you to think I was getting too old to do it."

"Hell, Judd, you won't know it when you are too old. That's what I love about you."

"I knew there must be something."

They both laughed. Celine stretched out onto her side to get a better view of him. He'd lost some weight. His jawline was as hard as an ax handle. His belly was so flat you could eat off it. *Careful girl*, she thought. *You're headed below the waist.* "Jack's in the Buffalo Wallow watching ESPN," she said.

"Jeez, what's he watching?"

"Water skiing, like he had money on it."

"Remember what he was watching the first time?"

"No," she lied.

"I'm surprised you don't remember, Cee. We were in the barn trying to make love away from the kids. Jack was getting interested, so you told me to turn on the TV. It was bowling."

"Well," she said, unable to resist the lure of old war stories, "you had a better view. You were on top."

"Oh no. You had me pinned, your hair flying over your face, lightning flashing outside, that wild smile on your face. What a banshee. You were dangerous, downright dangerous."

"Stop it, Judd," she said through her laughter. "You're embarrassing me."

"I think Jack's been looking for something like that on television ever since."

"Maybe you ought to rent him some porno movies."

"I'm afraid of what would happen to the television."

They laughed again, then wound down into an intimate silence.

"Cee," he said. "What're you doing?"

"What are you doing?"

"What do you mean?"

"Drinking, fighting, driving your car through walls, little things like that?"

He said nothing. The moment stretched to breaking.

"Well, Judd," she said, "it was great seeing you. I'm glad you're not hurt."

"There's something wrong happening," he said.

"You're telling me?"

"I mean about the cattle. I tried to tell you about it the day you came by but we got sidetracked. The Tsendai Corporation has leased that old plant of Harlow's, and the state says the cattle were killed by a mutant rabies virus no one has ever seen before."

"I don't know, Judd. I just can't imagine Harlow . . . "

"Well then imagine this. There was a man named Vandivier I found on the Internet. I met him and he told me about the virus before the state did. I was going to buy more information from him but they killed him first."

Celine looked horrified. "Judd, you can't get mixed up in this. You've got to go to the law, the government."

"I'm trying to get the EPA to take a good look at the plant, but Harlow's against me. He's made some kind of deal."

"Then go to the law."

"Who, Bob Wagman? He can't even shoot quail without radar."

"Somebody else, then. The FBI."

"Tsendai is a big investor in the economy. I have to get something on them before anyone else will get interested."

"This is just what you've been waiting for, isn't it?" she hissed.

"I have to," he said.

"Why, damnit?"

"The cattle died. Vandivier died. Things like this happen all the time and nobody does anything."

"Judd, why you?"

"You know why."

"Oh God! Not that again."

"I could have saved two lives."

"It was Vietnam, Judd. They were agents. They knew what they were getting into."

"Listen—I never told you all of it. Sylvie wasn't an agent. She was Lone's mistress. Lamh was the agent. After the two of them got to be lovers, he wanted to tell her. I told him no. She was still sleeping with Lone, and I didn't trust her. I told him I'd take him off the case, make sure he couldn't see her again. He was in love, so it was an effective threat. I shadowed Lamh to protect him, but I left her uncovered to make sure Lone didn't get suspicious. He shadowed her himself. He found them together. I've told you what he did."

"Judd," she said, touching his arm. "You were just doing the job the way you were taught."

He reached for her hand, took it in both of his, and leaned his head against their twined fingers. "There were no rules. I had to go on instinct. I should have believed more."

"I've never met anyone who believes more."

"It wasn't enough—not with them, not with you."

What could she do? He was a man out of time, the last cavalier. They didn't make them like him anymore, and they shouldn't. Men like him were foolish, prideful, dangerous—and goddamn irresistible to women like her.

She ran her hands into the thick of his hair and pulled his face to hers, kissing him deep and easy, tasting every year of their time together. She pulled at his shirt, pushed him backward on the grass.

It was like the time in the barn. Her hair flew wild over his face as horizon lightning flashed along the outer rim of the plains. She licked him, bit him, awakened him to a raging strength, which seemed to come out of the earth beneath his back, sending him so far into her that he flowed through every vein.

Afterward, they lay in the grass panting, not knowing what to say.

"Do you think Vinnie and Layla heard us?" she asked him.

"I don't care."

"I don't know what this means, Judd."

"It means what it's always meant."

"I can't come home with this . . . thing happening."

"Home might be tense for a while."

She was still atop him, head resting on his chest. She looked to the side and saw lightning strike the horizon and blaze up into an orange brushfire.

21

"JESUS God almighty!" yelled Donnelly.

He was lying naked on top of his station wagon when a bolt of lightning struck the dry brush not more than two hundred yards in front of him.

He'd been traveling in a northerly direction ever since the smoke from his cigarette pointed the way. He would bump the Celebrity overland until he had to get gas, find a station on the highway, then swing back to the plains.

The shocks were gone on the station wagon and the tires lopped over their rims, but that was okay. Soft tires cushioned the jolts, which had ruined the radio and loosened the steering until the car drove like a boat.

Every so often he checked himself in the rearview mirror and saw that his hair had been replaced by dust. There was nothing left of his face but the eyes. Sometimes when he looked in the mirror he thought he could see his soul.

The nuns said that your soul was you, but he had to wonder about that. He had wanted to do right by Elaine and the kids, but his soul didn't seem to give a good goddamn. Maybe when he died his soul would go to hell and he would get to heaven.

For now, though, the soul seemed to have won. The man Donnelly was disappearing into the plains, where his soul rose to the sky every night like a constellation.

He was watching it do just that when . . . BAM! Lightning roared over the car's roof.

He stood atop the car and saw that the brushfire wouldn't burn long, because there was only a couple square miles of it. The flames were moving fast, though. The blistering crackle was becoming a roar. His hair rose and his lungs strained for air as the fire created a whirlwind that pulled everything toward its center.

Dust, twigs, feathers, and rock floated by his face toward the swirling whiteness at the center of the blaze. He knew he shouldn't look into it, but he did.

Then he saw the eyes looking back. There were two of them, blinking and swirling in the center of the fire. They floated up and down in the blast and then lined up to stare at him as the flames curled past the edges of his vision.

There was something wrong, something he should do, but all he could do was stare into the fire. The eyes changed with each shift of the circling wind, never still enough for him to know them, yet telling him something, telling him to run.

He looked away from the eyes and saw that the fire had surrounded him.

"Christ!" he screamed. "I'm going to burn."

He jumped off the roof and started the car, needing to find a way out, but he was blind from looking into the fire.

"Don't let me burn yet," he prayed. "Let me get redemption. I can't die yet."

Around and around he drove, a dusty red horse at the center of a burning carousel, praying in screams, able to see nothing. He closed his eyes, straightened the wheel, and floored the accelerator. The old car bolted forward in a series of ratcheting bucks, shedding its light covers, bumpers, and Donnelly's clothes.

He was hanging on more than steering, his butt bouncing toward the opening where the driver's side door had been before it caught a rock and disappeared. He almost fell out, but managed to inch back to the center of the seat by pulling on the steering wheel, turning the careening car hard left toward an opening where the flames stopped on either side of a dry creek bed.

The car whomped into the creek bed and fishtailed along on its dead shocks until Donnelly felt cool air on the side of his face and opened his eyes. He was still half blind, and the car's bouncing had dismantled the headlights, but he was out of the fire and the radio was working again: a gospel station in Billings was playing "Amazing Grace."

Donnelly stopped the car, slid out the opening where the door had been, and the words of the song dropped him to his knees. He opened his mouth to the cool sky and sang:

Amazing Grace,
How sweet the sound
that saved a wretch like me.

I once was lost,
but now am found.
Was blind but now I see.

He could see. Everything had a halo around a blurry center, but he could see. He sang two more choruses of the song, then dropped face first into the dust.

"I'm not getting my car door fixed," he wept. "I'm never getting my car door fixed."

He raised his head and looked back over his shoulder. The fire was at least a mile away. He'd been saved, but why? What was there to do? Where was there to go?

His vision was almost normal now except for the afterimage of those eyes. They were still there, only now they were small and green and there were six of them. No, there were eight . . . sixteen. God! There were dozens of them, glowing green all around him.

Christ! Maybe they were animals. Snakes, hundreds of snakes slithering around looking for a warm body.

He hopped into the car and started the engine to scare them away, but they just lay there. All right then, he'd run over a few. He put the car in gear and rolled slowly forward until he felt it run over something small and hard—not like a snake at all.

He leaned out and picked it up. It was a golf ball, painted fluorescent green. There were fifty or sixty of them in a spray pattern lying below a large bluff. He eased the car toward the bluff. Then he stopped and got out. The golf balls shimmered all around him.

He stood in wonderment. Where had they come from? He was miles from the road and hadn't seen another soul for days, let alone a golf course. Had they been carried here by a windstorm, or fallen from an airplane? Had they been sent for him?

He climbed a little way up the bluff and sat on a rock. The shining green spheres were spread out beneath him like jewels for a king. Donnelly, king of the plains, with a working car and more magic golf balls than he could ever use. He leaned back against his rock and laughed, reached out a hand for balance and felt something hard and straight. It was a golf club. Was he the king of the plains or what? Magic golf balls, and now a staff—like Moses'.

The fact that he'd never played golf in his life made it perfect. He would have no idea what he was doing, which meant he would have no intent. Grabbing the club, he scrambled down from his perch.

When he got to the bottom, he waded into the carpet of golf balls and whacked away. The balls dribbled along the ground for a few yards, but that wasn't good enough. Spheres had to fly through space. All you had to do was look up to see that.

He worked harder, crouching so he could get under the balls. Finally, they started to fly into the air—not far, and certainly not straight. Every one of them curved sharply to the right, but it was a pattern, a direction. Donnelly threw the club onto the front seat and started scooping balls into the car. Then he turned the car in line with the balls he'd hit and started into the darkness beyond.

22

THE brushfire in the distance was a sign. There was a vision waiting, and it was time to go after it.

Far Lightning dug a pit—six feet long, three feet wide, and two feet deep. Just enough space to lie down in.

He didn't know how long he'd been there. One day? Two days? Time didn't exist in the vision pit. He'd eaten nothing, and had drunk only enough water to keep his brain from boiling.

But no vision had come. He knew it was there because he could feel wings beating around his head, but he couldn't see it. Maybe he was looking for something too big. That had always been his problem, anyway. He wanted to see something as big as Wovoka had seen.

But there was only one Wovoka. Way back in 1890, he'd had a vision like no other, a vision of the white man's world rolled up like a carpet and herds of buffalo stretching from river to horizon, Indians rolling free over the great plains again, families rejoined into nations but not through war—through the ghost dance and prayer; through a hard love.

There weren't many who believed anymore. The apples laughed. The drunks cursed. The hang-around-the-fort successes said that selling was the path to salvation. There were only a few, away from the towns, out in the empty, where you could hear the spirits that your fathers heard, the Father of all. Nothing fancy about it, really— just average miracles.

He had to scale down. Average miracles are all around. Space is curved. Anywhere you stand is the center of the universe. Black Elk said it. Einstein knew it. Things come around. You just have to look in the right place.

It was hot in the pit, early in the year for the sun to be so high and hot. He looked out of the pit and up to his glacier; far up in the pass, above where the wildflowers splayed, above the tree line where the evergreens never were, there was the glacier—mile-long sheet ice even in the sun. Even in a thousand years of sun there was the glacier, saddling the high mountain pass with ice as old as zero.

There were glaciers in every pass, but there was always one of everything with an Indian's name on it. Far Lightning's name was on the glacier nearest to the vision pit. The tip of its ice pointed to where his soul had walked from the center of the earth on the day he was born.

Since his boyhood, the evergreens had grown even with the north fork of the glacier. Now he looked closer. There was a one-tree space between the tree line and the ice. Always, the tree line had met the ice. Now it didn't.

But that was just a fact masquerading as truth. The truth of a vision lay beyond all the facts.

Two eagles circled above. It was late in the day, maybe five o'clock. Eagles rode on currents. The hotter the air, the higher they soared. These eagles were as high as midday and the sun was low, five o'clock low. Five o'clock thermals were now the same as midday thermals used to be . . . the air hotter than it should be.

Then a deeper vision: an eagle flew across the sun, veered, and headed for home. He banked and stroked with his wings, awkward and flailing, unlike an eagle. Then he was sucked into the sun, his wings turning black and melting, dying in flames.

There was something wrong with the air. It was too hot for five o'clock. The trees were advancing; the glacier was receding. The air in high spaces was deadly. It would melt eagles, and their death would fall on the people below.

Far Lightning knew. He knew what Jefferson didn't know and Harlow did know. He knew what Harlow's dogs must have known for a long time.

The vision was over. Far Lightning washed with the water in his hundred-year-old gourd. He ate jerk meat and choke cherries from his deerskin bag. He took four hits from the tequila bottle and lay down in his tent. He would sleep the rest of the day and the whole of the night, deep in the reality of ordinary miracles.

23

JEFFERSON knew he should feel good. What had happened on the golf course proved Celine still loved him, but he was as irritable as a pit bull. She wasn't home and she wasn't coming home "with this thing happening."

It was funny; she'd said that like there was a separate thing happening to her. He'd felt it in her voice, but just missed knowing what it was.

It was damn frustrating the way he was always just missing. He'd missed seeing into Sylvie, and he'd missed seeing how badly Layla needed something permanent.

Maybe he'd been looking at women with the wrong organ. He'd always thought of sex as a type of communication, but maybe it was just yourself you felt at the bottom of a woman's ocean. The thought made him almost grateful for his other problems.

It had been three days since he'd seen Celine on the golf course and four since he promised Chuck he'd back off. He'd done nothing except think about Tsendai and Celine and how each of them held his life in check. There must be something he could do without breaking his promise to Chuck.

What he needed was a way to shake out the rats in Tsendai without showing up on TV. He walked to his desk and picked up the *Wall Street Journal.* He opened it to the stock quotes and found that Tsendai Corporation was trading at fifty-three dollars a share. He folded the paper with a smile and picked up the phone.

Dave Grayson, his broker in New York, answered on the second ring.

"Dave, how's everything in the big town?"

"Well, if it isn't the Duke himself, John Wayne Jefferson. When're you going to come in for some civilization?"

"Maybe when you start making me some money."

"Judd, you're hurting me. What about Bio-free last quarter—in at twenty and then it split. Way I see it, you owe me your firstborn."

"He's at school in Switzerland. America is just a little too behind it for him. Seems they quit piercing their nipples over there two years ago."

"Guess I'll have to cancel that date with the mail room girl. Is this a social call, or are we into making money today?"

This part would be a little tricky. Dave was about as honest as they got in his line of work.

"Actually, it's payback for that Bio-free stock."

"Do I hear the rustle of money?"

"More like the quiet sound of money staying in your clients' pockets."

"You know something that's about to take a slide?"

"Yeah, and it's currently trading at fifty-three, up two points in the last month."

"Christ! I probably got my people in it, whatever it is. I'll have to move 'em."

That wasn't good enough. Dave had some big players, but not enough to affect the overall price.

"Dave, if I give you this, I want you to do something unusual for me."

"Uh-oh."

"I want you to pass it along the Street."

Silence on the other end.

"Dave, you there?"

"They got a name for that, Judd . . . manipulation. In case you haven't heard, you can go to jail for it—or to be more exact, I can go to jail."

"They'd have to establish a pattern. You don't have a pattern, do you?"

"I ain't about to get one, either."

"Listen, Dave. Something big is going on out here. Do this and you'll be a hero to your clients and the other brokers will owe you, not to mention me."

"You never been into this kind of thing before, Judd. Why now?"

"It's a personal thing."

"I don't like personal things."

"A man has been murdered. I'm trying to shake out who did it."

"Jesus! John Wayne rides again. If I do this, you owe me big. The next time I call, I want a big order with no questions asked."

"Deal."

"Awright, lemme have it."

"The Tsendai Corporation. A plant out here is spewing something lethal. There's going to be an EPA investigation and a mega-lawsuit."

"Tsendai has been very solid, Judd. You're not just blowing smoke?"

"They're going to have big trouble."

"How're you so sure?"

"'Cause I'm going to be the one giving it to them."

"You gotta do something about this lack of confidence, Judd."

"So?"

"Awright, awright. But it won't happen right away. I gotta take my time, establish a little deniability in case you're full of crap."

"Whatever."

"Keep watching the paper, and expect to hear from me. I'm thinking about getting into venture capital."

"I said it's a deal."

"Nice doing business with you. I think."

Dave hung up, and Jefferson felt better. Nothing like a little cutthroat capitalism to take the edge off a bad day.

24

"THIS is a picture taken from our helicopter," said Ling, pointing at an aerial photograph on Lone's desk. "It is of a place called Tony's Truck Stop."

The picture looked down on a rectangular box at the head of a larger rectangle, which extended into a third rectangle crossed by a series of straight lines.

Ling put a blunt finger on the second rectangle. "Notice the large parking lot, and the train yard across the road."

"What are the lines running perpendicular to the train tracks?"

"This group of buildings next to the truck stop is a coal-processing plant. The lines are conveyor belts carrying coal across the road into the train yard."

"And why do we like this place?"

"The truck stop is open twenty-four hours a day, and coal is loaded into the cars all night long. At four in the morning, there will be enough sound from the trains to cover any noise."

Ling was right. The truck stop was the perfect place to kill Jefferson, but it made him uneasy. The terrain was flat, and Lone had never forgotten that he came from the countryside. This Tony's was flat as a city block, and flat terrain favored Jefferson.

In the city, Jefferson had been able to follow Sylvie and take pictures of her. It was in those pictures that he saw something weak in her face and then aimed Lamh at her like a bullet. There were no curves to Jefferson's thinking: right-left, right-wrong, everything laid out square, like the picture of Tony's Truck Stop.

"Something the matter, Chu Chi?" asked Ling.

"Just thinking."

Ling walked to the window and looked out.

Lone stared hard at the picture, moving his head right and left. Then his heart skipped once and started to race. There. When you looked at it the right way—a face. The rectangles were eyes, the coal plant a nose, the tracks a vicious smile. The picture was staring at him, and when he looked into the hollow holes and zipper smile, the face became Jefferson's face . . . or, rather, the skull underneath.

Suddenly Lone knew what Jefferson would look like when he

was dead and the look felt like a curse. Curses from the dead stuck in your mind like the smell of burning flesh: Sylvie's body was a column of fire, her eyes cutting blue holes through red flames while her hair burned and her lips baked black, then flaked away. Her face had melted like peach gravy over the bone below, and then came the voice stretched by heat to a tight white wire, screaming one word until she could scream no more: *Jefferson! Jefferson! Jefferson!*

Five minutes later Jefferson had shot him in the chest. Then he stayed in his mind for twenty-five years. Now he had reappeared in the center of the ozone hole along with the viruses. Sylvie had cursed him, and Jefferson was the curse.

But if the man was a curse, why had he missed the kill shot? How could that be unless Sylvie had cursed him, too?

Maybe he and Jefferson should talk:

Don't you know you killed her, too?

I didn't burn her.

But she cursed both of us, and I've carried it alone for twenty-five years while you made your place in the world. I'm owed.

"I'm owed," he said aloud.

Ling turned from the window. "Chu Chi?"

"Nothing."

Lone walked away from Ling and stood against the far wall. He was still uneasy about Tony's, but it had one big advantage; Jefferson would show up. It was his country and he'd feel comfortable there. Macao, Phuket, Vegas, any casino you could name, luck always turned. C. K. Lone had carried the curse for twenty-five years and he was owed—by time and Jefferson and Hahn and the Communists and his damn stupid father, who had been too dumb to run to Hong Kong before they came for him.

Lone walked to the window and clapped Ling on the back. "You have performed perfectly. We'll do it tomorrow, with Tona, Lee, and Cho."

"You're coming?"

"Jefferson is going to put money in my hand and then I'm going to kill him. Make that clear to the men. No one but me!"

"Yes, Chu Chi."

. . . .

JEFFERSON WAS IN his den, pacing in front of the computer and mentally ordering Chuck to log on. When it happened, Chuck's words went through him like electricity.

```
Jefferson, are you there? It's Chuck.
```

Jefferson jumped into the chair in front of his computer.

```
Jefferson here. Go ahead.

Do you have the money?

No problem, as long as you have something
for me.

Are you familiar with Tony's Truck Stop?
```

Familiar? He owned 10 percent of it—repayment for the twenty thousand he'd loaned Tony Armitis when the bank was squeezing him.

The place lay across the junction of Interstate 15 and Highway 2, out in the middle of strip-mine country, a stretch that was lonely, barren, and ugly. It was a sprawling warren of bars, cheap motels, and a restaurants that served the belly-flop calorie bombs which reminded lonely truckers of their fat, warm wives.

From the outside it was drab, because it was covered with coal soot from the train yard across the road. Inside, it was bright and boozy, twenty-four hours a day of country music and cruising hookers, their Winnebagos parked outside. It wasn't promoted by the tourism bureau, but it was semi-famous anyway.

```
You're not from around here, are you?

I'm Canadian.

No, you're Asian.

I'm in Canada.

But you work for Tsendai and you're
Asian, aren't you?
```

Lone looked at the screen and paused. It was common knowledge that Tsendai was a Hong Kong corporation. Denying he was Chinese would only increase suspicions.

```
Yes. Does it make a difference?

No. But I want you there, not someone
else.

Of course. I've been wanting to meet you.

Why?

Some things can only be talked about in
person.
```

What the hell? Did Chuck know other things? Was he working a price hike?

```
A hundred thousand is as high as I go, no
matter what you want to talk about.

Don't insult me. When I make a deal I
keep it. Make sure you do the same.

I keep my deals too.

Then be at Tony's tomorrow night at
4 A.M.

Why so late?

Not many people at that time.

You don't know much about Tony's, do you?

I have what you want, so I set the time.
```

Something about the exchange reminded Jefferson of arguments with Celine—patterned, familiar.

```
Relax. I'll be there.
```

```
All right. But if you're not alone, I'll
leave. I'm taking a big risk.
```

There was that strange familiarity again. Chuck was probably just a guy who smoked too much and dreamed about big breasts, but Jefferson decided to take the magnum.

```
O.K. See you at 4:00.

How will I find you?

I'll find you. You'll be easy to spot at
Tony's.

Agreed.
```

When Lone clicked off the computer, he felt old and drained. He took the elevator to his suite, where he stood in front of the bathroom mirror and inspected his face. Fifty years old—skin still tight, but age in the eyes.

He didn't want to go tomorrow. It would mean a ride in the car and talking to the men. He hated thinking of things to say when words meant nothing, but it couldn't be helped. Face-to-face humiliation was the only way to cure himself of Jefferson's curse.

Still, it was possible they could miss and let him go crying to his beautiful wife. Unless there was no beautiful wife. Lone picked up the phone on his nightstand.

"Ling, do we know where Jefferson's woman is living? Good. Send Wu and Sula. Have them take Batiste and Nordgay from plant security and bring the woman here—whatever it takes short of killing her. I want her here alive."

Lone knew. There was no pain like losing a woman you really wanted.

25

IT was three in the morning and Jefferson was thirty miles west of Tony's. He pushed the rented Explorer up to eighty and hit the cruise control. He had a sudden impulse to run home, but this was where his life had brought him. He didn't like it, but it was better than trying to live someone else's life. He'd do whatever the situation demanded. That was the reason for the rental car: If something bad happened at Tony's, he could say a crazed cowboy had taken the Explorer and gone wild. He reached back and adjusted the pistol in his belt.

The parking lot at Tony's was five acres of blacktop, with cars on the right and rows of semis on the left, parked in lines like a development of box ranchers. To the left rear of the semis, hidden from wives and families, was a little section of hooker-occupied RVs.

Jefferson pulled into the lot and parked halfway down. He opened the tailgate and took out the fireproof metal case with the money in it. Carrying a hundred thousand in cash made the walk to the door feel like a mile.

You entered Tony's through a set of swinging doors, then a narrow hall to another set of doors, which opened into a circle of plastic palms. Tony's theory was that palms made people feel warm in the winter. They also covered up a lot of bad flooring.

The palm-tree corridor led straight back to another set of doors and two hallways, the right one leading to the rest rooms and the left to the kitchen.

Out front, there were two breaks in the palms. The right one took you into the dining room—an open space the size of a school gymnasium, with Formica tables in the center, a cafeteria line along the back wall, and a row of aquamarine plastic booths along the front.

On the left was the bar/lounge, a dark cave full of Naugahyde furniture, TVs, pool tables, and slot machines. The bar was full of truckers who were staying over long enough to get drunk or laid by the hookers in the RVs.

Presiding over it all from a plastic teakwood dais was Tony Armitas, a three-hundred-pound bald Armenian, who wore Hawaiian shirts and did a mean Don Ho impersonation. Tony only had five and a half feet of height to carry his weight, so he rarely got up, preferring to give orders through a microphone bolted to the arm of his reinforced swivel chair.

"Judd baby," he called out when Jefferson walked through the doors. "Have a cigar."

Tony lobbed a Macanudo through the air. Jefferson caught it and slipped into his shirt pocket.

"Look at this place," Tony said, spreading his arms. "Three-thirty in the morning, and there must be a hundred people in here. We're getting rich, partner. Of course you're already rich, thank God. What brings you way out here?"

"Just making sure you don't run off with the profits." Jefferson hopped up onto the dais and shook Tony's hand.

"And leave all this?" Tony said. "I guess you want to eat free since you own part of the joint. The meat loaf's good tonight, and we got some homemade bean soup."

"Nothing to eat, thanks. Actually, I've got kind of a business meeting set up."

"What kind of business you got at three-thirty in the morning, babe?"

"Quiet business. I'm going to wait for some people in the dining room. Send me over a Jack black."

"Sure, babe." Tony gave him a sidelong glance but didn't ask any more questions.

Jefferson sat in a front booth and drank his Jack Daniel's, the whiskey putting an edge of anger on his thoughts. Halfway through his second drink it occurred to him that someone really wanted his hundred thousand dollars, and here he was, holding it. What if it was the same bunch he'd run into at Vandivier's house?

He took the metal case and walked to the back hallway. "Think I'll say hello to Juan," he said to a curious Tony as he passed by.

Juan was the head cook. Jefferson headed for the kitchen, the quickest place he could think of to stash some money. He stuck his head through the doors and saw rows of stoves, deep fryers, and grills on his left, storerooms and walk-in coolers on his right, a back door at the end.

"Hey, Juan," he said as he brushed past him on the way to the door.

It was a warm night and only the screen was closed. Jefferson nudged it open and looked around: two big Dumpsters, a row of refrigeration units, and an access road for the garbage trucks. No way he was leaving that much money in a Dumpster. He turned and walked down the row of stoves to the double deep fryer on the end, hot grease bubbling like hell. No one would put an arm in there. He lifted the basket and dropped the metal case into the hot grease.

"Hey," yelled Juan. "What you doing, Mr. Jefferson?"

"Leave it there. Understand?" Jefferson said in his owner's voice.

"Okay," said Juan. "But . . . "

"Leave it," Jefferson said as he backed out the door.

When he got to the circle of palms, he saw three Asian men in suits standing by the entrance. The one in front was obviously the leader. He had a round, pleasant face with wrinkles around the eyes, and his bald head was shiny as waxed fruit. To his right rear was a little man with a pockmarked cobra face, and next to him was a taller man. That one was totally expressionless, as if his face had been painted on. Jefferson walked up to the bald one and stuck out his hand.

"I'm Jefferson," he said. "Let's go into the dining room."

Tony raised his eyebrows but said nothing.

Jefferson led the way and sat at the same booth as before. The little guy and the bald one sat across from him. The tall one sat to his right.

"My name is Ling," the bald one said amiably. "This is Mr. Lee. The gentleman beside you is Mr. Tona."

"You've come for the money?"

"Not exactly."

An unnatural heat ran from the bottom of Jefferson's feet to the top of his head. "Then what do we have to talk about?"

"You're not going to talk at all. You are going to sit in your seat and listen to someone who wants to talk to you."

"Either produce some information in one minute or I leave."

"You won't do that," said Ling.

"No?"

144

"If you do, Mr. Tona will take out his machine pistol and begin killing everyone in the room. Mr. Lee will go into the bar and kill everyone there."

Jefferson felt the sweat begin to roll from under his arms. "This is a bluff. You're not going to kill a whole restaurant full of people."

"Once you talk to this person, you'll have no doubt."

Ling broke into a broad smile. Jefferson felt an unnatural pain behind his eyeballs. Ling nodded to Tona, who rose and headed for the door.

"He'll be back in a few minutes with our guest," Ling said.

Jefferson stared silently at the two men across from him. The bald one smiled faintly. The other one's face was blank as plaster. Jefferson was facing the door, but he felt Tona and the other man enter before he actually saw them. The roots of his hair stiffened and the soles of his feet began to burn. He didn't want to look up. When he did, he was paralyzed.

"Jefferson," said C. K. Lone. He spoke with the quiet triumph of a man who's just reached the summit of Mt. Everest.

Jefferson was as stunned as if the man had crawled out of his head. He reached for the pistol in his belt.

"Do that, and everyone will die," said Ling.

Jefferson kept his hand on the pistol but didn't attempt to draw it.

Lee got up, and Lone slid into his place across from Jefferson. "Still protecting the innocents, I see," he said.

"I'll kill you," Jefferson answered.

Lone smiled.

"No, Jefferson. I'm going to kill you."

Jefferson felt a loosening in his bowels as he realized that this meeting had always been about his death.

"Then there's no reason I shouldn't start shooting."

"Go ahead," said Lone, spreading his arms.

A voice in Jefferson's mind said, *They're going to kill you anyway. Take him with you. His death is worth everyone in here.*

Jefferson's fingers twitched but he did nothing.

"I knew it," said Lone. "I give you a chance to kill me and you don't take it, because of these . . . people."

He said the word like it was the name of a bad smell.

"Fuck you," said Jefferson. "You're not going to do anything until you get what you need."

Ever so carefully, Lone lit another cigarette. "I'd say you're the one in need, Jefferson."

"But you need the hundred thousand."

Lone leaned forward but he didn't cross the center line of the table. "My yearly office rent is more than that."

"You don't need the money. You just need me to give it to you. Isn't that right?"

A shadow of almost carnal desire crossed Lone's face. "Yes, Jefferson," he said thickly. "You will get me the money and you will hand it to me and then I will kill you with my own hand."

"And I'll go along with this?"

"Yes. Otherwise all these innocent people will die."

Lone would do it. He had to blight your soul or die himself. Jefferson knew because he felt the same. He'd die if he had to, but he'd never give what Lone needed. He might pretend, though. He might just pretend.

"The money's in here somewhere, but you'd never find it."

"I don't want to find it. I want you to give it to me."

"You've got to show me you're not going to kill these people."

Lone was beginning to breathe heavily, a man on the verge of consummation. "What do you propose?"

"You take your men outside. Leave one man to be with me when I get the money."

"And then?"

"Then I come out and give it to you."

"And let me kill you?"

"Yes."

"Bullshit. You won't go that easily."

"No, but you'll have the manpower."

Lone thought for a few seconds, then made a decision. "Agreed," he said. "But first take out your pistol and hand it to Mr. Tona under the table."

Jefferson got the gun out of his belt and placed it on the seat next to him. Tona reached under the table and handed the bulky machine pistol to Lee. Then he stuck the magnum in his belt and buttoned his suit coat over it.

"Mr. Tona will go with you," said Lone. "The rest of us will be outside."

"You first."

As Lone pushed himself to his feet, Jefferson could see that he was wired. He wobbled a little as he walked to the door with Ling and the other one.

When they had gone, Jefferson got up and walked toward Tony's dais, trailed by Tona.

"Hey, Tony," he said. "I'm thinking of buying some imported jewelry from this gentleman—without any red tape or taxes."

Tony shook his head knowingly.

"We need a private place for him to show me what he's got. I was wondering if you could clear the kitchen for a couple minutes."

"Uh, okay," Tony said with a frown. "You okay, Judd? You look a little pale."

"Not used to staying up this late anymore. I'd like to get this over with and get home."

"Sure."

Tony motioned to a plump waitress. "Agnes, tell Juan and the boys to come out and take a break for a few minutes. Mr. Jefferson needs to use the kitchen."

Agnes nodded and went through the double doors. Then Juan came out followed by the four cooks. "I got biscuits in the oven, Tony," he said. "They be ready in five minutes."

"No problem," said Jefferson, and shouldered his way through the doors.

The kitchen: long, narrow, bright, back door still open. But there was no way to outrun a pistol. What, then? Something else. A weapon. Some kind of weapon. A kitchen full of them, like at Vandivier's. But this is no Smith, no junky con. This is a professional here, used to service, has probably never been in a kitchen in his life. Intense smells; burgers on the grill, biscuits in the oven, gravy, smoky bean soup, new pot on the oven, bubbling away, boiling, ham floating on top, ham bone sticking up past the rim, french fryer to the left. Close now and still no plan, nothing but the money in the fryer, grease hot enough to burn an arm to the bone.

"Get it," said Tona.

"It's in there."

Jefferson pointed down into the french fryer. Tona edged over and looked down into the grease, gun out, holding it chest high. "Get it."

"The grease is hot enough to burn my arm off."

Tona smiled a little lizard's smile. "Get it."

"I'm not sticking my arm in there."

Tona raised the gun.

"If you shoot me, you'll have to get it."

"How, then?"

"I'll have to drain the grease."

Jefferson stooped down, opened the metal door on the bottom of the fryer, reached in and up, feeling the fixture at the bottom of the reservoir, the lever that opened the drain, the long rubber tube that spewed the grease into a bucket. Lots of grease—maybe twenty gallons. Lots of pressure through the rubber tube. Bucket in the corner; mop sticking out.

"I've got my hand on the drain latch," said Jefferson. "Shove that bucket over here."

Nodding toward the bucket, Tona stepped right and aimed the gun, then pushed the bucket with his foot. Came closer—three feet, two feet, one.

Jefferson flipped the lever open on the bottom of the grease trap, whipped out the rubber hose, and soaked Tona's crotch with boiling grease.

Tona shrieked, raised up onto his toes, and jumped backward, dropping his arms, looking down in disbelief. Jefferson dropped the hose, rose, grabbed the ham bone out of the bean soup and jumped forward, swinging down with all his strength, the rounded ham bone head smashing Tona between the eyes. He had a shocked look, staggered back, and Jefferson swung again, grunting with effort, into his temple. Another shocked look. His body fell. Eyes open, he now had a dead look.

Jefferson dropped the ham bone and got his gun out of Tona's hand, rose, wadded three paper towels into a torch, stuck the torch into the stove's flame, kicked the bucket over, stepped up, and held the torch directly under one of the kitchen's sprinkler heads. As it began to whir, Jefferson jumped down, ran to the end of the kitchen, and pulled the fire alarm. The kitchen was now a blur of falling water, and the dining room would be the same. The crowd would stampede for the exits. Maybe Lone's men would, too.

Jefferson stuck the pistol in his belt and bolted out the screen door, running around the corner into the parking lot, where a crowd was gathering to look up for flames. A black stretch limo was sliding out from between some semis.

Jefferson put his head down and sprinted for the Explorer. He wrenched open the door, threw the gun on the seat, cranked it up, and gunned for the right exit. The limo was cutting across in front of him, getting there first and blocking his way. The sunroof was open. A man's torso appeared through the opening, arms stretching, aiming a weapon.

Jefferson aimed the Explorer at the limo's side, sped to thirty, hit cruise control, and jumped out, hitting the ground hard and rolling over three times before the Explorer slammed into the limo. He began running.

He looked over his shoulder and saw a man clambering out the top of the caved-in limo and remembered his gun was in the Explorer. Lone's other men were somewhere behind him, near Tony's. There was nowhere to go but the train yard. He put his head down and charged toward it.

The yard: half a mile wide, tracks running east-west, switching engines, rumbling steel and sparks, headlights carving the coal haze into drifting clouds of soot, and everywhere the burnt-metal smell of electricity. Long trains building momentum; the whole yard moved in slow motion.

Jefferson looked back and saw a man he didn't recognize. He was running awkwardly, carrying a machine pistol. He bent low, waited for a switching engine, and took off eastward, away from the man with the gun, running in a crouch, hoping for a hiding place or help. He saw gravel kick up to his right and looked back to see the man lower the gun and begin running.

It was now a foot race, and Jefferson was losing. The other man was smaller and faster. Soon he'd pull to within point-blank range. There was no place to hide except in the middle of traffic. Jefferson cut left into a stream of moving lights and rolling freight cars. Waiting until the last second, he leapt across the path of a string of coal cars and began running west, parallel to the cars and toward his pursuer.

Jefferson bent low and looked under the cars for the man's feet, but what he saw was light flashing off a face and the muzzle flash from a gun. He jumped up and began running again, but when he looked over his shoulder, he saw the same face crawling across the dome of coal in the car. The man had hopped the train and was coming over.

Jefferson broke right and sprinted across two sets of tracks to where another train was being pushed west toward a holding area. He matched his speed to the train's, caught the ladder, and began climbing.

It was a coal car, and it was empty. He swung over the side and dropped into the car as a bullet threw a shower of sparks off the place where his legs had been.

Inside the car, he dropped against the cold iron wall and gasped, every one of his forty-nine years stacked on his chest. He couldn't keep up the pace much longer. Then came the creeping temptation: lean back against the wall in a stupor, eyes glazed, think of snowy mornings in bed with Celine. Celine . . . the black limo . . . Jesus! Lone would go after her too!

Jefferson clattered wildly to his feet, looking around for the fastest way to Celine, but he was fifty miles away, in the bottom of a coal car, about to betray her by letting himself be shot. He ran to the front of the car and pulled himself up the ladder. Looking back, he saw the gunman drop into the car.

Jefferson hopped across to the car in front and climbed into it. He could hear the man's footsteps clanging along the bottom of the trailing car and there were only three more cars ahead, no engine. The train was a pusher. Three more cars, and his back would be to the wall.

Keep moving. Whatever happened, keep moving. Keep hoping.

But the gunman was already standing atop the trailing car, swaying, preparing to jump. Jefferson looked for a weapon—a lump of coal, anything. Then he saw the shovel in a rack by the ladder. He snatched it and ran toward the swaying man, reaching the end of the car before he could jump and thrashing the shovel back and forth, slashing the feet, breaking off the blade on the top of the car, but making the man jump back into the trailing car, buying time.

Jefferson turned and ran to the front end of the car, carrying the shovel, even though it was now just a stick. He climbed the side, swung over and down, reached the bottom rung, and stepped off. He hit the ground running but lost his balance anyway, falling and rolling. But he held on to the stick.

He came up onto his knees and saw the gunman hanging on to the outside of the car, struggling for a point-blank shot. Jefferson began to run toward the hanging man.

With a death scream, he shoved upward with the handle and felt a looming shape knock him over and back. He was rolling, sliding, tangled in the limbs of the man above him as they tore through the gravel and came to a breakneck stop against the steel rails of a parallel track.

Jefferson couldn't run. He couldn't even get up. All he could do was drag himself away from the weight, pulling himself with his elbows, then rolling onto his back, ready to accept whatever would happen. But nothing was going to happen, because the gunman was lying on his side with the shovel handle through the center of his chest.

Jefferson rose and stumbled toward the road. He heard sirens and saw red lights flashing in Tony's parking lot: fire engines, police cars, a milling crowd. He ran toward the scene, desperate to tell the cops that Lone would go after Celine, that he had to get to her first and they had to go with him. Then he came to a stop, reality shutting him down.

There had been a fake fire alarm, water damage, maybe a body in the kitchen. The cops weren't going anywhere until they figured out what was going on, and when they did, they wouldn't like it. They'd be looking to arrest someone. One thing they weren't likely to do was speed off into the night with the man who was the cause of it all—not until they'd gotten the facts straight, and by that time Celine could be dead.

Jefferson began running again, toward where he'd sent the Explorer into the limo. The limo was gone, but the Explorer was still there. He ran toward it, keeping his eye on the flashing lights at the far end of the parking lot. When he got to the car he saw that the front end was crumpled, the hood was raised, and the ignition wires had been torn out.

He ran toward Tony's and sprinted around to the side where the Winnebagos were parked. A bank of phones hung on the wall. He fished for his calling card, dialed Celine's number at the cabin, and got her machine.

"Celine," he bellowed. "It's Judd. Pick up! Goddamnit, pick up!"

Nothing. They hadn't had time to get to her yet, so she was out. *God, if she's with a man, please let her stay all night.*

He slammed down the receiver and ran back to the Explorer, yanked open the driver's side door, and found his gun wedged under the seat. He stuck the gun in his belt and looked wildly around the parking lot for a ride, any kind of ride. Then he saw a small Winnebago slide into the bottom of the lot, a hooker dropping off a customer. A trucker stepped out the back and adjusted his pants.

As the trucker walked away Jefferson sprinted to the back of the Winnebago and opened the door. She was a fortyish woman wearing nothing but a pair of lime green panties and a matching bra.

"Sorry, honey," she said. "But business hours are over."

Then she saw the gun. "Ohmigod, please don't shoot me! The money's under the seat. Take it, but please don't shoot me."

"Shut up," said Jefferson. "I don't want your money, but I've got to get to East Glacier."

"Oh no, please," she begged. "Not my 'bago. Please. I make my living with it. I'll be homeless. I'll take you wherever you want to go, but please don't leave me homeless."

The woman had stocky legs, skin like leather, and breasts on their way south. Not many years left to earn her stash.

"Sit down in the passenger seat," he told her. "Strap yourself in. If you unfasten the seat belt, I'll stop and throw you out."

The woman jumped into the seat and did as she was told. For a second Jefferson thought of calling Tony about the money in the french fryer. Then he thought of Celine and started the engine.

"Oh, thank you," said the woman next to him. "Thank you so much. My body and the 'bago is all I've got to work with."

"Shut up. I've had a rough night."

"Are you sure you can drive?"

"What do you mean?"

"No offense, but you look like you been run over by a lawn mower."

"Just stay in your seat and you'll get your car back."

"No problem. I can see you're in a hurry."

"Desperate, afraid, *and* in a hurry, so shut up and let me drive."

"Christ," she muttered. "Just like being married again."

26

IT was six in the morning when Celine stole a blanket from her own bed. She'd been out on the lawn since three-thirty because the thing was back. It had been gone for a week, but now it was here, choking her when she tried to sleep, with a smell like rotten meat.

She sidled into the bedroom, whipped the blanket off the bed, and hurried into the living room. Once there, she wrapped herself in the blanket and huddled in front of the television. Morning light poured into the room from a string of windows along the porch. Outside, the wide yard flowed into groves of poplar. The undersides of their leaves glistened in the early-morning gold like fish in sunlit water. The sight was so benign that for a few seconds she imagined everything was normal. Then the breeze blew a stray branch against the side of the house and she went stiff as a corpse. Something was trying to get her, and it was in her bedroom. She could parry it during the day, but when she slept, it covered her with a living stink.

She picked up the remote and began to surf through channels, stopping at a fishing show. A beefy guy in a flannel shirt stood in a boat tying a lure to his line. He was going on about what insects the fish would be looking for at different water temperatures. He was casting out into a blue lake bordered by white pine and spruce. It was morning there. She could tell by the fog rising off the top of the surrounding hills. It was Lake McDonald. She recognized it because it was only fifteen minutes away from the chair where she sat.

She and Judd had jumped at the chance to buy the two-acre spearhead stuck into the side of national park property. It had been early in their marriage and they really couldn't afford it, but the front yard floated above the water like a Buddhist dream.

She and Judd had gone into hock so they could own a piece of that dream and give it to their children. Whenever the vastness of the plains began to run away with their eyes or the hostility of commerce began to bargain its way into their lives, they'd take the children and go to the Sky Cabin, a name the children had invented and that they all used. There, the children would be born again every time they stood at the edge of the yard to throw rocks at the lake a mile below. She and Judd were newly married every time the kids were in bed and they stood warm in the night, smelling the pine in each other's hair. It was the best place Celine had ever been.

Only after the kids were away at school and Judd started acting weird had they ceased to go the cabin. It was as though neither of them wanted to soil the place. Maybe they should have gone, but Judd didn't mention it and she didn't want him to. It was her place more than anyone else's and she wanted to keep it clean.

Now it was being invaded by a living stain. She felt a red flush of anger sweep down her face and into her toes. Her hands dug into the arms of the chair and she almost launched herself into the bedroom to challenge the thing. She'd done that before, but nothing ever appeared. She'd end up naked and alone, screaming obscenities at the walls of a place she loved.

"Why?" she shrieked. "Why is this happening? Jesus Christ, why?"

Her voice bounced off the ceiling and hurt her ears. She felt like she was dying. She wanted Judd, but he had his own demon. What was there to believe in? Maybe the thing in her bedroom was the dead space where belief used to live.

Celine looked wildly from door to window to floor, sweating in the cold morning air and breathing like she was in an iron vest. Then she fell to her knees with her head against the chair.

"Hear me," she cried. "Hear me, someone. I'm in trouble. I'm in terrible trouble."

She leaned against the chair and sighed, unable to say any more. Turning her head to rest it against her arm, she saw the television screen. The man in the boat was holding up a string of fish and gesturing toward the lake with his arm. The sun turned the water to diamonds. The boat rocked gently. The man was flushed with happiness.

That was it. She'd go to the lodge, rent a canoe, go out on the lake, and let the water rock her to sleep, dream in the morning sun and wake up with a plan. Look how happy that guy on TV was. Maybe out on the water she could look up here and see herself and Judd and the children playing in the yard. She didn't even have to go back into the bedroom. There were some clothes in the dryer. Maybe she'd stay out the whole day.

27

FAR Lightning was playing the pinball machine in bar number three. It was one of three bars at the corner of Route 89 and East Glacier Road. Originally they all had names, but past winters had scrubbed the paint off the windows and knocked down the signs. By that time, none of the owners saw any point in advertising places everyone in Browning knew about anyway.

Far Lightning looked up from the pinball machine and stared at the bar's interior: cheap paneling, wobbly stools, faded tit calendars, and four bloated drunks kick-starting their livers with hangover vodka. A film of ancient dirt covered the plate-glass window, turning the morning light to dishwater.

Eight A.M. It was never too early for a drink in Browning or any other Indian town. All the white thieves and pale do-gooders had separated the Indian from his land, and the land was his soul. Without it, he was cut off from his God. The only way to reestablish contact was to die, so warriors poisoned themselves with booze and went down into the land.

But now Wovoka's prophecy was coming true. The white man's world would be rolled up and the land would be alive again. The shame of it was that he was surprised. He'd believed in it for twenty-five years, yet now that it was going to happen, he was surprised. Even a strong faith couldn't imagine the reality of the creator in action.

Far Lightning felt a surge in his heart that scared him. Then he recognized the feeling as joy. He traced it backward, trying to remember the last time his life had felt so light. Then he realized it was after the fight in the Buffalo Wallow, when he'd seen Celine Jefferson.

He laughed out loud at himself. Joseph Far Lightning, big-time believer, wearing cowboy boots, jeans, work shirt—white man's clothes—and he wanted a white man's woman.

He remembered her in the class. Every time she'd come close, his eyes had blurred with the smell of her. His hands had formed themselves into her shape. She was a wind curve of flower-petal white, made to be shielded by a warrior's back, someone who'd spent his life in moonlight and mountain snow, someone who could reach for her medicine.

"Aw, shit," he said, laughing again. Then he looked out the window and saw a big Lincoln swing left onto East Glacier Road. It was going fast enough to kick up a rooster tail of dust.

Big car. Four men. Going fast. Too fast for tourists. Wearing suits. Not tourists. Not kids. What, then?

Far Lightning left his beer on the machine and walked slowly toward the window. What were four suits in a fast Lincoln doing on the road to East Glacier? What was at the end of the road? Lake McDonald. A cabin. Jefferson owned a cabin overlooking the lake. He was at the ranch. She would be at the cabin . . . alone.

Jefferson causing problems with Tsendai . . . big corporation . . . scourge of the earth . . . business . . . dollar-mind . . . Jefferson poking at them . . . one stubborn man . . . a tough man . . . hard to deal with . . . unless you found a weakness.

They would do it. Hard for whites to believe, but easy for an Indian. The business mind went to the bottom line, and the bottom line was power. Paranoia? Maybe. But after the vision, only a fool would ignore his insides.

Far Lightning bolted out of the bar and jumped into his old pickup. Its untuned engine belched smoke as he sheared across Route 89 and headed up East Glacier Road, beer cans and blankets bouncing into the wind.

"Giddup, you son of a bitch," he said, and floored the accelerator.

28

LAKE McDonald was more than five miles long. It ran about a mile west of the lodge, then turned left where the shoreline narrowed. After that, it continued southwest between steep banks covered with pine and fir trees.

Most of the tourists stayed within sight of the lodge, paddling inexpertly around the widest part of the lake. But Celine knew what she was doing with a canoe. Within minutes, she had reached the point where the lake was sheltered by trees. Then she made the turn and paddled a half mile through the silence to a place where the world disappeared. She leaned back and looked up at the sky, nudging the canoe along by dipping her hands in the cold water.

Memory lifted away from her like mist. She felt weightless. At a point where all sounds blended into a gentle rush of wind, she fell asleep, sure she would awaken into a moment of complete innocence. It had always worked that way before.

LATER, SHE OPENED her eyes and blinked dreamily into the absolute blue, remembering the nameless terror of the night before as if it had happened to someone else. She felt almost sure of herself again.

Celine rose onto an elbow and looked hopefully over the edge of the canoe. She was expecting answers. Instead, she saw two canoes paddled by four Asian men wearing suits. They were about fifty yards away and advancing in the comical half circles produced by novice paddlers.

"Suits," she said aloud. "Why are they wearing suits?"

One of the canoes was making its way clumsily around her as if traveling farther down the shoreline. The other one cut behind her, floated forward, and stopped when it crossed the rear of her canoe.

Her body stiffened. The other canoe was no more than twenty yards away and coming toward her. Now she could see why the man in front was wearing a suit. It covered the ugly black pistol he was pulling from a holster under his arm.

. . .

FAR LIGHTNING SLID the truck to a halt in front of the Lake McDonald Lodge. He waved off the teenage doorman and loped into the lobby, slowing to a walk as he approached the desk clerk, a round-faced Blackfoot girl of about eighteen.

She told him that some Japanese land developers had been in asking about the whereabouts of the Jefferson cabin. It seemed there were a couple minor problems with a contract, and they needed to talk to Celine right away.

"I know Mrs. Jefferson," said the girl. "She comes in to rent a canoe sometimes."

"So you told them where she lives?"

"Didn't have to. She's out on the lake right now. I told them they could wait, but they paddled off in their suits."

"How long ago did they leave?"

"Just a few minutes. You might be able to see them out the window."

She came around the desk and led him to the twenty-foot picture window that faced the lake.

"Now, where could they have gone?" she muttered as Far Lightning bolted for the truck.

The road ran parallel to the lake for a couple miles, then turned left toward the western entrance to the park. Celine and the men had to be in the narrower reaches of the lake. They would have driven the Lincoln down one of the dirt access roads and would need a place to put her in the car. No way anyone could drag Celine Jefferson through a parking lot without attracting a lot of attention.

"Fight, Celine," he said. "Give me a little time to find you."

The only weapon he had on him was a hunting knife, but something would come to him if he could just get there.

"Don't go easy, Celine," he yelled against the truck's windshield. "Show some medicine."

CELINE EXPECTED TO be shot, but the man started gesturing with his pistol instead of firing. He was waving her toward shore . . . an Asian man in a suit . . . Tsendai. This had something to do with Judd and the computer plant.

159

For Christ's sake! First the thing she kept seeing, and now they were making her part of some rough business with Judd. Fuck them all.

She grabbed her paddle, turned right, and began stroking with all her energy. The four men couldn't paddle worth a damn. She'd be back at the lodge before they could catch her. No way they could do anything there.

The man in the front canoe kept waving his gun. He couldn't row with one hand, and his paddler had to do all the work. He was no match for her, but the rear canoe was moving toward the lodge to cut her off where the lake narrowed.

Think, damn you, think! The one in back is worse with the paddle than the one in front. Turn back, pass him, and head for a place where you can beach. If you're far enough ahead, you can make it through the trees to the road.

She turned the canoe around and began stroking with all her strength. The man with the gun was now at a right angle to her, but she would pass him before he could turn. His canoe was only fifty feet away, but it was floundering.

Celine picked up speed with each stroke, crossing their bow and pulling away. The first canoe was now far back toward the narrow spot. She was already picking out a landing spot on shore when she heard the shots and saw splashes in the water.

The hell with it. They'd have to shoot her. She wasn't going to quit paddling. But as she leaned into the next stroke, she felt an added weight and knew they weren't trying to shoot her. It was the canoe the man was aiming for, and he was too close to miss. She heard two more shots and saw water coming into the boat.

"Goddamn you!" she screamed, and paddled harder.

The canoe felt like it was loaded with iron, water now ankle deep, shoulders burning with every stroke, breath coming in dry gasps. She was determined to row the canoe or die trying, but then there was no canoe, just a long container for the water, which was now up to her waist. She was swamped.

She threw the paddle away and began swimming, but a hand caught the back of her shirt and held. She twisted her head and sank her teeth into the soft flesh between thumb and forefinger. The man screamed, and she tasted blood.

Free again and swimming, but this time the hand caught in her hair, twisted her face to the side, and smashed her with a fist. A blinding flash of red shot across the back of her eyes. Then she felt herself being pulled through the water by the back of her shirt, but could do nothing about it.

Her mind watched from afar as she lay limp in the water. Now it was over. Whatever her life had been before, it was over. There was nothing left but what would be. Something wanted her different or dead. So be it.

THE LINCOLN COULD be anywhere. There were goddamn access roads all over the place.

"Speak to me," Far Lightning said to the sky.

Ahead was the west entrance to the park. They had to be to the rear. He made a U-turn and roared back with the window down, his ear to the outside.

Then came the silence. All sound was sucked out a hole in the sky, and he was in a silence like the plains. His breath echoed against the limitless horizon. He saw the pines rushing by his window, felt his hair blowing weightless in the wind, but there was no sound. His hearing was high above, flying on the great blue. Then he heard the shots—two of them, and not far ahead.

He banked the truck off the road and skidded silently across a wash of brown pine needles. Then he was out of the truck and running through the trees, locked on to the direction of the shots. Branches whipped his face, but he kept his eyes ahead, stopping only when he heard the voices.

They were a hundred yards downhill through the trees, four of them yelling at each other in a foreign language as they paddled clumsily toward shore. One of them had an arm around Celine's waist, lifting her half out of the water and bracing her against the side of the canoe.

Far Lightning began working his way downhill. If he could get to the tree line before they reached shore, maybe he could . . . what? There were four of them, no doubt with guns.

Their car . . . he searched the shoreline and saw it a couple hundred yards away. He began running in a crouch. It was tough to keep from sliding, but he kept moving, passing above the men as they landed their canoes—and a limp Celine.

They dragged her out of the water and propped her on her feet. She stood unsteadily. A man tried to support her, but she slapped his arm away. The man in front held a gun on her while one of the others started toward the car. Far Lightning followed him. He intended to cut the ignition wires. Maybe then there would be time to go for the park rangers. His rushing them and dying would be no help to Celine. He looked up through the trees at the tall sky. *Father, make me invisible.*

He was working his way toward the car when the smell froze him. Thick, dank musk—a bear. He dropped to the ground and saw a grizzly, near two thousand pounds, ambling downhill toward the water, eating berries and sniffing the wind. It was rut season, and this was a male. He'd be in no mood to be challenged.

The bear was no more than fifty yards away, a distance he could cover in five seconds. Far Lightning thanked God for being downwind. The brown bulk kept on toward the shore. Then he saw the canoes.

Far Lightning tried to put himself in the bear's place: He was hungry and thirsty and hadn't had a female since the previous summer. It wouldn't take much to turn him into a fast-moving ton of teeth and claws.

CELINE'S TEETH WERE chattering, and she hugged her knees to keep them from knocking. She needed a blanket, hot coffee, and a cigarette. She needed to wake up from this dream and feel warm arms around her, to hear children's voices down the hall. She wanted to start all over and do the one right thing that would keep her from ending up here. God, it was cold.

Out of the corner of her eye she saw the shadow of a hand and felt a slap on the left side of her face.

"Stand up," said one of the men. "We have to go to the car."

"Where are you taking me?"

Again came the slap, enraging and humiliating. She tried to get up, but her legs wouldn't work. Two of them grasped her from either side and yanked her to her feet. Her legs still refused to work and they began dragging her; her toes trailed in the sand like a drunk's.

FAR LIGHTNING FELT a rage he had never experienced. He would rather die than be powerless. Between him and the beach stood a creature that could destroy his enemies, but the huge stinking hulk of a bear just stood and watched dumbly, sniffing the air and waiting for a sign.

The massive head turned toward him, and Far Lightning caught sight of the bear's eye: old and hard as the inside of amber. No hatred or mercy; power without purpose.

He reached down and found a group of rounded stones. When he had six of them, he waited until the bear turned his head toward the beach, then rose and threw. Two rocks missed. Two thudded against the animal's huge back, and two cracked against his skull.

The bear grunted and pawed the back of his head. Then he looked around for the source of his irritation, but Far Lightning was out of sight and still downwind. That left the people on the beach. While the bear's attention was on them, Far Lightning hit him with four more rocks. Two of them bounced off the back of his skull.

The bear owned the forest, and something was hitting him painfully in the head. He could see five figures who didn't belong on his beach and decided to make them pay for his headache. With a belching roar, he dropped to all fours and charged.

Far Lightning saw the two men drop Celine and begin to run. The bear ignored her and hit them like a small truck. A ten-inch-long paw swatted one into the air, gutting him like a fish. The other one tried to run, but the bear knocked him down and tore out his throat. The third man sent two shots into the animal's shoulder, causing him to stop and wonder where the pain came from. The remaining two men dragged Celine into a canoe and began paddling furiously out into the lake, screaming at each other to row harder.

CELINE BEGAN TO laugh. The men reminded her of a couple old-time comedians, steering in wobbles and blaming each other for their mutual stupidity. She looked back at the bear and hoped it would live. She had no such hopes for herself.

WHEN FAR LIGHTNING saw the two men leap into the canoe with Celine, he knew he had a chance. The bear was between them and their car, and they were paddling away from it. They'd have to beach the canoe up the shore and work their way back to the car. He had to follow the canoe and be ready when it landed. There were now only two of them. They had guns, but if he could surprise them . . .

29

THE Winnebago heeled over wildly as Jefferson pushed it along the winding lake road.

"Please be careful," pleaded the hooker, whose name was Blaze.

"Shut up," Jefferson growled.

"How do you know your wife's down here, anyway?"

"Because she wasn't at the cabin and she's not at her office."

Blaze shook her head sympathetically. "You say you two are separated?"

"She's not at some man's place, either."

"I'm sure you're great, honey, but you're not the only . . . "

"Her bed was messed up. She slept in her bed last night, and she'd never go a day without making it."

"Never?"

"No."

"Neat freak, huh?"

Jefferson glanced away from the road to give Blaze a look. Halfway down the interstate, he had allowed her to get up and put on some clothes. She was wearing cut-off jeans and a flannel shirt tied at the waist. She had scrubbed off the hooker makeup and now looked like any heftily attractive middle-aged woman. She'd been a pretty good sport about having her 'bago hijacked, and if he hadn't been so worried about Celine, he might even have taken the time to find out her real name, which surely wasn't Blaze Maize.

"Blaze 'cause I'm fiery, Maize to match my blue eyes," she'd said.

"Maize is yellow."

"It is not."

"It's yellow like corn. The Indian name for corn was *maize*."

She'd sulked about that for a while, but then brightened after she decided to bleach her hair to match the name.

"Yellow is a fiery color, too, isn't it?"

"Sure," Jefferson said.

"But you'd never think about things like that. You're a man—a good-looking one, too, under all that soot and blood."

"Thanks."

"Pull this wagon over somewhere and maybe I'll show you just how fiery I am."

"Shut up and sit down. My wife's alone in an isolated cabin and somebody's trying to kill her. Give me any crap, and I'll knock you out."

"Jeez, I wasn't trying to give you any crap."

"I'm sorry. I know you weren't. I'm just tense."

"You sure must love your wife."

"I do."

After that Blaze had been nothing but helpful. He'd maintained eighty on the way down and reached the cabin at eight-thirty. When he found it empty, he'd phoned Celine's office and Marylin told him Celine hadn't shown up. That froze him until he noticed there was no blood in the place. There were no signs of a struggle, either. Celine would never go quietly, so that left the lake. She loved to paddle out to a secluded spot and doze. She would be out there somewhere, alone and vulnerable. He pressed the accelerator and rolled around another curve.

"Please don't wreck my house," Blaze whined.

"If anything happens, I'll get you another one."

"Yeah, like you're a millionaire."

"I am."

"God, how many times have I heard that?"

"How many?"

"Uh, none actually."

"Well, I am. I wrecked my car in Tony's parking lot, and I had to find my wife in a hurry."

"And you're a millionaire?"

"Several times over."

"Maybe I should sue you."

"Maybe I should run your 'bago into a tree."

"No, no, it's okay. But I still don't see how you can be so sure your wife was there this morning."

"I could smell her."

"Right."

"We've been together twenty-five years. I can always pick up her scent in a room."

166

"Jeez! My three husbands couldn't even smell themselves, which was lucky for them."

"Quiet!"

Jefferson pulled the 'bago to a wide spot in the road and turned off the engine. There was too much area along the shoreline. Looking would be pure guesswork, but it was quiet along the road, and Celine would surely make some noise.

He turned and looked into Blaze's pale blue eyes. She'd been kinder to him than any car thief had a right to expect.

"I need a favor," he said.

"No kidding."

"I need to climb up on the roof and listen. Promise me you won't start the car and knock me off. There's a new RV in it for you, and you might be saving a good woman's life."

She shrugged her shoulders. "About time somebody did that, but I want the RV."

"You've got it. Write down your real name and address."

While Blaze was writing, Jefferson got out and climbed onto the roof, noticing that his hands and legs weren't working quite right. His forty-nine-year-old body hadn't been through so much since Nam, and he was running on pure adrenaline. When that gave out, he would fold up like an accordion. No way he was going to let that happen before he found Celine.

Blaze kept her promise. The RV stayed still as he sat on the roof and listened for any sound out of sync with the natural. For a while there was nothing but the soft whoosh of wind through the pines punctuated by songbirds warbling. Occasionally, a car would whine by, but it was still too early for heavy traffic.

His ears strained to sift sound from sound. His head nodded, then rocked forward as he willed himself to stay awake. The lull was cooling his fried senses. Maybe something had already happened and he'd missed it. The thought made him snap his head up in terror. How would he live if he let her down? His stomach roiled and he began to sweat. Then he heard a faint pop, followed by two more.

Jefferson was off the roof and behind the wheel in an instant. He jolted the 'bago forward across the blacktop to the nearest access road, where he skidded to a stop, grabbed the magnum from under the seat, and opened the door.

"What?" asked Blaze.

"Shots—somewhere down this road."

He plucked the slip of paper from her hand, hopped out, and began running toward the trees.

"My phone number's on there, too," she said as he disappeared into the brush.

30

AS he ran, Far Lightning searched the shore for the nearest landing spot. The forest went down to the water's edge for about a quarter mile, then backed away from a narrow spit of sand. That's where they would go. Neither one of them could paddle worth a damn, and they'd beach at the first opportunity.

He'd have to attack while they were beaching the canoe. They'd have their backs turned. He'd get one for sure, and maybe the other would be surprised enough to hesitate. No sense making a plan. See and react. They'd be wet, cold, and shaken from the bear. They'd make a mistake.

Be like the bear, he thought as he ran. *It's my forest.* He ran faster, panting heavily, leaping over fallen trees and dodging rocks. He felt his breath churn through his chest, heard himself grunt as he knocked limbs aside with his arms. The canoe was falling behind. He was going to reach the landing spot first.

A fallen tree in the way . . . left . . . uphill . . . digging in the heels . . . rounding the tangle of roots at the tree's base . . . then a tall shadow reaching out from the side of his vision.

Far Lightning dropped down and rolled out of the man's hold. Coming up with his knife out of its sheath.

"All my relations!" he said when he saw that the man in front of him was John David Jefferson.

"Where is she?" Jefferson asked in a tight voice.

Far Lightning pointed through the trees at the approaching canoe. Jefferson pulled a .44 magnum from his belt.

"Let's go," he said.

Both of the suits got out to push the canoe onto the bare spot. Jefferson was in the trees on one side of the narrow landing; Far Lightning was on the other. When the canoe was firmly on land, they stepped out.

"Move away from the canoe," Jefferson said to them, wading into the water, the magnum extended.

The lead man turned white but stood his ground. The other one started belching with mortal fear. Jefferson waded over to him and smashed his jaw with the butt of the pistol. Teeth flew out of his

169

head in a shower of white, and he went down into the water moaning incoherently.

The leader made a move toward his coat, but Jefferson leveled the pistol on him and he froze.

"I'm sending you back," Jefferson said as he got to him. "Tell Lone this is my land. Hear me?"

Jefferson put the barrel of the pistol under the man's chin. "Hear me?" he repeated.

The man nodded his head vigorously.

"Good," said Jefferson. "Because it's going to be the last thing you hear."

He pointed the gun out toward the lake, positioned it an inch from the man's ear, and fired. The man shrieked in pain and reeled in circles. A .44 magnum fired that close would be like taking an ice pick through the eardrum. Jefferson grabbed him by the hair and fired close to the other ear as the man flopped backward into the water and rolled around like a beaten dog. Anything he heard in the future would be from far away.

The man with the broken jaw helped the now-deaf one out of the water and they both hobbled up the hill toward the road, giving Jefferson a wide berth as they went.

Jefferson handed Far Lightning the gun and sprinted to the canoe, where he lifted Celine to her feet. Her knees buckled slightly, but she steadied herself on his arm and waded in. Her eyes were glazed and she was shivering. Far Lightning tossed Jefferson the wool range jacket he was wearing, and he put it around her shoulders.

Celine felt the tension in Judd's back and knew just how close he'd come to murdering the two men. God, she'd wanted him to . . .

"Cee," he murmured in her ear. "Cee, I have to tell you something."

He was placing her against the trunk of a tree, kneeling and holding her close, big hand stroking the back of her head.

"Goddamnit, Judd," she said. "Goddamnit anyway."

"I don't have time to talk about it," he said. "I have to get you out of this."

"Out of what?"

"It's Lone," he said. "From Vietnam. I saw him."

"The law, Judd. The police."

"Things have happened. I go to the police now, and I'll be the one in trouble."

"What things?"

"This isn't the time or place to talk about it."

For the first time she noticed his shirt was ripped, his jeans were torn, and his face was streaked with blood.

"Listen to me, Cee. You've got to go somewhere he can't find you. He's got connections everywhere but on the plains. I'm going to ask Joseph to take you out there with him. Understand?"

She opened her mouth to object but changed her mind when she thought of the men on the lake and the thing in her cabin.

"Okay," she said in a tiny voice.

Far Lightning could tell by Jefferson's pained expression that he was going to ask for something. White men didn't like to ask favors. They'd stolen a whole country so they wouldn't have to ask permission to live there. They'd invented clocks so they could pay each other for their time rather than ask for it. They didn't even believe in asking God for very much. That was why they gave money to drought victims rather than hold rain dances.

"Joseph, I want you to take Celine with you."

"Take her?"

"The man behind this is someone I know from the war, a personal enemy. He won't stop."

"He has something to do with the plant?"

"Yes. His name is Lone. He's with the Chinese mafia. I fought him during the war."

"You're sure about this?"

"I was supposed to meet a man at Tony's. Four men showed up, and one of them was him. He tried to kill me—and Celine."

"What happened to the four men?"

"One's dead; maybe two—but not Lone."

"This isn't some kind of patriotism thing, is it, Judd? You know, another chance to win the war?"

"Lone stole children and murdered them. Can you understand that?"

"Any Indian can understand that."

"Then help me."

"Why didn't you shoot these two men?"

"Does one thing have something to do with the other?"

"I'd like to know your intentions."

"My intentions are to make sure nothing happens to Celine."

"Until when?"

"Until it's over."

Jefferson was a decent man, but Far Lightning had thought about Celine for years. How would he be able to keep his distance unless she made him? And there would come a time when she would be shivering like now. She would call for him, and she had too much medicine for him not to answer. He tried to live an honest life, but there would be a lot of nights with her long legs moving through the darkness, the sound of them in his ears . . .

Jefferson could tell Far Lightning was asking himself the same questions any man would be asking. Things might happen out there, but as long as she was alive there was a chance she'd come back.

"Joseph, she's got to get out of here fast. The empty is the only place I'm sure he can't find her."

"What does she say?"

"Ask her."

Jefferson stepped aside.

Celine felt a thrill of dread when she saw Far Lightning coming.

"Judd told you what he wanted?" he asked.

"Yes."

"What do you say?"

His eyes were gray, like hers. "It seems like the best thing, for now."

Jefferson looked away from them, and the wind hit him in the face. His nose began to run. His eyes blurred. The sun had disappeared and a sheet-metal rain was passing over the mountains onto Lake McDonald. He knelt at the water's edge and sculpted some ramparts into the moist dirt. The water broke through and flooded the inside. He knew what it must have been like in Richmond after the Civil War and why bourbon was invented in the South.

31

LONE'S head was in a box of silence, dark as the night, big as a room, his head sticking through a hole in the bottom of the box, clamped so tight that he couldn't move anything but his eyes. He couldn't tell up from down, and the quiet was squeezing his head from all sides. His eyeballs were popping like grapes from the skin. He opened his mouth to scream, but the silence came rushing in and swelled his head, pressing it against the walls of the box. He tried again to scream, forcing air through his throat with a popping sound as he woke into a fit of coughing.

Lone rolled off the bed and landed on his back. He found his cigarettes on the end table and lit one. It was two in the afternoon. He'd meant to sleep all day, but it had only been four hours since his worst experience in twenty-five years.

Not only had they missed both Jefferson and his woman, but three men were dead and Tona was probably going to be a vegetable for the rest of his life. Jefferson still had the joss. Nothing would be right until that changed, but how could you fight joss?

Lone got to his feet and opened the curtains. His residential suite was two floors below the office, but it had the same southern view of the Rockies. He pulled a chair to the window and sat staring at the mountains, hating them for what lay beyond. Montana was Jefferson's land. He owned enough joss there to make Sylvie's curse stay right where it had been for twenty-five years.

Lone jumped to his feet and walked in a tight circle, lighting one cigarette off another and massaging the back of his neck, trying to stop the impulse to fly down to Montana and kill everyone he could find. They didn't want him—not Montana, not Hahn, not Sylvie, not the whole dung-heap insect society of them. They didn't want him, but they owed him. That's what had stopped him from telling Ling to break out the machine pistols. He had to look hard at the curse and decide if it was fate or something he could change. He owed that to himself.

He poured a drink and looked at the mountains again. After a few minutes, he felt more in control of himself. You had to have control. You had to balance what you wanted against what you needed. Last night he'd wanted Jefferson dead, but had he needed him dead? Lone pondered that question while he had another drink, and decided that maybe the problem wasn't altogether joss.

Things with Harlow were at a stalemate. He could have waited to move on Jefferson. He could have been more subtle, drawing the noose tight before pulling on it. Last night had been too soon. He'd been too eager. Eagerness always led to a loss of control.

So if the problem was a loss of control, then the answer was to transfer the problem to Jefferson. He'd saved his wife, but now he'd have to hide her, which meant she'd be gone for as long as this business lasted. Jefferson would go back on television and scream to the EPA, but governments measured time in months, not days. He'd be impatient for his wife. Maybe next time he'd be the one who was out of control.

He walked into the living room and picked up the *Wall Street Journal*. He checked the stock quotes and his optimism turned to lead. In five days, Tsendai had dropped from fifty-three to forty-five. At first the slide had looked like institutional profit-taking, then small investor response to the institutions. Now it was threatening to become a full-scale selling frenzy. Hahn would be calling his men on the Street for answers, and then he'd be calling Calgary for an explanation.

Hahn would have to be told an edited version of the problems with Jefferson, one that left out the deaths at Tony's. If he heard about the deaths, he'd want a meeting, maybe even a trip to the plant. Then he'd talk directly to some of the Russians, who'd be pleased to tell him how well things were going. If that happened, Hahn would have to suffer a helicopter crash before he could get back to Hong Kong. Then the brothers would send people to check on the crash. It would be a nightmare.

But Hahn was lazy. He'd be looking for an excuse to stay where he was comfortable. The stock problem would disturb him much more than problems at the plant. Keep the focus on the stock problems—that was the way.

Ling's voice came over the speakerphone.

"Mr. Hahn on the line, Chu Chi."

"Put him on."

"Choi Khan?"

"Yes, Mr. Hahn."

"Have you been following the stock prices?"

"I have. What do you hear?"

"A conspicuous silence. Then hints."

"Hints?"

"There has been a well-regarded rumor. An EPA investigation. Huge liability suit. No one will say where the rumor originated."

"I believe I know the original source."

A pause while Hahn remembered not to sound too eager. "Go on."

"The problem is a man named Jefferson, a wealthy rancher who is having a personal feud with another rancher, Harlow Rourke. Rourke holds the lease on the plant I'm using for my project. He's also an investor in Tsendai. Jefferson knows this, and he would have contacts on the Street. I believe he started the rumor to hurt Rourke."

There was another pause while Hahn digested this mix of fact and fiction. "What is the nature of this feud between Jefferson and Rourke?"

Lone took a deep breath and remembered his luck was due to turn. "I don't know the original cause, but some of Jefferson's cattle died and he thinks Rourke poisoned them. He's threatening an EPA investigation of the plant to force Rourke out of a moneymaking lease with us."

"That could be dangerous."

"I'm getting ready to distract Jefferson with some business losses of his own."

"I have to wonder, Choi Khan. Is your project worth this amount of discomfort?"

"I promise you, Mr. Hahn. The project will be the most important event of your career. It also represents a considerable investment, which will have to be written off as a loss if we close."

It's sink or swim, you old bastard. And you're in the water with me.

"Yes, it seems that we're committed to this course unless things get worse. I will engineer some buying to rehabilitate ourselves on the Street, but I expect the cost to be returned."

175

"Of course."

"You're getting expensive, Choi Khan."

"An investment, Mr. Hahn."

"All right, but remember that the purpose of investment is production."

"Always, Mr. Hahn."

"I have every confidence that you will eventually present me with a startling success."

Lone pictured Hahn lying among Jefferson's cattle, surprise locked into his dead eyes.

"I strive constantly toward that end, Mr. Hahn."

"If I had a son he could be no more dutiful than you, Choi Khan. One day my position will be vacant and you will be rewarded."

"Yes, Mr. Hahn. I'll keep that in mind."

"Good-bye, Choi Khan."

"Good-bye, Mr. Hahn."

Lone started to light a cigarette, and then realized his palms were sweating. It had been close, but he'd neutralized Jefferson's attack on Tsendai stock. Now it was time to tighten the pressure on Jefferson. He'd already be boiling because of the attempt on his wife. A little more prodding and maybe he'd lose control. And if he lost control, he'd lose his joss. That's the way it worked. Sure it was. Lone's palms were still sweating, but he lit the cigarette anyway. He had control.

32

FAR Lightning's shack sat by a stream and was shielded from the sun by two large cut-banks. Blankets now separated the one-room structure into his and hers.

It was two in the afternoon of the fourth day. A cool breeze was coming out of the east, where a storm was starting to form on the horizon. Celine and Far Lightning were sitting in lawn chairs by the stream. They'd been talking about the approaching storm when suddenly an overwhelming fear pinned her arms to her sides and paralyzed her neck. Then came the brown stain inside her head, pulling her another inch toward isolation. It was on her again, pressing her heart, stealing her breath, turning her inside out. She tried to look at Far Lightning, but her vision was dimming toward blindness.

Then she felt something cool and wet on her face, something that smelled of yeast and grain and water. The smell went into her nose and unlocked her brain. She remembered how to breathe. Her vision widened. She could see the ground and her feet and Far Lightning's hands reaching from behind her, rubbing moist dirt onto her neck and face.

"What are you doing?" she shrieked, jumping out of her chair.

Far Lightning began circling while he threw handfuls of wet earth at her. They pelted her face and clung to her hair. He began to shout in a rhythmic sing-song:

"Bigfoot sightings, low-fat recipes, Sally, Geraldo, Garbo gab from waiters who served her a drink once in Denmark. Preachers wearing aftershave selling you savior haircuts so they can look closely for the souls of whores. It's the news. Murder in the city and killers stalking country roads for foreclosed farmers' daughters. Charles Manson T-shirts bought by men living next to nuclear waste dumps who think they're in love with their wife's sister's husband's girl-friend who works at the insurance office where they'll have to kill everyone because love's impossible in a world where she won't come to Alaska and open that muffler shop. Single-parent sitcoms and family-abuse dramas told by bubble-haired women on CNN who turn up in slick magazines telling about the time they were raped in the lobby of their doctor's office by a security guard who kept telling everyone it was only a movie, and now he has an agent. I see what's happening to you, Celine. Things ride in on the infocrap highway, spirits of the things you see. Look at this."

He reached down and picked up a handful of dirt, then he bent his face to his hands and sniffed. "We can sniff the earth and learn what's attacking you," he said.

Celine gaped and stammered. "I don't know what you mean."

"Something's been attacking you, and I don't mean the men at the lake."

He couldn't know, but he did. "I think I might be going crazy," she said.

"You probably are. The question is why." He stepped close and looked down at her shoulders. "Your neck is becoming permanently bent from it."

He placed his hand on the back of her left shoulder. The hand was big and warm. It squeezed lightly and the warmth extended through her neck and down her back. "It's inside you, but it doesn't come from you."

"How can you know that?" she asked in a hoarse croak.

He smiled and his face softened into leathery crinkles. "Well, you're nothing like it. You're not ugly or shapeless, shrunken or pinched. It couldn't come from you."

"Unless I'm going crazy."

"Craziness is loose brain chemicals. Anything else is a spiritual problem."

"So?"

"You can shoot a gun, right?"

"Judd taught me. I'm good."

"Then you know that when you squeeze the trigger, it has to be like caressing the thing you're killing. You have to almost love it."

"I've only shot targets."

He looked back at her, a slow appraisal that started at her toes and went steadily to the top of her head.

"Killing is about truth. You have to look right into the thing's center."

"How do I find its center before it finds mine?"

He flopped into his chair, produced a leather bag with the makings, rolled a fat joint, lit it, then held it toward her.

"No, thanks."

"Afraid?"

"It's been a long time."

"Time might be the thing that's after you."

Celine laughed for the first time since the lake. "You have the cure for time?"

Joseph pulled a bottle of tequila from his pocket and took a deep drink. He offered it to her, but she waved it off. A cold wind blew across her neck and then turned warm again. The storm was coming closer. Black fingers reached across the sky.

"You go to the ground," he said. "The soil of Montana is prehistoric: tribal feuds in the bedrock, dead dinosaurs, inevitable sadness."

"Damnit, Joseph. I'm already scared enough."

He came over to her and dropped to one knee so she could look him in the eyes. His face was broad and big-browed, framed by long straight hair. His gray eyes rested cool on her face.

"I'm sorry," he said. "It's just . . . you're a powerful person. It's a crime for you to be held in fear."

She bent forward and ran her hands through her auburn hair, taking solace in its thickness. "What, then?" she asked.

"A vision quest," he said, reaching out to take her hand. "It will bring you into your power."

"You mean I should actually . . . what?"

"I dig a pit in the ground, deep enough for you to get in. You take a sweat bath first to purify yourself and then you get into the pit. You take a little water but no food. I cover up the hole and you stay there until your vision comes. You stay there for as long as it takes—two days, four days, whatever. It will come, and when it does, you'll see your demon clearly and how to kill it. When you get out of the hole, you'll know your true name."

She looked up into the sky, searching for the familiar Celine Jefferson, the one who wore a tailored suit and showed plots of the Jensen property to easterners.

"Joseph, it's just too . . . "

"Too primitive? Too Indian?"

"Maybe. Don't be insulted."

Joseph leapt toward the stream and yelled, an angry wail muffled by the oncoming wind. He leaned forward with his hands on his knees, long hair touching the dust.

"Whites," he said mournfully. "They'll accept any piece of nonsensical bullshit as long as it's dressed up in statistics. You bought phony quiz shows, scorched-earth housing, boxed-glop food, and Reaganomics, but you won't believe this because I can't bring out a guy in a white lab coat to tell you it's true."

Celine walked to the edge of the stream and looked east over the moving emptiness of the plains. The grasses reached away to the horizon, ebbing and flowing in the restless air. There was a life in the earth she'd never noticed before, a quality of breathing in the turning of leaf to sky, a running like blood in the venous patterns of blowing grasses. She heard Joseph's footsteps behind her.

"This is the center of the earth, Celine. All the power you need is right below your feet."

"Would you be there?"

"Just a few yards away."

"I need some time," she said. "Things are happening so fast."

"Sure," he said. "I'll ride out for a while and leave you to think about things. I'll be back by tonight."

"Where are you going?"

"Somewhere high. I'll take a rifle and my new golf club, maybe hit some balls."

"You're not angry?"

"No, of course not. You need time to think."

"Okay."

"You won't be afraid if it storms while I'm gone?"

"No. It keeps . . . other things away."

"The earth is the answer, Celine."

"I'll see you later, Joseph."

He rode into the darkening evening without a backward glance. Nothing she could remember had felt like such an end, or so swollen with beginning. How long had it been since her life felt like a beginning? A lightning bolt stabbed out of the east, causing her to crouch next to the ground, where Joseph said salvation was buried. She picked up a handful of earth and smelled it, rubbed it against her cheek as he had done. Where else did she have to go for answers but to the earth? By the time Joseph was out of sight she knew she was going to do what he asked.

33

DONNELLY now drove naked while sitting on a T-shirt. The station wagon was more of a carcass than a car—doors gone, headlights empty—but still it ran. Whenever it occurred to him that he didn't know where he was going, he'd get out the golf club and whack away at the green balls. Then he'd point the car in their direction and drive until nightfall.

On the day following the brushfire he'd driven to a K-Mart on the highway and charged five gas cans. Now he could stay out in the empty for long stretches. That was good, because the open sky talked to him on the radio. He knew because he could pick up just one station, WJOY out of Billings: "your big sky church of the air." His favorite song was "Take Me Jesus, Just as I Am."

Who else would take him just as he was? Even if Elaine forgave him for running away, there was still the $27,000, which he didn't feel that sorry about anymore. He also didn't seem to mind being alone and wild in Montana, though he didn't like it that much, either. He was just doing it.

Donnelly stopped the car and climbed onto the roof to look around. He was parked in a small depression with a rise of scrub behind him and a green hill in front, where the terrain changed from mesquite to pasture. He looked closer and saw he was stopped on a barbed-wire fence he had run over while thinking about Elaine. The wire stretched away in two directions for as far as he could see.

"Property," he mumbled.

He lit a cigarette and noticed a bank of dark clouds moving in from the east as the air collapsed into a sticky calm.

Donnelly was about to lie down on the roof when he saw two horsemen approaching from the front. He had an impulse to leave, but the golf balls had pointed him in this direction. He got down from the roof and sat in the car. The air was close and dank. He broke into a standing sweat.

The two men dismounted on either side of him.

"Would you look at this shit," said the one on the left. He was a short block of muscle and wore a T-shirt stained with tobacco juice. Tattoos covered his football-sized biceps, a goat's head on the right, a cobra on the left. He had a flat face and tiny eyes that looked like metal.

The man on the right was tall and thin and had eyes that seemed to meet at his hooked nose. A stringy fringe of hair hung from the sides of his greasy cowboy hat and touched his narrow shoulders. He wore a black vest that hung open over his bare chest. His navel formed the genitals of a woman tattooed on his stomach.

"Hey, pardner," said the one with the muscles. "You steal this car for parts? 'Cause I know you can't be driving it."

The man leaned his head into the driver's side, smiling through a grate of tobacco-stained teeth.

"Son of a bitch, A.C.," he yelled to the other one. "We got us a nudist, sittin' out here naked as his birthday, with his dick hangin' over the seat."

The other cowboy peered into the back of the car. "Yeah," he said. "A real nudist. Ain't got much going for him in the possessions department."

"Wait a minute," said the burly one. "I seen you somewhere before, ain't I?"

Donnelly looked away at the sky, which was now the color of a bad bruise.

"Hey, I'm talkin' to you."

Donnelly kept looking toward the sky. He wondered if God had talked to the Israelites by using the clouds.

"Elaine liked my dick just fine," he said.

The muscle man spat a stream of tobacco juice onto the wagon's front fender. "Well, buddy," he said. "I don't give a shit about Eee-laine or your dick neither. What I care about is why you're on Rourke property and where I seen you before."

"Rourke property?"

"That's right, Harlow Rourke, biggest man around here, and you done busted his fence."

The clouds were darker now, an early night. Donnelly felt a sticky thrill in the hair of his arms. "It was the balls," he said.

"I told you I didn't give a shit about your balls."

"I can say what I want."

The big man took a step back from the car and squinted. "That's it.

That's the same thing you said back in the Buffalo Wallow. You're the sumbitch jumped me when I was about to cut that Indian. This is him, A.C., the one who jumped us."

"Yeah, Rodney. I believe it is," answered the skinny one. "Underneath the beard and all that dirt."

"I was pissin' blood for a week," Rodney said through clenched teeth. "Now I'm gonna cut you like I was gonna cut that Indian."

"Rodney," cautioned A.C. "The law."

"This is the plains," Rodney bellowed. "The buzzards will have him picked clean before anybody misses him."

Rodney reached to his belt and unsnapped a leather case, which contained a lockback knife.

Donnelly thought about the Israelites and dark clouds over the desert. "This is the valley of death," he shrieked.

Rodney moved forward, knife out. Donnelly grabbed his golf club and stabbed hard with the end of the shaft. Rodney whooped in pain and staggered backward, clutching his left eye, while Donnelly jumped out of the car to face A.C., who was coming around the hood waving a short branding iron.

Donnelly began swinging the golf club's metal head back and forth with all his strength, and A.C. moved backward, using the branding iron as a shield.

Donnelly advanced but was acutely aware of his testicles dangling. Thoughts of emasculation supplied him with a wild energy, and he began to swing the club so fast that it sounded like the blade of a helicopter.

"Aborigine," screamed Donnelly. "I'm am aborigineee."

"Goddamnit, A.C., stand your ground," Rodney bellowed. "All the bastard has is a golf club."

A.C. began to notice that every time he blocked one of Donnelly's blows with the branding iron, he put a dent in the golf club.

"Come on," he said. "Come on and swing on me."

Donnelly did, but the club was rapidly developing a U shape, and Rodney could now see well enough to close in from the rear.

"We got him now," he said. "I'm gonna cut his nuts off."

That prospect caused Donnelly to jump onto the car's hood and run down the roof to the open back, where he reached in and grabbed his bag of golf balls. He took a ball from the bag and threw it at A.C., who was coming around the right side of the car. The ball smacked squarely into his forehead, and he dropped to his knees.

Donnelly sprinted away toward the ascending embankment. As he ran, he saw a rocky outcrop near the top and headed for it. Rodney was chasing him, but he stopped long enough to kick A.C., screaming at him to get up.

Donnelly had time to duck behind the chest-high rocks and let loose a barrage of golf balls, which thumped off the cowboys' chests and faces. They stopped and backed down the hill a few steps.

"Whyn't we just get the rifles and shoot the sumbitch," A.C. said, rubbing his head.

"Cops might trace the bullets back to us."

"What're we gonna do, then?"

"We're gonna wait until he uses up them golf balls and then we're gonna cut him."

Donnelly began gathering loose rocks into a pile. "I'll put out your eyes," he yelled. "This is the valley of death!"

"He's crazy as a shithouse rat," said A.C.

"All the more reason nobody'll miss him," Rodney said.

Donnelly knew he was like the Israelites who had committed suicide rather than surrender to the Romans. "We all die alone," he yelled at the cowboys.

"You ain't alone," said Rodney. "You got us."

He took two steps forward, and Donnelly pegged a golf ball at his groin. Rodney dropped the knife and sank to his knees.

"That sumbitch is really crazy," A.C. said. "Maybe we could claim self-defense if we shot him."

Rodney was sitting down, knees pulled up to his chest. "Nah," he groaned. "Now I want the fun of cuttin' him."

He rose and began moving forward, followed by A.C. Donnelly peppered them with golf balls and rocks, but this time they kept coming, backing up a few steps when they were hit, but moving forward.

Suddenly, Donnelly knew he had come to Montana to die. "I'm sorry, Elaine," he said quietly.

The cowboys were almost on him when they stopped and stared.

There was a smell in the air, gamey and wild, then a quiet rumbling.

Donnelly jumped into the air as something cold touched him on his bare buttocks. He looked around and saw dogs, ten or twenty of them in a semicircle at his back. They were like no dogs he had ever seen; they had high shoulders like hyenas and long legs like wolves. They shifted nervously from side to side, holding their massive heads low, curling their lips and snarling. They had too many teeth and ivory-yellow eyes. Every few seconds, one of them would lunge at the cowboys, then return to the pack. The pack would inch forward and the next lunge would be a little closer.

"Christ almighty," said A.C. "It's those wild dogs of Harlow's. Let's get the guns."

"Can't," Rodney answered. "They've spooked the horses."

Donnelly looked up and saw their horses heading back over the hill where they first appeared.

"What're we gonna do?" A.C. whined.

"Let's ease down to the bum's car," Rodney told him.

The two men began backing down the hill, the dogs following in a stalking crouch.

Donnelly began hopping to and fro, staring wild-eyed and growling in a nervous response to the dogs. Two of the animals cocked their heads and watched, teeth bared in wicked grins. Donnelly kept jumping and growling. The dogs began to take turns stalking the cowboys and watching him, two at a time, sitting six feet away with a baleful sparkle in their eyes.

He kept jumping and growling. The cowboys kept backing toward the car. The sky was black as evening. A wild musk filled the air. Donnelly threw back his head and howled a long good-bye to his old life. The two watching dogs also began to howl. Then the rest of the pack joined in with a purple sound that put an edge on the day's cloud-darkened light.

"Jesus, this is too weird," murmured A.C.

"Get in the car," ordered Rodney. "We're gettin' out of here."

Donnelly was going to lose his car. His howls changed to a sad tone, and the dogs' changed with him, blending into a sound like wind in winter trees.

An ugly noise cut through the dog music, and Donnelly looked up

186

to see an open jeep coming over the hill. The driver had a thick mane of white hair that streamed behind him in the wind. The dogs fell silent.

The jeep came to a jolting halt beside the station wagon, and the cowboys edged out to stand by the rear fender. The white-haired man eased his legs onto the ground and stood. Then he walked directly toward the dogs.

"Mona," he bellowed. "Rico!"

Two of the dogs pricked up their ears and paced nervously.

"Jose! Dana!" the man roared. "Vamoose! Vamoose!"

In a few minutes, four of the dogs loped past Donnelly, followed by the rest of the pack. Then they all melted into the scrubland.

"You called them by name," Donnelly said to the old man.

"Some of 'em I know. Who the hell are you?"

"Used to be Donnelly."

"Used to be?"

"Yes."

"He's crazy, boss," said Rodney. "He drove over your fence an' then started throwin' golf balls at us. Ain't that right, A.C.?"

"Yeah, Mr. Rourke," agreed A.C.

"Hell, just look at him—naked as hell, and he smells like meat left in the sun."

"I'm an aborigine," Donnelly said.

"You from Australia?" asked the old man.

"Maybe."

The man looked straight into Donnelly's eyes. Looking back, Donnelly could see a fever there. He'd seen eyes like that before—in the mirror, when he was thousands of dollars down with no way out. The man in front of him was doing something wrong, and he would die from it, but before that he might do anything.

"The dogs didn't go after you," said Rourke.

"They thought I was funny."

"What are you doing on my property?"

"Following the golf balls. They're how I find my way."

"Your way where?"

"I don't know."

"See, boss?" said Rodney. "Crazy as hell."

Rourke pulled a handkerchief out of his pocket and mopped his brow. "Warm for this time of year," he said. "I suggest you get the balls to take you in another direction."

"I broke my club." Donnelly pointed at the bent driver laying on the ground.

"Jesus," said Rourke. "This is making me tired."

"It's killing you," Donnelly said without thinking.

Rourke jerked his head as if someone had hit him. "What's killing me?"

"Something you're doing."

The color drained from Rourke's face. "Who sent you here?" he asked hoarsely.

"Just the balls."

"Rodney, you say you were in a fight with this man?"

"Yeah, boss."

"Anyone else with him?"

"Yeah, an Indian."

"An Indian. What did he look like?"

"Tall, gray hair."

"Far Lightning," Rourke said. "What did he tell you?"

"He told me I was a Heyoka."

"Why did he call you that?"

"I will take a sword to your high places. Your altars will be broken, your images smashed."

Rourke made a coughing sound. "Rodney," he said. "Put this man in his car and drive him a few miles away from here."

"He won't get in no car with us, boss."

"I didn't say ask him, damnit. I said *put him.*"

"They're going to kill me!" Donnelly shouted at the old man.

Rourke stared hard at him but said nothing.

"It's what I know about you, isn't it?" Donnelly asked.

Rourke dismissed him with a wave of the hand and started toward his car.

Donnelly sprinted around the rocks and caught up with Rourke.

"You're going to hell!" he shouted. "You're not looking well because you're going to hell."

Donnelly could smell the old man's sweat, and it was like piss.

Then the cowboys came for him. He sprinted around Rourke and headed for the station wagon, Rodney and A.C. right behind him. He jumped onto the roof and began kicking at them.

"You'll go to hell," he screamed to Rourke.

Donnelly darted from one end of the roof to the other, kicking at the two cowboys.

"We gotcha now, buddy," said Rodney. "We're gonna put you in the car just like the boss said and drive you away from here."

"You're going to hell."

Then A.C.'s hand was on Donnelly's leg, pulling him off balance. He saw Rodney bolt up onto the roof. He saw the blade of a knife. Then he saw metal and paint fly into the air and heard a loud crack. His leg came free. Two more cracks . . . gunfire. Then a voice from the direction of the rocks.

"Everybody stay right where you are. I'm coming down."

34

FAR Lightning had been thinking of Celine as he rode. Had it been right to mention the vision quest? Was it really possible for her, or was it nothing but his romantic fantasy? Show the white woman some Indian power?

He shook his head in disgust. Celine had only been with him for a few days and already he was asking questions about himself. Women made you look for answers to questions you thought they'd ask. Then they asked things you didn't expect. Your feelings became like money, constantly calculated. She was going to complicate his life, and life should be simple. He was about to stop for a drink of tequila when he heard Harlow's dogs howling.

He listened for a few seconds, then rode off in the direction of the noise. A few minutes later he topped a rise and saw the Heyoka hopping around naked on the roof of his station wagon. Harlow Rourke was watching as two of his cowboys tried to get Donnelly off the roof. One of the cowboys had a knife. Later, Harlow would say he hadn't known they were going to cut anyone. Far Lightning slipped his .30-.30 out of its saddle case.

Everyone froze when he fired. Then he nudged his horse down the hill while keeping the rifle on the cowboys. As he rode closer, he could see it was two of the three who had jumped him in the Buffalo Wallow.

"Where's your other friend?" he asked the big man.

"He doesn't like getting this close to Indians. Can't stand the smell."

"Too bad all you scumbags don't feel that way. Now, back off and let the man down."

"You ain't going to shoot nobody."

Far Lightning rode over to Harlow.

"Tell them," he said.

"Back off, Rodney," said Harlow. "Or one day he'll catch you alone out here and back-shoot you."

"That's exactly what I'll do, Rodney."

"You dog son of a bitch," Harlow said.

"I told you it was never going to be over, Harlow. And it's not, is it?"

Far Lightning rode back to the station wagon and spoke to Donnelly. "Come on down, Heyoka. Remember me?"

Donnelly jumped down and walked closer. Far Lightning could smell his musk—bull elks in rut. The man was developing some powerful medicine.

"They were going to kill me," Donnelly said. "I ran over their fence."

"Why?"

"That's where the golf balls led me."

"What golf balls?"

"Glowing ones. I ran into a whole valley of them one night, and a golf club to go with them."

Far Lightning was speechless. Just when it was getting hard to turn off MTV, something would happen to keep you real, a choice you made when you weren't looking.

"They were going to kill me," Donnelly said again. "The balls protected me."

"How are you going to find your way now?"

"Just keep going the way I was, I guess." Donnelly pointed across the fence to Harlow's land.

"That crazy son of a bitch is not going across my land," Harlow bellowed.

"Why not?" asked Far Lightning.

"I don't have to give you any goddamn reasons. It's my land."

"For now."

"Custer was the last person you people kicked off this land, and that was a long time ago."

"Everything comes around, Harlow. You're finding that out now, aren't you?"

Harlow backed away with a shocked look on his face.

"You heard me right."

"I should have killed you the first time I saw you," Harlow said.

"Why didn't you?"

"You were just a boy."

"Wouldn't stop you now, would it? Something's coming, and you're going to lose the land."

"He's going to die of it," shrieked Donnelly. "He's going to hell." Donnelly was hopping around with a maniacal smile shining through his dirty beard.

"See?" said Far Lightning. "He knows too. Your world is going to be rolled up like a carpet. I've seen a vision."

Harlow choked out a fake laugh. "Save that bullshit for the girls."

"The land doesn't want you on it anymore."

"The land, hell," Harlow answered. "The reason you dumb bastards lost it in the first place was because you were full of dreamy-time horseshit about being part of it."

Harlow picked up a clod of dirt and crumbled it. "It's just dirt," he said. "You plow it. You dig it. You buy and sell it. It's nothing but god-damn dirt."

He picked up another clod and threw it at Far Lightning's head. "Dirt!" he screamed.

Far Lightning ducked away from the clod and fired a shot to calm Harlow down. "You think everything's dirt, and you made some kind of dirty deal for that old fertilizer plant. Jefferson knows it, and he wants me to help him screw you up."

"But you won't."

"Depends on if it would get rid of you faster."

"You want him off, too."

"Yeah, but I like him, and you're the most evil man I know."

"Stay out of it, Far Lightning. I beat you people once. I can do it again."

"That sounds almost like a dare."

"Take it any way you want."

Far Lightning fired another shot into the air. "Get out of here and take your boys with you," he said. "If anyone fucks with the Heyoka, I'm going to paint my face and come for them."

He fired two more times, coming closer to the two cowboys with each one. When the jeep had disappeared over the hill, he untied his Big Bertha driver and tossed it to Donnelly.

"Here, you'll need this. I'd tell you to hit them in some other direction, but a Heyoka always does the opposite of what other people do."

Donnelly stared awestruck at the driver. "Thank you."

"No. It's me who should thank you for reminding me how things work."

Far Lightning turned his horse toward the rise, thinking that sometimes life was simpler than you thought.

35

THE sun was coming up when Jefferson slammed the Rover to a stop in front of his house. He leaned back in the seat and rubbed his grimy face, coming away with a handful of black soot. He looked down and noticed for the first time that he was covered by a greasy black film, all that was left of his Red Dog gas field.

The fire had been like the birth of hell—a ten-square-mile tornado of flame sucking everything toward its center in a roaring vacuum of dirt and debris.

The best well-fire outfit in the country had been on the scene for three days, and they were just now getting a handle on it. The field was gone, of course. Nothing to do but get a percentage on the dollar from the insurance company.

These things happened, but this time it had happened for a reason. When the lead firefighter told him it looked like arson, Jefferson knew who had done it and why. It was Lone, switching from all-out to limited war. It was Lone, and he was here.

Jefferson had been standing on a rise a couple of miles away from the burning gas field. Fire shadows struck the bluffs with orange lightning that blazed white with each new explosion, and in one of those flashes Jefferson saw something that made him stop breathing. A half mile away, on the point of the nearest bluff was the figure of a man. He was nothing more than a connection of pencil lines silhouetted against the flashing sky, but Jefferson was sure it was C. K. Lone. He knew the slant of shoulder, the angle of arm, and he knew some dark inner thing that rose off the distant figure like black wings, a thing that had existed before he was born. He knew in a second of insight that his ancient relatives must have recognized it, too. He was programmed by genetics to hate Lone on sight.

Then Jefferson remembered what Vandivier had told him: *The immune system is programmed to recognize and destroy invading viruses.* He could hear an echo of the man's dying words: *All life is a virus.*

That's when Jefferson turned and ran for his car, thinking of a trunk in his attic. If all life was a virus, then maybe Lone could get sick too. He was about to come down with a bad case of Sylvie.

JEFFERSON SHOVED OPEN the Rover's door and ran for the house. Once inside, he made for the long hallway to the master bedroom. There, he lowered the folding stairs from the ceiling and climbed into the attic, where he tossed aside anything that lay between him and the green footlocker with his name stenciled on it.

He hadn't opened the trunk since he closed it over twenty years ago. He couldn't even recall what was there except for the pictures of Sylvie he'd stolen the day after Lone had killed her.

That night, at the suggestion of Jack Daniel's, he'd decided to take Sylvie's surveillance pictures home with him. He'd stuffed them into his briefcase and proceeded to get completely drunk.

Now he knelt and opened the footlocker. In descending order were several sets of jungle fatigues, a well-worn pair of boots, his Bronze Star, and a black Naugahyde pouch. He opened it and dumped the contents on the floor.

There she was: Sylvie, picking out melons in the marketplace; getting out of a chauffeured Citroen; coming out of a bar with Lone on one side and Lamh on the other. Lone was wearing the smile of a man who'd just taken a bite out of the world and was enjoying the taste. He held a cigarette in his right hand; his left was around Sylvie's waist.

Lamh was a little taller than Lone, with shoulder-length hair, a narrow mustache, and a white silk tie. He was smiling the crooked smile he admitted copying from old American movie stars.

Sylvie was smiling proudly but looking past the frame of the picture. It was the same wistful look she had in all the pictures. It was the look of someone who wanted to get past the edges of her life. She wanted out badly enough to beat her head on the floor, but all she could do was hope the gods sent someone to save her.

Jefferson knew he could have been that someone if only he hadn't been so intent on Lone. He slumped against the wall and rested his head on his knees. The morning was hot, but his sweat ran cold. Everything could have been different. All he would have had to do was tell Sylvie that Lamh was a plant and make a deal with her. It was easy to see that now, after he'd seen the same desire for freedom in Celine's eyes.

Jefferson slipped Sylvie's pictures into the pouch, tucked the pouch under his arm, and headed for the bedroom. He needed some sleep before the drive to Great Falls.

36

AT seven o'clock the following day, Jefferson was headed north out of Great Falls on Highway 83. The early evening vibrated with the quiet shimmer of an empty church, a thought that made him uneasy, because he was pretty sure body snatching was a sin.

Well, not body snatching exactly, more like body embezzling. Coroner was an elected office in Cascade County, and Jefferson had helped finance Harold Thorsen's successful campaign. Harold had balked when Jefferson asked to be repaid with a body, but the woman had been homeless, with no family, and a debt was a debt.

John Baakerwilde, the owner of Baakerwilde's Funeral Home, hadn't balked at all when Jefferson asked for a three-thousand-dollar cremation for his aunt Sally from Seattle.

Now Jefferson was headed home with Aunt Sally's urn next to him on the front seat of the Rover. When Lone got the ashes in the mail, he'd have them tested. Then, when he found out they were human, he'd spend a lot of time wondering if they were really Sylvie's. Then he'd remember Sylvie when she was alive. Then he'd get sick when he remembered the smell of Sylvie's body burning.

Jefferson knew that because he shared the same memory. It was time to admit the truth: He and Lone were connected at a level as old as death.

The falling sun threw a golden spray into the air over the backs of the passing cut-banks. Owls sat ruffling their feathers on shaded fence posts as smaller birds dived across the peach-colored light into the charcoal smudges of darkening trees.

Jefferson shifted uncomfortably in his seat and thought of Celine. He was beginning to fear the difference between dying alone and being alone when you died. Sure you had to go by yourself, but the presence of an earthly love might carry you away easy. He'd counted on taking a look from Celine with him into the beyond. If he left without the feel of her, he might become a ghost lost between worlds. In the chilliest part of himself he already felt that way. Lone was near, and wherever he went, so did death. The beyond might be closer than ever, and Celine was slipping away like a shadow.

The sun was down now, and Jefferson rolled up his window against the damp air. The road ahead ran due north into the oncoming night.

37

FAR Lightning sat cross-legged under the noon sun. Using a razor blade, he cut small squares of flesh from his shoulder. He placed each square onto a handkerchief, where the sun turned them to leather. Blood dripped off his elbow and dried in the dust. The pain was intense, but that was part of the medicine.

His grandmother had cut forty squares from herself for his first vision quest. When you were in the pit, it helped to feel part of someone else in there with you. Celine would need help. She'd also be shocked.

It had seemed a little excessive to Far Lightning when he first considered it, but then he remembered his grandmother. All through the terror of 1945, when Harlow's riders came at night, she'd hold young Joseph close and sing the old songs. She always said the old days would come back, even when the others told her that the whites were devils and there was no way to beat them.

Grandmother said love was a flower in the middle of a thorn bush. When he told her about Van Gogh cutting off his ear for a woman, she said: "A brave act, but a woman wants a man who will listen to her."

If Celine saw his self-mutilation as craziness, he'd remind her that it was only a shoulder. He hadn't cut off his nose to smell the rose. He cut another square and winced. Only five more to go.

It had been a busy morning. He awoke before dawn and rode to the power spot where he had hit golf balls with Jefferson. There he built a sweat lodge—willow branches bent into a small frame, six feet in diameter and four feet high. He covered the frame with blankets, then dug the vision pit. It was nothing more than a grave-sized cave in the side of the hill. Then it had been time to cut the squares of skin.

After cutting the fortieth square, he poured on hydrogen peroxide. An explosion of pain lifted his rump a foot off the ground. A red lightning bolt shot through his head, then turned white like the eagles in his vision. He took the best drink of tequila he'd had in a long time.

When the squares of skin had dried hard as pebbles, he poured them into a hollow gourd and glued on the top. He shook the gourd. It rattled like rain on a roof. Time to go for Celine.

· · ·

SHE WAS SITTING on the bed wearing a pair of jeans and a white linen shirt. Her red hair was clean and wild against the cloth. She had her knees drawn up, and there were small white lines at the corners of her wide mouth.

"What happened to your arm?" she asked, pointing to the square of gauze on his shoulder.

He lifted the gourd and rattled it.

"If things get rough, shake the rattle. It'll remind you that you're not alone."

"You mean you . . . "

"Same thing my grandmother did for me my first time."

She blushed and looked away.

"It's not that big a deal. Just remember to shake it."

"When things get rough?"

"Yeah."

She stood and threw out her arms in exasperation. "What am I doing, Joseph? I have no idea what I'm doing."

"It's simple. You're going to find a vision. The vision will bring you power. Afterward, you will know your true name. I chose Far Lightning because my vision took me into a storm. The lightning went into me. I went into it. I was twenty then, and my hair's been gray ever since."

"Excuse me, but . . . "

"Don't confuse what's possible with what's usual."

"You're scaring me, Joseph." Her face was pale and her hands were shaking.

"You know how you catch a mountain lion? You stake out a goat as bait. Fear is just bait for your courage."

"Very imaginative."

"Hey, I've taken this trip lots of times. Here's the way it goes: You take a sweat bath to prepare your body and empty your mind, then you get in the pit with the rattle and a blanket. I cover the pit, and you stay there."

"How long?"

"As long as it takes. My first time, I was there four days. I won't leave you."

She turned away and lit a cigarette, then put it out.

"You could try a psychiatrist for your problem—a year of sessions and drugs. Or you could hide for the rest of your life."

She made a fist and ground it slowly against the wall; strong veins protruded from the back of her hand. She turned and faced him.

"When do we do this?"

"Now."

FIRST HE HAD to find the right kind of stones, then he had to heat them in the fire until they glowed red. The floor of the lodge had to be covered with sage and sweetgrass. They needed water from the stream, which was a quarter mile away.

When he was done, the sun glowed the same red as the stones. Celine was sitting in a small stand of cottonwood trees. He knelt in front of her. This was the part he'd been avoiding.

"Celine, there's something else."

She looked up with a wan smile. "Why am I not surprised?"

"Sorry. I know you've had a lot to handle. I think you're very brave."

"You're leading up to something."

"Yes."

"Well?"

He took a deep breath and plunged ahead. "Okay. I want you to get rid of the thing that's dogging you, but for this to work we have to do it right."

She raised her eyebrows, a hint of mockery in her eyes. This was going to be as embarrassing for him as for her.

"The sweat lodge is important to the process. It empties your mind and body of toxins. You have to smoke the pipe with someone. There's a person outside to pass in the hot stones and the water. Today, I'll have to do both."

"Yes," she said, knowing there was more.

"To do it right, the ones inside the sweat lodge have to be naked."

He rushed on before she could say anything. "It's dark in there, full of steam. All you see are people's outlines. You have to expose your body to the steam and the smoke. You have to let the spirits get to know you. It's the true way."

200

Her gray eyes covered him with an appraising stare. "Well," she said. "You first."

First he placed the hot stones in the small pit at the center of the lodge. He didn't look at her as he removed his clothes. Inside, he sat next to the pail of cold water. Then he heard the zipper of her jeans. She crawled quickly through the lodge's low opening, but for an instant she was caught in the light from outside.

Racehorse woman; long tight flanks, firm and round in the rear. He sucked in his breath as her hair touched him on the way past.

When she was seated across from him, he filled his pipe with red willow bark. The pipe had been his father's and his grandfather's.

"The steam will make you light-headed," he said. "You'll feel like you're floating. Then we'll pray. If you can't take any more heat, tell me and I'll open the flap to let in some air. Ready?"

"Yes."

Her voice was soft as the smoke. He took a ladle of cold water and poured it over the hot stones. The tiny lodge was filled with an enveloping cloud of heat, which went through his lungs and outward into every inch of his body. He felt his head float away with the steam.

He heard Celine breathing in hoarse gasps.

"Breathe it freely," he said. "It won't hurt you. It'll only make you clean inside."

Her gasps were replaced by soft rushes of air. He lit the pipe, smoked, and passed it through the darkness to her. When she leaned forward to take it, he could see the white sway of a small firm breast. He could make out the shape of lacy shoulders and easy-curve belly, but his head was detached from his body and he looked without wanting. The pipe came back and he caught the smoke, rubbing it over himself. He could hear her doing the same, whispery sounds like falling snow. He began to pray:

"Let us see ourselves as you see us. Show us the path we should take."

He went out to the fire for six more stones. The steam became a physical weight. Celine panted loudly, and he prayed in time with the sound.

"Let us fly when we should fly, crawl when we should crawl. Let us be air, water, fire, and earth."

They smoked again, and he put in the last group of stones. His mind seemed to raise above the ground and go to her like the steam. He flowed over her and became one with her smell: perfumed earth; a loam of sugar-salt.

When he stepped out of the lodge, he put on his pants and located her clothes, but before he could pass them to her, she stepped out too.

She was something out of a peyote dream—hair glistening in a silver web of water droplets, fine-boned face streaked with soot, charcoal trails from eyes and lips, her body striped the same, a lean body fulfilling itself with oncoming age: slight fat bending long over legs, converging at the little belly bulge left by departing children, then sloping down into the auburn triangle between her legs, wet and shining from the steam.

He looked at her with a delight untouched by lust. Still dizzy, she stumbled slightly and a quiver ran up the back of her leg into the roundness of her behind. It flexed and tightened as she caught her balance.

The sun had left a cantaloupe-colored band of light along the top of the Rockies. She walked toward it, moving her head from side to side as though she were listening to music. She stopped and wiggled her toes experimentally, then raised her head to breathe the cool evening air.

The backs of her shoulders shook with a chill. He picked up his blanket and placed it around her.

"I feel . . . younger," she said. "I can't find the words."

"There aren't any."

He turned her toward him and looked into her eyes. "Now's the time to begin."

She got into the pit, drew her knees up into the blanket, and pulled it tight around her shoulders. He handed her the rattle.

"Don't forget to use it."

He placed a willow frame covered in porous cloth over the top of the pit. The band of light was gone from the mountains. A smell of sage filled the air. He walked a few yards away and sat on a mound of grass.

THE SWEAT BATH had left her exhilarated but limp. The second she curled into Joseph's blanket, her head became heavy. The dirt around her was dry, and he had lined it with sweetgrass. She spread the blanket under her head and dropped immediately into a cushioned sleep.

Then there was light coming through the cloth but no sound. She thought she might be dreaming, but it hurt when she pinched herself on the leg. She felt foolish to be taking this so seriously.

There was nothing stopping her from taking the roof off her little cave and saying hello to Joseph. The idea was appealingly irreverent, and she laughed aloud . . . maybe. It was hard to tell in such isolation. She was a tree falling in the forest.

Why didn't she just jump out of the hole and wave? Unless she couldn't. But that was ridiculous. It was only the rules that said she couldn't, but exactly what were the rules? What was it Joseph had said? Four days? Yes, he said he stayed in his hole four days. God, what about bodily functions? But there was no food and very little water. The need might not arise. Quite the opposite, in fact. She would become dehydrated and have convulsions. Jesus, her heart would stop!

That's when you'd have your vision. Damn right. Everybody had visions when they were dying. The dumb savages thought they were having visions when they were actually having near-death experiences. It was a scientific fact that you would be near death after four days without food or water. The vision seekers were almost dead. Some of them probably did die, and the rest of the tribe said they flew away.

It was so obvious. No one could stay four days in a hole. But Joseph wasn't dead . . . far from it. He was fifty-something, but when he took off his clothes, he had a younger man's body—short-waisted and thick in the leg, but solid. There was an overall sleekness to him, a smooth bronze color. He had a bit of a belly, but it was tight, not flabby. He was a more symmetrical person without clothes than with them—big arms, powerful head, interesting penis; there was an inquisitive head on it, which made it seem as alive as a second person.

Jeez! She was imagining his penis as a puppet. Why didn't she get out of this hole? You couldn't stay in a hole four days. Just like you couldn't eat bacon or get to the stars on a rocket or see the future. Sure, and Abe Lincoln was really a racist; Malcolm X wasn't. Women were stronger than men, which was why men were always beating them up, and breast cancer was detectable by mammogram unless you were under fifty, over fifty, or some indeterminate age along the line toward eighty which they hadn't found yet but were working on. And you needed water or your heart would stop.

Experts knew these things. Death was real, and heaven was just a rumor. Her heart would stop. It was black in the blanket, and her heart would stop if she didn't get out. She had to get out or her heart would stop, but she couldn't move because it was beating so hard. If she moved it would burst. She had to move but she couldn't. It was black and she couldn't see, but she could hear and what she heard was the walls of her heart bruising themselves against her chest.

She was trapped and couldn't move. It was black and she was blind and her heart was choking. There was no air. You couldn't stay in a hole without air and now she was paralyzed. The only movement was in her eyes and she didn't want to move her eyes because something was there . . . in the corner.

She tried to look away from her own eye, but it was no use. The thing was there, sliding out from the corner, slithering with rhythmless pulses, the belly of a snake on glass. It was crawling out of her eye and across her face, pushing tendrils into her nose. She had to move, but there was no blood in her legs.

The thing was spreading out of her like a slow uncoiling of vomit. She gagged and now it was a hovering shroud between her and Joseph. She tried to call out, but her tongue was coated with brown bathroom stink and she couldn't move. An oily gauze was all over her.

Don't forget to use the rattle.

She moved her hand and heard a small scattering of pebbles, but the thing heard it too and she could feel it looking. She shook the rattle again and felt it probing for the sound, under her arms, between her legs.

She gagged. Every hair curled away from the thing like burning grass, but instead of heat, she felt the air go numb and disappear. A vacuum tore at all her joints. The rattle sounded again and the thing kept pulling her apart. It was as real as dying, and there was no tunnel and no light. There were no friendly faces to show her the way.

It was inside her now, cold as doctor's steel, looking for the rattle with the rotten slowness of a maggot's crawl.

Look. To kill, you have to look into the center.

Where were its eyes? If it was looking, it had to have eyes. But her own eyes were sewn shut. It took all her strength to pull them apart, and then a searing pain lanced her head, forcing her to see what she didn't want to see.

The thing had no eyes because it had no body because it was the center of another vision. Someone else was having a vision of her swallowing herself, drowning in the corruption of every lame, sickening, shameful hatred she'd ever had for guilty girlish fascination with nasty wants: rodeo cowboy butts and bull penises hanging into the dirt; the momentary desire for the labial taste of submission; the lick of blood, the sting of the whip, the harness of slavery, the absence of mind, the language of grunts, the downward prayer of moans. She looked now and knew it saw in her everything she never wanted to be but couldn't help imagining, all desires she had cast aside but couldn't help remembering.

She came to understand in a second of pure death that she couldn't look into the eye of the thing because all it saw was every weak, sick graveyard impulse she'd ever had. It was her the thing was seeing and herself she saw when she looked into its center.

It didn't care about the rattle anymore. The rattle had stopped. Her lungs were iron. She couldn't breathe. She would die, and they'd say it was because she was white and weak. Joseph said she had the medicine, and they'd say he was wrong. But he'd been to the lightning and he believed. She had to believe, too. She had to believe or die.

What did she have of her own that was beyond the rattle and above the terror? What could guard the last living part of her? She was naked in a foreign grave, paralyzed by a raping terror, and unable to move anything but the tips of her fingers. There was nothing left but the movement of a finger and Joseph's fading words: *It will come to you.*

She moved one finger and felt a weight that gave it heft. With an effort that felt like it would snap her neck, she pulled her head toward the finger, curling her body into a circle and pulling her hand toward her mouth, pulling in the finger with her lips, feeling the foreign weight, sucking it, pulling it off her finger and onto her tongue. It was hard and circular. A ring. Her wedding ring—the only thing that remained of summer rooms and soft sighs, hard choices, chances taken, victorious laughter, the grace of conception, sweat of labor, pain of childbirth, fear of loss, reality of difference, wrench of fear, loss of union, mortal separation. All that was left of her was contained in the hard, warm, unbreakable circle. She moved it under her tongue.

An infinitesimal point of light appeared in the surrounding darkness and gave enough space to allow a sip of air. The point expanded slightly. She took a larger breath. The light grew. She breathed again, and with each breath the light grew concentrically larger, moving into the darkness like a sun in space, burning a hole in the black big enough for her head, then her body. Then she was lying in morning sunlight as it fell through a window of her parents' house. She was alone upstairs dreaming a young girl's dream of being safe haven for future children and their father. She breathed easily, deep and long, floating in the window on waves of salty air, looking for something out past the window in the place where water became sky. Then it was there: a child, a boy child toddling sturdily toward her, his eyes bright with intelligent laughter, a smile on his shining face, full of knowing innocence, a springtime child full of sultry delight.

He wasn't her own child, but she knew him by his motion and the light in his eyes. He knew her, too, and reached for her with stiff baby arms, waiting to be lifted and snuggled, a smiling little boy who was unbelieving of death, laughing at it . . . banishing it. She reached for him and came up out of the pit into warm wind on her face.

The boy disappeared, but a world took his place; a wide, bright, limitless world. She shed the blanket and twirled to feel the breeze on her body. It blew through her pores, lifted her eyelids, and stroked its way through the hair between her legs, replacing terror with an immaculate tingle, which spread into her blood. She was alive!

She whirled and whirled, thrilling herself with the sight of the sun on her body. She whirled some more and saw a large figure approaching carefully through the light.

"Celine," said the figure. "I was coming to check on you. It's been two and a half days."

It might have been two and a half minutes or two and a half years. She was timeless and alive in every nerve of her body.

Joseph retrieved the blanket from the pit. He shook the dirt off it and moved close behind her to place it around her shoulders.

"You'll need water," he said.

But it wasn't water she needed. She was alive, and he had cut out part of himself to be with her in death. Now he was with her in life, close and warm. She could smell his skin and his hair and the male smell from under his arms.

She shrugged off the blanket and ran her hand up his chest and through his long hair. What she needed was another human warm and deep inside her, filling her with the light of day after the long night.

She ripped at his shirt and felt his chest with her face.

"Celine," he said deep in his throat. "No, I . . . "

"Yes, goddamnit!" she hissed, tearing at his belt buckle.

He tried to protest, but she pulled him down with her, over her, into her, bright and deep, driving out the last of the darkness, spreading and flowing, light in her veins, heat to her toes, dirt on her back, sting of small stones welcome and hot, sending her wildness into him.

He reared to his knees and covered her face with his hands, pulled at her hair, causing tears to brighten her vision. She rose upward onto the man above, feeling the spirit inside him and knowing it was both male and female, the same as hers. Two into one and genderless as joining waters, they flowed to the sea and subsided, leaving them back in their separate bodies sharing the mud made by their sweat.

"Celine," he said, about to apologize.

She covered his mouth with her hands. "Shh. You have to trust the medicine."

"Now what?"

"Now I need water. You can't go without water. It's a scientific fact."

Then she laughed.

38

IT was three in the afternoon when Lone drew the blinds of his office. He switched on the fluorescent desk lamp, tore off the top of the envelope, and extracted a note from the lab where he'd sent the contents. He skimmed the form until he saw what he was looking for:

". . . DNA of enclosed bone fragments shows them to be that of a human female, age undetermined . . . carbon-dating at an appropriately equipped facility possible, but certainty of results likely to be less than normal due to charred condition of bone fragments . . ."

Lone tossed the note aside and dumped the envelope's contents on his desk. The ashes glowed silver under the lamp. He opened his desk drawer and pulled out the letter from Jefferson.

> *Lone,*
>   *I saved Sylvie's ashes because I knew someday I'd see*
> *you again. Wherever she is, she hates you. Back off my*
> *property or I'll send you more to remind you of what a*
> *mutant freak you really are.*
>
> *J.D.J.*

Lone looked at one of the pictures: himself and Sylvie and Lamh coming out of a bar, arm in arm. Sylvie was wearing a peach-colored silk dress a little lighter than her skin. It had a high collar buttoned at the neck. Her hair was wound to the top of her head, allowing her long neck to show. He and Lamh were smiling. So was Sylvie. Everyone was happy until you looked long and hard. Then you noticed her eyes. They weren't part of her smile. They were focused far past the edge of the picture, on something she could barely see but wanted very much. There was sadness in the way her head was cocked a little to the side. Whatever she wanted, it was something she couldn't have.

Lone knew he'd seen that look, but he couldn't remember where. It was familiar, though, and it was important. If he knew where he'd seen it, he might know what she was thinking. He looked up and away from the picture, remembering the carpeted floor in back of the Citroen and the times Sylvie knelt there in front of him, giving him the red warmth of her mouth: *blinding light from her tongue, his head on the gray plush seat, a private shore, surf-like lapping sounds, oncoming tide rising through his groin, motion within motion, swallowed, protected, world without end, but knowing the end was coming, seeing it come in the shine of blurred window light, brighter with each movement of her head, watching it come for him like water, drowning him in timeless time, up through his legs and over him until the last things left were his eyes, staring up and away out the window at the feeling as it left, looking for the place it was going, wanting to go there too.*

Lone jumped out of his chair and brought his fist crashing down on the desk.

"Yes," he said softly, and sank back into his seat.

He now recognized the look in Sylvie's eyes. It was the same as the look in his own eyes when she took him away from the earth and then let him fall. It was the look of knowing that the good never lasts.

The good was short and the bad was long and things would happen as they pleased. Everyone was cursed, and both he and Sylvie knew it.

But Jefferson still believed he protected the innocent, still believed he was innocent, too. He hadn't learned what a thirteen-year-old whore learned in one day, the thing Lone had learned at Hahn's: Everyone was cursed. What Jefferson called guilt and innocence were just good luck and bad luck.

Jefferson should have gone back to America and left Vietnam to its joss. But no, he had to keep trying to separate the bad from the good, and somehow he had gotten Sylvie to do the same thing with her lovers. She had begun to think Lamh was good and he was bad.

It was that false separation that led to the end: flames throwing shadows on the walls, no sound but a searing crackle with voices at its center, their screams shrinking away, vocal cords stretched by the heat, a peeping as they melted, then nothing but the stink and the ashes.

After that came the hospital and surgery, nights spent vomiting up his grief in pools of bile at his feet, eating tubes of Sylvie's lipstick to remember her taste, caressing her nightgown to remember her touch, becoming a boy again, crying for Sister and family. Then the savior came—the self. That's all you had, but it would save you if you listened to it.

Lone looked down at the ashes on his desk. Jefferson expected him to be afraid of Sylvie's hatred, and he was. But behind the fear was something more powerful—joy at having her back in any form at all.

He rolled the silky ashes through his fingers and thought of her skin. He felt the bits of bone and remembered the light in her eyes and the way that light warmed his blood. He wanted her back in his blood.

The ashes in his palm were soft and glowing, faintly scented with a dry sweet perfume, a concentrated memory of wet sheets after times with Sylvie. The smell made him erect. He wanted more. He wanted her as part of himself, and he would have her any way possible.

He brought the ashes to his nose and inhaled as hard as he could. A roiling cloud slammed into his sinuses and blinded him with lightning behind his eyes. His ears rang and his head lashed against the back of the chair. He rose and staggered backward, coughing and sneezing, gritty slime in his mouth and nose. There was a tightness in his chest that made it hard to breathe, but then it eased and his vision became sharp as a diamond. He could hear the wires humming inside the walls of the room and feel the carpet on the bottoms of his shoes. He laughed out loud and was surprised at how young he sounded, how strong he felt. Sylvie was alive in his brain. He could feel her, and she felt young, strong, and beautiful.

He laughed again when he realized Jefferson was right: He was a mutant. He'd just mutated into part-Sylvie, and he felt better than he had in twenty years.

In a few minutes he became certain he'd found the answer to Vanek's problems with the virus. They had to let it take any mutant path it wanted—no stopping or stabilizing; just let it go. They could start with a likely combination and let it run until it stopped on its own. One of the combinations would soon end up just where they wanted it. He wasn't a scientist, but he was a mutant. He knew.

There was something else he knew: Jefferson was the one who felt guilty. He'd used Sylvie as a pawn, and she had died for it. He hadn't cared who got hurt as long as he got his man.

Lone took another noseful of ashes and this time the storm cloud was shorter and the elation came faster. He'd forgotten what it was to feel good—the warmth and the shower of ideas, like the one he was getting now. He pressed a button on his phone.

"Ling, get me Vanek on the phone. I've thought of a way to solve his problem. When I'm finished with him, get me a pickup truck of some sort, one with a cover on the back."

39

THE two children were walking together down a one-lane road that cut through a sea of golden wheat. The wheat belonged to the boy's father, Zachary Weyand, Sr. The girl's name was Wanda Sixkiller. She was eight years old and a Blackfoot. Her father worked the wheat for the boy's father.

Zachary Weyand, Jr., was ten years old and walked home with Wanda every day so she could meet her father. Neither of the two children thought anything of walking the three quarters of a mile from the bus stop to the Weyand gate. They didn't talk much but Zach was supposed to watch out for the girl as if she were his little sister, which was why he pushed her gently to the side of the road when he heard the truck. It was a nice truck, a maroon Ram V-8 with a silver cap on the back.

"There," said Lone. "Those two. All we had to do was wait for the school bus."

Ling, who was driving, looked nervously around, but no one else was in sight. The wheat was tall, and the road curved away from the school bus stop.

"Should we watch for a day or two, to make sure it's safe?" he asked.

"When things are right you know it," Lone answered, taking a noseful of Sylvie's ashes from a plastic liquor flask. Ling cast a worried look but said nothing. If C. K. Lone wanted to use drugs, it wasn't his place to ask questions, especially when things were going so well.

The sky was as blue as any sky over China, Sylvie was caressing the inside of his forehead, and the children were there for the taking. "This is perfect. Pull ahead of them and stop. I'll take the girl. You get the boy."

When the boy saw the two of them get out of the truck, he ran toward the fields. Lone was closest, so he chased him. The boy was quick, but Lone had done this before. You didn't have to catch children. All you had to do was get close enough to knock them down. In four strides he was near enough to slam the boy in the back, making it easy to grab the back of his shirt and get an arm around his waist. At this point, the boy started to scream, but Lone quickly shut him up by choking him. The kid was kicking and scratching, but Lone lifted him off the ground and threw him into the back of the truck, where Ling was waiting with a syringe of sodium pentathol. The girl had been no problem. She was already unconscious.

Lone hopped into the back of the truck and prepared to close the gate, but the boy made one last rush toward the exit. Ling caught him by the back of the neck, leaving his feet and legs free to kick and push as Lone caught him around the head and injected him in the neck. Then they hauled him in and shut the tailgate.

"The boy was slippery," said Ling.

"Not slippery enough to lose the master." Lone grinned. He hadn't had so much fun since Vietnam and was already thinking of having another noseful of Sylvie.

They climbed out of the back and got into the truck's cab. The whole thing had lasted only two minutes, and there was no sign anyone had heard or seen a thing. It would be clear sailing to a spot by the border, where the helicopter would pick up the children and fly them to the stockyards. Then they would drive the truck safely across the border.

"Are you going to use them in the shows?" Ling asked.

"Not now. Hostages are only useful if they're unharmed."

"What do you think Jefferson will do?"

"One thing he won't do is risk the children."

"He will do nothing?"

"Nothing except ask himself a lot of questions with unpleasant answers."

Ling looked at him quizzically.

Lone laughed out loud and reached into his pocket for the flask. He felt as if he could walk to Canada the way he used to walk the trails of Vietnam. He held the flask to his nose and snorted. He felt whole again.

40

JEFFERSON was slumped in his leather office chair staring at the computer monitor. He'd been there pretty much nonstop since he'd sent the ashes. He knew it would take the bastard some time to get over the shock, but it had been five days now.

The light at the bottom of the computer let Jefferson know that he had an E-mail. A pain knifed its way through his chest as he read the message.

> Jefferson. If it hadn't been for your
> gift I wouldn't have thought of taking
> Weyand and Sixkiller.

The story of the missing children had been all over the news for two days. It would be nice to believe Lone was bluffing, but Lone didn't bluff and kidnapping was his profession.

> Any more negative news stories, any
> contact with the EPA about the plant, any
> trouble at all, and the children will die.

Jefferson dropped to his knees in front of the monitor, weak with guilt. He'd wanted to unhinge Lone with the phony ashes, but he'd forgotten that an unhinged Lone was especially dangerous.

> You hurt those kids in any way, and I'll
> dynamite your plant myself. Then I'll
> come for you.
>
> If they die, it will be because of you.
>
> How long do you intend for this to go on?
>
> Until you issue a public apology on
> television. You will say you overreacted
> to your dead cattle and you are sorry.
> After that, no one will believe anything
> you say and I will give back the

children. But you will do what you want,
no matter who gets hurt, like you've
always done.

You killed Sylvie, not me.

And you didn't care what happened to her
as long as you got to me.

Jefferson started to type, then paused. Had he been suspicious of
Sylvie all those years ago, or was Lone right? He couldn't remember
anymore. His fingers froze over the keys and then more words from
Lone marched across the screen.

Think as long as you want. The children
stay with me until I'm satisfied.

Another month or two and Lone would get bored and start asking
the kids to do special things for special favors, then there would be
no point in their coming home.

Agreed, no more publicity.

And the apology?

It will take a little time to get it on
the air.

Take too long, and you'll be responsible
for what happens.

Jefferson left the computer without answering and walked out of
the room. His house was low and rambling, made of fieldstone,
glass, and beams of yellow pine. Its twelve rooms were shaped into
a U, with a swimming pool in the center. He liked the front great
room the best. There was a fifteen-foot fireplace along the back wall
and a twelve-foot picture window in front, where he could look out
on five miles of sloping grassland bordering his entry road.

He'd sent Matilda home because she kept giving him advice on health and marriage. Pete was up on the northern range, and Ernie, the groundskeeper, was at a paintball war in Wyoming. The house's emptiness sat as heavy as an accusation: The children had been caught in his private war.

Colonel Jack's favorite song had been "Onward, Christian Soldiers," and he'd insisted that young John D. pray regularly. As usual, Jefferson had done what the Colonel ordered, but he quit when he got to Vietnam and found out he wasn't sorry when he killed. His religion stressed forgiveness, but forgiveness took time and a bullet was easier.

Jefferson dropped to his knees in front of the window.

How did you pray after such a long time? Then he remembered something Far Lightning had said: *I don't say anything; I listen.*

He stopped trying to think of anything to say and just looked out at the sky . . . blue on white, then black at the edge of space. Then he heard a short series of bell-like rings, and it took him a few seconds to realize it was the telephone. He rose and picked it up.

"Hello."

"Hey, cowboy. It's Vinnie. Where you been?"

"I've been busy."

"Yeah, I heard about the gas wells."

"I'm handling it."

"You got to have people, cowboy."

"I'm all right."

"No you ain't. It's time you got over this shit about me stealin' Layla. Can't lose what you never had, know what I mean? You're a one-woman man, cowboy. No shame in that."

"So?"

"So me and Layla are bringin' you a pie. You know how good she does a cherry pie. We're bringin' you one. Maybe we can make some plans."

"I've got some things to do."

"Damn right you do. We're comin' out later tonight. Is nine all right?"

Jefferson shrugged and looked out the window. What had he just been asking for? "Yeah, nine. I think I have some ice cream for the pie."

41

THE pie looked great, and so did Layla. She'd cut her hair, and it fell in a curved line over her straight jaw. She wore jeans and a Mexican peasant top.

Vinnie had lost the rhinestone-cowboy look. Now he wore plain brown boots with his jeans, a white linen shirt, and a flat-top Stetson.

Things were a little awkward at first, so they ate the pie. Layla went around the table ladling mounds of vanilla ice cream. She licked the juice off her fingers while giving Vinnie secret glances. All of this had no effect on Jefferson. Layla seemed like someone he'd known in a more innocent past.

After two cups of coffee, Vinnie announced he had to take a leak and left the room. When he was gone, Layla moved to a chair next to Jefferson and took his hands in hers.

"Judd, there're no hard feelings about Vinnie and me, are there?"

"Nah, I'm glad you're happy. Any hard feelings about your house?"

"The construction guys you sent over did a great job. It's better than new."

A concerned frown wrinkled her smooth forehead. "Judd, if it's any comfort, I think Celine still loves you."

"Thanks, but that might not be enough."

A troubled look clouded her face. "Judd, where is Celine? No one's seen her around lately."

"She's away for a while."

Layla raised her eyebrows. "Kind of sudden."

"Yeah, it's a sudden kind of world."

Vinnie came back in the room and sat down across the kitchen table. He swiped a finger through his pie residue and licked it before lighting a cigarette. "So, cowboy. What's going on?"

"Life and life only."

"Seems to me maybe things are a little more unusual than that."

"You talking about anything specific?"

Vinnie and Layla glanced at each other and Layla gave him a nod.

"Yeah," Vinnie said. "I like to keep up with the news, and I noticed in the local rag there was a dead body found in a train yard across from a joint called Tony's. The dead guy had a shovel handle through his chest. It also seems like—and this is on the same night, mind you—the sprinkler system in Tony's went off accidentally. Cops and fire trucks all over the place, like somebody wanted them there. Then there was the two Asian guys got killed by a bear up on Lake McDonald. And before that, there was a guy to the west of here named Vandivier who they found pulverized in his house. That seemed like a lot of bodies in a short time to me, so I asked Layla and she backed me up. Oh yeah, there was your gas wells blowing up—sorry about that. And before that, there was the dead cattle you went on TV about. By the way, I ain't seen any follow-up on that. Last of all, there's the two kids gone missing."

Jefferson drank some coffee and drummed his fingers on the table. "Now that you mention it, that does seem like more news than usual."

"And to think I left New York for someplace quiet."

"Be careful, Vinnie, people might blame it on you."

Vinnie studied Jefferson's face through his cigarette smoke. "That's funny. Me and Layla were thinking the same thing about you."

"What were you thinking, exactly?"

Vinnie gazed out the kitchen window for a few seconds before answering. "Well," he said, "knowing Tsendai, and knowing you from the night you drove through Layla's house in your truck, I started to think maybe all this unusualness is because somethin' nasty is going on between you and the Tsendai boys."

"You think I killed that man in the railroad yards?"

Vinnie looked down into his coffee then into Jefferson's eyes. "Yeah, cowboy. I think somebody was trying for some payback on your TV story and you iced him."

"You're calling me a murderer?"

"I'd call you resourceful."

Vinnie kept staring at him with big eyes—half priest, half piranha.

Jefferson didn't know what to say. Admitting any of it would lead to a discussion of the kids. Layla would want to call in the cops, and Lone would kill the children rather than try to hide them. "I guess you'll have to call it whatever you like."

Vinnie shook his head, disgusted. "I told you he'd stonewall didn't I?" he said to Layla.

"Judd," she said. "You can't go on like this."

"Like what?"

"Alone."

"Tsendai's a big outfit, cowboy," Vinnie said. "They blew up your gas wells, and I got a suspicion they snatched your wife, maybe even the kids."

Vinnie's eyes bored through the smoke. Jefferson remembered he was partly responsible for the children and looked away.

"It's the kids!" Vinnie yelped. "The bastards have snatched the kids, and you're afraid to say anything. That's it, Layla."

Layla put a hand on Jefferson's arm. "Judd, don't you know you can trust us?"

"You need some people on this one, buddy," said Vinnie. "And I can get the kind of people you need."

Jefferson launched himself out of his chair with a push that spilled Vinnie's coffee.

"Goddamnit, stop it! Both of you. Even if it was true, I couldn't tell you anything."

Vinnie jumped back from the table and mopped coffee from his pants with a napkin. "You're scared they'll kill the kids, ain't you?"

"What the hell are you so interested for?" Jefferson bellowed. "You just got here a few months ago and now you're in a hurry to bring in guns from New York. What do you get out of it?"

"Damn you, Judd," shouted Layla.

Vinnie held up a hand to Layla and shook his head.

"It's okay, honey," he said to her. "What I get out of it is a home, buddy. I'm gettin' married here. I'm gonna have kids here, and I don't want no button men from Hong Kong screwin' it up. What you get out of it is a friend, somethin' I notice you ain't exactly over-loaded with."

Layla went to Vinnie and curled herself around his upper arm. It made a nice picture, and Vinnie made a nice speech, but Jefferson wasn't sure he was buying. Vinnie was still a New Yorker, no matter what he thought, and Layla was a blonde in love. They didn't know C. K. Lone.

"Neither of you have any idea what you'd be getting into."

Vinnie came forward like a dog catching a scent. "What is it I'd be gettin' into?"

Jefferson decided to tell him, if only to shut him up. "The name of the man who runs Tsendai is C. K. Lone. I was an army cop in Vietnam, and he was in the black market. He peddled girls and children. He made snuff films. He burned his own girlfriend and her lover alive when he found them together. Her lover was an agent of mine. I almost killed Lone that day, but I blew the shot."

"Mother of Christ!" Vinnie said. "I knew Tsendai was a triad outfit, but I didn't know they were into the slave trade."

"It's Lone's specialty, and now I've pissed him off. There's nothing he won't do."

"What are the triads?" Layla asked.

"Biggest syndicate in the world, babe," Vinnie told her. "They control all the drugs out of Asia and now they're moving into the U.S. of A."

"Call the cops, Judd," Layla said angrily. "It's their job."

"Tsendai's a legitimate company, and I've got no proof Lone's done anything."

"The cops gotta have a ready-made case to fool with the big boys, honey," Vinnie said.

Layla slapped her thighs and looked offended.

"There must be something that would get them interested."

"Yeah, I could raise hell until the EPA came and looked at their plant."

"But you can't raise hell because he's got the kids," Vinnie snapped.

Jefferson just looked at him. The matter of the kids was like a hand grenade with the pin out. If he let go, there was no predicting the result.

Vinnie came up close and stared hard into his face. "I agree the cops are out," he said. "Which means you need me and the help I can get."

Vinnie was talking about professional shooters out of New York, and the idea was appealing. But Jefferson had learned in Nam that men with guns are hard to control. The two kids were his responsibility, and he wasn't going to lose them.

"Listen, cowboy," Vinnie said hoarsely. "Nobody ever gives back on these deals. You want those kids, you're gonna have to take someone of his."

"The only person he ever had is dead, and he killed her himself. Besides, I didn't say he had the kids."

"You think I'm stupid or somethin'?"

"No, but I know the territory and I know Lone."

Vinnie looked like he was going to spit. "So that's it. You don't want no one crashin' your private party."

"Vinnie," Layla objected. "He's not like that."

Vinnie backed away and looked at Jefferson like as if he were a piece of cheap furniture.

"Yeah he is. He's the old soldier still fightin' his private war. Don't even matter to him who wins anymore long as he can pretend he's twenty-five."

"What is . . . is," said Jefferson.

Vinnie smiled crookedly and shook his head.

"The last guy I heard say that went out for a meatball sandwich and got blown away before he could eat it."

"Look, Vinnie. I appreciate what you're saying, but Tsendai is located in Calgary. What do you want to do, run up there with a carload of hit men and start shooting up the place?"

"Get your stuff, honey," Vinnie said to Layla. "We're leavin'. You know, Jefferson, there's somethin' I like about you, but right now I can't think what it is."

"It's nothing personal, Vinnie."

Jefferson looked to Layla, but she was no help.

"He was only trying to help you, Judd. Enjoy the rest of the pie."

She gathered up the shawl she'd brought and went to Vinnie's side.

"I'm in a bind, damnit," Jefferson said dejectedly.

"At least you know that much," Vinnie answered. "If you wise up, gimme a call."

No one said anything as Jefferson walked them through the kitchen. "Really," he said as they went out the front door. "Thanks a lot. It's just that I . . . " He shrugged helplessly.

"Yeah, yeah," Vinnie said over his shoulder.

"Be careful, Judd," Layla said as she followed him down the walkway to his Bronco. "You're a great guy, but sometimes you don't see too good."

42

IT was 10 P.M. and Far Lightning was back in bar number three drinking a little more tequila than usual. It wasn't every day a man did something as hard as telling Celine to leave him.

The boy child in her vision wasn't him. If it had been, their second time at sex wouldn't have been so awkward. They'd both been thinking too much, trying too hard. The third time was worse. They'd been paying so much attention to their thoughts that they hadn't finished at all, just rolled apart and held hands.

Now he thought he had it figured out. The first time she was partly in her vision and they'd been together like sky and wind. It was sex without the usual hint of nastiness. Afterward, he'd realized that her vision made her a kind of sister, and you kept your hands off sisters.

Yesterday morning he'd been at the table waiting when she awakened.

"Last night," she said sheepishly. "I guess I didn't realize how tired I was."

"We have to let that go, Celine."

She dropped her eyes and looked away.

"The first time was part of the medicine."

"Ahhh, but that was . . ."

"Yes it was, but I think there's no going back to it."

She got out of bed and pulled on her jeans and shirt, with no seduction or self-consciousness. "We could try again," she said.

"You're looking for an answer. I'm not it."

She leaned up and kissed him on the cheek. "So what do we do, act like it didn't happen?"

"The vision's not complete. You still have to find your true name."

She lit a cigarette. "Joseph, I don't know who the child was. All I know is that no one can tell me he wasn't there."

"The answer will come to you, but you have to be by yourself."

She stared blankly over his shoulder, not wanting to hear him.

"You'll be fine. You know how to camp. You can shoot a fly out of the air, and you've got medicine. When you find your name, you'll find your power."

She smoked more and looked around the room for another way.

"Take the rattle I gave you. Shake it if you want me near."

She picked up the rattle, looked at him, and shook it. He went to her, and she rested her head on his shoulder. Their feet made soft shuffling sounds as they swayed together.

"What about those men at the lake?" she asked.

"The thing between Judd and them will end. You have to be ready for what comes after. Go find your name."

She moved out of his embrace and began collecting her camping gear.

FAR LIGHTNING RAPPED the bar with his shot glass, and Ed Proudfoot, the owner, walked down to refill it.

"Putting it away pretty good tonight, Joseph," he said.

Ed was right. If he kept on like this, he'd be in jail by two, but maybe that's what he wanted. He'd just thrown away the most precious gift of his life. The goddamnedest most irritating thing was that he felt more relieved than sad.

He'd always been a liar to his women, loyal but unfaithful. His ex-wives had all known that and maybe even expected it. Celine was a woman with the rhythm of the East still in her. He hated the East and its dollar-mind above all things. He wanted it gone from his land. He wanted to raise horses, barter for objects, and kill his food. He wanted his woman to depend on him for her life. Celine would never need him that way. He might even wind up needing her, and that would be the end of what he believed. He was afraid of her. Better to admit it now than resent it later.

So he'd kept his mouth shut while she finished packing, remembering something he'd heard around a campfire: Part of being a man is learning that sorrow and regret are not the same thing. As she was getting ready to leave, he thought of the softness of her skin and became fat with sorrow, but he kept his mouth shut.

The front door of the bar opened, and Silas Sixkiller came in. Silas was in AA and hadn't had a drink in four years. Life was going good for him, but now he'd lost his daughter. It was like a devil didn't want to let him go. He slid onto the next stool and lit a cigarette.

"Joseph, I heard you were in here."

"I'm sorry to hear about Wanda, Silas."

"That's what I wanted to talk to you about."

Silas ordered a Coke. The skin around his eyes was white and tight. He probably hadn't slept more than a few hours since it happened.

"How you holding up, Silas?"

"Haven't had a drink, if that's what you mean," he said, gulping the Coke and waving for another.

"That's not what I meant."

"Sorry, Joseph. The booze has been on my mind. If it wasn't for Hattie and little Cy, I'd be on the floor."

"Any news?"

Silas lit another smoke off the butt of his first. "No. The cops and the National Guard are trying to give me a line of shit, but I can tell they got doubts about finding her."

His voice broke like the leg on a chair and his head fell into his hands. He breathed deep, then looked at Far Lightning with red-rimmed eyes. "That's why I've been looking for you, Joseph."

"Wanda?"

"Yeah. We've tried every way but the old way. I know you see visions. I want you to tell me what's happened to her."

Far Lightning's first impulse was to say no. It was a complicated procedure. You had to lay out some holy objects, then the pipe and special blankets. Then you had to be tied into a blanket, in the dark and with a roomful of believers who were willing to sing until the spirits came and lifted you to the rafters, telling you things as they carried you. It was tough on your energy, and it been a long time since Far Lightning had done it.

"I don't know, Silas. You can't just up and do it. There's preparation."

Silas squirmed on his stool and then slammed his fist onto the warped Formica bar. Mel Quince was sitting at the end of the bar, and a ripple knocked over his glass of draft.

"Hey," he bellowed. "Somebody looking for trouble?"

Mel was a Crow and bar number three was Blackfoot territory, so naturally he was half expecting a fight. He was a bulky boy who'd been laid off his job as an oil roughneck in Oklahoma. He still wore his orange hard hat, and his biceps were big enough to show the mushroom-cloud tattoos on each of them.

"Hey, Mel. This is Silas . . . Sixkiller."

Mel squinted hard through the beer glaze in his eyes and slapped the side of his hard hat.

"Oh God, Silas. I'm sorry. I didn't recognize you. I'm sorry about your daughter."

"No problem," muttered Silas, then grabbed Far Lightning by the sleeve. "Please, Joseph. Help me. What good is being Indian if you can't help me?"

Silas had put the sledge to the spike with that question. What the hell was being Indian all about if it wasn't trusting your religion? Hadn't he just given up the woman he'd always wanted because of that religion?

"All right, Silas. But we've got to have a whole circle to smoke and sing, and a place. That could take several days to round up."

Silas rubbed a hand back and forth over his buzz-cut head and chewed the inside of his cheek. Then he hopped down from the stool, hitched up his jeans, and pointed to the floor.

"Here, Joseph. Do it here. The place is full of Indians, and we need to do it now."

Silas was exaggerating a little in his excitement. The place wasn't exactly full, but there were ten men. They were all Indian, and with the exception of Silas, they were all half-drunk.

"My name is Silas Sixkiller and my daughter is missing," he said to the room. "Joseph Far Lightning is going to do the blanket ceremony and we need all of you to help. You'll help, won't you?"

Silas was going down the bar pulling on sleeves and twirling bar stools, sweating and pouring on the power. Pretty soon he had everyone in the bar standing in a circle in front of Far Lightning waiting for directions.

Great Father, Far Lightning silently prayed. *Time to put up or shut up. Please help me.*

He always carried the pipe in his pickup truck, so he went and retrieved it from under the seat. As holy objects they used a pocket watch that Ed's great-grandfather had stolen during a train robbery in 1901, Mel's snake-skull key chain, and Silas's wallet with a photo of Wanda inside. Far Lightning placed the objects in a circle on the bar, then taught them two old chants.

"We need a blanket with some medicine," he said, looking around the room.

"Just a minute," Mel yelled, and went out the door. When he came back, he had a large black tarpaulin and some rope.

"I got my Harley out in the pickup," he said proudly. "I was using this to cover it."

"The man says he needs something with medicine," objected Silas.

"I rode that Harley flat-out from Lawton, Oklahoma, to Wild Gap, Montana, and the cops never tagged me once."

"Good enough," said Far Lightning.

The ceremony had to be done in the dark, but before it could start, Far Lightning had to be tied like a mummy into the tarp. When it was over, he would be in a different place in the room. The spirits would put him there, and while they did, they'd tell him the whereabouts of Wanda Sixkiller. Maybe.

The men spread the tarp flat on the floor, and he stretched out at its edge. Then four of them rolled him up in it. After he was rolled tight, they would go around him with ropes. It was dark inside the tarp, and it smelled of grease.

They were starting around him with the ropes when things were interrupted by a crash and an animal shriek. The room broke into a bouncing jumble of shouts, curses, and flying barstools as a herd of men raged back and forth kicking and trampling him.

He started writhing away from the noise in a panic. He felt a group of men hit the floor behind him in a collective whump of expelled air and bruised ribs.

Far Lightning struggled upright and flapped himself out of the canvas. When his eyes cleared, he saw four men pinning a bare-chested man to the floor while a fifth got ready to club him with a long-necked bottle of Bud.

Far Lightning jumped forward and grabbed the bottle just as it started toward the man's head.

"Don't hit him," Far Lightning screamed. "He's a Heyoka!"

The man with the bottle backed off, and Far Lightning looked down into Donnelly's face. "Hey, remember me?"

Donnelly looked at him like he was the one who was crazy. "Sure. You saved my life. Just trying to pay you back."

Far Lightning laughed. "You mean you . . . "

"I was walking by . . . saw them tying you up."

"It's okay, Heyoka. It's a religious ceremony."

"Oh. Never mind, then."

Far Lightning reached down and pulled Donnelly to his feet. He was wearing a pair of khaki pants cut off at the knees and sneakers with cut-out toes.

"You know this man?" Mel asked.

"Yes. He helped me in a fight with some Rourke cowboys at the Buffalo Wallow. His name is Donnelly, and he's a Heyoka."

"But he's white," Mel said.

"True, but he's a Heyoka. A vision brought him here from Philadelphia, and he saw into Harlow right off."

Everyone in the room knew Harlow's history with Indians and hated him for it.

"I haven't had a drink for a while," Donnelly said, gazing lovingly at the bar.

Ed poured him a shot of bourbon, and he drank it down with a satisfied grimace.

"What are you doing in Browning?" Far Lightning asked him.

"Looking for gas. Then I saw the tepees."

The Museum of the Plains Indians was in Browning, and it included some tepees in a field outside the building.

"You been sleeping in them?"

"For a couple days," Donnelly said.

Donnelly sleeping in tepees. What better sign could there be?

"Joseph," interrupted Silas. "The ceremony. My daughter."

He was right. Donnelly had completely stalled the momentum of the blanket ceremony, but maybe this was the ceremony.

"He's a Heyoka, Silas."

Silas looked at him blankly.

"One of the things they do best is find children."

"Looks to me like he can barely find his own ass," Silas answered.

"Maybe, but he knew something about Harlow."

"It's going to kill him," Donnelly said.

"What?" asked Far Lightning. "What's going to kill him?"

The room got quiet, and Donnelly nodded toward the bourbon bottle. Ed poured him another drink.

"Something he can't stop doing," said Donnelly. "Something he can't stop doing."

"What about my daughter?" demanded Silas.

Far Lightning looked directly into Donnelly's face.

"This man's daughter is missing. Can you tell us anything about where she might be?"

Donnelly's face narrowed to a puzzled frown. "Your altars will be broken, your images destroyed," he said.

Silas looked like he was going to punch Donnelly, but Far Lightning put a hand on his arm.

"It's a vision he saw on his computer."

Jefferson had seen the same thing. Then there was Jefferson on the news, and then Jefferson's gas wells had blown up. And then . . . nothing.

Donnelly was firing down his third drink. His offshore-blue eyes were beginning to go round and wide.

"Tell me about Harlow," Far Lightning asked him. "What did you see when you looked into his eyes?"

"I was a computer programmer," answered Donnelly.

"Yes."

"I was a gambler, too. Hacked into my credit records, covered my debts. I had two daughters."

"And Harlow. What was in his eyes?"

Donnelly took a huge hit of a Camel and watched the smoke slide up to the ceiling.

"I smelled piss in his sweat, the same way I smelled when I was losing."

"His eyes?"

"Same as my eyes. He's losing, and he hates everyone."

Harlow wasn't losing to the Indians or Jefferson or anyone else

Far Lightning could think of, except maybe Tsendai. Could be he'd made a deal he couldn't get out of.

A little trouble with Tsendai. Check the sequence. First the plant, then dead cattle, then an angry Jefferson, then the TV story, then the gas fire, then Wanda and the white boy missing, then . . . nothing. A little trouble with Tsendai. Damn! Could it be?

"My daughter, Joseph," Silas said through gritted teeth. "Ask him about my daughter."

Far Lightning held up a hand to Silas. "One minute, please. I have to make a phone call."

43

JEFFERSON slumped into a chair in front of the window and watched Vinnie's lights cut a path down the entry road. The silence of the big house rolled into the room like a tide. His chest felt heavy and his head was light. He had to think, but his mind kept seeing two grainy photographs from the newspaper: a round-faced little girl with serious eyes and a handsome blond boy with a mischievous smile.

What would happen to that smile after a month with C. K. Lone? How long would it take the serious eyes to become dead? Jefferson was drowning in the fact that he was responsible for the answers to those questions. He had to get out from under and breathe. There were decisions to be made. Was he going to accept Lone's terms or talk to the EPA, handle the situation himself or take Vinnie's help? And if he decided to handle it himself, what would he do?

He was walking in circles, just as Far Lightning had predicted. He needed a way to go. He needed a vision. But how did you get one when you didn't know if you believed in them? Then he thought of Far Lightning again: *I don't say anything; I listen.*

He leaned his head against the back of the chair and looked out the window, riding into the stars, breaking their shapes into syllables, then into letters and the spaces within the letters, to a triangle of darkness inside Orion, the same one he'd noticed the night he talked to Vandivier.

Unwanted DNA, Vandivier had been saying . . . a theory that viruses are actually bits of human DNA we cast off eons ago.

Jefferson found the North Star and stared hard at the narrow blue aura that surrounded it. He relaxed more, and the aura expanded like the iris of an eye, pulling his sight deeper into the whiteness around the blue, thin as light filament but widening now to reveal an even thinner ring inside, thin as an idea of pale peach, the color of sunset over the tidewater when he was ten and losing himself in the edge of the world, the color that was there a hundred thousand years ago, when some stooped, hairy creature had looked at it the same way.

. . .

BENDING HIS NECK *hard against the ape curve of his back, the creature widens its eyes and searches the blond light for a voice he can see but not hear. He wants to float away but feels staked to the earth by something inside himself.*

He squats against the ground and feels a small dark presence hiding near his groin, a shadow burrowing toward the ground and trying to take him with it.

The thing inside is not him, but it soon will be. Its shape will become his, and he'll be chained alone to the earth by something in him that's afraid of the light. He rubs a matted hand along the hairless place where his lips meet and groans because he's afraid of himself.

Suddenly he sees bent shapes creeping over the ridge to his left. They rise and come screeching toward him, swinging bones and throwing rocks, baring their teeth and howling for blood. It's a group from across the river and they've come to kill him.

He stops thinking about himself and remembers the others inside the cave—the old and young, babies and females. He grabs a length of tree branch and begins to run, keening a horrified warning that lights up the night. His mind flies ahead of him to the tribe. He feels their eyes pleading with the distance for his return, and he runs faster, fearing the sadness in those eyes if he falls, knowing it's only in their sight that he lives.

The two fastest chasers almost get him as he reaches the top of the rise, but he leaps to the top of a rock and swings backhanded, shattering the first one's head and causing the second to stop long enough to have his shoulder smashed by a two-handed swing from above.

The creature sprints away along the rocks at the top of the hill, drops down into a ravine, and runs up the side of the opposite hill, where the tribe is waiting with rocks and clubs. They've heard his warning and they're ready. When the pursuers reach the ravine, they fall under a rain of rocks thrown by the females, and while they're still looking for shelter, the males descend on them with their clubs.

It's a meat storm: teeth, eyes, brains, and blood shower the little valley. When it's over, the tribe walks through the attackers smashing the heads of the ones still alive.

Then there is the celebration: howling, roaring, touching, jumping, and slapping. Each member is lost in the eyes of the tribe. Separate becomes whole in the elation of survival. Then the noise quiets and the males sink to the ground with the females, moving together while sensing the others, the tribe blending into a carpet of pleasure that warms the frost into dew along the moonlit hillside.

The creature awakens with the warmth of the female's back against his chest. He rises and walks toward the strip of color now cutting a path between ground and darkness. He walks toward it through the sleeping bodies of his tribe and the broken shapes of their enemies. He moves without feeling his feet on the ground. His eyes float out to the light, riding with it as it pushes away the night. He can read the colors as they spell out the dawn. He's wide as the world, deep as the sky, and alive as the changes in the sunrise.

When he's alone at a place by the water, he lets go a stream of gold urine that arcs through the sun and strikes rainbows off the rocks below. When he's finished, the dark thing that kept him small has been flushed out with his water.

Last night he was the tribe and this morning the tribe is him. He can feel all of them, and they make him bigger than himself. The self is gone, and he's the light and the color and everything that will never die. The shadow has been excreted.

JEFFERSON SLAMMED HIMSELF out of his chair and walked to the window, knowing now that Vandivier had been right: When man was first forming, his DNA was forming too, cells making choices through fights won and babies made afterward.

If that was true, it brought up a question that both thrilled and terrified. What about the ones from across the river? They would be afraid they didn't have what it took to survive, afraid they would cease to exist. Then they'd look inside for something to hold them on the earth, the only thing that could—the self. Each one would slink away ashamed and lick his blood, tasting for himself. They'd sneak back toward the victors sniffing for the secret of success.

They'd drink the water where the urine floated, lapping up the ex-creted self of the winners. They'd take in more of the shadow, and it would increase their connection to the dirt, and then they'd need more and more of it.

When they felt fit enough, they'd attack again. And if they won, they'd credit the self. If they lost, they'd face their first fear and lap up more of the winner's waste. In a few generations they'd be locked inside themselves, and mankind would be two different species. For one, violence would be a rare sacrament. For the other, it would be a way to feed the self. Each would recognize and hate the other, both of them locked into a pattern of attack and defense. Jefferson sighed and remembered what Vandivier had said as he died: *All life is a virus.*

Jefferson turned away from the window and faced the fireplace, where Celine had insisted on placing a picture of his father; a blow-up of him on the retreat from the Chosin Reservoir. He was standing next to a jeep, looking over his shoulder at the snow-covered hills where two hundred thousand Chinese troops were waiting. Colonel Jack was wearing a heavy coat and a hat with ear flaps. All you could see were his stud jaw, his eyes, and his mouth. The amazing thing, the frightening thing, was the smile. Colonel Jack was looking up at all those Chinese and he was smiling like a hungry hyena. Way back in his eyes was a stony light. Jefferson had always assumed it was a reflection off the snow, but now he knew it had been there since the first Jefferson had pissed in his enemy's river.

Now Jefferson was sure he knew what Colonel Jack knew: You had to fight the external enemy or you'd soon have an internal one. There was an eternal war between the Lone kind and the Jefferson kind, and there was a real difference between them. All life was a virus.

The phone rang and he grabbed for it reflexively. "Hello."

"Judd, it's Far Lightning here. I'm in Browning in bar number three."

"Yeah?"

"Silas Sixkiller is here with me looking for a sign about his daughter. Donnelly's here too."

"Who's Donnelly?"

"He's the guy from the East who lives in his car. You haven't noticed him around?"

"I've been preoccupied."

"Well, he's a Heyoka. Silas wanted me to tell him where his daughter is. Then Donnelly showed up. Then I got an idea where she might be. I think you got an idea, too, don't you?"

"I know who but not where."

"Maybe we can work that out. Donnelly's an expert at computer hacking. I want to bring him out to your house."

"Come on."

"Now?"

"Sooner if possible."

"You sound like you got a fire under you."

"I've had that vision you were talking about."

"We're on our way."

Jefferson hung up and was suddenly hungry. He decided to eat the rest of the pie while he waited for Far Lightning.

44

IT was one in the morning when Far Lightning showed up with a bearded little man who stood blinking in the foyer like a rodent pulled from its hole. He wore torn khaki shorts and a flannel shirt with no buttons. The muscles in his arms and neck were thin and tight. He was a walking sheath of nerves, moving around the room eyeing the paintings and mumbling to himself.

"You had a vision?" Far Lightning asked.

"I can't explain it."

"But you saw it?"

"Just say I know who I am and what I'm doing."

"Good enough. This guy can help us."

"Where's Celine?"

Far Lightning backed away a step and held up his hands. "She's got a rifle, my best paint horse, and my camping gear. She needed some time to think things over."

"What things?"

Far Lightning lit a cigarette and looked blankly through the smoke. "Something she saw. You'll have to ask her."

"When am I going to see her, Joseph?"

"Judd, she's strong. It's those kids who need help."

"How did you know Lone had them?"

"They couldn't get Celine. I figured the kids were the next best thing."

"And this guy can help?"

"He's a hacker from Philadelphia. Used to get into his own credit card records to pay off gambling debts."

"We use him to take a look inside Lone's computer files?"

"That's what I figured."

"What did you say his name is?"

"Donnelly."

"Hey, Donnelly, let me ask you something."

The rodent yanked his head around as if he were on a leash. "Me?"

"Yeah. You understand our problem?"

237

Donnelly blinked hard and shifted from foot to foot. "Uh, children."

"We need you to help us find them."

"Donnelly my friend," said Far Lightning. "We need to get into some computer files."

A new light came into Donnelly's eyes and he stepped quickly across the room. "Private files?"

"A company," said Jefferson.

"Bank?"

"No, a holding company with offices in Calgary. Can you do it?"

A wistful smile worked its way out of Donnelly's matted beard. "You have a telephone number?"

"I've got the E-mail address of the company's CEO."

Donnelly's smile broke all the way through his beard. "I'll need some whiskey," he said.

JEFFERSON GOT A bottle of Old Grand Dad and took Donnelly into the den. The stringy little man brushed off the chair like a concert pianist sitting down to play. Then he keyed in Lone's E-mail address. He typed a message to see if Lone would answer, and when he didn't, Donnelly typed a series of commands. In a few minutes Lone's electronic telephone directory was displayed on the screen.

"That's Harlow's number," Jefferson said, looking over Donnelly's shoulder.

"What are you looking for?" Donnelly asked.

"The man who uses this directory has stolen two children," Jefferson said. "We're hoping to find out where he might be keeping them."

"How?" Donnelly asked.

"You're the expert."

"Garbage in, garbage out," Donnelly said. "Have to know what I'm looking for to find it."

"He's a businessman," Jefferson said.

"What kind of business?" Donnelly asked.

"Illegal business," Far Lightning answered.

Donnelly swiveled in the office chair and looked at them. Before sitting down, he had seemed perpetually stunned. Now he had the calm assurance of a pilot in his cockpit.

"Bills," he said. "Businesses have to pay bills."

"This business is illegal."

"Doesn't matter."

"But his bills would be on the Tsendai database, not Lone's," Jefferson said.

"He'd have access," Donnelly answered.

"But there would be a password."

"What's the company's name?" asked Donnelly. "And what's his name?"

"Tsendai is the company. His name is C. K. Lone."

"C.K.?"

"He's Chinese. I don't know what it stands for."

"Hmm," said Donnelly. "Chinese only has phonetic spelling in English. Doubt if he would use it."

"Why?"

"Businessmen like to do things fast. They think up their passwords on the spur of the moment."

Donnelly began a singsong chant: "Anagrams or literal references. Anagrams or literal references, anagrams or . . . "

He kept up the refrain as he typed and deleted, humming it to himself as the cursor darted around the screen.

Jefferson looked at Far Lightning and raised his eyebrows.

"Heyoka," Joseph said with a shrug.

"That's it," Donnelly chirped. "Onesend. Part of his name, part of Tsendai's, and he's number one at the company. Businessmen are very hierarchal."

"You mean you're in already?" Jefferson asked.

"Hmm, yes," said Donnelly. "Security program here, though. Might take a little while."

Jefferson and Far Lightning retired to the other side of the room, where they sank into leather chairs and smoked. A cloud of smoke cut the low-lit room into layers. Donnelly's head looked like it was floating in the air. Far Lightning's eyes blended with the sifting grayness and became invisible. The atmosphere was cryptlike.

"Where'd you say you met him?" Jefferson asked, to break the gloom.

"I got into a little scrape in the Buffalo Wallow and he helped me."

"What's he doing in Montana?"

Far Lightning hunched forward in his seat, glancing toward Donnelly. He lowered his voice. "He's looking for redemption."

"That's completely nuts."

"Oh, I'd say it would pay for a few sins if he helps us find those kids."

Jefferson resisted the urge to ask Far Lightning if he thought adultery was a sin.

"Celine will be all right," said Joseph.

Jefferson's mouth dropped open and he gaped at the Indian.

"Don't look so surprised, Judd. I could see you thinking about her."

Suddenly Jefferson was blood-angry at the whole world. "Everybody's got to have an act," he said disgustedly.

"It's no act."

"Then why didn't you know something like this would happen and help me when I first asked?"

Far Lightning picked his words carefully. "I did know. I just didn't want to help you. Later I saw a vision—the destruction of the white man's world."

"Oh come on . . . "

"Listen to me, damnit. The glaciers are melting. I saw it. It must be global warming, just like they've been saying, and it's causing death in the air."

If Far Lightning was right, it could answer a question that had been gnawing at the edge of things since the beginning: What was Harlow getting out of his alliance with Tsendai? If Vandivier's report backed up Far Lightning's vision and the report went public, Harlow's land would become a tough sale.

"Tell me what you saw."

"An eagle. It flew high and then died. Something is wrong with the air."

Jefferson remembered Yohiro and his balloons. Something was happening in the air over Montana that gave Jefferson a mighty dread.

"Now, tell me your vision," Far Lightning said.

"Two different species of man. One kills because that's its nature. The other kills to defend itself from the first. All life is a virus." He paused. "Maybe I'm just crazy from the stress, though."

Far Lightning's face came to within inches of Jefferson's. "The things you really know are too old for words. They're a sound you feel instead of hear, out of the earth . . . bone music."

In the shattering of a second Jefferson understood everything Colonel Jack had ever told him with his silences.

Then they were interrupted by a shout from Donnelly.

"Not feeling too well, 'cause he's going to hell."

Jefferson jumped across the room to where Donnelly was pointing at the computer screen.

"Not feeling too well, going to hell," Donnelly chimed, pointing to a list of names on the screen. Halfway down the list, Harlow's name was accompanied by a figure—250,000—and a notation: Thai-VN-15-20-complete.

"What is it?" Far Lightning asked, peering over Jefferson's shoulder.

"A customer list," Jefferson answered. "Just like the ones he kept in 1969. It means Harlow likes fifteen- to twenty-year-old Thai and Vietnamese girls. The word *complete* means he likes to kill them when he's done."

"I thought I knew how bad Harlow Rourke was," Far Lightning said.

"Looks like you knew him better than I did."

"He needs to die."

"Now you know what my vision was like. How's it coming, Donnelly?"

"This is the CEO's personal files. Got to get out and into company files."

"How long?"

Donnelly played a ten-fingered staccato on the keyboard for thirty seconds and looked up through his beard. "About that long," he said with a watery giggle.

On the screen were two rows of pictures.

"That one," said Donnelly, pointing to a lightning bolt.

He moved the cursor to the lightning bolt and tapped the mouse.

Immediately, a list of addresses flashed onto the screen. Under each address was a monthly grid showing amounts owed and paid for gas, water, telephone, and electricity.

"Donnelly," said Jefferson. "I think you are a holy man."

"Cheesebox security," Donnelly mumbled. "Not like the banks. I'm too old for banks."

Jefferson scanned the list, knowing what he was looking for. Lone would keep his merchandise in a dormitory warehouse. Some he'd ship right away; others he'd use in the circus. The place would have to be big enough for both rooms and a small arena. It would use a lot of electricity, and it would have to be out of the way.

"Look at the bill on that one," he said, pointing to 21 Brahma Way.

"A lot of juice," Far Lightning said.

"Two thousand dollars' worth, and it's not even winter."

Jefferson pulled a book map of Canada from the bottom drawer of his desk. He thumbed through it until he found the page for Calgary and the grid number for 21 Brahma Way.

"The stockyards," Far Lightning said. "I remember from when I used to ride bulls. They call it Brahma Way because it runs by the place where the breeders show their bulls."

"That's where he's keeping the kids."

"How can you be sure?"

"Another country, another warehouse. Trust me."

"Okay. You thinking of the police at all?"

"What are they going to do—get a warrant, bang on the door, and ask to search the place? Meanwhile, the kids get their throats slit."

"I'm against cops on principle."

"All right then. Donnelly, we need one more thing, a scientific study by a man named Vandivier. It would probably be in Lone's personal files, maybe under a camouflaged heading. Think you could look around?"

Donnelly was muttering about banks and baseball. "A fool to bet the favorites," he was saying.

"Donnelly, can you . . . "

"Lone's file," he answered. "Vandivier."

Donnelly started thwokking away at the keyboard.

"We have to get a look at that report," Jefferson said to Far Lightning.

"We already know pretty much what's in it."

"Maybe, but we can't go to the EPA with visions and hunches."

"Whites are crazy for science."

"Like I said, we need that report."

"Won't do us any good until we get the kids back."

"So, what do you think?"

"I think we're going to Calgary."

"Yeah, come here."

Jefferson led Far Lightning to a window that looked east toward the plains. He wondered if Celine was out there looking back. If so, was she looking at him or at Far Lightning?

"What makes you so sure she's all right out there?" he asked.

Far Lightning could tell Jefferson knew about him and Celine. He'd be no good in a fight over that. Guilt made you slow in a fight, but lying made you weak and he'd need all his strength in Calgary. *Don't ask, Judd. Leave it to a bigger power.*

"I asked you a question," Jefferson said.

"What?"

"How can you be sure she's all right?"

Jefferson's jaw was twitching and the veins in his neck were beginning to bulge.

"She has a strong will."

Jefferson knew what Far Lightning was trying to tell him. Anything that happened with Celine was because she wanted it to. *What would you have done in his place?* "Maybe too strong for anybody's good," he said.

"That's a question best left to time," Far Lightning answered.

Jefferson drew the curtain over the window and turned back to Donnelly.

"Nothing," said the stringy little man. "Not here. Zippo. Empty. No can do. Bye-bye. Gotta go."

Donnelly got up and started fidgeting around the room. "Gotta go," he said again.

"You can stay here if you want. I've got plenty of space."

"My car's alone," Donnelly said. "Can't leave her alone."

"You can bring your car here."

Donnelly stopped moving and stared at Jefferson as if he'd just farted in church. "I go where the balls say."

"What the hell?"

"It's a long story," said Far Lightning. "He's got his own way."

"But he's crazy as a bug. We ought to see he's taken care of."

"Box him up in a room? Feed him drugs until he shuffles down the hall peeing in his state pajamas?"

"Maybe they could help him get back to what he was."

"He told me there's people want to hurt him, a debt or something."

"Okay, take him back to where you got him. Then we've got to figure something out about Calgary."

"Yeah. We can't just bang on the door."

"And we don't know how many men are inside or where they're keeping the children."

"Seems like it would be best if they brought the kids out."

"That would be damn nice of them."

"Hmmm," said Far Lightning, stroking his chin.

"What?"

"I might be getting an idea. Let me check a few things, and I'll come by in the morning."

"If you've got something, tell me now."

"No, you think on it too. Maybe you can come up with something better than me."

Far Lightning took Donnelly by the arm and guided him down the hall to the front room.

"Thanks," Jefferson said to the wiry little man in torn clothes.

"Two girls," said Donnelly. "'Night, honey. Daddy loves you."

He was staring at a place far away from the room. Tears were squeezing their way into his dusty beard. Jefferson turned away quickly and heard the door shut behind him. It was going to seem like a long time until morning.

45

THEY decided to do it in the evening, when it was dark enough to be confusing but light enough to see the children. They left Wild Gap at three-thirty, towing a horse trailer behind Jefferson's Rover. Inside the trailer were Jack and Far Lightning's big roan, Drumhead.

They reached the outskirts of Calgary at five-thirty. The stock-yards were on the north side of town, so it took another half hour to get there. When they saw rising yellow dust, they parked the Rover in a lot and led out the two horses. Jefferson had his magnum in the saddlebags. Far Lightning stuck a sawed-off shotgun into a holster hanging from his saddle and tied a large burlap bag to the pommel. Each of them had a lariat on his saddle apron.

"You're sure it'll work?" Jefferson asked.

"You're the rancher. You know what bulls are like."

"Semen for brains."

"That's right."

"Let's go."

Jefferson mounted Jack and moved down a hill toward the three square miles of tin buildings and wooden corrals.

The yards were a teeming mixture of motion and smell encased in a cloud of dust. Hay trucks clanked down the narrow streets and turned onto dirt paths between the barns. Cattle crossed from pen to pen, urged along by men on horseback. Limos carrying buyers rolled through the din of bawling animals and the earthy odor that hung in the air like a color. Two more horsemen were unnoticeable.

Twenty-one Brahma Way was at the extreme western side of the yards, close to an entrance off an outside road.

Jefferson stood in his stirrups trying to see where it went. "It bears left and goes west," he said.

"They could get out that way."

"The idea is they won't have time."

"That's the idea, all right."

"Let's go."

Jefferson was tight as fence wire, and he knew Far Lightning felt the same way. What if the bulls didn't respond? What if the security crew got them rounded up before they caused any trouble? There were probably a hundred other things they hadn't even thought of, but hell—bulls were bulls, and the animal control riders were just a bunch of crippled-up old rodeo drunks. The plan made sense. After that, you just had to have faith.

"I told you," Far Lightning said, pointing to a series of pens across the road from 21 Brahma Way. "They like to keep the bulls out here, where they can't smell the cows."

"Not far to the warehouse."

"Maybe fifty yards."

They had stopped their horses across the road and oblique to Lone's warehouse, a windowless square of corrugated metal painted pale blue. Like most of the other warehouses, it had no sign announcing the tenant. The side of the building faced the bull pens. The door faced back toward the main section of the yards. A white stretch limo was parked in a turnaround by the door.

Jefferson nudged Jack across the road and circled the warehouse. "There's another door at the far end," he said when he returned.

Far Lightning nodded toward the limo. "They'll come out the door closest to the car."

"I don't want to count on it."

"Okay, I'll go around by the other door. If they come out my end, I'll fire a shot in the air."

"I don't want to attract the security people."

"Hell, Judd. If those bulls are acting right, the sound of a shotgun's going to be like pissing in the ocean."

"Yeah, okay."

They looked at each other uneasily, each knowing what was on the other's mind. Finally, Jefferson decided to say it.

"Listen, if something happens to one of us, the other one leaves with the kids. The kids are the thing, right?"

Far Lightning nodded. "Might as well get started," he said.

The bulls were rodeo riding stock, which meant the breeders had taken the normally nasty nature of bulls and made it worse. These bulls weren't just nasty; they were homicidal. They'd knock a man down and gore him just because he had the nerve to be on the same planet.

246

To keep the bulls from killing each other, they were kept in individual enclosures, which were about the size and shape of a horse trailer with a rising gate in front. There was a catwalk along the line of pens so that an attendant could let them into a central corral without risking any of his favorite parts. There were eighty occupied pens, and they had double gates. Jefferson figured it would take fifteen minutes to get them all open.

It was six-fifteen. A purple dusk fell through the haze, imparting an underwater blur to the movement of men and beasts. Jefferson and Far Lightning made a circuit of the corral, attempting to look aimless.

"I saw a control shed on the far side with one man inside and three brokers talking business over on the east side. Nobody by the corral gate."

"Yeah," said Jefferson. "That's what I saw. Where's the security boys?"

"They don't patrol on foot until after dark. During the day, they just ride by in jeeps."

"Okay, then. I take the catwalk, and you do the main gate?"

"Okay, but first the medicine."

Far Lightning pulled a set of rubber gloves from his pocket and put them on. Then he untied the burlap bag from his saddle and opened it.

"Whew," Jefferson said. "I can smell it from here."

"Better start from across the street and work back."

They rode across the street and dismounted. Far Lightning reached into the bag and pulled out a handful of rags covered with moist rusty stains. The stains were caused by cow estrus. They had been soaked in it by Far Lightning's rancher friend Michael Owleye.

Far Lightning threw Jefferson a set of gloves and handed him some of the rags. Then they urged their horses up against the warehouse and began rubbing its corrugated sides with the sexual scent of cow. When they had covered a forty-foot square, Far Lightning dismounted and, while Jefferson followed with his horse, walked away from the building and across the road, dragging the rags along the ground. When they reached the pens, a few of the bulls were already becoming restless.

"We'll have to be fast," Far Lightning said. "They're going to start making a hell of a racket."

Jefferson jumped down from Jack and tied him to a fence post. Then he took more rags and went down a row of pens, smearing scent on the gates. Far Lightning went in the other direction. Within a minute, the bulls had begun bellowing and ramming into the gates of their pens with the force of small cars. The line of pens was now shaking from end to end.

Jefferson dropped his rags and climbed the ladder to the top of the catwalk. He saw a man's head appear at the door of the control shed, then duck inside—probably heading toward the phone. Hunching low into the dust from the pens, Jefferson ran around the catwalk raising the gates. The bulls charged out like locomotives and went straight for the open corral gate.

There were eighty bulls—sixty moving tons of sex-crazed purpose. They exited the corral in a ground-tilting stampede and headed for the wall of Lone's warehouse, where they began rutting and ramming into the scent-coated wall with a blind drooling fury that made the wall shake and the roof vibrate. Far Lightning hopped on his horse and rode to the back door. Jefferson ran Jack to the front door, dismounted by the limo, and punched holes in its tires with an ice pick. Then he mounted up, pulled out the magnum, and waited.

The bulls kept on ramming and jamming. Hard-dicked and heavy-headed, they expended themselves against the wall with such maniacal force that it began to develop an inward bow. The sound inside had to be like hell on Judgment Day. It also had to be obvious that a sound like that was going to draw a lot of people, and soon. Already, Jefferson could see arms waving and people running. The warehouse sounded like it was exploding.

Then two stocky Asian men rushed out the door carrying children under their arms like suitcases. Jefferson waited until he saw Far Lightning start from the other end of the building before he kicked Jack forward and ran him toward one of the men, intending to knock him to the ground and pick up the little girl he was carrying. But he heard something behind him and turned to see a pounding mass of bellowing flesh coming for him—a Brahma trailed by two others, wild for the scent he still had on his hands and shirt.

The men with the kids saw the bulls at the same time and ran hard toward the limo. Jefferson realized there was no way out of the parking area except back toward the bulls, and Jack was having none of that. He'd keep running in circles until the bulls nailed him, and now there were three more splitting off from the crowd at the warehouse and heading toward them. Jefferson wheeled Jack to the limo's right side, jumped off, and headed for the door. Out of the corner of his eye he saw Far Lightning pull Drumhead around and make a run for the end of the building. He was followed closely by a group of bellowing bulls.

When Jefferson's bulls saw Jack separate from his rider, they milled for a few seconds until they picked up the scent again, then they charged. Jefferson opened the door to the limo and threw himself inside, pulling the door shut just as one of the bulls slammed into the car's side, rocking it like a boat on rough water.

Then the opposite door opened and one of the men chucked the two kids onto the rear seat and sailed onto the floor inches ahead of a bull's horn. Jefferson rolled to the right in the four-foot space between seats. He heard a man in the front start the car and scream in Chinese.

At first, both Jefferson and the other man were too surprised to do anything, but then a look of hatred came over the other man's face and he reached under his suit coat for the gun that dangled from a shoulder holster.

Jefferson pulled the magnum from his belt, but he realized the kids were only three feet away, in his line of fire. He reached over and caught the man's arm with his left hand, then drove a fist into his ribs. The man fell to the floor as the driver stopped the car and looked back over the seat. He reached for his own gun, but turned back to the wheel as two bulls slammed into the side of the car and smashed the door against his ribs. He turned the car toward the road as Jefferson hung on to his man with one hand and whaled away at his ribs with the other.

The man whaled back, slamming a fist into the side of Jefferson's jaw. The car was still working through four bulls, which were attempting to ram it to a stop. Jefferson raised up to get leverage for his next blow and saw Far Lightning head around the back of the building. He was trailed by six bulls.

The driver was still screaming in Chinese as he worked the limo through the bulls. The car's flat tires flapped against the ground, causing it to thump along as if it had stiff knees.

The limo was out on the road and heading slowly for the back exit. Jefferson knew that if they got out of the stockyards, the driver would stop and shoot him. He had to do something about his man and do it fast, but the guy was young and tough, still trying to get his gun out while pushing Jefferson back against the seat and trying to pin him there with a knee. Two bull rushes rocked the car and the driver swung left, causing the man's knee to fall away and giving Jefferson a second to feel the wet bar against his back and the liquor bottles above it. He reached back, pulled out a bottle, and slammed it into the man's right knee. The pain made him forget his gun long enough for Jefferson to reach in and snatch it out of its holster. The kids were two feet away and he couldn't risk a shot, so he jammed the gun under the front seat and swung the bottle again, clipping the man's elbow as it protected his face, but the other arm was coming out of his pocket with a knife.

Jefferson blocked the knife with the bottle while feeling around on the floor behind him for his gun. If it was going to be a knife against him, he'd have to chance a shot, but instead of the gun he felt something thin, round, and flat—a CD that had been knocked to the floor by the car's evasive tactics.

Jefferson managed to get his bottle between the knife and his face as the other man lurched close to him. Then he brought the CD around and sliced across the man's eye with its edge. The man screamed, lowering his guard long enough for Jefferson to slam the bottle into the side of his head. The man sank limply to the floor as the car ran into an impassable number of bulls and stopped, bulls slamming into it from all directions, driver screaming, pulling the emergency brake, something landing hard on the roof, driver turning with hand under coat, Jefferson looking up, seeing Far Lightning on the roof, driver pulling gun from holster, Jefferson pressing sunroof button, seeing driver look up too late to stop the rope noose from catching him around the neck and pulling tight.

The driver dropped the gun onto his seat and clawed at the noose with both hands, but it was no use. Far Lightning was using the edge of the sunroof for leverage and held tight long enough for Jefferson to get the gun from the seat and put it against the driver's head.

"We gotta get out of here before these bulls tear the car apart," said Far Lightning as he lowered himself through the sunroof, pushed the driver aside, and took the wheel.

"Where'd they all come from?"

"They followed me. I saw you heading for the exit and led 'em that way."

The car rocked sickeningly as the bulls slammed into it from both sides. A horn smashed through a back window and both children screamed.

"We got to get out of here," said Far Lightning. "We'll head overland back to their pens. They'll get the scent mixed up with their own and simmer down."

"What about these two guys?"

"Throw 'em out. If they run long enough, the bulls will lose interest."

Far Lightning eased the dented limo onto a grassy field that marked the outer edge of stockyard property and began bumping slowly along, gathering speed as he continued a wide turn to the left. Jefferson jerked a thumb at the driver. The man looked out the window, eyes wide with terror.

"You heard the man," said Jefferson. "If you run long enough, they'll give up."

Jefferson opened the side door and jerked his thumb again. Far Lightning slowed to a crawl and the man stepped out and began running. Five bulls began chasing him as he sprinted toward the highway, but the rest stayed with the car and the scent that floated around it.

"What about the other guy?" asked Far Lightning as he sped up.

The man wasn't dead, but he was bleeding from the nose and moaning gibberish.

"He's in no shape to go anywhere."

"Let him stay with the car, then."

"What do you mean, stay with the car?"

"We need horses to get out of here."

"I know that."

"Drumhead ran off from the bulls. You got any idea where Jack is?"

"No."

"Then we got to steal a couple. I say we put a little distance between us and these bulls, then we get out, aim the car toward the bull pens with the cruise control, and head for the horse pens on foot. Security will be over there dealing with the bulls."

The thought of leaving Jack was painful, but he was only a horse. The main thing was to get the kids home. Jefferson reached out and patted the boy on the arm.

"Zack, isn't it?"

The boy looked as dumbfounded as if he'd been abducted by aliens, but he managed to nod his head.

"We've come to take you home. Sorry about all this, but we thought things would go smoother. You trust me?"

The kid looked at the unconscious man on the floor and nodded his head. Jefferson reached over and lifted the little girl off the seat, hugged her, then placed her on the front seat next to Far Lightning.

"Hey, Wanda," he said. "Remember me? I'm Joseph Far Lightning. I showed you the crow dance at your house last year."

Joseph made a couple dancing motions with his shoulders and the little girl smiled.

Jefferson looked out the back window and saw that the bulls had fallen back. Some of them were just milling and pawing the ground. "Now's the time," he said.

"Okay," said Far Lightning.

He stopped the car, and Jefferson got out with the two kids. Then Joseph aimed the car toward the bull pens, ran up a little speed, and jumped out onto the soft grass.

"Look at it," he said as he walked back toward Jefferson. "Like a ship about to run aground."

The dented white limo lurched off toward the bull pens, tacking right and left on its bent rims but moving ever forward.

252

"Come on," said Far Lightning. "The horse barns are about a quarter mile over there to our right."

He swooped the little girl up into his arms and started across the field. Jefferson gave Zack a pat on the back to urge him forward and followed.

When they got to the horse barns, Jefferson saw something that he should have predicted: Jack, cantering back and forth between the barns, whinnying to the females inside.

"That Jack doesn't have but a couple things on his mind, does he?" said Far Lightning.

"No he doesn't, bless his heart," answered Jefferson.

All the control riders and security men had gone to round up bulls and look for whoever had set them free. It took Far Lightning about three minutes to slip into the barn and pick out a roan and a saddle.

"Nice horse," he said when he rode out of the barn and swung Wanda up into the saddle. "A good trade for Drumhead."

Jefferson whacked Jack on the side of the head to get his attention off the mares and swung up into the saddle. Zack knew how to hang on behind without squeezing the breath out of him, and Jack barely noticed the extra weight.

"All right," said Jefferson. "We're out of here."

46

LONE stepped out of the helicopter and waved away the car that was waiting for him. The Unitel plant was only two hundred yards away, and he wanted a few minutes alone. He patted the flask in his jacket pocket and realized that what he really wanted was a few minutes alone with Sylvie.

As he neared the blue building, he turned away from the gravel path and walked along the back wall. He turned the corner and stood looking across a field of grass. The only feature of the wall behind him was a windowless fire door.

Lone knelt next to the door and took the flask out of his pocket. He shook it and watched a small cloud of dust rise and settle inside the clear plastic. The ashes were a distillation of Sylvie, and they intoxicated him as fully as any other distilled product. After the initial suffocation, they gave the whole world a peach-colored glow that made him feel like he was looking out from inside Sylvie's skin, seeing simple answers to complex questions. It was as if he were thinking with both his mind and Sylvie's.

He could see, think, touch, and feel with her, all without fear that she would lie or leave. The only part of her left was the part that fit into his brain cells. The physical acts were things he could have with anyone. Lately he'd been inhaling a headful of Sylvie before screwing some of the merchandise, and he'd performed like he was twenty-five again.

The problem was that the ashes were now half gone. Someday soon he would lose her all over again. He was going to talk to Vanek about making an unlimited supply, but first there was the immediate crisis. Sylvie would help.

Lone took the cap off the flask, snorted mightily, and slammed backward into the tin wall, gasping as the smoky essence sifted into the front of his brain. He was ready now to tell Chang it was time to shut down the plant. Then he'd talk to Vanek. Vanek would understand what he wanted.

Lone decided to try the fire door. He grasped the handle and pulled. It should have been locked, but it swung wide open. There was a defect in the lock. Very convenient, though. Sylvie made everything easier.

HE SAT BEHIND Chang's desk when he gave him the news. Chang paced the room and tried to keep from raising his voice.

"We only have two containers of virus," he protested. "If something goes wrong in Argentina, we'll have no way to make more."

"There are only two things that could go wrong—the virus might not reproduce itself or it could mutate further. Vanek says that won't happen, doesn't he?"

"Yes, but scientists can be wrong like anyone else."

"He's not wrong."

"With all respect, Chu Chi, how can you know that?"

"Lately I have a gift. Did Vanek tell you it was an idea of mine that led to the successful virus?"

"I find it hard to listen to anything he says."

"Well, it was. The point is that lately things are revealed to me. I know it's time to leave. Jefferson will soon be all over the television. Then the government will get curious."

"This is Jefferson's doing?"

"We had leverage. Now we don't."

"Why don't we just kill him?"

Lone had asked himself the same question more than once since the stockyard disaster. Jefferson's home was only a few miles away, but what if they succeeded? The media would love the story of a prominent Montana citizen being murdered after complaining about Unitel. And what if they failed? It had already happened three times. Either way, attention would be drawn to the plant, and they'd have to leave anyway. Better to go now, reproduce the virus in Argentina, and come back later for Jefferson.

"Jefferson will still be here a year from now. We came to Montana to make a virus, and that's what we've done. I'll take no chance of losing it."

"You know best," Chang said, without conviction.

"Good. You will begin dismantling the plant today. Leave the plant's safety system intact until we remove the virus. Pay off all the

Russians but Vanek. He doesn't know it yet, but he's going with us. Be ready to leave within three days. I want to see Vanek now. I'll be outside, near the south side of the building."

A hint of puzzlement crossed Chang's face, but this time he just nodded. "Right away," he said, and turned toward the door.

WHEN VANEK CAME out the fire door, Lone was staring east at the miles of blowing grass and thinking how glad he'd be to leave Montana. It was Jefferson's land, and there was something in it that made Lone sick in the deepest part of himself.

"You vanted to see me?" Vanek said timidly.

He was even paler than usual and his hands were shaking. The man was scared to death.

"Dr. Vanek," he said, extending his hand. "Congratulations on your success."

Vanek looked surprised at this show of friendliness but not displeased. He smiled nervously and shook Lone's hand more vigorously than was necessary.

"Thank you," he said. "A large part of the credit is yours. That vas a really useful suggestion you gave us. Sometimes in science one needs the fresh viewpoint of a layman . . . "

Vanek was suddenly terrified at having called Lone a layman.

"Relax, Doctor. That's exactly what I am, which is why I would like to ask you a question that may seem stupid."

"Oh no, I'm sure it . . . "

"It probably is stupid, but I want an honest answer. I promise you there will be no penalty."

Vanek seemed to breathe a little easier. He even looked mildly interested.

"The question is this: Is it possible that certain people have . . . a chemical connection to each other?"

Vanek attempted to suppress a slight smile. "Are you referring to love, Mr. Lone?"

"Let me put it another way. If a person were cremated, could the ashes of that person contain a chemical that would bond with the cells of another person?"

Vanek ran a hand through his sparse hair and stared off into the distance. "This is not really my field," he mumbled.

"I'm not going to hold you to your answer."

"Vell, people do have distinctive glandular secretions called pheromones, and these pheromones do account for a large measure of sexual attraction, but if the person vere cremated . . . "

"His glands would be cremated, too, but would they still be chemically, ah . . . ?"

"Distinctive? I suppose it is possible that, although changed by heat, they vould still be chemically peculiar to the person. The equipment has not yet been invented that could test such a theory."

"Suppose for a minute it's true, and suppose someone who had known the person inhaled the ashes. Could these pheromones or some other chemical join to that person's nerve endings or cells?"

Vanek looked genuinely confused. "Vell, there are things vich do bond to neurons—dopamine, cocaine, endorphins. But as to vether they are still present in ash . . . "

"Suppose they were. Could they get inside a person's actual self, his body cells?"

"Vat you are describing is a virus, Mr. Lone."

"But is it possible?"

"Ve know it is possible for viruses, but a chemical compound vould need a vay to join with the host's DNA. That is highly unlikely."

"Isn't everything a chemical compound, Doctor?"

"Yes of course, but . . . "

"But what?"

"Nothing. Vat you say is vithin the bounds of theoretical imagination, but the compound vould have to contain bits of DNA that resembled the host's."

"Doesn't everything contain bits of DNA?"

"Yes, but . . . for a compound to act like a virus, it vould then be a virus."

"Then it's not impossible."

"As a . . . leap of faith—no, it is not impossible."

"A leap of faith, you say. Let me ask you a more practical question.

If a person had the ashes of someone who was cremated, could they be synthetically reproduced?"

Vanek was now sweating profusely. "I'm not sure I understand."

"I mean, could you reproduce the ashes of a particular person if you had some of those ashes to work with?"

"Ve could reproduce ash, but nothing of the particular person. To do that ve vould have to clone the person and then cremate him or her."

"And if you did that . . . "

"I don't know. It is only a concept, and unlikely ever to be tested."

Lone turned away and looked into the distant field of empty green. It swirled like rough water, patternless and shadowed by dead spots . . . so much empty space. There was a secret to it all, one that would protect him from the sickness he felt in Montana. He could feel it hiding behind the wide light of the plains.

"Refresh my memory, Doctor. What is immunity? How does the body protect itself against a virus?"

"Against ours there is no defense."

"I mean normally."

"Simply put, the body's cells are programmed to recognize the arrangement of surface proteins on a virus. Corresponding immune cells lock on to those proteins—capture them, as it vere."

"And what does a vaccine do?"

"There are some invaders the body doesn't recognize. A vaccine introduces those cells to the immune system in a dead form so that ven they encounter a live virus, they vill recognize it."

Lone stared up at the sky and repeated the words to himself.

"A dead form . . . recognize and destroy it . . . but it needs a dead form."

Then it came to him as brilliantly as his solution to the mutation problem. The DNA in Sylvie's ashes was bonding to his DNA. It was a vaccine against stupidity and depression. What he needed was a vaccine to protect him against the sickness he'd felt since encountering Jefferson in 1969.

Then another flash of genius shot through his brain with an intensity like pain. For over twenty years he'd been wondering how he'd kill Jefferson when the time came, and now he knew. He would burn him alive and his ashes would become a vaccine against everything he represented when he was alive. Jefferson would be a dead form of bad luck. It was so logical, so scientific, that it had to be right. It might be a year before he could act on it, but now he had the answer. In the meantime, he'd put Vanek to work on a synthetic form of Sylvie's ashes.

"So," said Vanek anxiously from behind him. "Is that all you vanted, Mr. Lone?"

Lone turned and smiled at him. "For now, Doctor. For now."

Vanek backed toward the door. Lone reached for the flask.

47

JEFFERSON lay in bed remembering his vision of the ancient tribes, knowing he was across the line into the land of Colonel Jack, whose picture was now on the night table.

He rolled over and looked at his father's hungry smile as it ate through the frosted Korean air. Two hundred thousand Chinese up in the hills, but there was no doubt in the Colonel's mind: He was where his history had put him, and he'd do what it told him to do—kill the enemy until there were no more to kill.

Jefferson got out of bed and carried the picture to the mirror over his dressing table. He looked down at the picture and then smiled into the mirror.

" 'Onward, Christian Soldiers,' " he said.

TWO HOURS LATER Jefferson yawed the Rover left at eighty miles an hour and roared under the wooden arch at the entrance to Harlow's property. The turn made the five-gallon gas can fall against his leg. He pushed it upright and readjusted the magnum in his belt.

He'd called Harlow before he left, just to make sure he'd be there. Said he wanted to talk, wanted to get sensible. Harlow agreed as quickly as a wolf invited to lunch with the three little pigs. He even offered to send Emmabelle into town for a few things so they could talk uninterrupted. That was good. Jefferson had always liked Emmabelle.

He rolled the Rover into the turnaround in front of Harlow's door and slid to a halt. Snatching the gas can and a handful of rags, he walked to the door and opened it without knocking. Harlow was rising from behind his desk when Jefferson kicked open the study door.

"It is I," he said, "John David Jefferson, and I've come for the Vandivier report."

Harlow's ruddy face went white as a used-up Popsicle. He lost his balance and sat back in his chair to keep from falling.

"Christ, Judd. You trying to give me a heart attack?"

Harlow's voice sounded faint when heard through the rush of blood pounding through Jefferson's ears. He put the gas can on the floor, pulled the magnum out of his belt, and walked to the front of the desk. When he got there, he swept the desk clean with a slash of his hand, leaned on it, and put the pistol's barrel against Harlow's forehead.

"You drunk or somethin'?" Harlow stammered.

"Give me the Vandivier report."

Harlow's lower jaw was shaking so hard he could barely speak. "What the hell are you talking about?"

Jefferson took the gun away from Harlow's head and rapped him sharply on the bridge of his nose. Blood streamed onto the front of his shirt and he tried to stand up, but Jefferson grabbed a handful of hair and pulled him back into his seat. Still holding on to Harlow's hair, he walked around the desk and looked down into the old man's watering eyes.

"Tell me, Harlow. What's the pleasure in killing young girls? Tell me."

Harlow's face flushed and sweat began to roll down his forehead. "You're crazy," he said, his eyes slithering to the side.

Jefferson smacked Harlow's mouth with the gun, splitting his lip and knocking out a tooth. "Do I have to ask you again?"

Harlow coughed and spat a wad of bloody phlegm onto the floor. Jefferson stepped away from the chair, and Harlow wiped his mouth with the back of his hand. He spoke while looking at the floor.

"All the getting of a lifetime, and then there's nothing left to get except a hole in the ground. Every one I put away is like she's going in my place."

Instinctively, Jefferson moved away from Harlow, wondering what you did with a thing like this. "How does Emmabelle stand for a corpse like you to touch her?"

Harlow's face collapsed into gray folds. "You got no proof," he said.

Still facing Harlow, Jefferson backed toward the can of gasoline. "You can bet Lone's got proof, and one day he'll use it. Now, give me that report."

"You're makin' a mistake."

Jefferson unscrewed the top of the gas can and began splashing the contents around the base of the room. Then he soaked the curtains and the furniture. Finally, he drenched the rags he'd brought with him, placed one in the center of the floor, and dropped a match on it.

Harlow made a croaking sound when the rag whumped into bright blue flames.

"What I'm going to do," Jefferson said, "is put another rag down where this one ends and light it. I'm going to do that until they reach the baseboards. When that happens, this whole room is going up, then the whole house."

He lit another rag and dropped it at the end of the first one, starting a trail toward the curtains.

"A fire will draw the ranch hands in here," Harlow said. "They'll call the law."

"Nah," said Jefferson, pointing the pistol at Harlow. "You'll just say you were careless, 'cause if you don't, I'll shoot you."

He lit another rag and dropped it. Harlow jumped out of his chair and came around the desk, flapping his arms and stepping on the rags, one of which stuck to the bottom of his shoe and caught his pant leg on fire.

"Oh goddamnit, Jesus Christ!" Harlow bellowed as he shucked the pants and kicked them away from him.

"Give me the report," Jefferson said, lighting another rag.

Harlow was standing on one leg to examine the burns on the other one. His face was turning the color of an eggplant.

"Put down the goddamn rag, you son of a bitch," he roared. "I'll give you the report! Put the rag down, and I'll give it to you."

Jefferson lit the rag and held it over the trail of gas. Harlow ran to the wall and pulled back an oak panel, revealing a safe. He dialed the numbers and threw a ring binder at Jefferson's feet.

"Fool," he said. "That information will hurt you, too."

Jefferson put the rag down by his foot and stamped it out. He thumbed through the binder and saw it was filled with formulas and graphs. Vandivier's résumé was appended in the back.

"Keep your eye on the news, Harlow. You can watch your deal with Tsendai going to hell."

"You won't get away with this."

Jefferson laughed at the sight of the old man threatening him while standing there with his blue-veined legs hanging out of baggy boxer shorts.

"You won't be around long enough to cause me any trouble," he said. "When Lone sees this report on TV, he'll think you double-crossed him."

Jefferson put the magnum in his belt and pointed his fingers at Harlow like a gun.

"Good-bye, Harlow."

JEFFERSON WHEELED THE Rover out of Harlow's drive in a spray of dust, catching sight of his smile in the mirror. Once and for all, he was Colonel Jack's boy.

"Fuck 'em," he said. "Fuck the whole Chinese army."

48

IT had been three days since Jefferson's attack at the stockyards, three extra days of life that Harlow Rourke didn't deserve. The old bastard had betrayed them. There was no other way Jefferson could have known where to look for the missing children. Somehow he'd persuaded Harlow to change sides, and for that, Harlow would die.

Lone took a nine-millimeter Beretta out of his desk drawer and worked the slide. He'd leave in an hour with Ling, pick up Chang at the plant, then take a van to Harlow's ranch. They'd drive him out in the wasteland somewhere and leave him there when it was done. Montana was good land for killing. He'd give it that.

Lone turned on the television and flipped through the channels until he got the Great Falls station. It took him a few seconds to realize what he was seeing, and when he did, he muttered a curse. It was the same reporter who had appeared with Jefferson. She was sitting at a desk holding a black ring binder and wearing a serious expression. She appeared to be savoring the importance of each word.

"This study by a respected physicist, the late James Vandivier, forecasts the melting of Montana's glaciers and a subsequent rise in the water table of the Rocky Mountain basin."

Lone turned up the sound and felt a pain start in his forehead. The woman frowned and made eye contact with the camera.

"An even more disturbing element of the study is its contention that mutant viruses are being formed in Montana's upper atmosphere. It claims that the ozone layer, which shields the earth from ever-present radiation, is becoming seriously depleted and that a resulting increase in radiation is mutating familiar viruses into new and potentially deadly strains. Viruses are . . . "

Not only had Harlow told Jefferson the location of the warehouse, he'd given him Vandivier's report. Lone switched off the television and slammed his fist onto the desk. He knew Vandivier's report would cause things to happen. Dead cattle were nothing. The ozone layer was old news. Viruses, however, were something the average idiot knew enough to be afraid of and the average TV executive knew enough to put on the air. Other stations would pick up the

264

story. Mothers would call, worried about their children. Montana would be this month's doomsday, and doomsday was good politics. There would soon be an investigation. It was the end—for the project and for Harlow Rourke.

Lone picked up the phone. "Ling, we're going to Montana."

He patted his pocket to feel Sylvie's ashes. Until Vanek came up with a synthetic, he was going to have to save them for special occasions. He'd have some in twenty-four hours, when he was on the plane to Argentina. He'd deal with Harlow, then go to the plant for the viruses. After that, he'd fly back to Vancouver and take the Learjet south. The office in Calgary could stay just like it was. Hahn wouldn't know where he'd gone until he had enough money and power to take over. He'd always wanted Sylvie with him when that happened, and now she would be inside his body inoculating him against loss. Science was the one true religion.

49

AFTER leaving Jefferson's house, Donnelly had decided to become a dog. Far Lightning had dropped him in Browning, where his car was parked behind a bingo hall. He'd walked back to the Indian museum, where he wandered into a field and looked up at the sky.

"'Night, girls," he said. "Daddy loves you."

He said it again three or four times, but there was no answer. Daddy was gone. Elaine was an attractive woman. Someone else was probably telling them stories by now. He wasn't Daddy anymore. He wasn't Donnelly anymore. Far Lightning liked him and Jefferson was grateful, but there was no love from anywhere, except maybe the dogs. They had saved his life.

They'd smiled at him, too. Maybe they thought he was one of them. Maybe he was. He was furry and smelly and naked and on his own in the wild just like they were. Suddenly he was seized with a desire to find them and be one of them. He'd never been able to understand humans anyway. Hadn't Elaine called him animal names on so many occasions? Pig; son of a bitch; dog.

Donnelly ran to the station wagon and drove out to the plains. Once there, he drove in aimless circles for days, whistling and growling and barking. When the dogs didn't answer, he left the car and wandered for two days and nights, drinking water from a canteen and eating roots.

On the third night, he trotted over a rise and saw them in the moonlight below. A stream ran through the low ground and the dogs had encircled a small antelope that had stopped to drink. The antelope was lunging to and fro looking for a way out of the circle of dogs. Each time it tried to break out, one of the dogs would run at it from the front and turn it back toward another dog. In this way, the dogs tightened the circle until one of them was able to dart in and bite down on a back leg. The antelope tried to kick at the dog, but when it did, another came in and seized a front leg. It went down, and a big dog was instantly at its throat. The whole thing couldn't have lasted more than five minutes.

Donnelly fell to his knees. In the blended faces of dog and antelope he thought he'd seen the face of the Almighty, and he wanted a closer look.

Moving in a slow crouch, he began to creep down the hill. At first, the dogs were too busy feeding to notice him, but when he was within thirty yards, one of them caught his scent and raised its massive head. It snarled softly but didn't come toward him.

Donnelly crept to within twenty yards, then ten. He could see the yellow gleam in the dogs' eyes. Antelope blood dripped black off their jaws and pooled in the hollow cavity that had once been the animal's belly. Its head was twisted upward, an expression of wonder in its eyes. Donnelly had seen that expression before somewhere. He inched closer, trying to remember where. Two of the dogs snarled, but he kept moving.

Soon he was only several feet away. He could smell them—a damp musk. It smelled like the beard on his own face. He could also smell the blood of the antelope, like copper and salt. He crept closer.

One by one, the dogs left the carcass and went to the stream to drink. As the last one moved away, it looked back at him and growled softly in its throat.

He crept toward the carcass and crouched over the antelope's face. It looked resigned and a little ashamed of being caught. Had he really seen the expression before? It seemed important to know. He looked away from the head to the chunks of meat still hanging from the animal's flanks. A black dew of blood congealed on their surfaces. He could see teeth marks in a big piece of meat attached to a rear leg.

He heard soft snarling from the stream. He felt the breeze blow past his ears. He heard crickets in the grass, a frog's croak from the water. He was alone on an ancient plain under moonlight a million years old.

His head shot forward, and he bit into the chunk of thigh meat, gnawing and shaking, tearing it loose and chewing. It was hard and tough and rich, tasting of iron and the strength of twenty-foot jumps. Blood flowed out the corners of his mouth and onto his beard. He swallowed and felt stronger.

He ate until the piece of meat was gone and then went to the stream, where he took up a position close to the dogs. He bent to the water and let its coolness take away the iron taste of blood. Then he sat back and smelled the moonlight.

The dogs began to move. He rose and started to move with them. In the distance, he could see an orange glow against the sky. The dogs were moving toward it, and he followed. When the dogs reached the top of the hill, they stopped and sat. Donnelly charged up the hill to a spot twenty yards to the left of them. When he got there, he saw they were looking down into a small valley and that the orange glow was caused by the parking lights of a brown van.

Two men were pulling another man out of the van's rear. He was a tall old man with flowing white hair. Donnelly recognized him from the day with the cowboys but didn't remember his name. His hands were tied behind him, and he stumbled as they pushed him away from the van. He regained his balance and turned to another man, who was getting out of the front passenger seat. He pointed a pistol at the old man while the two others got shovels and dug a shallow pit in the loose ground. The man with the pistol motioned the white-haired man to the edge of the pit, but he wouldn't go. The men with shovels grabbed him under his arms and dragged him there. The man with the pistol stuck it against the old man's face and fired. His white hair turned black in the moonlight, and he jerked backward into the pit. The men with shovels refilled the pit with dirt. Then they all got into the truck and drove away toward the mountains. The whole thing couldn't have taken more than ten minutes.

Donnelly felt like he was floating high above with the moon, a barren satellite with a fixed, rocky smile. Then the lead dog began to howl in an arching siren, which rose long and then fell back. A second dog did the same thing, then a third. Soon they were all howling in a modulating wail that broke the cool blue sky into sections, which fell into Donnelly's ears and went to his heart.

Tears began to stream down his cheeks, and he remembered when he'd seen the face of the dead antelope. He'd been in an art museum with Elaine and seen a painting of a dying Spanish saint. His face was an elongated antelope shape, and he was lying on the ground with his head in the lap of a merciful woman. The head was twisted up like the antelope's.

Donnelly threw back his head and began to howl with the dogs. He howled for the antelope and for the man in the pit. Most of all, he howled for himself, because he wasn't a dog after all. He was a man in need of a merciful woman to cradle his head. He kept howling until the tears stopped. The dogs had gone, along with his wife and his life. There was nothing left but the need for mercy.

Donnelly crabbed his way down the hill and began to run. He ran until a blade of morning appeared along the edge of the night and his legs collapsed under him. He crawled to the side of a cut-bank and rolled into a grassy depression.

"Mercy," he mumbled. "Mercy for the lost."

50

CELINE had ridden aimlessly for a week, then she spotted the little clump of cottonwoods by a stream. The high green oasis seemed to be calling to her, and she was supposed to be looking for something.

It wasn't until she was watering the horse in the stream that she noticed the balloons in the distance. There were three of them, and they were bobbing in slow circles but stayed in one spot. Someone had probably anchored them to the ground with lines she couldn't see.

The balloons were oddly beautiful against the deep azure sky. Back-lit by the sun, they were pale pink in the circling breezes and kissed against each other like pleasant memories.

Maybe this was the beginning of the answer Joseph had promised her. She smiled, and wondered what she would she have done if he'd asked her to stay. It was surprising how tempting the idea was, and how foolish. He'd called her a sister, and she supposed he was right. There was a connection between them closer than lovers and the realization left her free to follow his advice without fear.

Your power will come with your true name.

The time with Joseph had convinced her that there was no such thing as chance. There had to be a reason the balloons affected her so personally, but the threads of causation were thin. The harder you stared, the less visible they became. Somewhere in the tapestry of balloons and sky was her name, but finding it would be like finding the truth in an optical illusion.

She picked up Joseph's rattle and shook it. Would some antenna in his DNA pick up the sound? She looked up to watch the balloons weave like lovers in a dance. She shook the rattle to summon Joseph, but instead she was jolted backward by the sudden presence of Judd.

In a millisecond she saw his lean dark face and the black flash of his eyes. She could smell him and feel his dark curls. She heard his growling chuckle and felt the sweat drops from his brow, saw his white, even smile and his strangely delicate feet.

He was there and then he was gone, leaving the balloons still as painted stones. Just visible over the top of the rolling land was the top of a building. She sear`ched her memory and decided it might be Harlow's old fertilizer plant.

How strange that Judd should appear so vividly. During her time with Joseph, he had receded to a weightless mist. Now he'd exploded in her mind like a bomb and it had something to do with the balloons. She had to see them up close. Maybe they made sounds in the wind that spoke her true name. She decided to ride closer to the balloons, but not until she'd had a nap. Taking a blanket from her pack, she walked to a grassy spot in the shade of a cottonwood, rolled the blanket into a pillow, and closed her eyes.

IT WAS DAYLIGHT when Donnelly awoke and began moving again. A molten yellow sun circled slowly in an ink-blue sky. He was weak and dizzy, unsure whether he was awake or dreaming. Then he found himself high on a windy lake of grass from which the horizon appeared as a great circle. The ground led downhill to a rocky plain. Between him and the plain, he could see the tops of a few small trees showing over a bluff. Their leaves glinted like the green in Elaine's eyes. He began walking slowly toward the bluff. When he got close, he dropped onto his belly and crawled to the edge. What he saw made his heart beat so fast he thought he would pass out. There was a tethered horse, and a few yards away from the horse was perfection: an angel with long legs and a mane of auburn hair that captured the sun.

It was the woman from the Spanish painting—God's mercy on earth. Except for one thing. To her right, propped on a log, was a large rifle.

51

CELINE raised her head with a start and looked at her watch. It was five o'clock. She'd been asleep for an hour and a half. A profound uneasiness was lodged in her bones, left there by her vision of Judd.

The balloons were still waving in the deepening sky and there were over two hours of daylight remaining. She decided to ride over and see what kept them aloft.

DONNELLY LAY IN the grass above and knew he had to follow her. She was the beautiful woman in the Spanish painting, sent by God's mercy to make him human again. And he was human again. He knew it was true because he could see Elaine on their wedding day, looking up into his eyes and saying, "I feel so close to you, Joe. I've never felt this close to anything before."

She was so light and warm in her white lace dress that she seemed to melt right into his body when he held her.

Once, she'd believed in him. All the bitchiness was just her way of trying to fight off the Devil. She'd tried to be his angel, but he'd refused to believe. Now he did, but the only way he could show it was to be an angel himself. He'd be an angel to the beautiful Spanish woman. Somehow Elaine would know it and understand.

A thrill went through him when he knew it was possible to repent of his sins. The woman below would be his charge. He would watch over her and keep her from harm. He would follow her, but he had to stay hidden. If she saw him she might shoot, and to hurt your angel was to hurt yourself.

The woman was up on her horse and walking into the valley. Donnelly followed at a slow trot, trying to keep trees and rocks between them. He was weak and winded, but he had to keep up. There weren't enough angels to go around.

THE BALLOONS WERE a little farther away than Celine had imagined. By the time she got to them, it was nearly six-fifteen. She was on a rise of rocky ground looking down into a grassy plain. To her left she could see the dark blue building rising from a dome of gravel about a quarter mile away. In the distance to the left was

272

Glacier National Park, and to her right was the outer edge of Jefferson property.

She looked up at the balloons. They were directly overhead and anchored by steel winches. From underneath, she could see they were as large as weather balloons and a thousand feet in the air. Looking up the length of all that cable made her dizzy, so she dismounted and sat on a nearby rock.

From a distance, the balloons had been beautiful and evocative. Now, seeing the greasy cable to which they were attached, she found them oppressive. Instead of the singing sounds she had imagined there was a grating squawk as the cables tugged against the winches. Flakes of rust fell onto the grass, and every so often one of the cables would snap taut with a gunshot crack.

The ice on top of the Rockies was turning a rusty red as it was touched by the falling sun. The sky was going black at the edges and blending with shadow stains spreading down the mountainsides. Cold rushes blew through the warm air like currents through water. One of them crossed Celine's shoulder. She shivered and looked at her watch—6:45, time to head back to the campsite. She was about to rise when she heard the voice.

"Stand please, Mrs. Jefferson, but don't run."

Celine's head snapped left and she saw a man in a suit standing above her. He was a stocky Asian man, and he was smiling.

"My name is Wu," he said. "You probably don't remember me, but we met at Lake McDonald."

Celine took one step toward the gun on her saddle, but the man's voice snapped like one of the cables.

"Another step and you die."

Celine stopped and looked back. He was still smiling, but his arm was extended and he was pointing a large black pistol. With a nauseous emptiness, she turned toward him.

"So very glad to see you again," he said.

THERE WAS NO cover between Donnelly and the square building, but it was now almost dark and the man with the gun had to drive his jeep around a perimeter road. Donnelly struck out toward the building in a straight line and knew he would get there first.

273

When he saw the man with the gun, Donnelly almost jumped down from his perch in the rocks above, but it was too far. Instead, he closed his eyes and willed the man to take her to the building rather than shoot her.

He loped to the side of the square steel structure and dropped to the ground. The lights of the jeep circled left around the building and then up to the front door. Donnelly crawled to the corner and saw the man take the woman by the arm and pull her from the jeep. The he pointed toward the door with his pistol, and the two of them went inside.

He was her angel and hell was inside the building. He would follow the beautiful woman there and watch over her until God's other angels came for her.

He stood and saw a door at the far end of the wall. Pressing himself close to the corrugated metal, he sidled to the door and pulled gently on its small handle. It swung open without resistance.

He stepped inside the door and found himself at the base of a set of metal stairs. He went up the stairs and found himself in a long hallway. To his left was an elevator across from a set of double doors. In five quick steps he was down the hall and next to the doors. By the elevator was a stairwell, and he could hear voices from the second floor. He needed a quiet place where he could call down his powers of protection.

Gently, he opened the door to his left. Inside was a large sunken room lit only by red EXIT signs. A metal walkway ran around the perimeter of the room, and there were two sets of stairs leading down to the floor. Donnelly stepped through the door onto the walkway. As his eyes adjusted to the dim light, he could see that the room below consisted of an open square in the middle, computer stations on the sides, and glass panels on each end. Behind the glass panels were rows of worktables. In front of each panel was a bank of joysticks, which controlled a set of robotic arms. There were large wooden crates scattered around the room, as if someone were going to pack up the computer modules. Across the room in a corner was a large square cabinet, which looked like it was made for the central processing unit. The cabinet would be the perfect place to gather his energy.

Donnelly went around the walkway and down the stairs into the room. The floor was wood parquet. He crossed to the large cabinet, knelt, and crawled inside. It was just high enough for him to sit with his knees drawn comfortably up to his chin. The door swung out onto the central floor, so he reached out and pulled it closed. There was a locking hinge on the inside that could be opened simply by pushing on it.

It was a refuge at the bottom of hell—quiet, righteous, and lonely, like Elaine's space when she was married to him. She was released from him now, and if he could protect the redheaded woman, he would be released too. He had heard her voice from up the stairwell. She sounded frightened, but she was alive. He closed his eyes and began to cover the room with protection.

52

LONE paced Chang's office and told himself for the thousandth time that he was doing the right thing. The two containers of virus waiting downstairs were the important thing. Jefferson would still be here a year from now—no need to kill him until the virus was sold. But all those thoughts were at war with the idea of Jefferson as a pile of ashes.

Sure there was time to come back, but the plane could crash on the way to Argentina or Jefferson could die in a car wreck. What good was a vaccine if you couldn't get it when you needed it? And when would he need it more than now?

Lone sank heavily into Chang's chair, admitting something to himself he wouldn't admit to anyone else: He was afraid to leave without the protection of Jefferson's ashes. Sylvie's essence was for pleasure, but Jefferson's would be for war. Without those ashes, he'd still be prey to the bad luck that had sucked his blood since 1969.

Lone felt dizzy and knew his throat was on the verge of closing. He was heading shakily for the scotch bottle when the door swung open and Wu pushed a woman into the room.

She had red hair, a slim figure, and a beautiful face, the same as in her photographs. Ten seconds passed before he could get his mouth to say her name.

"Mrs. Jefferson?"

She was calmer than he would have expected, staring at him with fixed gray eyes. He got up and circled her, checking the long legs and firm rear. She was in her forties and had small breasts—not what the Arabs liked but what the English and the Germans did. Yes, the Germans. But selling her would be like selling a genie who could grant your number one wish.

"My name is C. K. Lone," he said. "I know your husband."

"People know where I am."

"Wu, how did you find her?"

"When I went out to get the balloons, she was sitting under them."

"Alone?"

"Yes."

276

"People are looking for me," she said.

"If there is one thing I've noticed about Montana, it's the size. I doubt if anyone ever finds anything unless they know where to look."

"I told them where I was going."

"But you weren't going here, were you?"

"My husband knows you own this place."

"Fine. Let's tell him you're here."

Celine realized what Lone intended to do and tried desperately to think of a way to stop him. "He won't come. We're getting divorced," she said.

"He would come even for a total stranger."

"He hates me for leaving him."

"He'll come even if he does, especially if he does."

Celine fought back tears of frustration. The man knew Judd, all right. "He'll bring the law."

Lone looked into the woman's face and smiled, as real a smile as he could remember giving anyone. He almost liked her. She was a gift, finally, after the swill of Kowloon and Hahn's sweaty shows and his puke-faced customers and Sylvie and the wide black box of Montana, after his whole life since Father was dragged away by the Communists with his stupid glasses hanging from his stupid ears. A gift.

There would be no law, because Jefferson knew what would happen if he brought the police: The woman would die on the roof, where they could all watch, and she'd die the triad way—by a myriad of knives, with ritual cuts across all the main muscle groups, and then the meat cleaver. He'd hook up a loudspeaker so they could hear her scream, and the hell with the consequences. Jefferson would come alone.

"Your husband knows what will happen to you if he calls the police."

Other women would be wetting their pants, but not this one. This one was staring at him with a look of control in her eyes, the same way Sylvie had stared on the morning she died.

"Mrs. Jefferson, things will happen when your husband gets here, but until then I will treat you well."

She stared past him out the window.

"Wu, have someone lock all the doors, especially the fire door on the south wall. No one goes out or comes in unless I say so. But wait here while Mrs. Jefferson and I make a phone call."

THE GAME ROOM of Jefferson's house contained the "Space Invaders" machine, an eight-foot pool table, several leather sofas, and a four-foot television. A set of sliders offered a look at the pool and the Rockies beyond. Jefferson sat on a sofa watching the evening news. WGFL in Billings had just done a follow-up piece on the Vandivier report in which they asked for a response from the EPA. It wouldn't be too long before the networks started asking for the same thing.

Jefferson rose from the couch, missed a three rail bank shot at the pool table, and walked outside to look at the mountain reflections in the pool. The sun was down and the blue water was turning jagged and dark with shadows. It was the time of day when Celine used to come through the door carrying two cups of coffee. She'd hand him a cup, then they'd look from the pool to the mountains and smile at each other like two kids playing a trick on the rest of the world. He stood with head bowed, trying to remember the last time they'd done that. When the phone rang, it made him jump.

"Jefferson," said the voice. "I'm calling because E-mail is too indirect for this situation."

The hair rose on Jefferson's arms and neck. "What situation is that?"

"You know who you're speaking to?"

"The world's biggest piece of shit?"

Lone laughed, and Jefferson heard a small clicking on the line.

"The situation is this. I'm at the Unitel plant. Your wife is here with me. Either you come, or she'll wish you had."

Jefferson sank to the floor and leaned against the side of a sofa. "Bullshit," he said, knowing he was wrong.

"Here, you can speak to her."

"Judd?"

"Celine, are you all right?"

"Yes. I'm sorry, Judd. I rode too close to the plant."

"Celine, I . . . "

"Get the police, Judd. Don't pay any attention to what he . . . "

Her voice faded away and was replaced by Lone's. "You know what will happen if you bring the police."

There was a feeling in Jefferson's stomach like the pull of deep water. "If you kill her, you do it without me there. Then I come for you."

"I'll do it the triad way—a myriad of knives."

"But it's me you want."

"Make me a proposition."

Lone would break any deal if he could. Celine had to get away from the plant in a way that would prevent Lone's men from following. "Okay, here it is. I ride in on a horse. I stop on the southern edge of plant property, the side with the trees and high ground. Celine walks out of the plant alone. She takes the horse and leaves. Then you've got me on foot."

"I've seen western movies, Jefferson. Two people can ride one horse."

"All right, I leave the horse at the edge of the trees and walk toward her. We pass. She gets on the horse and rides into the trees. You can't follow her with a jeep, but I'm close enough that you drive to me before I can run to the woods. Same thing if we both run."

Lone could put a man with a rifle on the roof of the plant to shoot both of them, but they'd be moving targets at two hundred yards. Jefferson doubted any of Lone's goons were that good. There was a long pause while Lone thought it over.

"Agreed," he said. "But before she comes out, my men will search the property for cops."

"I'll make my own search sometime during the night, and I'll have a man covering me. If anyone moves before my wife is on her horse, I'll make a fight out of it. You may get both of us, or you may get neither." He would make a fight out of it no matter what he said, but he'd be alone and in the open. It was the best possible deal.

"I've been waiting twenty-five years, Jefferson. Nothing will happen before your wife is on her horse."

Lone would try for Celine, but once she was on a horse no Hong Kong city boys would catch her. "Okay, when do you want to make the switch?"

"Tomorrow morning at seven."

Jefferson started to turn off the phone, but listened for a second and heard the little click again, as if someone were hanging up an extension phone.

"Hello," he said. "Somebody there?"

There was no answer, and he had much bigger things to think about. Talking to Lone had been like negotiating a deal for cattle, but there was no way he was going peacefully to the slaughterhouse. He'd take the magnum with him, and after Celine was on the horse, he'd shoot whoever came for him. Lone would send more jeeps and the thing would turn into a firefight. If he went down, it would be quick. Maybe he'd even make it, but he'd need a man to make sure Celine got away. Jefferson had another drink and dialed Far Lightning's number.

"I don't like it," Far Lightning said when he called. "You're going to be out in the open with nothing but a pistol."

"It's a big pistol."

"I can get some other men. We'll put 'em up in the rocks with rifles."

"He's going to check things out first. He sees anything wrong, the deal's off and he kills Celine. Do you hear what I'm saying, Joseph? He kills Celine."

"There's got to be another way."

"Goddamnit, she didn't ask for this. Now, do you love her or not?"

Jefferson hadn't meant to say it, but now that he had it was okay. Things would move faster if the cards were on the table. "You don't have to answer that. Just be there at five so we can get you into place before the sun comes up. You're good enough that they won't spot you."

"I know others just as good."

"If you won't do it my way, I'll do it alone."

Silence again.

"All right, Judd. Your way."

"Joseph?"

"Yeah?"

"You hear anything funny on your end of the line?"

"Funny?"

"I keep hearing a noise, like someone else hanging up."

"I don't hear anything."

Jefferson stared at the phone again, then turned it off and tossed it away. He went into his study and looked at pictures of Celine and the kids. Then, at two, he lay down and tried to sleep. He even dozed off a few times, only to awaken in a pool of sweat when he saw the bullet coming at him.

53

JEFFERSON rode Jack and led a bay named Lance. The bay was strong enough to carry two people but not as temperamental as Jack. When he was a half mile away, he tied Jack to a tree and rode Lance the rest of the way. It was 5:15 when he nosed through the trees to the south of the plant. He tied Lance to a limb and walked to where the land fell away over a stretch of rocks, then broke into a field of scrub grass. The distance to the plant was about five hundred yards—250 until he met Celine, a two- or three-minute wait until she reached the trees and then . . . he'd been in fights before. He turned and walked back into the forest.

As he made his way through a grove of spruce, a shadow rose from the ground and spread its arms.

"You were within six feet and never saw me," said Far Lightning.

He had pine boughs stuck in his clothes, so he was invisible when he lay in the shallow depression he'd made.

"That's good," Jefferson answered distractedly. "But make sure you're lying down when the sun comes up. They'll have binoculars on the roof, and they'll send jeeps around the perimeter."

"You should have let me bring the others."

"She's only got one chance. There's no way I could live with myself if I blew it."

"I know."

"I know you know."

The two of them looked at each other through the morning's early gray, aware of what they were saying.

"Listen," said Jefferson. "You're here for just one reason—to get on the damn horse with her and get the hell out of here."

Far Lightning nodded.

"Let me hear you say it."

"I'll get her out, Judd."

"No matter what else happens."

"Right."

"And after that . . . if things don't . . . "

"Shut up."

"If things go bad, you make sure she's all right."

"You don't have to say it, goddamnit. And don't be so sure about what you think you know."

The sun was running red along the eastern ground when Far Lightning stalked back to his hiding place and lay down. Three jeeps pulled away from the building and began to cruise the perimeter. Jefferson walked back into the trees, pulled the magnum from the saddlebags, and stuck it in a holster at the small of his back. Then he took out a palm-sized 25-caliber Beretta and put it in a leg holster on the inside of his left calf. It didn't have much range, but it could be lethal within thirty feet. He cinched the holster tight around his calf and knelt down in the pines.

The jeeps made a slow circle of the plant property, moving in opposite directions while shining their searchlights through the trees, rolling slowly, with the drivers and riders talking Chinese into their radios. Then they drove back to the plant and went inside.

It was six o'clock. An hour to wait. An hour to think about his life with Celine and how much pleasure she'd brought him. Then he remembered that if she'd married someone else, she wouldn't be in the blue building with C. K. Lone.

His stomach knotted when he thought of what was likely to happen within the next hour. He began to sweat, and his mind searched again for another way, but this was what life had come to. All the thinking in the world couldn't alter choices already made. He edged over to Far Lightning's hiding place and tapped him on the shoulder.

"Listen," he said. "I know you're doing this for Celine, but I want you to know I appreciate it."

Far Lightning stared up at him. "I'm doing this for all of us," he said. Then he chambered a round into his scoped deer rifle and looked toward the plant. Conversation over.

A side door opened and two figures emerged—a man and a woman. Jefferson's heart clutched when he saw the morning sun turn her red hair to gold. He tapped Far Lightning on the shoulder. "I see them," he said.

Jefferson fingered the three speed loaders hooked to his belt and stood up. "See you later," he said.

"Absolutely."

Jefferson stepped out into the sunlight. They walked toward each other slowly, as if in a dream. His eyes darted left and right, looking for any sign that Lone would break the agreement, but as she came closer, he could look away no more and lost himself in the unconscious grace of her walk. He remembered how easily that walk had carried two babies. He remembered how she looked with the sun in her hair as her head lay on his pillow. He moved in time with the sway of her arms and remembered how automatic it had been to catch one of her hands and hold it.

When he was within sight of her face, he locked on to her eyes and guided her to him. Then she was there in front of him, lean, tan, smelling of wild grass, sugar-sweat. Her eyes went wide, and she leaned her forehead against his shoulder.

He plunged both hands deep into her hair and cradled the back of her head. "Did they hurt you?"

"No."

He pushed her away far enough to look into her eyes. "Did they tell you how this is supposed to work?"

"You're not going in there, Judd." A current of wild panic ran close to the surface of her voice.

"No, of course not. But we have to make it look good. Far Lightning is in the trees. You keep walking, and I stand here until you're safe."

"You can't go in there." She grasped the front of his shirt as if to drag him with her.

"I'm not. But those jeeps would get to us before we could make the woods. You have to keep walking."

"Then what?"

"Get on the horse with Far Lightning. When you're gone, I run for the trees. Jack's in there."

Celine looked past him to the forest and then back at the building. "It's too far, Judd."

"I've done this kind of thing before."

"A long time ago."

"Don't argue with me, damnit," he said. "This is the only way. Now, start walking toward the trees and don't stop."

"Judd, I can't . . . "

"Don't screw this up, Celine!" he shouted. "Think of the kids, and get the hell out of here." He turned her toward the trees and pushed her. "Think of the kids, damnit!"

She stumbled, and he thought she was going to fall, but then she started walking—slowly at first, then faster.

As Celine moved away, he turned sideways and crouched, one eye on her and the other on the side of the building. When she was fifty yards from the trees, a jeep began to move slowly toward him.

"Hurry up, Celine," he said, even though she was too far away to hear.

She was still climbing the rocky slope as the jeep coasted to a stop in front of him.

One man driving, just like Lone had promised. He was young, with the greasy forelock and gangster mustache all the Hong Kong punks liked to wear. The top was down on the jeep, and Jefferson could see the Mac-10 machine pistol in his left hand. A cigarette dangled from the corner of his mouth and some of the smoke got in his eye, causing him to squint and turn his head. Jefferson yanked out the magnum and shot him twice through the chest. The kid's gun flew out of the jeep in an explosion of blood and bone.

Jefferson leapt into the car on the passenger side, tossed the body, and slid behind the wheel. He popped the clutch and the jeep bolted toward the trees, but seconds later two men popped up in front of him and began spraying automatic-weapons fire. Jefferson ducked his head and wheeled right as bullets clanked off the rear of the jeep. He floored it parallel to the woods, intending to cut left, but two more men appeared and started raking him broadside. He cut back toward the plant, but there were three more jeeps fanning out toward him, and then he felt the back tires blow as automatic fire slammed into them from the rear. The jeep began fishtailing as its flattened tires deflated and the rims dug into soft ground. He whipped the nose back toward the trees and floored it, running straight through them, his head low. Then the left front tire caught a slug and blew, dropping the fender into the ground and rolling the jeep over like a falling horse.

Jefferson clutched the magnum and jumped, hitting the ground and rolling, running toward the men in front of him, screaming and firing and dropping the closest him. His machine pistol clanked to the ground only a few yards away.

Jefferson dropped the empty magnum and zigzagged toward the machine pistol. He took two steps before something hot and hard knocked his legs out from under him and he fell, rolling toward the gun, getting to his knees, making it to his feet, and managing three halting steps before falling again and lying there as footsteps and Chinese chatter crackled through the dusty air.

Goddamn! Men hidden in holes, just like in Nam. Why didn't I remember that?

CELINE CLAMBERED OVER the rocks and up onto the roan. Then she saw Joseph rise from the ground with a rifle in his hand. He was motioning her forward when two shots sounded. He dropped to one knee, aiming the rifle into the valley below. She turned and almost fell out of the saddle when she saw Judd hop into the jeep and begin driving.

Delirious joy froze her in place as she saw him coming toward her, but then six small figures rose from the ground and began firing. Judd veered toward the building, but a pack of jeeps was closing out of its shadows.

Joseph was running toward the edge of the trees, kneeling and firing, but it wasn't enough. Steel sparks raked the sides of the jeep as it reversed course and came straight at her, wobbling pitifully on wounded tires until it nosed over and threw Judd into the air.

The small figure arched into a freeze-frame tumble. Nothing else existed but the slow-motion spin of Judd through the air and onto the ground, slower still as he lifted himself and moved toward the men in front of him, stop-time slow as his legs waved free in a spray of red and he fell to the ground, rose in still pictures and walked one step, halting and stiff, another step, arms-out innocence, toddling for childlike balance, lame and bleeding and reaching out for her. Then she knew. He was the child in the vision pit who'd saved her with a smile. Judd was her vision, and Jefferson was her true name. She'd taken it once, and now she took it again.

· · ·

FAR LIGHTNING WAS trying to get his scope on the men to the front of the jeep so Judd could get through. He dropped one of them, but then the jeep nosed over and rolled. Nothing to do now but what he'd promised.

"Celine," he shouted. "This way."

Once he was on the horse with her, they'd head through the trees, where the jeeps couldn't follow, and then back to the shack.

"Come on," he screamed, but she wasn't listening.

Almost imperceptibly, Celine was turning the horse's head toward the valley below. Far Lightning sprang out of his shooting crouch and ran toward her.

"No, Celine. No, goddamnit! There's nothing you can do."

She turned her head and looked at him with dazed eyes. He was only a few steps away. If he could just grab the reins . . . then he was there and had the horse in hand, but she was backing the animal away, kicking at its flanks and whipping its head back and forth until it was wild-eyed and frothy. He was pulled over the open ground but held on.

"Let go," she yelled. "I'm going down there."

"No!"

"Goddamnit, let go."

"I'm getting you out of here."

"No . . . the boy in the vision was him," she said. "I saw him again just now."

Far Lightning tightened his grip on the reins. "I promised him," he said.

"My true name is Jefferson. I promised him first. Now, let me go or, I swear—one day I'll kill you."

"What can you do?" he asked lamely.

"Be there."

Did he believe or not? He let go of the reins, and she kicked the horse down into the valley.

Far Lightning watched helplessly as the men below lifted Judd into the back of a jeep and pushed Celine into another. He knew Judd would hate him for letting her go, but she was a free person and knew her true name. You either believed or you didn't.

He wasn't giving up, though. Lone was a man who had waited a quarter century to lay hands on his enemy. You didn't just kill someone that important and go on with the day's business. Lone would take time to gloat before he killed them.

Far Lightning didn't want to imagine what form Lone's gloating might take. Instead, he had to concentrate on getting into the building with a weapon. The first thing was to get across the open valley without being seen.

He began working his way through the trees to his left, trying to get a view of the building's rear, knowing he had to get in and that Lone would kill both Celine and Judd if the police showed. He was stepping fast down the ridge toward the back of the building when he passed a small gully and saw a movement to his left. He whirled and saw a man rise up out of the gully. He was dark-haired and medium-tall, wearing brown jeans and a matching hat.

"Hold it a minute," the man said, raising a pistol. "I ain't nobody you want to shoot."

It was the Italian, Gionfredo. Far Lightning had seen him a few times in the Buffalo Wallow.

"We got here just at the end," he said. "Couldn't do nothing."

"We?"

"I told Jefferson I could get help outta New York, but he turned me down. I had to get a man to tap his phone so I'd know what was going on. Me and my men came straight from the airport."

"Your men?"

"Professionals. Four of 'em."

"We got to get into the building."

Gionfredo lowered the pistol and sat down. "I think I got that covered, but we gotta wait for the van to get here from Billings."

"What van?"

"The EPA van."

288

54

LONE'S nerves were electric with the heat of vindication. His theory was absolutely true: Sylvie's ashes had bonded to his cells and changed the way the world treated him. How else could this have happened? Not only did he have Jefferson, he had the woman. No special privileges now for saving children, no last-minute rescue for either of them. Jefferson was now just one more bag of guts, and so was his wife.

They pushed the woman into the room first, then Jefferson, who slid to a sitting position against the wall. His left leg was clearly broken, bone sticking out near the knee. The right calf was also seeping blood, but the bullets appeared to have gone through without contacting bone.

Lone knew he should say something, but what he was seeing left his throat muscles paralyzed. Jefferson was staring up at him with an immense pain in his eyes, a pain that came from somewhere deeper than his bones. He was wondering what he'd done to bring him here. Lone leaned over and took a good look at the man who would soon be a vaccine against himself.

Jefferson's jaw was hard as the side of a safe. He had a full head of graying hair, big shoulders, and black eyes like bullets at night.

"Jefferson," Lone said. "It's good to see you again, and I mean that."

JEFFERSON WAS TRYING hard not to vomit. Right now he hated Far Lightning worse than Lone. The son of a bitch had promised, promised twice.

CELINE BEGAN TO shake, but then a trick came to her. She curled her mind inward and looked for the moment she'd experienced with Judd in the vision pit, both of them reaching for something that wouldn't come until they were grown.

"I'm told you came back voluntarily," Lone said to her.

"That's right."

"Why?"

"I had to."

"Why?"

"You wouldn't understand."

"If I do, it might affect what happens here today."

"A vision," she blurted. "It was a vision."

While she was talking, Celine sneaked a look at Judd, to remind him that Joseph was somewhere outside. If they gave him time, enough he'd find a way in.

JEFFERSON SAW THE little eyebrow hook Celine always gave him at parties when she wanted to speak privately. Then he remembered. Far Lightning was still outside, and Joseph was the most stubborn man he knew. They had to give him time.

LONE SAW A look pass between Jefferson and his wife, but was more interested in other things. "Tell me your vision," he said to the woman.

Celine knew she needed time, anything for some time. "I saw my husband as a small child, and me thinking of him when I was a girl, like we knew each other before we met."

"Yes, like the cells of your body knew the cells of his."

The woman looked shocked that he would know.

"I knew a woman in that way once," he told her. "Now, thanks to your husband, I know her that way again."

JEFFERSON DECIDED THEIR best hope was to keep Lone talking. "Her name was Sylvie, and he burned her alive," he said. "I was there that day and kept the ashes to remind him of it."

CELINE STRUGGLED TO comprehend what Judd was saying. It was impossible that he could have kept a woman's ashes for twenty-five years without telling her. He nodded imperceptibly as he spoke, telling her to believe him.

LONE SMILED WHEN he remembered the letter that came with the ashes. "To remind me that wherever she is, she must hate me. But she doesn't hate me, Jefferson. She loves me now more than ever. She's my vaccine against bad luck."

Lone quit speaking and stared into space, stunned again by the reality of his own words. "I think it's time we moved downstairs," he said. "This room is a little too flammable."

TWO MEN LIFTED Jefferson to his feet and began dragging him toward the door. The pain in his mangled left leg went off like a bomb, and he could feel the pieces of broken bone grating against something hard. The feeling made him retch until he remembered what it was: the little Beretta in the leg holster. They hadn't searched his pants leg because it was such a mess. The gun might be a mess too, but if he got the chance, everyone was going to find out.

55

DONNELLY thought maybe he had died. Then he moved his head and saw light through an empty lock hole in the cabinet. He looked down into the darkness and saw his legs drawn up to a sitting position and his arms resting on his knees. He moved his hands experimentally and wiggled his toes. Then he heard a voice in the room and put his eye to the hole.

The Spanish woman from the painting was sitting in the middle of the room across from a big man who had blood coming from his leg. Four men were standing over them with pistols. A fifth man with a burr haircut was sitting close to them in an office chair with wheels. Something was going to happen. Heaven was close, and so was hell.

"NOW THEN," LONE said to Jefferson. "First, let me say that you were right about this plant. What we've done here is manufacture an airborne rabies virus that will kill an army within minutes. It's going to make me head of all the triads when we move to the United States, but that isn't your concern, because you won't be here. What should concern you are Sylvie's ashes. They have joined to my body's cells. They're a vaccine against age and depression. I feel better than I have in years. But what I need now is a vaccine against people like you. Do you know that a vaccine is just a dead form of the disease? But I don't want to bore you with science. The point is this: I'm going to reduce you to a dead form of the disease. I'm going to burn you and then inhale your ashes just like I've been inhaling Sylvie's. You're going to be a vaccine against people like you."

JEFFERSON LOOKED INTO Lone's eyes and saw the glassy conviction of the truly crazy. Pictures flashed through his mind of monks burning themselves in Vietnam, sitting placidly in the flames as their skin turned black and crisp. But he was no monk. He wouldn't be able to do it that way. He'd scream and cry in agony until his face melted and he could scream no more. He'd die broken and humiliated, with Lone laughing at him. The thought was worse by far than the thought of death, and he racked his brain for a trade—some way to die with his soul intact. Then he thought of the little Beretta strapped to his shattered calf. There might be a way to bargain—for his death and Celine's life.

"What about my wife?"

"I haven't decided what I'll do with her."

"Jesus, my leg," said Jefferson, reaching for his left calf.

AT FIRST CELINE was too stunned to accept what she was hearing. Then it came home with a rush that made her dizzy. She was sitting in a room with a man who fully intended to burn Judd alive . . . because of some ashes . . . ashes that, as far as she knew, didn't even exist. It was insane, but it was going to happen, and she was going to have to watch.

"WU," SAID LONE. "Go downstairs to the emergency generators and bring me a can of gasoline. Three liters should be enough to do the job without burning down the building."

JEFFERSON COULD SEE Lone was in a hurry, and there was no sign of Far Lightning. This was going to be the last day of his life. *Accept it. If you accept it, you can dictate the terms. You can still get Celine out.*

Jefferson groaned as a pain shot through his left leg. He massaged the thigh and then reached gingerly to his calf, ran a hand experimentally under the pants leg, feeling a shard of bone and then the smooth grip of the little Beretta, intact and undamaged.

DONNELLY COULD FEEL his internal organs quivering with excitement. Elaine would know it was all right that she'd once felt close to him. All he had to do was protect the redheaded woman. But he didn't know how. *Tell me*, he said to the darkness inside the cabinet.

LONE SAW THE PAIN on Jefferson's face as he felt his shattered leg.

"Don't worry," he said. "In a few minutes you won't even notice that."

"Notice this, motherfucker," Jefferson said as he leveled the Beretta at Lone's head. "Any of your men moves a muscle and you're dead."

THE GUN WAS small, but it was less than ten feet away. Lone didn't want to gamble his men's speed against Jefferson's.

"No one move," he said. "Jefferson, you know this is a losing proposition. If you shoot me, my men will kill both of you."

"What if I don't shoot you?"

"Then we have a stalemate—until you pass out from blood loss or fall asleep."

"I'll shoot you before then. You can count on it."

"It would take a head shot to kill me with that little thing, and you would only have a split second."

"Want to bet I can't do it?"

"You're going to die either way."

"I know that."

"Then what . . . Ah, your wife. Of course. One last act of self-righteous bullshit before you die."

"Think it over," said Jefferson.

"I don't have to think it over. I don't really care about her. Let's hear your proposition."

"Let her leave. When she's gone, I give you the gun."

"Once she's gone, you'll shoot me."

Jefferson hadn't thought that far ahead, but Lone was right. Once Celine was out the door and on her horse, he would shoot. And then he would die when Lone's men shot him. Lone wasn't going to let it happen that way. He was crazy, not stupid. Jesus, just a little time— a half hour, maybe. He didn't want to burn. God, he didn't want to turn into a screaming pile of ashes just because Lone believed that a drunken old woman was Sylvie.

Jesus, that's it. Tell him the truth about the ashes. But it won't work. Believing it's her makes him feel lucky. He's not going to let his worst enemy rob him of that. But maybe Celine could knock a hole in him, get him arguing about it. You've got to tell her. Somehow you've got to tell her what to do.

"Okay, how about this," Jefferson said. "My wife walks toward the door, slowly. You roll your chair away from me at the same speed she's moving. By the time she gets to the door, you'll be forty feet away. I could still shoot you, but it would have to be a damn good shot, and you've got Sylvie's ashes to help you. You said the ashes made you lucky, didn't you? You said Sylvie's ashes were in your cells and she loved you more than ever. I've got to shoot you in the head from forty feet with a little pop gun, and you got Sylvie's ashes down in your cells. You willing to trust her? You willing to trust that the ashes love you? Test her love. Make the bet. Sylvie's ashes against my skill. What do you say?"

Jefferson was talking to Lone, but he was looking with all his might at Celine, pulling at her with all the intimacy of twenty-five years in the same bed.

CELINE WAS SO tense she was choking on the clenched muscles of her neck. There was nothing she could do but pray for the medicine to come to her like Joseph had said it would. It had been easy to believe that when she was with him, but now she was in here, watching the man she'd slept with for a quarter century negotiate the end of his life. She looked at him and saw a light in his eyes, liquid black, shaded water, pulling her in, the same whirlpool as when he was over her and in her, one big arm underneath her back while he talked to her with his body, rocking her and lifting her to him, urgent, violent, things in his mind he couldn't say, the same as now, spewing words at Lone but talking to her, Sylvie and ashes . . . ashes . . . Sylvie's ashes. God, it was a lie! There were no ashes. She'd have known. Judd sent some ashes, but he didn't have them lying around for twenty-five years. He was lying, talking about ashes but looking at her with the black fire in his eyes like when he wanted to make love or fight. That was it. He wanted to fight. Fighting took time, and he wanted to fight.

"Bullshit," she blurted.

Both men stopped talking and looked at her as if she were speaking a foreign language.

"My husband is bullshitting you to get me out of here, but I'm not leaving him."

"Bullshitting me how?" asked Lone.

"Those ashes aren't whose you think they are."

"Shut up and get out of here, Celine," Judd growled.

"I'm not letting him burn you up over some phony ashes."

"What makes you say they're phony, Mrs. Jefferson?"

Lone was trying to sound casual, but his voice was a little too tight.

"You think he had a woman's ashes lying around the house for twenty-five years and I didn't know about it? I'd have known. He got some ashes somewhere and sent them to you."

"I had them tested," said Lone. "They are the ashes of a human female."

That was undoubtedly true, and Judd certainly hadn't killed anyone to get them, so the person was already dead . . . and Judd had bankrolled Harold Thorsen's campaign for county coroner.

"Shut up and take the deal," Judd shouted at her. "Get out of here."

He was staring at her with the hot hard look, and just the slightest blink of one of his eyes to tell her he was lying.

"The county coroner owes Judd money," she said to Lone. "Obviously he got an unclaimed body and cremated it."

"She thinks she can protect me if she stays here," Judd shouted as he looked down the barrel of the small automatic. "Get her out of here, and let's get on with this."

LONE THOUGHT JEFFERSON was probably right. His wife was trying to make the ashes seem unimportant to save her husband from being burned. But if he knew the coroner, he could have done what she said. The protective-virus theory was so logical, though. Could an insight like that be wrong?

"Get her out of here," Jefferson said again, and there was a note of desperation in his voice.

If the ashes were phony, the theory about them was wrong. He had to know before he inhaled the remains of his worst enemy.

"I'll make the deal you offered," he said to Jefferson. "But only if your wife calls this Harold Thorsen and asks him if he gave you a body. I'll put him on the speakerphone so I can hear the answer."

"No," said Jefferson as Lone turned to Celine.

"Mrs. Jefferson. If what you say is true, then your husband's ashes are no good to me. I'm in a hurry. If the ashes aren't real, I'll simply shoot him. Surely you realize that there is no way, even at a risk to myself, that I'm going to let him live. You have to see that. This way, your children will still have a mother and he will die with some dignity. You must know how important that is to a man like him."

CELINE LOOKED AT Judd.

"Don't do it, Celine," he said, but his eyes were pushing her toward the phone. He wanted her to do it, and when she looked at her watch, she knew why. Harold's office didn't open until eight-thirty.

"All right," she said. "But the coroner's office doesn't open for forty minutes."

56

IT was eight o'clock—thirty more minutes until the call. The pain in Jefferson's left leg was a constant red presence. His neck was getting stiff, and his back felt like it was in a vise. Only a desperate will was keeping his gun hand level with Lone's head.

His mind was grasping at anything to get away from the pain, and finally it settled on Celine's face. He lost himself in the memory of her jaw as he smoothed the hair out of her eyes after sex, and the way her back curved under his palm as he let it flow amidst the lace muscle and willow bone. He took his left hand off the gun and moved it through the air at his side.

CELINE SAW JUDD'S left hand make a curving stroke through the air and felt it move along her back, the way it did when she was lulling her face into his shoulder, eyelids drooping, his hand keeping time with her breathing. She'd turn her back to his front and, half in a dream, she'd smile, beachtime at sunset, her back always spooned into his front, the one smile he never saw. Now she floated that smile across the room.

JEFFERSON SAW THE smile and knew that if he had to die today, it would be with that in his mind. It was eight-fifteen.

THE DARKNESS AROUND Donnelly quivered with the howling of dogs, and in his mouth was the taste of antelope. He put his face to the peephole and saw the woman reach for the big man with her eyes. This had to be the one who would take him back to Elaine.

LONE SAW THE woman smile and wondered if she was losing her mind, not that it mattered. No matter what he'd told Jefferson, there was no way he was letting her go. He'd take his chances and he'd survive—maybe with a wound, but he'd survive. Jefferson was too weak to pull off a head shot at forty feet. First, though, he had to know the truth about the ashes.

If the ashes were really Sylvie, he would burn Jefferson and breathe his ashes as a vaccine. If not, he'd burn him anyway. Things could attach themselves to your cells. Jefferson was a disease. Things attached. Vanek had confirmed it. Jefferson had to burn. The woman had stopped smiling now. Jefferson was looking gray and tired. It was eight thirty-one.

"It's time, Mrs. Jefferson," he said. "There's a phone at the computer station to your left. The speaker is next to it."

57

"IT'S eight-thirty. Where the hell you been?" Gionfredo snapped at the driver of the van.

"Hadda wait till they went out on a job," said the driver. "Government guys start late."

"You hijacked it?" asked Far Lightning.

"Nobody got hurt," Gionfredo answered. "These guys are pros."

The van was dented white, with the blue logo of the Environmental Protection Agency on its side. Three of the four men inside wore dark suits, white shirts, and gold chains. The fourth was short and wore a dull brown suit with a mustard-colored tie; he had glasses. He looked like a typical government pencil-neck until he pulled up his left coat sleeve to check an eight-inch stiletto spring-mounted against his forearm. He flicked his wrist and the stiletto was instantly in his hand.

"That's Diblasio," said Gionfredo. "He's the one's gonna get us through the door . . . take this." He handed Far Lightning a silenced .22 magnum.

"I'm used to this," Far Lightning said, lifting the deer rifle.

"Suit yourself, but you and me gotta cap anyone we see until we find Jefferson. The other four back us up."

Far Lightning looked at the snub-nosed machine pistols carried by the men in the van and had second thoughts. "Listen, ah, Gionfredo."

"Call me Vinnie."

"If we go in there like an army, he'll kill them for sure."

"That's why we waited for the van. We pull up. They check us with their TV surveillance. They see the EPA label. They don't want no problems, so they send someone to the door to tell the little man in the brown suit there ain't nothing to inspect. Diblasio handles the entry quick and quiet."

At first, Gionfredo looked like just one more paleface geek in cowboy clothes. Then, as they'd driven overland to Highway 83 and stopped at the edge of plant property, Far Lightning noticed that he wasn't exactly pale and he wasn't at all nervous.

"Let's hit it," said Vinnie.

300

Diblasio drove the van up the entrance road and pulled into one of the executive spaces by the front door. The EPA logo would be clearly visible to the camera mounted halfway up the side of the building.

THE VOICE WAS small and tinny over the speakerphone, but every word was understandable.

"Hi, Celine," said Harold Thorsen. "Been a long time. How are you?"

"Fine, Harold, but this isn't exactly a social call. I need to know if Judd picked up a body from you recently."

Her question was followed by fifteen seconds of silence that said more than the words which followed. "Uh, that's a funny question, Celine."

"I need to know, Harold."

"Does this have something to do with, you know, a divorce?"

"No, it has something to do with getting back together. I hoped you'd be rooting for that."

"I am. Everybody is."

"Then please, Harold. Tell me."

The man stammered an answer that pretty much told Lone what he wanted to know. "Celine, I . . . I'd like to know it was okay with Judd before I told you anything."

Celine gave Lone a triumphant glance, and he nodded.

"Harold, let me just ask you this. If Judd came in and asked you for a body, you'd consider it, wouldn't you?"

"Well, only if it was unclaimed."

"Unclaimed?"

"You know, a homeless person with no known family . . . if he asked me . . . which I'm not saying he did."

"Are you saying he didn't?"

"I'm not saying anything until I talk to him."

Celine covered the receiver with her hand.

"Enough?" she asked, and Lone nodded.

"Thanks, Harold. See you."

The woman placed the receiver gently on the hook, and Lone turned away so she wouldn't see the look on his face. This was as bitter as losing Sylvie the first time, more bitter now that he'd felt how good it was to have her back. For a few seconds he felt like asking Jefferson to pull the trigger. Then he remembered that he was going to be leader of all the triads. His vaccines would be gone, but so would his disease.

"All right," he said to Jefferson. "I'll keep the deal, but first I want to know one thing. Why the ashes?"

"I thought you'd feel guilty. Excuse me for not knowing how fucking crazy you really are."

LONE THOUGHT JEFFERSON was the one who was crazy. The man was going to die this morning, and still he was able to crow over a trick he'd played. But of course: He thought his wife would leave and then he'd make the shot to the head. He thought the day would end with his offspring healthy and his enemy's line at an end. He and Jefferson were two different forms of life, made to kill the other. They would go on fighting long after they were both dead.

For the first time in his life, Lone was sorry he didn't have any children. He'd have to fix that—use some of the merchandise, five or six of them, get them all pregnant, and send the children to good boarding schools. First, though, he'd save them from their worst enemy.

"All right, Jefferson. I'm ready to keep the deal. Mrs. Jefferson, you can stand up and walk toward the exit door to my left rear. Move slowly. Make sure you don't get ahead of me."

REALITY FELL ON Celine and pinned her to the floor. Judd was going to die when she left. This would be the last time she ever saw him or heard him or smelled or touched him. Her world was going to change from round to flat, nothing but empty space. She couldn't move. Her legs wouldn't work. She could barely even see. Then she heard his voice.

"Get up, Celine. You have to go now."

She couldn't speak. Her throat was paralyzed.

"Scoot over here a minute," he said. "Just push yourself over here next to me, come on."

. . .

JEFFERSON KNEW HE had to get her to leave. If she was all right, he'd feel alive, even at the end. The thought of her out there with the children made things all right, but the thought of them both dying made him too scared to breathe.

She pushed her way across the floor and stopped when her hip touched his.

"Celine," he said, still looking down the gun at Lone. "You have to do this. I'm getting weak. There's no more time. There's no other way. If you're alive, the family's alive."

At first her voice was just a choked gurgle, but she swallowed and started again. "My legs won't work."

"If you don't go, I'll lose control and he'll have us both. He'll make you watch while he burns me. Please don't let me die like that. I don't want you to see me like that."

JUDD'S VOICE WAS strained and hoarse. He was close to breaking, and she knew he was right. The thought of seeing him in flames made her more afraid than living without him. The blood flowed back into her legs, and she moved into a crouch next to his shoulder. She leaned her head close to his ear and whispered.

"Thank you. Thank you for everything. I'll see you again." She kissed him lightly on the side of his neck and stood up.

LONE COULD SEE Jefferson was ready. He thought he could make the shot, and maybe he was right. His eyes were hard as a cobra's. He wasn't going to get the chance, though, because he loved his wife and it made him soft inside. When the time came to make a choice he'd save her, even if only for a few more minutes. Lone glanced at Ling, who nodded. The woman started walking.

ONE FOOT IN *front of the other. Don't think about anything else.* She concentrated on the door, a fire door with a red EXIT sign over it, dark there except for the sign, shadows in the dark, boxes and crates, a path through them to the door, Lone at the corner of her vision, chair rolling slowly backward, staring at Judd, whom she could no longer see . . . ever.

No thinking. Move.

. . .

DONNELLY WATCHED THE redheaded woman coming toward him, her face saintly with a halo of sadness. She was the woman in the painting, and she was going to pass within a few feet as she left forever. There was nothing she needed from him, no way back to Elaine, nothing to do now but stay in the box. It was as good a place as any. He would die there. What else was there to do?

LONE ROLLED THE CHAIR smoothly over the wooden floor, almost three feet with each push of his legs, keeping pace with the woman. She was halfway to the door, walking a little faster now, Jefferson twenty feet away and receding, a computer station coming up on the right, glass wall to the rear, behind it the cubicles and in them the rabies virus, waiting for him. Thirty feet away from Jefferson now, the computer station only five feet to the right.

Lone looked past Jefferson and spoke to Ling. "Kill her," he said as he dived off the chair.

DONNELLY LOOKED PAST the woman and saw the bald-headed man reach inside his coat. *NO!* The Spanish woman wouldn't die while angels could fly.

Donnelly opened the door of his box and flew through the air, his arms spread wide, turning as he went, chest out to the bald-headed man as something hit him. It didn't hurt. Nothing hurt. All his pain was back in the box.

JEFFERSON SAW LONE dive, heard a shot from his right, swung that way, and put two bullets into the side of Ling's head. He swung back to Lone and fired three more shots, which slammed harmlessly into the computer station. Then Lone's other men were around him with guns and he was yelling for them to shoot, but Lone was yelling louder as he ran across the room waving his hands.

"No-no-no-no-no. Don't shoot him." Then Lone was standing over him, panting and flushed. "You're going to burn, Jefferson, and so is your wife. Some bum was nice enough to save her for me."

Jefferson looked and saw one of Lone's men bending toward a naked body lying on top of Celine's. Then he saw her foot move.

God. This isn't right. This can't be right!

Then he heard a bonging sound, then three of them, then three more.

"The door," Lone said disgustedly. He swore in Chinese, walked back to the same computer station that had saved him, and flicked on a television monitor. He swore again and then laughed.

"Jefferson, you finally got your wish. It's the EPA."

58

FAR Lightning, Vinnie, and the three other men stood near the door with their backs against the building. The surveillance camera rocked down far enough to sight Diblasio and the van, but its bracket kept it from going farther.

Diblasio adjusted the clipboard in his left hand and pushed a button on the door frame.

"They don't answer the door, we drive the truck right through it," said Vinnie.

Diblasio stepped away from the door and looked up at the surveillance camera. "EPA inspection," he said, holding up the clipboard. "If you don't answer the door, I'm authorized to come back in one hour with the sheriff. Take a look."

Diblasio switched the clipboard to his right hand. Far Lightning could hear a security chain and see the door open slightly. Diblasio held the clipboard up to the opening.

Far Lightning blinked and almost missed it. Diblasio dropped the clipboard, reached through the crack for some hair, and stuck his stiletto through someone's throat. There was a slight gurgle, and then Vinnie snipped the security chain with a pair of bolt cutters. They eased the dying man to the floor and ran down a long hall, Vinnie and Far Lightning leading the way around a corner into another hall, where they stopped by a set of double doors. Far Lightning put his ear to the door, heard voices, and nodded to Vinnie, who eased it open a crack and then kicked it aside.

JEFFERSON WATCHED AS Lone's man pushed the naked body off Celine and pulled her to her feet. There was a noise over his head and the man dropped Celine and swung his gun toward the noise. The room became a hurricane of wood, blood, and screams.

WHEN LONE SAW the door open a crack, he sensed what was happening and leapt for the glass wall behind him. As furniture splintered around his head, he crawled behind the wall and into one of the glass cubicles. When he got there, he took a deep breath and relaxed. He was still in charge, still on track to be head of all the triads, still able to come back for another try at Jefferson. The virus and he were partners, and his partner was about to save him.

WHEN VINNIE HAD said his men were pros, he had meant it. They murdered Lone's men in fifteen seconds, chewing gum as they did it, calm as telephone installers. Far Lightning dropped his rifle on the catwalk and ran down the stairs to Celine. As bullets splintered the floor, he snatched her up and made for the catwalk.

The firing had stopped when he reached the top of the stairs and pulled Celine close to listen for breathing, heard it, and breathed again himself.

"Joseph, you're here," she said as if waking from a dream.

"It's over."

"Judd," she screamed, jumping out of his arms and looking over the railing. Then she saw Jefferson lying facedown under a desk. He moved, and she began to run.

WHEN THE FIRING started, Jefferson had rolled under a computer desk. His legs stuck out into the maelstrom but went untouched. He was inching out from under the desk when Celine grabbed him by the shoulders and pulled his head against her chest. A pain shot through his broken leg, but it didn't matter. Then he heard the voice, metallic and distant but unmistakably Lone's:

"Listen to me, or you'll all be dead before nine o'clock."

Vinnie and his men stopped checking bodies for signs of life. Far Lightning stopped in the middle of firing up a cigarette, and Judd stopped trying to lose himself in Celine.

"Now that I have your attention, listen carefully."

Jefferson looked to the far end of the room and saw Lone standing in one of the glass cubicles, a microphone dangling over his head. He was holding up a glass cylinder about eighteen inches long.

"No one come near me, or we all die," he said. "This is what killed Jefferson's cattle." He held the cylinder higher. "If you don't think I'll do it, ask Jefferson."

. . .

THERE WAS SOMETHING about the voice that terrified Celine. It had a brown and stifling color, nauseatingly familiar . . . the thing in the pit. She released Judd and threw herself against the floor, hoping it would go away. Then she remembered again what Joseph told her. *To kill it you have to look into its center.*

She raised her head and saw Vinnie's men standing between her and the glass partition. She could barely see the top of Lone's head, which meant he couldn't see her, either. Then something was trying to work its way into her memory, something she'd seen from the catwalk, something important. She began to crawl away from Judd toward the back set of stairs, wriggling over the bodies of two men until she reached the stairs and was out of Lone's sight.

LONE WAS FEELING better by the minute. The five men were obviously professionals, and they'd already done what they were paid to do. A deadly virus couldn't have been part of the deal. The Indian didn't look ready to die for anyone, and Jefferson had just been reunited with his wife. He'd be looking forward to life.

"If I drop this cylinder, we all die," he said. "So I'm going to walk out of this cubicle, then out of the building. Either I drive away or you shoot me and kill all of us."

CELINE CREPT TO the edge of the catwalk, wondering desperately what she'd seen in those few seconds when she was searching the floor for Judd. It was something about the part of the room where Lone was standing. She looked down and saw a thick glass wall in front of six glass stalls . . . robot arms with metal pincers hanging inside the stalls . . . each stall connected to a front aisle by open doors. Along the front aisle were work stations to control the metal arms . . . a glass roof enclosing the entire layout. Lone was standing in the center stall.

If he was allowed to leave, the war would never be over. What the hell was her brain trying to tell her? She looked frantically around the room and back to the glass boxes, then the alarm went off in her head . . . a red alarm . . . red buttons on the wall of each stall. She saw them through ventilation slots in the glass roofs, fire-engine red beneath yellow words: RAPID CONTAINMENT.

"I'm going to give you thirty seconds to think about it," said Lone. "Then I'm going to start walking. If anyone makes a move we all die. I have nothing to lose."

Containment. Work stations . . . robot arms . . . glass booths . . . each booth with an arm . . . each booth with a door . . . a door that could close . . . conatainment.

Celine looked frantically around the catwalk and saw Far Lightning's deer rifle lying where he'd dropped it. She snatched it up and snugged the butt into her shoulder. *Close range, but the most difficult shot ever . . . the only shot possible from this angle . . . through the ventilation slot and into the button of the last work station . . . put the slot on top of the sights . . . then down a half thought to allow for the bullet's rise . . . love the slot . . . feel the button . . . sad about it all . . . then caress the trigger.*

As the bullet slammed into the red button, the stall doors snapped closed and locked. A horn began sounding and a mechanically calm female voice floated eerily from speakers throughout the plant: "RAPID CONTAINMENT SEQUENCE NOW IN OPERATION. SEN-SORS CONDUCTING TEN-MINUTE EXPOSURE SEARCH. NON-ESSENTIAL PERSONNEL SHOULD EVACUATE THE BUILDING. SENSOR SEARCH NOW NEGATIVE AT NINE MINUTES AND THIRTY SECONDS."

Lone saw the door to his station slam shut, ran to it, and tried the handle, but it wouldn't move. Then he heard the computer's voice and relaxed. When the message ended, he spoke into the hanging microphone and gave them his own message.

"It will take the computer nine minutes and thirty seconds to check for contamination. When it doesn't find any, the doors will open and I'll be leaving."

He wanted a cigarette, but the cubicle was now airtight and would fill up with smoke. Plenty of air for nine minutes, though. He leaned against the wall and looked at the faces staring at him. He tucked the cylinder under his arm and gave them the finger.

. . .

WHEN JEFFERSON HEARD the recorded voice, he lifted his head from Far Lightning's arms and looked at Lone in the glass stall. Then he heard the voice, and everything in the world disappeared but the face of C. K. Lone.

The pain in his leg disappeared and the dizziness and the intervening twenty-five years. It was a hot August morning in Saigon and there was no one in the world but the two of them. He didn't have an M-16, but he did have something else—something he hadn't noticed until he stared at Lone's cubicle: The controls for the robot arms were almost exactly like the ones on his "Space Invaders" game. He began to crawl toward Lone.

Far Lightning stooped and held him. "Hold up, Judd. That leg's bleeding bad."

Then the voice of the computer: "EIGHT MINUTES AND THIRTY SECONDS."

"Get me to the work station," he said to Far Lightning.

"Judd, he's locked in."

Jefferson reached onto the back of Far Lightning's neck and pulled his face close. "He's locked in with the virus . . . 'Space Invaders.' "

Far Lightning looked at him as if he were delirious.

"EIGHT MINUTES."

"The arms," he said. "Get me over to the controls."

Far Lightning frowned down at him, and then Celine's face appeared.

"The controls," he said. "They're like the ones for 'Space Invaders.' "

He nodded toward the work station, saw her look, and knew she understood.

"Get me over there, then get out."

CELINE KNEW THE safe thing was to let Lone leave with his virus, but then nothing would be changed—and things *had* to change. This had to be over. She looked into Judd's eyes and saw twenty-five years of trust.

"Get him over there," she said to Far Lightning. "I'll help you."

"SEVEN MINUTES."

. . .

LONE SAW AN oncoming darkness—Jefferson, bleeding and unable to walk, but coming, being dragged but coming, black eyes like the morning in Saigon.

"THANKS," JEFFERSON SAID to Celine. "Now, get out."

"Come on," she said to Far Lightning.

Jefferson felt her touch his arm, but he was looking into the cubicle. Then she moved away.

"Celine," he said.

"Yes?"

"You know."

"Yes. Always."

"FIVE MINUTES THIRTY SECONDS."

Jefferson eased onto a stool and stretched his broken left leg to the side. He looked into the cubicle and saw a worktable in the center and a small black box against the front wall. The box had a hinged lid, which was thrown back showing honeycomb baffling and molded wells for two cylinders. One well was empty, and in the other he could see the top of a metal cylinder, like the one lying empty on the floor of the cubicle. Lone was standing against the back wall holding the glass tube that fit inside.

The control panel consisted of two joysticks with three buttons on each of their finger grips. *Three buttons. Three prongs on the end of each arm. One more button than the "Space Invader" sticks, but otherwise exactly the same.*

Jefferson flipped a switch marked POWER and fingered the buttons.

Lone jumped when he saw the prongs move, and then looked at the black case in the corner.

Jefferson took both arms up to the ceiling and whipped them back and forth, noticing that they moved as fast as a living arm.

As Lone moved his eyes toward the case in the corner, Jefferson brought the right arm down on top of his head. His knees buckled slightly, but he jumped left and stood rocking on the balls of his feet. Jefferson swung at his head with the right arm, and he jumped backward away from the real target, the black case.

Jefferson knew that if he could get the case up next to the ceiling, the game was over. He could take out the cylinder, drop the case, unscrew the top, and set loose the virus. There would be nowhere for Lone to run if he could do it before the computer unlocked the work station doors.

"FOUR MINUTES THIRTY SECONDS."

LONE KICKED THE box away from the robotic arm and pushed it along the wall toward the back of the cubicle. There, he knelt and levered the case upright. He was about to get both tubes back in the box, and then all he'd have to do was dodge the arms until the computer opened the door to his cubicle.

JEFFERSON SLID THE left arm between Lone's legs and pressed all three buttons on the control stick. Lone's scream was audible through the glass as he scrabbled backward with the control arm locked onto his genitals.

Jefferson let go and swooped in on the black box, lifting it to the ceiling with the left arm and working the metal cylinder out with the right. When he had the cylinder out, he dropped the box and began unscrewing the metal cap.

"ONE MINUTE THIRTY SECONDS."

Lone saw the black box hanging in the air and, despite the pain in his groin, jumped for it, holding his glass tube against his chest. Each time he landed, it was like being kicked all over again. He vomited down the front of his shirt, then backed shakily toward the wall. Jefferson had the metal cylinder out and was trying to unscrew the cap.

"SIXTY SECONDS . . . FIFTY-NINE . . . "

Lone set his vial on the floor and reached into his pocket for the pistol.

JEFFERSON COULD BARELY see through the sweat in his eyes. Some lamebrain idiot moron had cross-threaded the cap. It was moving an eighth of a turn at a time, and there was less than a minute to go. He wasn't going to make it. He knew he should give it up for Celine's sake, but he'd been waiting for this since stooped creatures roamed the opposite sides of a riverbank. There was no turning back.

"FORTY-FIVE ... FORTY-FOUR ... "

TEMPERED GLASS COULD stand through an earthquake but maybe not through a clip of nine-millimeter bullets. Lone fired three shots straight at Jefferson's face.

AN EXPANDING WEB of cracks appeared in front of Jefferson's eyes. *Jesus! Where's the vial? If the gun's in his hand, where's the vial?*

He looked wildly around the cubicle, saw the vial at Lone's feet, and went for it with the right arm.

"THIRTY-NINE ... THIRTY-EIGHT ... "

LONE WAS GETTING ready to fire the rest of his shots when the arm streaked past his eyes. He tucked the gun under his left arm and snatched up the vial as the arm crashed down.

"THIRTY ... TWENTY-NINE ... "

Twenty-eight seconds and seven shots left ... cracks widening; chances good. Lone tucked the vial into his inside coat pocket, raised the pistol, and fired three more times.

"TWENTY-FIVE ... TWENTY-FOUR ... "

CRACKS SPREADING IN front of his eyes ... where was the cylinder ... where was Lone? Through cracks and sweat and tears of rage, Jefferson saw Lone's arm, torso, and bulging coat pocket. He drew back the right arm and levered it forward at full speed into the front of Lone's chest.

"TWENTY ... NINETEEN ... EXPOSURE ALERT ... WORK STATION LOCKDOWN NOW IN EFFECT."

Lone knew he was dead but held his breath anyway. The cracks in the glass were wide, and four more shots might do it. He and Jefferson ... dead together. He could still do it.

. . .

JEFFERSON SAW LONE walk forward, cheeks puffed, refusing to breathe . . . raising the pistol with a smile. Jefferson dropped the metal cylinder from high on the left arm and brought the arm down into the back of Lone's head, popping his mouth open, and knocking him forward into the glass.

LONE TOOK A breath and felt a red-metal dust flow out his arms and down his legs, where it hardened into rods in the soles of his feet and the tips of his fingers. The gun disappeared as his head cracked back against his spine and he saw the ceiling rise away as he fell to the floor, snapping his jaws to loosen the steely smell of his blood as it congealed into cables that pulled his eyes to the inside of his head, where they saw red brain looming over vomit-green plain, cut through by urine-yellow river, then coiled upward to cut through dripping red sky with black helix tunnels of electric shock that made him bite blind against the rasp of paralyzed lungs and the flail of death-grip arms as he rolled and snapped and bit through tongue and lips and cheek, and then his brain rotted apart and ran red out his mouth and all he saw was his own eye looking back with a crooked brown iris that opened with teeth and . . .

LONE WHIPPED AND slashed on the floor as if he were connected to a high-tension electric cable. He bit the air and the floor and his own shoulders. Then his eyes rolled back in his head and his body spasms accelerated into continuous vibration. He began to chew his own face apart, then spewed blood out his mouth in a gusher, arched into a spine-cracking arc, and died.

Jefferson sank back onto the stool and felt the weight of genetic history lift from his shoulders. Now he was free of an enemy who was closer than a friend, free of a father who knew something impossible to express.

59

OUTSIDE, Celine sat in a spray of purple heather under a butter-yellow sun. Far Lightning stood above her, and Donnelly lay with his head in her lap. Vinnie took Far Lightning by the elbow and walked him a few yards away.

"We're lookin' at a suckin' chest wound over there. The guy will be dead inside of ten minutes."

"Why do you think I'm not calling 911?"

"You gonna tell her?"

"She'll know soon enough."

"What then?"

"She's strong."

Vinnie studied Far Lightning's face for a few seconds, forming the answer to a question he would never ask.

"Right," he said. "Look, I gotta get these guys to the airport in Billings by one o'clock."

"How do I say thanks for a thing like this?"

"You don't . . . ever."

"Thanks."

"You ought to move Celine outta here, just in case."

"She wouldn't leave without Judd."

Vinnie shifted nervously from foot to foot. "I hate to run out on you."

Far Lightning gave a short laugh. "Run, hell."

Vinnie shook Far Lightning's hand and hurried across the field toward the EPA van. Far Lightning turned back to Celine, who was stroking Donnelly's head while she stared fixedly at the plant.

DONNELLY LOOKED UP and saw the woman from the painting. Her hands were warm on his face as it rested in the soft circle of her lap. She smoothed back his hair so he could see the sky. He moved and she looked down.

"How're you doing?" she asked gently.

He couldn't speak, but it didn't matter. He was inside the painting, an angel ready to fly, ready to be close to Elaine in lace, ready to fold together in a new wedding, two angels together . . . forever . . . gone.

Celine started CPR, but Far Lightning reached down and stopped her.

"His chest is full of blood," he said. "There's nothing to pump."

"I've got to do something!"

"You gave him a chance to live his vision. That's all he wanted."

She stroked Donnelly's face one more time and then stood up next to Far Lightning.

"Judd will be out," she said.

"You know?"

"I know."

"Bone music."

She was about to ask him what he meant when Judd dragged himself out of the building, willed himself to take a few more steps, and fell. She started to run.

"MY GOD," JEFFERSON said when she knelt to hold him against her. "I think I've died and gone to heaven."

"Shh," she said. "You don't have to die to do that."

60

ELAINE Donnelly's mouth fell open when she saw a big Indian standing on the front steps of her two-story Colonial. When he'd phoned from the airport, she said the sheriff in Montana had already told her: Joe had been killed in some kind of shooting spree and they were sending the body home. She said she didn't want it but that she'd take it anyway, so the kids would at least have a grave to visit.

"I know what really happened," Far Lightning said. "I think you and your kids should know, too."

She'd given him directions.

She was dark-haired, small and pretty, with a trim figure and bright green eyes. When she offered him coffee, he took it.

"Your husband and I had something in common."

"I didn't know Joe had anything in common with anybody," she said bitterly.

"He hurt you."

"Only if you count gambling away twenty-seven thousand dollars and the drinking and the whores that went with it."

Donnelly undoubtedly hadn't deserved her, until the end.

"I have two friends," he said, "a married couple. They were . . . kidnapped. Your husband was hiding in the same building where they were being held. The short of it is, he stepped in front of a gun for the woman. He gave her enough time for her friends to get there. You won't hear any of this from the sheriff, because he doesn't know. I was there."

Elaine Donnelly stared as if he'd slapped her in the face. "You're talking about Joe?"

"In my religion, there's a person called a Heyoka. They do everything backwards. They're clowns, but they're also holy men. I think your husband became one of these men."

"Jesus," she said. "Joe never did an unselfish thing in his life."

"He had a vision. Then he acted it out."

"He was crazy."

"Maybe we're just using different names for the same thing."

She took a Kleenex from a green box and wiped her eyes. "Joe," she muttered. "I kept trying to show him there was a good man inside if he'd just get out of his own way. Then he goes two thousand miles and proves me right, the crazy bastard." She laughed a little and then cried.

"One more thing," he said. "The situation—it turned out good, but not exactly . . . legal. If you mention it to the sheriff, people will have to deny it."

"Why should I say anything? Tell your friends good luck, especially the woman."

"Thanks for letting me talk to you."

"Thanks for coming," she said, holding out her hand. "I'm sorry if I sound bitter."

But why should she be sorry? Life had taken what it wanted from her, and it wasn't sorry.

"A holy man, you say?" she asked at the door.

"I think he had a vision."

"A vision of what?"

"Visions usually end up being about things you love."

"That's funny," she said. "I was his wife for ten years, and I don't have any idea what he loved."

AT THE AIRPORT, Far Lightning walked to the boarding area and looked out the window, hoping Vandivier's report was right about the effects of global warming.

In front of him in line was a man wearing a fishing hat. The man turned and stuck out his hand.

"Al Walker," he said. "You going to Montana?"

"I live there."

"I'm going for the fishing. Lots of fishing out there, huh?"

"Wait a while and there might be more than you think," Far Lightning said with a smile.

61

JEFFERSON got out of the hospital on the last day of September. The doctors said he was a lucky man. With a break like his, sometimes they couldn't save the leg.

They'd asked a lot of questions about how he'd come to shoot himself in both legs. Sheriff Bob Wagman had asked some questions, too, but he was already pretty busy trying to figure out what had happened over at that old plant of Harlow's and who had dumped Harlow in a shallow grave and why the government had come in and told him the plant was off-limits to everybody but Jesus—and while he was at it, how had that crazy bastard Donnelly managed to get himself shot, too?

Jefferson thought Bob might have a few more ideas than he pretended, but they were hunting buddies, and who was he to question the judgment of a guy who owed him five hundred from poker?

The newspapers were pissed about "the apparent gang war in Montana," but nobody thought Vinnie Gionfredo had anything to do with it. Hell, he was a Montanan now, married to the Bright girl and ranching up a storm.

The first frost had come on the fourth of October. It snowed a little on the fifth, then cleared up and stayed in the eighties for about two weeks. Things were back to normal now, though.

It was the twentieth, birch and aspen turning gold against the high, clear blue, flutes of cold air frosting the edges of a warm overhead sun.

Celine had dismounted and walked eagerly to the top of the hill overlooking the ranch. Jefferson eased himself down from Jack and walked to her with the limp he would have forever.

"It seems impossible that all this might change," she said.

"Maybe it won't."

"What will we do if it does?"

"Deal with it."

"Joseph thinks the government would give most of the land back to the Indians."

"But they'd base the taxes on downtown Denver."

They laughed, and he bent down to inhale the fall smell in her

319

hair, then threw his coat on the ground and nudged her onto it, looking steadily into the calm gray of her eyes' horizon.

"Here?" she asked.

He answered by unbuttoning her shirt, reveling in the lightly freckled skin between her breasts. She lifted her hips as he pulled off her boots and jeans, and then she was naked. He looked down as he removed his own clothes, letting the flow of her long body arouse him . . . the arch of her foot, the slide of scissored legs as they moved against the chill, the smooth slope of white from rib cage to auburn autumn between her legs.

She looked into his face as he entered, moving slow and listening to her eyes as they told him what she wanted. Her look moved them together into the rhythm of speech as he pillowed her with his arm, brought her closer to his face so they could talk without words, lips against lips, bodies rocking, eyes beginning to rage as the silent talk became sound and she pulled him down her spine and into her center, her first, her life within life, where she'd been waiting forever and he met her in a burst of fire that made his body hard as marble, his hands soft as life, covering her face, feeling the come of her breath on the palm of his hand.

They lay together living the smell of each other. She felt a chill and drew her coat over them, kissed his neck and spoke in a half whisper.

"Yessir. You're sure the man I've always known."

"From the vision?"

"You've never asked me about the rest of it."

"What?"

"On the plains . . . with Joseph."

"Do you want to tell me?"

"Maybe someday, when we're old."

He raised his head and looked into her eyes, where he'd always lived, always would live.

"Never happen," he said.